THE OMEGA AGENCY

Top Secret Government Agency charged with keeping peace throughout the world—by just about any means possible. With a few exceptions, the operatives generally live their own lives until they are called into action.
They work under the direction of special envoy Adam Ridgeway—and they *always* get the job done.

Jaguar: At home with guerrilla warfare, there's nothing this loner likes better than a solitary mission. But Jake Mackenzie doesn't always get what he wants....

Cowboy: His relaxed stance and charming drawl disguise his tireless efforts and cool head in the face of danger. Yet Nate Sloan's toughest challenge might be escaping the pursuit of a camp of determined women!

Doc: Book smarts matched by physical strength give David Jansen an edge, but he hides both behind a diffident air. What will happen when his resolve is truly tested...?

Chameleon: With an ear for languages and a quick mind, Maggie Sinclair can be anyone she wants to be. But will she let Adam see her true self?

And don't miss the adventures of the next generation of OMEGA agents:

Artemis: Like the huntress, Diana Remington always bags her prey. But her arrows miss the mark when she's sent to recover a downed pilot in *Hot as Ice*, a February 2002 release from Silhouette Intimate Moments.

Renegade: The last thing ex-marine Rick Carstairs wants is to act as bodyguard to the Mexican president's fiery niece—especially after he meets her.... Watch for his story, coming later this year from Silhouette Intimate Moments.

PRAISE FOR

MERLINE LOVELACE

"Wow! Clear your evening...
you'll want to read this all at once."
—*Affaire de Coeur* on *Night of the Jaguar*

"This story is a fantastic tale
of danger and love in wild surroundings."
—*The Paperback Forum* on *The Cowboy and the Cossack*

"Unforgettable characters and scintillating romance..."
—*New York Times* bestselling author Debbie Macomber

"Merline Lovelace delivers top notch
romantic suspense with great characters,
rich atmosphere and a crackling plot!"
—*New York Times* bestselling author Mary Jo Putney

"Merline Lovelace writes with humor and passion."
—*Publishers Weekly*

MERLINE LOVELACE

DANGEROUS TO HOLD

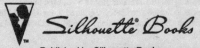

Silhouette® Books

Published by Silhouette Books

America's Publisher of Contemporary Romance

SILHOUETTE BOOKS

DANGEROUS TO HOLD

Copyright © 2002 by Harlequin Books S.A.

ISBN 0-373-48468-2

The publisher acknowledges the copyright holder
of the individual works as follows:

NIGHT OF THE JAGUAR
Copyright © 1995 by Merline Lovelace

THE COWBOY AND THE COSSACK
Copyright ©1995 by Merline Lovelace

Visit Silhouette at www.eHarlequin.com

Printed in U.S.A.

CONTENTS

Dear Reader,

I'm thrilled that Silhouette has decided to release this special collector's edition of the original CODE NAME: DANGER series. I had a ball with this series—I never knew where OMEGA's intrepid undercover operatives would take me or what hairy situations they'd get into next.

In this edition you'll meet the cool, unflappable Jaguar and rodeo-rider-turned-secret-agent Cowboy. And of course there's the irreverent Maggie Sinclair, who continually strikes sparks off OMEGA's chief.

If you enjoy the first two books in the original series, be sure to watch for the next two. *Dangerous To Know* hits the bookstores in July 2002.

And—long drum roll here, please!—in response to your many letters and requests, the adventures continue in a whole new set of CODE NAME: DANGER books. The first book in the new series, *Hot as Ice,* is a February 2002 release from Silhouette. A new title follows later in the year, with more books coming after that.

Happy reading,

Merline Lovelace

NIGHT OF THE JAGUAR

To the man who has always been my dark, handsome hero—the one, the only, the wonderful, Al.

Special Acknowledgments

With special thanks to my super "technical advisers":

Dr. Larry Lovelace, whose medical expertise is exceeded only by his great sense of humor;

Colonel Bob Sander, U.S. Army (Ret.), who spent far more days in the jungle than he cares to remember;

and

Lt. Bill Price, Oklahoma City Police Dept. (Ret.), friend, security expert and a Jaguar at heart!

Prologue

Cartoza, Central America

Oh, God, please don't let them find us!

The terrified woman squeezed her eyes shut, as if that might block out the horror that had shattered the night.

A rattle of machine-gun fire assaulted her ears. Hoarse voices shouted. Someone screamed—a long, agonized cry for help. A pig squealed horribly.

The woman hunched lower behind the screen of spiky palmettos, her arms wrapped around the small, trembling bodies she was trying to shield, and prayed as she'd never prayed before.

The gunfire stuttered to a halt. Low, guttural voices called in the village. Then nothing. Heavy, dark, suffocating silence, unbroken except for a small whimper from one of the children cowering against her. A silence that lengthened, causing hope to claw at her chest. Maybe they were gone! Maybe the attackers would melt back into the jungle they'd crept out of.

She drew in a ragged breath and tried to shush the child pressed against her side.

She flinched at the muted thud of footsteps nearby. A low voice. More footsteps, only a little way from their hiding place. Men trudged past. For a few moments, a few heart-stopping, desperate moments, she thought she and the children were safe. But then, a parrot screamed a protest at the passing men, startling a frightened cry out of little Teresa.

The footsteps slowed, then stopped. Stillness descended, heavy and waiting.

She pressed Teresa into her side, against the thick, sweltering folds of the robe she'd thrown on in the desperate hope it would give her and the children some protection. The little girl's terror infected the others. Ricci, only three, sobbed.

The palmetto fronds rattled, parted. Moonlight glinted on the evil-looking gun barrel that pointed right at her heart, and cast the lean face above it into sharp, shadowed angles.

They stared at each other, her eyes wide with terror, his narrowed and deadly.

Another face appeared at his shoulder. "What is it, gringo? Who's there? More of these peasants who resist our cause? Kill them!"

The man holding her in his line of fire drew in a deep breath. "It's a nun. For God's sake, it's a nun."

Chapter 1

On a quiet side street just off Massachusetts Avenue, in the heart of Washington's embassy district, an elegant, Federal-style town house stood dark and silent in the pre-dawn April chill.

A discreet bronze plaque beside the front door caught the dim, fading glow of the streetlamps. Anyone brave enough or foolish enough to be wandering the capital's streets that early might have peered curiously at the plaque and learned that the structure housed the offices of the president's special envoy.

Those in the know—political correspondents, foreign diplomats, cabdrivers, and the bag people who slept on the subway grate on the corner—could have told the curious wanderer that the position of special envoy was another of those meaningless ones created several administrations ago to give some wealthy campaign contributor a fancy Washington office and an important-sounding title.

Only a handful of government officials with the highest compartmentalized security clearances knew that the offices of the president's special envoy occupied just the first two floors of the town house.

Still fewer were aware that the third floor served as headquarters for a covert agency. An agency whose initials comprised the last letter of the Greek alphabet—OMEGA. An agency that, as its name implied, was activated as a last resort when other, more established organizations, such as the CIA or the State Department or the military, couldn't respond for legal or practical reasons.

And only the president himself knew that the special envoy also acted as the director of OMEGA. The director alone had the authority to send its agents into the field.

One of those agents—code name Jaguar—was in the field now.

His controller paced OMEGA's high-tech communications center on the third floor of the town house. Her pale gray linen slacks showed the effects of a long day and an even longer night, as did her wrinkled red silk tunic, with its military-style tabs at the shoulders and pockets. Tension radiated from every inch of her tall, slender body as she took another turn, then stopped abruptly in front of the command console

Dammit, why didn't Jake report in?

Maggie Sinclair shoved a hand through her thick sweep of shoulder-length brown hair and glared at the unwavering amber light on the satellite receiver. "Are you sure there hasn't been any interference with our signals?"

The communications specialist seated at the side console sent her a pained look. "No, ma'am," he drawled in his soft Texas twang. "Not unless somebody's got something a whole lot more sophisticated than baby here."

He patted the steel gray console tenderly. "And no one does. If one of our agents in Saudi Arabia or Afghanistan or anywhere else on the planet so much as sneezes into his transmitter, I'll pull it down for you. No one, not even the *U*-nited States Air Force, can interfere with my signals."

Warming to his subject, Joe Samuels began to describe in loving, excruciating detail the power and frequency spectrums he could call up at will. Maggie listened with half an ear, having shared the small hours of the night with him and his baby many times before. She stared at the amber light, her thoughts on the man she was waiting to hear from.

Where was Jake? What was happening in Cartoza?

After more than two years as a special agent for OMEGA, Maggie had spent enough time in the field to develop keen instincts about an operation. Every one of her instincts was screaming that something had gone wrong with this one.

She should have heard from Jake hours ago. She was his control, his only contact at headquarters, and he hadn't missed a prearranged signal yet. The last transmission he'd sent had indicated that the big arms shipment would be tonight.

They were close, so close, to breaking up the international consortium that specialized in selling stolen U.S. military arms to unfriendly governments and revolutionary forces. Posing as an expatriate mercenary, Jake had infiltrated one of the rebel bands some weeks ago. The information he'd sent in so far had detailed how the weapons were being smuggled from various military arsenals across the U.S. He'd even pinpointed the isolated airstrips where the arms were being delivered.

But until tonight he hadn't been able to identify the middlemen, the Americans who arranged the shipments and took payment in drug dollars. Tonight, Jake had learned, the big money men were flying in with a special shipment. Tonight, he'd planned to be part of the group that met them. Tonight, OMEGA would take the middlemen down.

Maggie had placed surveillance aircraft on orbit and put a strike force on full alert, waiting for his signal. It hadn't come.

Resuming her seat in front of the command console, she reached for a foam cup with a neat pattern of teeth marks around its rim. She took a sip of cold coffee, then grimaced and set the cup aside. With a last, frowning glance at the amber light, she tugged a black three-ring notebook toward her. She flipped through the tabbed sections until she found the parameters for mission termination.

Maggie knew the criteria for ending an operation by heart. As the respective control and field agents for this mission, she and Jake had drafted them together weeks ago. But with his life on the line, she wasn't trusting anything to memory.

Ten minutes later, she pushed the notebook aside. She still had some latitude within the agreed-upon parameters. She'd sweat it out a few more hours yet, she decided. There was still a chance they could pull it off. The drop could have been delayed by weather, by mechanical problems with the plane, by any one of a hundred unexpected events.

Besides, Jake was good. Damn good. He had more field time than anyone in the agency, two years more than Maggie herself. He'd been one of the first operatives recruited for OMEGA, a CIA transplant who'd helped train the dozen other transfers from various military and government agencies. He'd salvage the operation…if it was salvageable.

Still, the sixth sense Maggie had learned never to ignore in this business kept nagging at her. Her brows puckered in concentration, she stared at the console and willed herself inside Jake's head.

What was going on down there?

She was so intent on the unwavering yellow light that she didn't see Samuels acknowledge a positive palm-and-voice print. Nor did she hear the near-silent hum as the heavy oak door to the control center—protected by a bullet-proof titanium shield—slid open.

"Nothing yet?"

The deep, quiet voice, with its distinctive Boston cadences, made Maggie jump. She swiveled her chair around, thinking ruefully that she should be used to the way her boss moved by now.

And, she decided with a quick intake of breath, she certainly ought to be used to the sight of Adam Ridgeway in formal dress. She'd seen him in his special envoy persona often enough, looking incredibly distinguished and darkly handsome in white tie and tails tailored to fit his broad shoulders and lean, athletic body. Adam usually stopped by the

OMEGA control center after attending one of his many diplomatic functions. Maggie had expected him tonight. Nevertheless, she had to force trapped air out of her lungs as she shook her head.

"No, nothing yet."

He flicked a glance at the row of clocks above the command console. "It's almost 4:00 a.m. down there."

"I know."

One of Adam's dark brows notched at her clipped response.

"I'm giving him another few hours," Maggie added, in a more measured tone.

He studied her face for a moment, then nodded. "All right."

The tight knot of tension at the base of Maggie's spine loosened an infinitesimal fraction at his quiet acceptance of her decision. She and Adam had had their disagreements in the past over her somewhat unorthodox methods in the field. But he'd never yet questioned her instincts about an operation. That he didn't do so now reinforced Maggie's confidence in her decision to delay terminating the mission.

Adam turned away, pulling at the ends of his white tie. "I'll be in my office downstairs. Call me if you hear anything."

The mischievous grin that was as much a part of Maggie's nature as her intense dedication to her job tugged at the corners of her generous mouth. She snapped a hand to her forehead. "Aye, aye, Skipper!"

Adam paused, his blue eyes gleaming at her atrocious approximation of a salute. "It's obvious we didn't recruit you from the military," he commented dryly.

Maggie grinned as she watched him stride across the room with the smooth, controlled grace of a man who had crewed for Harvard and still sculled on the Potomac every chance he got. She often teased him about his choice of a sailing craft, suggesting that someone with his wealthy background could afford a real boat—one with an engine, maybe, or at least an anchor.

When his black-clad frame disappeared into the darkness outside the control center, Maggie swung back to the console. Her lingering smile faded slowly.

The amber light emitted the same unblinking glow.

Where the devil was Jake?

Two thousand miles away, Jake MacKenzie cursed viciously as he slashed at the strangler-fig root that had wrapped itself around his boot. His machete sliced through the thick elastic root with deadly efficiency, then slid back into the worn leather scabbard attached to his web belt. Jake reached up to adjust the night-vision goggles that photomultiplied light some forty thousand times, changing the inky darkness around him to an eerie luminous green. He plowed ahead, hard on the heels of the shadowy figure in front of him.

Christ! Everything that could've gone wrong tonight had! Not only had the plane they'd come to meet failed to show at the small airstrip hacked out of the jungle, but government troops had unexpectedly arrived in the area. Someone had better have a damn good explanation for that colossal screw up, Jake thought savagely.

As if that weren't bad enough, he and the band of revolutionaries he'd infiltrated had spent half the night detouring around the troops to get back to their camp, high in the mountains. Then, outside a sleeping village, one of the rebels had stumbled over some pigs. Startled, the stupid bastard had sprayed the squealing animals with his AK-47. Within moments, the night had erupted. Shouts from the nearby village, scattered small-arms fire and the answering stutter of the rebels' automatic rifles had split the darkness. Before Jake could stop them, the rebels had charged through the cluster of huts, firing on the peasants, who had so far stubbornly refused to support their cause.

They'd wanted to kill the terrified woman they'd found hiding in a stand of palmettos, too. Until they'd seen her black robe and veil and the kids clutched in her arms. Even these sleazers hesitated before pulling the trigger on a nun and three children. Still, Jake's acid observation, in quick, idiomatic Spanish, that a medical sister was the closest thing to a doctor in this remote part of the interior was probably what had saved her life.

So far.

Dragging the woman with them, the rebels had melted back into the jungle. The children, clinging to her like frightened monkeys, had stumbled along, as well. Within moments, an impenetrable wall of darkness had swallowed them. Not even the rugged all-terrain vehicles the *federales* used could navigate through the dense tropical rain forest.

And now he was stuck with them, Jake thought in disgust. Three orphans, according to the woman's frantic pleas to spare them. And a nun! An American nun, if her mangled, broken Spanish was any indication. As if he didn't have enough on his hands with this botched mission.

"Don't touch him!"

At the sharp, sudden cry, Jake dropped into an instinctive crouch and spun around. Through the thin lenses of the goggles—stolen from a U.S. military base, along with a shipment of high-tech arms—he saw the spectral shape of one of the rebels tugging at a child's arm.

"No! No, let her go!"

The man spit out a response, but obviously the sister didn't understand the guttural patois the rebels used. She snatched at his shirt, demanding that he release the child.

Jake straightened, his stomach clenching. The woman's black robe and medical expertise wouldn't protect her much longer if she riled these men. Or if they got to drinking. Or if—

A muted snarl from the man holding the child's arm told Jake things were fast getting out of hand. Cursing once more, he stalked back along the narrow, overgrown trail. He shoved up the goggles, which tended to blur items at close range, curled a hard hand around the woman's arm and jerked her away. The child, a girl of about five or six, cried out.

"Let me go!" The woman yanked against his tight hold, intent on the child.

Jake's grip tightened. "You may not realize how close you are to getting a knife in your ribs, Sister."

She swung toward him, her face a pale blur in the murky gloom. "You're an American?" she gasped in disbelief.

"More or less," he snapped.

"Wh-what are you doing with them?" She gestured to the group that now surrounded them, dim shadows against the darker blackness of the night, then repeated helplessly, "You're an American."

Jesus! Jake's fingers dug into her arm. "This is no time to be discussing nationalities. In case you aren't aware of it, my associates don't like *norteamericanos* much more than they do their own people who resist their cause. Come on."

She dug in her heels. "Tell that…that murderer…to get his hands off Teresa."

The wiry rebel understood English a whole lot better than the sister understood Spanish. He spit out a phrase Jake was glad the woman didn't grasp. The situation, he decided, was rapidly going from dangerous to nasty.

"The children are slowing us up. He's only going to put the girl on the packhorse, for God's sake."

She panted with a combination of fear and desperate determination. "For *his* sake, that's all he'd better do."

Jake released her arm, wondering what the hell she thought she could do if any of these men did try to harm the children. Bludgeon them with her rosary beads?

"Look, Sister," he warned, his voice low, "you'd better understand that you're in a pretty precarious situation here."

She drew in a ragged breath. "No kidding."

Jake sliced her a quick look, surprised at the terse response. Either convent life was an even tougher boot camp than he'd realized, or this was one gutsy lady. Unfortunately, he'd found over the years that gutsy tended to get people killed. If he was going to keep this woman alive long enough to figure out what to do with her, he'd better make damn sure she understood what was ahead.

"Don't think that veil you're wearing will protect you if you get their hackles up," he stated with brutal candor. "The only thing that saved you back there in the village is the fact that one of their pals died last week from a nasty case of gangrene. They've decided that it might be nice to have a *médica* around the camp to prevent such little unpleasantries in the future."

She gave a small gasp and put a shaking hand up to her throat. Even in the darkness, Jake could see the way her eyes went round with fear. Good, he thought savagely. She needed to be scared. He sure as hell was.

"I'd advise you not to push them too far," he added softly.

Muttering under his breath, the rebel beside them stooped and swung the girl onto the horse. Jake slung his weapon over his shoulder and lifted the littlest, a boy of about three or four, up behind her. The third child, a thin, wide-eyed boy of about eight, would have to hoof it.

The men drifted into the darkness to take up their positions in line. Jake tucked his weapon under his arm once more and waited for the signal to move on. The woman beside him glanced at the automatic rifle, and a look of revulsion crossed her white face, visible even in the darkness.

"How...how many of the villagers did you kill?"

Jake bit off an oath. He couldn't tell her that he'd tried to prevent the rampage. Hell, he didn't dare tell her anything. Talking to her at all was risky, given the group's simmering frustration over the missed drop. Although Jake had managed to convince these men that he'd sell his country or his soul or both for the right price, he was still a gringo, an outsider they didn't quite trust. With the least provocation, they'd turn on him like jackals after raw meat.

"How many?"

His hand tightened over the gun barrel. "As many as got in the way."

She put a hand over her mouth. "God will have to forgive

you for what you've done," she whispered. "I can't. Those people were my friends."

Jake refused to allow any hint of sympathy or remorse to creep into his reply. "Yeah, well, I just might be the closest thing to a friend you've got left right now. And I'm telling you that if you want to survive the next twenty-four hours, you'd better keep moving and keep your mouth shut."

She swallowed and clutched the boy's hand.

"Stay in front of me from here on, where I can keep an eye on you," he ordered. "Don't step off the path, and keep a tight hold on the kid. There are a few surprises along the trail for anyone unwise enough to try to follow us. Now move it, lady…Sister."

Gripping her skirt with one tight fist and the child with the other, she turned and fell into line.

As the small group traveled in heavy silence, the night sounds of the jungle they'd disturbed slowly resumed. Leaves rustled in the tall trees. Whistles and chirps seemed to come from every direction. Bats whirred through the branches high above, while whining mosquitoes circled Jake's ears. The crunching, tearing sounds of small animals and insects feeding drifted to him through the darkness. Once, far off in the distance, a jaguar screamed.

Jake managed a grim smile.

As the echo of the animal's cry died away, he mentally reviewed his options. There weren't many at this point.

He could abandon his mission right now and try to take out the dozen men with him on this botched operation. He calculated the risks to the woman and the children and abandoned the idea. It wasn't any more feasible now than it had been back in the village.

That left trying to brazen it out. When this little band got back to camp, Jake would have to convince the desiccated fanatic who led them that the aborted airdrop and the proximity of government troops were both just coincidence. That Jake himself had nothing to do with either—which he didn't.

At the same time, he'd have to find a way to protect this

nun and her charges without blowing his cover. That might be a bit tricky, given the fact that he was supposed to be a conscienceless mercenary.

Still, he had no choice. There were already two other women in camp, one hard and pitiless and as dedicated to the revolution as the intense leader she slept with. The other was the vacant-eyed wife of one of the men, who didn't mind sharing her, for a price. Jake's gut wrenched at the thought of the games the men played with the uncomprehending, unresisting woman. His fingers clenched around the gun barrel at the thought of what they could do to the woman stumbling along ahead of him.

At that moment, he heard her call a strained reassurance to the little girl atop the plodding packhorse. Despite her own fears, and what she must know was a very uncertain future, she managed to soothe the whimpering child. A reluctant admiration for the woman's ragged courage tugged at him.

Maybe, just maybe, they could pull it off, Jake thought. More than just their lives was at stake here, he reminded himself. An entire country teetered on the brink of civil war, and all the horror that came with it. Cartoza was a small nation, but one of the United States' staunchest allies in Central America. Its government was dedicated to wiping out the drug traffickers whose insidious products were destroying the social fabric of all the Americas.

The U.S. President himself had activated an OMEGA response based on the information that the drug lords were financing shipments of stolen U.S. arms to the insurgents. The shipments had to be stopped before the friendly government toppled.

There was still a chance, a slim chance, of accomplishing that mission. If his controller at OMEGA didn't jump the gun and send in an extraction team, Jake might yet take down the middleman who was supplying the arms.

His lips twisted in a small, grim smile at the thought of his controller. By now, Maggie Sinclair would be pacing the floor, those long legs of hers eating up the cramped space in the communications center. Her brown eyes would be narrowed in intense concentration, her dark cloud of hair would be tangled from her unconscious habit of raking a hand through it whenever she was deep in thought. For all her worry, however, Jake knew, Maggie wouldn't panic.

The tight, coiled knot of tension between his shoulder blades loosened imperceptibly. Maggie wouldn't terminate the operation. Nor would she send in an extraction team. Not until she heard from him or figured out for herself what had happened. Jake had worked with most of the agents assigned to OMEGA, and Sinclair was one of the best.

Chapter 2

One more hour, Maggie thought. Two at the most. That was all she could allow herself. And Jake.

She took another sip of coffee, unmindful now of its cold, sludgelike consistency. Holding the cup at her lip, she began tracing a second ring of circular indentations around the rim. Suddenly a light flashed on the upper left portion of her console.

The front legs of Samuels's chair thwacked down on the tiles. "It's Big Bird!"

Maggie's heart pounded in sudden excitement. Big Bird! She should have known the surveillance craft orbiting high above the Caribbean would be the first to break the wall of silence surrounding Jake. The huge air force jet, with its Frisbee-like rotating radar dish, was officially termed the USAF Airborne Warning and Control System, but everyone had a different tag for it, some affectionate, some irreverent. No one, however, made fun of the vital information processed via its banks of on-board computers.

With the speed and skill of a magician performing sleight

of hand, Samuels flipped a series of switches. The clear, calm voice of an air surveillance officer came over the speaker. Maggie hunched forward in her chair, listening intently.

An aircraft meeting the specifications Jaguar had called in earlier had taken off from a deserted airstrip in Alabama, Big Bird confirmed. Two F-15s had scrambled from a base in Florida to make a visual ID, then shadowed the slower-moving plane across the Gulf of Mexico. At the last minute, the aircraft under surveillance had aborted its landing in Cartoza, for reasons unknown at present. The report went on to provide a wealth of technical detail on the suspect's flight pattern, air characteristics and radar signature.

Maggie acknowledged receipt of the transmission and sat back, thinking furiously.

"So the drop didn't take place?" Samuels asked.

She met the communications specialist's steady gaze and shook her head. She wasn't surprised by his question. Everyone in the OMEGA control center during an operation was briefed on every detail. They worked as a team, together, twenty-four hours a day, throughout the duration of the mission. Everyone involved had a personal stake in the outcome.

"Get me a voice link to those F-15s," Maggie said. "I want to talk to the pilots and find out what—"

Another flashing light interrupted her.

Samuels verified the caller's credentials, then sent Maggie a wide grin. "It's the on-duty rep at the State Department crisis center. He has a report of some action in your sector of operations."

Maggie picked up the handset, adrenaline pumping through her veins. Although she far preferred fieldwork to acting as a control agent, she had to admit that being stuck at headquarters had its moments. Like now, when the reports started to flow in from a dozen different sources. From CIA, from Treasury, from any and all agencies whose intelligence networks OMEGA tapped into. She'd need a cool head, and the insight gained only through years in the field, to piece together the fragmentary and often conflicting bits of information that would soon pour in.

"State Department, this is Chameleon," she rapped out, identifying herself with the code-name she'd earned by her ability to melt into whatever locale she was sent to. "What do you have?"

Forehead furrowed in concentration, Maggie listened as the on-duty operations officer relayed information about a rebel raid on a small village in the interior of Cartoza.

"How many casualties?" she asked when he paused to consult his notes.

"Four. Three villagers and one suspected insurgent."

"Any positive ID on the insurgent?"

"No, the locals are still running their checks. I've got some vitals, though, if you want them."

Maggie gripped the handset. "Let me have them."

"Five feet seven. Black hair. Brown eyes. With an old, jagged scar on the left thigh, possibly from a knife. That's all I have right now."

Maggie slumped in relief. Jake certainly sported a shaggy head of black hair, and he'd acquired more than his share of scars over the years. But his eyes were a flinty shade of gray, not brown, and he stood a good five inches taller than the dead man.

"There's one more thing."

"What's that, State?"

"The villagers led the government forces to a newly dug, shallow grave containing the remains of a woman…an American woman, according to the garbled reports we got. With all the confusion of the raid, we haven't been able to confirm who it is. Was."

Maggie frowned at the console. "Who did you have down there?"

"We're not sure. The personnel folks are screening our data files now. Assuming she's not some tourist who took a wrong turn at Cancún and ended up in the middle of a revolution, we should know something within the next hour or so."

"Keep me posted, okay?"

"You got it."

Maggie replaced the handset, her eyes thoughtful. At this point there was no reason to assume a connection between the dead woman and Jake's operation. But she sensed instinctively that there was one, just as she knew that Jake wouldn't want her to terminate the mission until she was convinced it was necessary.

Twenty minutes later, she still wasn't convinced.

Although she hadn't yet heard from Jake, she'd sifted through enough fragmentary information to form a picture of what must have happened. The presence of the government forces in the area was a coincidence, an unscheduled military exercise. But their presence would have been enough to scare off the drop aircraft. Maggie guessed that the rebels had raided the village as a target of opportunity when the drop was aborted. There was a chance, a slim chance, that Jake's cover hadn't been compromised yet.

"Call me immediately if anything else comes in," she instructed Samuels. "I'm going to update the chief with this latest information."

She strode across the communications center and waited impatiently for the palm- and voice-print scanners to verify her identity. When the heavy door slid open, she took the stairs two at a time. She was in the the special envoy's reception area within seconds. Another synthesizer activated the door that led to his office. Maggie passed through a short corridor that contained every lethal protective device the enthusiastic security folks could devise.

The inner door stood open, but the sight of Adam on the special phone that recognized the distinctive voice patterns of only two men in the world stopped Maggie on the threshold. He waved her inside, listening intently, one hip hitched on the edge of the half acre of polished mahogany that served as his desk. Although he'd taken off his formal coat and white tie, he couldn't have shed his well-bred, aristocratic air even if he wanted to, Maggie thought. When she stepped inside his office, she caught the gleam of diamond studs winking amid the starched pleats of his shirt.

She also noted the slight narrowing of his vivid blue eyes. That was as close as Adam Ridgeway ever came to frowning. Not for the first time in the past two years, Maggie wondered just what it would take to shatter Adam's iron control. She herself had managed to strain it severely on more than one occasion, she acknowledged with an inner grin.

"The reports are just beginning to flow," he said calmly. "We still don't have a clear picture of what happened."

Maggie suppressed a smile at Adam's Kennedyesque pronunciation of *clear*. A gifted linguist, she delighted in the idiosyncrasies of American dialects as much as in the foreign languages that were her specialty.

The only child of an Oklahoma-bred "tool-pusher" whose job as superintendent of an oil-rig drilling crew took him all over the world, Maggie had spent her childhood in a series of exotic locales. By the time she won a scholarship to Stanford at seventeen, she'd been fluent in five languages and conversant in three more. Until two years ago, she'd chaired the foreign language department at a small Midwestern college. Then a broken engagement and the sense of adventure she'd inherited from her parents had left her restless and ready for change.

Three months after a call from her godfather—a strange little man her father had once helped smuggle out of a Middle Eastern sheikdom—she'd been recruited as an agent for OMEGA. Only later had Maggie learned that she was the first operative drawn from outside the ranks of the government. And that her godfather, now retired, was one of OMEGA's most intrepid agents.

Adam's conversation soon drew to a close. "I understand the urgency, Mr. President. I'll get back to you as soon as we know what happened in Cartoza."

Replacing the receiver, he folded his arms across a wide expanse of crisp white shirtfront. "All right, Sinclair, tell me what we have so far."

Briefly, succinctly, Maggie recapped the information she'd synthesized. When she mentioned the shallow grave and its occupant, Adam stiffened.

"We should know within an hour who she is," Maggie added. "State's running through their data base of all known citizens in the area. They've requested checks from Canada and the European nations, as well." She paused, chewing on her lower lip for a moment. "I don't know that there's any connection between the woman and our operation, but I have this…"

A small smile curved Adam's lips. "Tingling feeling in your bones?"

"More like a prickly sensation at the base of my spine," Maggie replied solemnly.

The smile disappeared. "Well, whatever it is, this is one time I hope your instincts are wrong."

"Oh-oh. Sounds like the call from the president added a new piece to the puzzle."

"Several pieces. Tell State to check the status of a medical sister who was working in Cartoza. From the Order of Our Lady of Sorrows."

"*Madre Dolorosa?* I read up on those sisters as part of my prebrief for this operation. It's a large order, headquartered in Mexico City, with branches throughout Latin America, the United States and Europe. Although the order is still very conservative in matters of dress and convent life, the sisters have been active in Central America. I'm not surprised one of their people was in Jake's area."

"Apparently the sister wasn't the only American woman in the area. Tell State to also check the status of a Peace Corps volunteer by the name of Sarah Chandler."

"Sarah Chandler?" Maggie wrinkled her brow. "Why do I know that name?"

"She's only been in the Peace Corps a short time. She arrived in Cartoza less than two weeks ago, in fact. Before that she was a rather prominent political hostess here in Washington."

"Oh, Lord! Not that Sarah Chandler!"

"Yes, that Sarah Chandler. The senator's daughter."

As she made her way back to the third-floor control center, Maggie's mind was racing. No wonder the president wanted to know what had happened in Cartoza. Senator Orwin Chandler of North Carolina was one of the most influential and powerful men on the Hill. According to Adam, the senator had already heard through his own intelligence sources about the rebel raid and had pieced together enough to know that the U.S. had some involvement or interest in the action. He didn't want any damn details, Chandler had informed the president. He only wanted assurances that his daughter was safe.

There wasn't any way the president could give Senator Chandler those assurances, Maggie thought grimly.

Not yet.

Tucking the sweep of her hair behind her left ear, she reclaimed her seat at the command console. "Okay, Joe, let's get back to work."

Despite his years in the jungle, Jake had never become accustomed to its lightninglike transitions from light to dark. In the evening, there was no dusk. Just a sudden graying of the air, then a blackness so swift and intense he couldn't see his hand in front of his face.

Dawn sliced through the canopy of fig and mahogany trees with the same startling speed. One minute he was stumbling along the narrow trail, straining to see the faint moving shadows of the men in front of him with the aid of the low-light goggles. The next minute those shadows had taken on context and contrast and the goggles instantly became superfluous.

Or at least that was the way it usually worked.

This morning, however, the figure directly in front of him refused to take shape. Jake shook his head, unable to appreciate the dedication that would lead someone to don a heavy, shapeless black robe in the oppressive heat of the jungle. His own khaki shirt already clung to him like a second skin, and the sun had only been up a few minutes. His jaw tight, he watched the woman lift her arm to wipe her face with a corner of a voluminous sleeve. She had small hands, he noted. Small and fine-boned, with short, blunt nails and work-roughened skin.

Frowning, he moved up alongside her. "That habit may have saved your life last night, but it's the worst possible getup for this climate. Your superiors ought to have more sense than to send you sisters into the interior wearing something like that."

She looked up at him then, and Jake saw her face for the first time in daylight. Framed by the limp white wimple and black veil, it was a composite of high cheekbones, an aristocratic little nose and a firm, pointed chin. Dirt streaked her forehead. Sweat and the pallor of exhaustion filmed her skin. But nothing could dull the impact of the most stunning eyes Jake had ever seen. Wide and luminous and a clear, translucent aquamarine in color, they shimmered like jewels in the morning light. They also, Jake noted, raked him with undisguised scorn.

"I wouldn't expect someone like you to understand matters of the cloth, Mr....Mr...."

"You'd better just call me 'gringo,'" Jake replied, recovering slowly.

She turned away, declining to call him anything at all.

He fell back into line behind her. Jake swore under his breath, slowly, savagely. The beads of sweat clinging to his cheeks suddenly felt clammy. All hell was going to break loose when the men with him got a good look at the woman they'd taken.

It was too late now to even think about taking out the patrol strung out ahead of and behind them. They were within a mile of the camp. The intrusion-detection devices that ringed the hideaway had signaled their arrival for the past half hour. If gunfire broke out now, the rest of the rebels would be on the scene before he had the exhausted woman and her charges halfway back down the winding mountain trail they'd spent the past five hours trudging up.

His mouth grim, Jake reviewed his options.

He had only one, he decided as the narrow trail suddenly emerged from the tall, heavy forest into a debris-strewn clearing. He'd have to bluff it out.

The rebel camp sat high in the foothills of the Teleran Mountains, a line of jagged peaks extending from the Canadian Rockies all the way down through Central America. Dry and barren on the Pacific side, the mountains were greened by the trade winds on the Atlantic side. The moisture-laden winds dumped up to three hundred inches of rainfall a year on the steep slopes. The lush rain forest that resulted made for harsh living conditions and difficult travel, but, as Jake well knew, it provided excellent cover.

In classic guerrilla style, the band he'd infiltrated made maximum use of existing land features. They traveled under the screen of the thick forest canopy and carried with them only what they needed to fight with. For their base camp, they'd appropriated a cluster of tumbledown shacks that had once been an outpost of a vast coffee plantation. Abandoned by workers seeking more lucrative employment in cocaine-processing factories, the outpost had long since been re-claimed by the jungle. Only a few of the tin-roofed huts still stood, their wooden shutters gaping. The rebels used the most secure one to store their supplies. Their leader had claimed another for his personal use.

A narrow, sluggish stream cut across the far edge of the clearing, providing the only source of water for sanitation and drinking. Thin, barrel-ribbed packhorses, still the primary means of transportation this deep in the interior, cropped beside the stream. Overhead, camouflage netting stretched across the entire camp, shielding it from observation.

As the small group straggled into the clearing, Jake moved alongside the woman. "Keep quiet," he murmured. "And keep your head down."

She immediately flashed him a wide, startled look.

Christ! Those eyes were going to get them both killed. "Keep your head down," he all but snarled.

Stepping in front of her, Jake skimmed the gathering crowd for the thin, hawk-eyed leader who'd taken the name of the revolutionary hero he revered. He didn't have to search long. The only one in camp who adhered to any standards of discipline in his dress or personal hygiene, Che stood out among his scruffy band. The woman with him stood out even more. Her lush figure strained the fatigues she wore, but Jake knew better than to equate her rounded curves with stereotypical concepts of feminity. He'd seen her use the automatic rifle slung over her shoulder to deadly effect.

Stiff and unbending in his camouflage uniform, the leader stopped a few paces away and listened while the man nominally in charge of last night's fiasco stumbled through a muddled explanation in his thick mountain dialect. They'd already radioed in a brief report, but Jake could see that Che was tight-lipped with anger over the loss of the shipment of shoulder-launched heat-seeking missiles he'd been expecting.

When the man's muttered excuses ran out, Che turned cold eyes on Jake. "So, gringo, why do you think the government troops were near the drop zone last night?"

"Beats the crap out of me," Jake drawled, "but you'd sure better find out. I'm not risking my ass with these trigger-happy bastards of yours again unless you get some reliable intelligence that the area's clean."

Che's lip curled. "Or unless we up your fee, eh?"

"My fee doubled last night. I don't like working with amateurs."

A wash of color rose in the man's olive cheeks. "Watch yourself, gringo."

"You want me to show you how to arm these little toys you're collecting," Jake replied steadily, "you pay for it. The price goes up with every botched drop."

A muscle twitched on one side of Che's jaw. Jake held his look with a cold one of his own. After a long, tense moment, the rebel's gaze slid to the silent, black-clad figure. "Why did you bring her?"

Jake's voice deepened with disgust. "Because these fools you call soldiers of the revolution almost left her lying in the dirt in the village."

The leader sneered. "And that offended some long-lost religious sensibility of yours?"

"That offended my sense of self-preservation," Jake shot back. "The public outcry over a *religiosa*'s death would've caused a massive government manhunt for her killers. I didn't think you'd appreciate that, at least not until we get our hands on those missiles you want and even the odds a bit."

"You could've left her body in the jungle, where no one would find it."

"And the children's, too?" Jake shrugged. "You aren't paying me to murder nuns and children. If you don't want them here, you get rid of them."

Che's eyes went flat and black. For a heart-stopping moment, Jake feared he might have overplayed his hand.

"We might have need of a *médica*'s skills sometime in the near future," he offered casually.

Che made no effort to hide his suspicion as he glanced from Jake to the woman, then back again.

"You brought her, gringo," he said at last. "You're responsible for her. If she escapes or puts a knife through one of my men, you die."

Jake bared his teeth in a slow, twisting, menacing smile. "Then tell your men to keep away from her. Or they die."

Jake turned without another word and gripped the nun by the arm. The quick, questioning look she slanted him from beneath lowered lids told him she had understood little of the exchange. Just as well, he decided grimly.

The milling men parted as they walked to where the eldest boy stood protectively beside the packhorse. Jake reached up and lifted the little girl down first. She ran to the sister, burying her face in the black skirts. He scooped the toddler up, tucked him under one arm and jerked his chin toward the hut that served as a storage dump for the camp's supplies and the few personal belongings the men had with them. "Over there."

When he shoved open the door, trapped moist heat hit Jake in the face and sucked the air out of his lungs. He stepped inside and gestured to the others to follow. Setting the boy down, he nudged him toward the now-wilting sister, then tossed the bundles of gear belonging to the others out the door. That done, he knelt beside a military-style backpack propped against a crate stenciled with U.S. markings. As he dug through the knapsack, Jake rapped out a series of low, hurried orders.

"Listen, and listen well. I'm going to go get some water and round up some food. Don't show your face outside this hut, and for God's sake don't try anything stupid, like slipping into the jungle while I'm gone. This camp is ringed with more booby traps and explosive devices than a nuclear storage site."

He straightened, canteens dangling from one fist, and eyed her for a moment. "I don't suppose you know how to use an AK-47—or, better yet, an APG?"

She ran her tongue over dry lips. "What's an APG?"

"Never mind."

A ripple of comprehension crossed her pale, strained face. She glanced at the crates, then back at Jake. "It's some kind of weapon, I gather. That's why you're here, isn't it? You sell guns to these men."

"No. I sell myself, or rather my expertise. These goons don't know how to operate half the weapons they're supplied by the drug lords who keep them in business. I show them."

A look of scorn settled in her eyes, deepening them to a shimmering blue-green that reminded Jake of a lake he'd once fished in upstate New York. It held cold, crystal-clear water, with a deceptive, unplumbed depth. The kind that invited a man to strip off and plunge in. The kind that invigorated and enticed and—

Jake pulled himself up short. Jaws tight, he whirled and

slammed the door of the hut behind him. As he strode toward the sluggish stream, he couldn't decide what irritated him more. The fact that she hadn't made any effort to disguise her contempt, or the fact that such incredible, expressive and downright seductive eyes were wasted on a woman who'd taken a vow of celibacy.

Pushing the sister's image out of his head, Jake dropped to one knee beside the stream. He dragged the canteen in the slow, rippling water with one hand. The other he hooked in the web belt he wore low on his hips. His fingers drummed an impatient tatoo on the buckle.

Only Jake knew that the metal gusset next to the belt buckle doubled as an encrypting device, and that the pattern he tapped out formed a digitized code. The transmitter sewn into his belt was too small for anything other than a short emergency signal. But that signal would be picked up by the U.S. Navy ships cruising offshore and relayed to the OMEGA control center within minutes.

Chapter 3

"**Y**es!"

Joe Samuels's shout brought Maggie running from the crew room, where she'd gone to splash cold water on her face.

"It's Jaguar," he told her, his eyes snapping with excitement.

Maggie expelled a whoosh of pent-up breath. Jake MacKenzie had survived the disaster of the night before. She headed for the command console. "Is he on the satellite receiver?"

"No. All I got was an emergency signal, relayed by the navy. Here it is."

Maggie's pulse leaped when she saw the three numbers Samuels had scrawled. Although she knew the emergency signals she and Jake had devised by heart, she went immediately to her black operations notebook and verified the individual digits.

Agent in place.

Stand by for further word.

"Way to go, Jaguar," Maggie murmured, grinning broadly.

Her finger slid down to the clear-text explanation of the third digit.

Neutral on board.

Thoughtfully, Maggie tapped the notebook with her fore-finger. Well, at least now she knew the location of the missing American woman. State had verified just moments ago the sketchy information the president had passed to Adam. There had been two American women in the village at the time of the raid—one a medical sister from the Order of Our Lady of Sorrows, the other a Peace Corps volunteer by the name of Sarah Chandler.

But which one had been buried in the shallow grave, and which one was now smack in the middle of Jake's operation? Until she gathered that rather vital bit of information, Maggie decided she'd better find out all she could about both of them.

Twenty minutes and as many contacts with various agencies later, she sat back in her chair and frowned at her two pages of scribbled notes. Scanning the profiles she'd pieced together, Maggie decided she didn't much like either one.

Sister Maria Augustine, age thirty-four. Formerly Helen Peters. Born in Pattersonville, Ohio. Joined the Order of Our Lady of Sorrows a year after graduation from nursing school. A highly skilled nurse practitioner who'd spent nearly half her life in Central America. As well known for her clashes with the bureaucratic government officials who regulated her medical station as for her outspoken criticism of the rebels who preyed on the people she served.

And Sarah Chandler, twenty-nine, daughter of Senator Orwin Chandler. Graduate of Sweet Briar College, with a degree in education she'd never put to use. A wealthy, pampered socialite whose affair with a married diplomat had caused a feeding frenzy among the Washington press corps when it was uncovered six months ago. And whose drunk-driving conviction a few weeks later had led to her disappearance from the Washington scene.

According to Maggie's sources, Senator Chandler had used his influence to convince the judge to give his daughter com-

munity service instead of a jail sentence. Again because of
her father's influence, Sarah Chandler had been allowed to
perform that service as a volunteer with the Peace Corps.

Maggie groaned and shoved a hand through her hair. Great,
just great! Jake was stuck down there in the jungle with either
a scandal-ridden socialite or a social activist of a nun on his
hands. At this point, she wasn't sure which one she hoped it
was.

Sarah Chandler sat on a fifty-pound sack of dried beans, an
arm around Ricci's small body. Teresa clutched at her other
sleeve with both hands, while Eduard, his face solemn in the
sweltering haze of the hut, stared at her with wide black eyes.

Desperately Sarah tried to stifle the fear that had gripped
her since the stutter of machine-gun fire had torn her from
sleep so many hours ago and even now made her hair slick
with sweat under the limp veil. Despite her best efforts, a
series of tremors racked her.

Oh, God, what was she doing here? How had her life turned
upside down like this in such a short time?

Humid, suffocating heat seared her lungs with each gulping
breath. She glanced around the hut in mounting dismay. The
panic she'd held at bay all through the long, terrifying night
clogged her throat.

Her father was right! She could have worked out her shattering guilt over the consequences of her actions at home just
as well as in the Peace Corps. She could've done community
service in D.C., or in their home state of North Carolina, for
that matter, anywhere other than some remote little village in
the middle of the jungle. Sarah squeezed her eyes shut, seeing
Orwin Chandler's big, hearty figure as he paced the paneled
library of the Bethesda home they shared, puffing on the one
cigar he allowed himself each day.

If she'd listened to her father, if she hadn't pitted herself
against him for perhaps the first time in her life, she wouldn't
be here in an airless shack, pretending a medical knowledge

she didn't possess. She wouldn't be bound by horrible chance and circumstance to a steel-eyed mercenary who—

"Sarita?"

Ricci's wobbling voice pulled Sarah back from the brink of a hysteria engendered by delayed shock and total exhaustion.

"Sarita, tengo que ir al baño."

She stared at him, uncomprehending. Her formal Spanish, sketchy at best, seemed to have deserted her completely. Nor had she been in country long enough to gain any real understanding of the local dialect. The people she'd lived with these past weeks had hidden their smiles at her faltering attempts to communicate and replied politely in English. Even these children had a better command of her language than she did of theirs. Somehow, that made Sarah feel even worse.

"I'm sorry, Ricci," she said shakily. "Please, tell me again."

"I have to make the pee," he announced in English.

"Oh."

"Me also," Teresa chimed in.

Their simple needs steadied Sarah as perhaps nothing else could have. After a dark night of terror and a morning that had brought them to the grim reality of the rebel camp, they needed to make pee. Sarah reined in her incipient panic, reminding herself that she'd promised Maria she'd watch over these abandoned children until the church authorities came for them.

Maria! A stab of regret lanced through Sarah for the woman she'd grown so close to in such a short space of time. Strong, competent, no-nonsense Sister Maria, with her skilled hands and sympathetic brown eyes. Maria, who'd died so needlessly, so tragically, just two days ago after the Jeep she'd been hauling medical supplies in hit a tree root and overturned, crushing her underneath.

Ricci tugged impatiently on her sleeve. "Sarita!"

"Okay, honey, okay."

The…the gringo had said not to go outside. Biting down

on her lower lip, Sarah glanced around for a vessel the children could use. The hut was too small and too airless for them to just relieve themselves on the hard-packed dirt floor.

Aside from the stacked wooden crates she'd been warned away from, the only contents of the hut were sacks of coffee, rice, and the black beans that formed the main dietary staple in this region. Some dirty, ragged bedrolls had been tossed in one corner, along with a wadded pile of mosquito netting. Her gaze fell on the gringo's backpack, propped against the wall. Maybe there was something inside she could appropriate.

Tugging her arm free of Teresa's clutching hands, Sarah pushed herself off the cot and crossed to the bulging brown-and-green knapsack. Inside she found a cache of items necessary for survival in the tropics—quinine, a first aid kit, snakebite antidote, a plastic bottle of water-purifier capsules. There was also a shaving kit that held a few toiletries, as well as two small travel toothbrushes. Greedily grabbing one of the toothbrushes, Sarah set it and a squeezed-up tube of toothpaste aside, then dug deeper. She pulled out a poncho, vital in a country where torrential rains pounded out of the sky for at least an hour every day during rainy season, and a spare pair of the high, flexible rubber boots with thin soles necessary for walking any distance through the streams and soggy layers of vegetation in the rain forest.

Frustrated, Sarah turned to the side pockets. Her rummaging fingers extracted a clean, if wrinkled, khaki shirt from one pocket, a thick wad of socks from another, and from the last a couple of pairs of white cotton men's briefs.

Sarah fingered the soft cotton. To her consternation, a flush added to the heat bathing her cheeks as she stared at the Jockey shorts. Size 34, she read on the label. Unadorned, utilitarian, and utterly masculine.

For the first time, Sarah visualized the man she'd spent the past five desperate hours with as…as a man. A startling mental image of his lean, muscled body clothed only in these briefs gripped her. She remembered suddenly how his sweat-dampened shirt had clung to wide shoulders and delineated the taut muscles of his upper arms. How the web belt sporting a long, lethal-looking machete and a plain leather holster had hung low on his narrow hips. How...

"Saritaaaa!"

At the small, desperate wail, Sarah jumped. She crammed the briefs back into the side pocket and scrabbled in the dirt for the likeliest receptacle.

"They used my *boot?*"

The gringo's voice rose incredulously. He stood just inside the hut, canteens dangling from one arm, a mounded plate of beans and rice in either hand.

At the sound of his harsh exclamation, Teresa whimpered. Sarah wrapped an arm around the girl's thin shoulders and pulled her into her side.

"Well, they had to use something," she pointed out.

"They used my *boot?*"

"Oh, for—" Sarah bit off the impatient exclamation. What was the big deal? "You can rinse it out in the stream. After you provide something more suitable for the children to use."

He slammed the tin plate down on one of the crates. "There's a whole damn jungle right outside. They can use that!"

"You *said* not to leave the hut," she retorted, then belatedly remembered her role. "And I must ask you to refrain from taking the Lord's name in vain."

Under the dark stubble that shadowed his face, his jaw worked. Narrowed gray eyes glittered with an anger he made no effort to disguise. "Look, lady—Sister—we're going to lay a few ground rules here."

The unmistakable menace in his voice turned Teresa's whimpers to outright sobs. She burrowed into the smothering folds of the black robe and sent sharp little elbows poking in Sarah's side.

The scowl on the man's face deepened at the girl's sobs. He looked so fierce and threatening that Sarah's brief spurt of defiance evaporated. She gripped Teresa with a sudden feeling of panic.

His effect on the boys was no less dramatic. Little Ricci whimpered that they would die and buried his face in the thick black skirt. Eduard rose from his cross-legged position on the floor, sidled next to Sarah, and put a hand on her shoulder.

She wasn't sure whether the eight-year old meant to draw comfort from her or reassure her. Eduard rarely spoke. Even the skilled, patient Sister Maria hadn't been able to draw the boy from the silent shell he'd encased himself in since one of the villagers found him in the jungle several years ago, thin-ribbed, hollow-faced, and starving. His flat black eyes gave no hint of his thoughts or his emotions.

The touch of Eduard's small hand on her shoulder sent a wave of confused emotions through Sarah. She was ashamed of her sudden panic, yet too exhausted to summon the courage to combat it. And, worse, she was swamped by the enormity of the responsibility that had been thrust upon her.

She didn't know anything about children! She knew even less about jungle survival. How could she hope to escape and make it back to civilization dragging three kids? How could she defend herself, let alone them, from the furious man who confronted them? She wanted to burst into tears and bury her face in Teresa's tangled hair.

The gringo must have seen that he'd pushed her to the limit of her resources. The glittering anger in his eyes gave way to disgust. He rattled off something in Spanish that Sarah didn't catch and turned to dump the canteens beside the plate he'd slammed down a few moments ago. Reining in his temper with a visible effort, he shrugged off the weapon slung over his shoulder and propped it against the wall next to his back-pack. He settled himself on the wooden box, his long legs sprawled out and his back against the stack behind him.

Whatever he'd said seemed to reassure the children. Or maybe it was his less threatening stance. In any case, Teresa's cries dwindled to gulping hiccups. Ricci's face appeared from the folds of Sarah's skirt. He glanced at the gringo, then at the food. After a moment, he pulled himself up and waddled over to the plates. Digging a grubby hand into the combination of rice and cold black beans, he proceeded to stuff the mixture into his mouth.

Wearily Sarah unwrapped her arm from the little girl's body. "Go on, Teresa. You must eat. You too, Eduard." She sent the older boy a glance she could only hope was calm and confident.

"You, also, Sarita," Teresa insisted, refusing to relinquish her tight grip on her sleeve. "You come, too."

Sarah nodded and started to push herself to her feet.

"Sarita?"

The deep voice rasped like rough sandpaper along Sarah's frayed nerves. She froze, wondering wildly if she should tell this man her real name. Did she dare trust him with the knowledge that she wasn't the medical sister he believed her to be? She straightened and brushed the straggling veil out of her face to look at him.

No. No way. Not this hard-eyed mercenary. If he bartered his despicable skills for the drug dollars these rebels paid him, she shuddered to think of the price he'd demand for the daughter of a United States senator.

"Sarita is what the children call me." Pulling the first name she could think of out of the air, she met his gaze. "I'm Sister Sarah Josepha. From the convent of Our Lady of Sorrows."

She managed to roll the convent name off confidently enough. In the few weeks they'd worked side by side in the small clinic Maria ran, Sarah had learned a great deal about her companion's religious background. Open, friendly, at times blunt and outspoken, Maria had held nothing back. Sarah had found herself envying the woman her dedication and sense of purpose.

"Our Lady of Sorrows," he murmured. "Appropriate."

Sarah stiffened. "What's that supposed to mean?"

He flicked a glance at the children, now crouched down in front of the food and busy filling their empty bellies. "Only that we're both going to experience a lot more sorrow than we can handle if we don't keep a real cool head for the next few days."

A sharp splinter of hope pierced Sarah's heart. "The next few days? Do you mean we'll only be here a few days? Then you'll let us go?"

"I don't know how long you'll be here," he replied flatly.

The hope in Sarah's chest exploded into tiny shards of a disappointment so painful she choked.

His brows drew into a dark slash. "Look, Sister Sarah, if it was up to me, I'd put you and the kids on a packhorse right now and get you the hell out of Dodge. I'm not exactly thrilled to have the four of you on my hands while I'm trying to conduct a...business operation."

The hesitation was so slight that Sarah almost missed it. Bitterness and frustration curled her lip. "A business operation? Is that what you call it? There's a word for people like you, you know, and it's not *entrepreneur*."

He rose to his feet and took a slow step toward her.

Sarah swallowed, but refused to back away.

"You've got a real mouth on you, for a nun," he commented softly.

He was so close Sarah could smell the tang of healthy male sweat emanating from his chest. She stared up at him, seeing the hard line of his jaw under the stubble that shadowed it. She realized suddenly that tall and lean translated into overpowering and rather dangerous at such close quarters. Rubbing damp palms down the sides of her skirts, Sarah took a deep breath and summoned up the last tattered remnants of her courage.

"Is that so? Just how many nuns do you know?"

Something glimmered in his eyes. Sarah couldn't tell whether it was surprise that she refused to let him intimidate her, or reluctant admiration at her stand, or amusement. The thought that her desperate struggle to contain her fear might amuse him sent her chin up another notch.

"Not many," he admitted. The ghost of a smile tugged at his lips. "In fact, I've only met one other. She caught me snitching fruit from the corner grocery store and whacked me over the head with her umbrella. When she marched me home, my staunch Methodist father agreed with the good sister that I needed a little more forceful guidance and took me out behind the garage. Since then I've tended to avoid your kind.''

Waves of relief coursed through Sarah. She just might make it through this mess after all. Lifting her chin, she gave a disdainful sniff. ''Obviously, both the whack over the head and your trip to the garage failed dismally to curb your ways.''

''Obviously,'' he drawled, turning away. ''Go eat. Then we'd better get what sleep we can before the heat gets too unbearable. I'll string some hammocks for the kids, and we can make do with the bedrolls.''

''You're going to sleep here? With us?''

''Right the first time.''

''I don't think that's either necessary or appropriate, Mr….Gringo.''

He didn't even bother to turn around. ''What you think in this instance doesn't matter a whole lot, Sister Sarah. You see, that ferret-faced little runt out there who leads this band of so-called revolutionaries isn't exactly pleased that I dragged you back here. He's made me personally responsible for you, and I'm not a man who takes his responsibilities lightly.''

Ignoring Sarah's inelegant little huff of derision, he looped the end of a hammock rope around an exposed wooden roof support. ''Go eat,'' he ordered, in a voice that brooked no further argument.

While he moved about the small hut, Sarah joined the children. They scooted aside to make room for her around the impromptu table. Remembering his warning about things that went boom in the night, she lowered herself gingerly onto the edge of the crate, then glanced around for something to eat with. There wasn't anything except her fingers. Sarah wiped them on her robe and tried not to think of what might be clinging to either her skin or her skirts.

Her first scoop of cold beans and rice lodged in a throat still dry with the residue of fear and exhaustion. Sarah unscrewed the plastic top of one of the canteens and washed the lump down, grimacing at the taste of tepid water laced with chemical purifiers. She wiped the mouth of the canteen with her sleeve and passed it to little Teresa, then scooped up another few fingerfuls of food. Within moments, she was gobbling the hearty fare down as hungrily as the children.

After half a lifetime of dining at Washington's elegant restaurants and quaint eateries, Sarah had been surprised at how well she adapted to the steady diet of rice and black beans that formed the basis of every meal in this part of the world. In the evening the villagers augmented the dish with chicken or, occasionally, pork cooked in a spicy tomato sauce. When scooped up in still-warm corn tortillas and finished off with the plentiful fruits of the area, the food was nutritious and filling.

Or maybe Sarah's easy adjustment to it had stemmed from the fact that, for the first time in her life, she wasn't giving much thought to either her weight or her appearance. The humidity had wreaked such havoc on her once-shining cap of long platinum blond hair that she'd taken to simply dragging it back with an elastic band. Moreover, she'd found a degree of comfort and a strange sense of freedom in the baggy cotton trousers and shirts her Peace Corps sponsor had told her to bring. Sarah smothered a silent groan, wishing she could shuck the hot, sticky black habit and pull on one of those lightweight shirts right now.

Even Maria herself had rarely worn these suffocating robes, donning them only for infrequent visits to her chapter house in the capital city. In the interior she wore sensible lightweight cotton work clothes—and the bright red ball cap with the Washington Redskins logo emblazoned on the front that Sarah had given her.

At the memory of the ball cap, Sarah's fingers stilled halfway to her mouth. She closed her eyes against the familiar wave of pain and guilt that washed through her. André had bought the ball cap for her on one of their delightful, illicit outings. Sarah had thought to use the anonymity of the huge crowd at a Skins game to teach the suave, sophisticated Frenchman a little about the American national pastime. Instead, he'd shaken his head at her incomprehensible enthusiasm for what he considered a slow, pedestrian sport and whisked her away during the third quarter to a discreet little hotel to demonstrate what he laughingly called the French national sport.

She'd been so in love with him, Sarah thought in despair. She hadn't stopped to think about the pain and tragedy her selfish need for him could cause. She'd believed him when he caressed her and adored her with his skilled hands and clever mouth. She'd—

"Don't forget to shake your bedroll out before you lie down."

Sarah blinked and slewed around to see the gringo stretched out, his long legs crossed at the ankle and a floppy-brimmed camouflage hat covering his eyes.

"What?"

"Shake out the bedroll," he murmured, without removing the hat. "It's a safe bet the last inhabitant was a snake, either the slippery, slithery variety or one of his two-legged cousins."

Sarah eyed the stained mat beside his in distaste. "Maybe I'll share a hammock with Teresa."

"Suit yourself."

After the children finished their meal, Sarah wiped ineffectually at the smallest ones' faces with the dampened tail of her sleeve. Eduard disdained her ministrations. He folded his thin body into the hammock, then pulled Ricci in beside him. Sarah draped a tent of mosquito netting the gringo had rigged over both of them.

She approached the second hammock with the assurance of a woman who danced with a joyful, natural grace and played

a mean game of tennis. She soon found, however, that ne-
gotiating her way into a swinging hammock with a child in
one arm and heavy skirts draped over the other took more
than grace or coordination. It took a skill she didn't seem to
possess.

On her first attempt, the lightweight net swung out from
under her, nearly dropping her on her bottom. On her second
attempt, the knee she'd lifted to anchor the net swayed away,
causing her to hop a few steps across the dirt floor on one
foot to keep from losing her balance. Six year old Teresa
clung to her neck, like one of those stuffed toys with the long,
strangling arms, and giggled.

The sound tugged at Sarah's heart. She smiled down at the
child. "Think that's funny, do you?"

Teresa put a dirty hand to her mouth to cover the gap from
her lost front teeth. Her black eyes sparkled.

"Let's try this again. We'll do it scientifically this time.
One step at a time."

Grasping the edge of the net in a firm hand, Sarah rose up
on tiptoe and swung her hips into the net. She gave a startled
squawk as the hammock rolled high up in the air and dumped
her on the floor.

Teresa came down on top of her, giggling helplessly. Childish snickers from the other hammock told Sarah that Ricci
was getting as much enjoyment out of this as Teresa. Even
Eduard was smiling, she saw when she sat up and shoved
back the once-starched white headband that held her veil out
of her eyes.

So was the mercenary. He leaned on one elbow, the floppy
hat pushed to the back of his head. Even through the draped
mosquito net, Sarah could see the crooked slash of white teeth
that cut the darkness of his unshaven cheeks.

Sarah had perfected a lot of skills during her years as a
Washington political hostess. One of the most valuable was a
ripple of musical laughter that went a long way toward minimizing any social disaster. André had often told her that her

ability to smile and shrug off domestic crises that would mortify other hostesses was among her most charming traits.

So the answering smile she gave the gringo began as a well-learned, deliberate response to an embarrassing situation. But as her mouth curved, Sarah found relief from her fear and fatigue in the simple act. Her smile deepened.

For a moment, their eyes met, his gray and shadowed by black lashes, hers free of the fear that had haunted her for so many hours. They weren't mercenary and nun, but simply a man and woman enjoying a ridiculous moment. He broke it off first. Still grinning, he lay down again and tugged the hat over his eyes.

Sarah dragged herself to her feet and plunked Teresa into the hammock. ''It's all yours, sweetheart.''

The little girl grabbed at her hand. ''Sarita!''

''Don't worry. I'll be right here beside you.''

Gently disengaging her hand, Sarah pushed aside the mosquito netting draped over the stained, uninviting bedroll. She lifted the sleeping bag by one corner and shook it once, twice. Something fell out and scurried away between the stacked crates. Sarah gasped, then grabbed the other corner and shook the mat for all she was worth.

The man on the other bedroll grunted and rolled over on his side, his back to Sarah.

After a vigorous shaking, she laid the edges of the limp bedroll down and sat back on her heels, eyeing it distrustfully. When nothing moved under its surface and no hissing lump appeared, she smoothed it out with short, swift and very cautious pats.

''For Pete's sake, will you lie down?''

Sarah threw his broad back an indignant look. Slowly, gingerly, she stretched out, then reached up to tug the mosquito netting back down. It settled around them both like a white cloud, enclosing them in an airy, strangely intimate cocoon. After a few moments, the exhaustion seeping through her bones caused her rigid muscles to relax. She dragged her sleeve across her face to wipe away the moisture generated by her exertions and closed her eyes, sure she'd be asleep within moments.

She was wrong.

As tired as she was, her body wouldn't, couldn't, slip into blessed semiconsciousness. Instead, an insidious need crept through her, stiffening her limbs and keeping her eyes wide open in the hazy light.

The boys' breathing evened out. Little Teresa whistled once or twice through the gap in her front teeth, then snuggled down in the hammock and grew still.

Sarah stared up at the rusted tin roof. She listened to the scurry of forest mice scuttling up and down the walls in their never-ending search for insects. From a few feet away came the rumble of deep, sonorous breathing. Not a snore, exactly, but pretty darn close to it.

Desperately Sarah willed herself to ignore the sounds around her and go to sleep. She squeezed her eyes shut and began to count, as she'd done so often as a child, when her father had gone to some political fund-raiser or another and she'd lain awake in her big, flower-patterned bedroom, waiting for him to come home and read to her.

At two hundred and forty-seven, she gave up. Worrying her lower lip with her teeth, she rose up on her knees, then inched to her feet. She lifted her skirts and moved as quietly as possible across the hut.

She didn't even hear him move. She was just bending toward an object near the wall when a hard hand spun her around. The veil whipped at her face, causing the headdress to tilt haphazardly to one side of her head.

"What the hell are you doing?" Suspicion blazed in his eyes and singed his low, furious voice. "I thought you said you didn't know how to use a weapon."

"I don't!" Sarah gasped.

"Then why were you reaching for it?"

Sarah glanced down at the automatic rifle propped against the wall beside the backpack. "I wasn't reaching for your precious weapon!"

"So what were you after, lady?"

No *Sister Sarah* this time. No crooked grin that coaxed an answering response from her. At this moment, he radiated a hard, cold authority that made Sarah gulp.

"Tell me," he growled, giving her a shake.

The veil tilted farther over her ear, then fell off completely. He sucked in a quick breath, his narrowed eyes on her hair.

Sarah raised a hand defensively to the limp, sweat-slicked blond strands. "We...we don't cut it anymore. We haven't since Pope John's Vatican Council."

There'd been a Pope John. She was sure of it. And the Italian ambassador had talked at great length about a Vatican Council at one of the dinner parties Sarah had given for her father. She held her breath, waiting for the gringo's response.

His flinty gaze shifted to her face. "So you don't cut your hair anymore. That still doesn't explain what you're doing creeping around the hut."

She opened her mouth to reply, then shut it. She opened it again, but couldn't force out the words.

"I'm fast running out of patience," he warned softly, "and you don't want to be around when I do."

"I have to use the boot," Sarah muttered through clenched teeth.

Chapter 4

She needed to use the boot!

Drawing in a deep breath, Jake ran through his options.

He could risk taking her outside to go downstream, as the other inhabitants of the camp did. Or he could escort her into the jungle, no doubt with a trail of interested spectators tagging along behind.

No, options one and two weren't smart. He'd heard the murmurs among the men when Sister Sarah walked into camp. He'd caught the swift, slashing male assessment they'd given her when she glanced up at him, her eyes gemlike in a pale and dirty face.

Option three, he could let her use the damned boot.

What the hell? No doubt the acid from the kids' urine had already eaten through the special lining and destroyed the satellite voice communications device concealed there. One of the other OMEGA agents, a former air force jock, had told Jake about a C-130 transport plane that had gone down in Vietnam. Seemed the effluent of the farm animals being evacuated with desperate villagers fleeing the Vietcong had destroyed the cables under the aircraft's flooring. If urine could destroy the 130's metal-and-wire cables, Jake's transmitter-receiver was a goner by now. So was his boot, he decided wryly.

Releasing the sister's arm, he stepped back. "Be my guest."

Bright spots of color flaring in each cheek, she snatched up the rubber footwear. After a quick look around the hut, she marched behind a stack of crates.

Jake smiled grimly, wondering how he was going to explain this one to Maggie Sinclair—when, and if, he ever found a way to slip out of the camp and retrieve the backup transmitter he'd buried in a cranny of a towering strangler fig.

He settled back down on the bedroll and bent an arm under his head, thinking about the unexpected complication to his mission in the form of Sister Sarah Josepha. As he'd admitted earlier, he didn't know a whole lot of nuns, but the few he'd seen here in Central America were sure different from little Sister Sarah. Most of them wore sensible work clothes and no longer covered their hair with veils. They didn't drape themselves in old-fashioned, uncomfortable habits in an excess of zealous piety.

Although… Jake was forced to admit that none of the sisters he'd seen around these parts possessed quite the same combination of luminous eyes, tumbling white-gold hair and unconsciously seductive smile, either. At the memory of the way her smile had softened the angled planes of her face into a breathtaking beauty, he felt a slow, involuntary tightening low in his groin—followed immediately by a wave of self-disgust.

Maybe it wasn't overzealousness that kept her in those shapeless robes, he thought wryly. Maybe Sister Sarah exhibited a whole lot of common sense by covering up her undeniably attractive attributes so that they wouldn't distract her—or others—from the vocation she'd chosen.

Only the strategy wasn't working. Not right at this moment, anyway. Not for Jake.

He'd been in the jungle too damned long, he decided grimly. He'd forgotten the basic tenets of civilized behavior. He had no business thinking the thoughts he was about the woman who emerged at that moment from behind the crates and moved quietly toward the mat next to his. Jake heard her give the bedroll a few cautious pats before she settled in.

He came awake an hour later with the swift, instant alertness that had saved his life more than once. His senses collected immediate impressions for his brain to process. Heat, humid and oppressive against his skin. The scent of his own sweat. The sound of shallow, regular breathing. The feel of a hand on his arm.

Jake glanced down at the small white hand that rested palm up against his sun-browned skin. Sister Sarah was a restless sleeper, he noted with a tight smile. She lay sprawled on her back, her face turned away. As he watched, she twitched a little and twisted her head toward him. He sucked in a swift breath at the pallor of her face under its sheen of sweat.

Well, hell. So much for common sense. That heavy black habit had to go, before Sarita succumbed to heatstroke. Jake had better find something more suitable for her to wear in this stifling hut.

He rolled off the mat with the lithe, noiseless movement that had become second nature to him and reached for the webbed belt that was always within reach. It settled around his hips with the familiarity of an old friend. The leather holster slapped against one thigh, the machete against the other. Clamping the hat down on his head, Jake left the shack.

Sarah awoke after a few hours' of restless sleep, groggy and disoriented. She wasn't at her best in the mornings—if it still *was* morning. Especially, she remembered slowly, when she'd spent most of the night tramping through the jungle.

She lay still, unwilling to move, unwilling to face what came next. Maybe if she just kept her eyes closed, she could convince herself she wasn't lying in an airless little shack. If she didn't breathe in too deeply, maybe she could keep the searing heat out of her lungs.

"Sarita."

Maybe if she just feigned sleep a little longer, Teresa would stop tugging at her sleeve.

"Sarita, *el gringo* is gone. Is he coming back?"

Sarah opened one eye. The little girl's worried face hovered against the filmy background of mosquito netting. Sarah turned her head to survey the empty bedroll next to hers.

"Will he come back?"

The fear in Teresa's voice tore at Sarah's heart. According to Maria, the six year old had lost both parents and two siblings in a devastating flash flood that all but destroyed the village last year. Since then the child had attached herself tenaciously to whoever offered security.

Maria had taken her into the clinic while church and government officials worked through the lengthy, complicated adoption process. In the interim, the little girl had become the nun's second shadow, following her everywhere. After Maria's death, Teresa had immediately transferred her attention to Sarah. For the past two days, Sarah hadn't been able to take a step without the dark-haired girl in the faded blue flowered dress beside her. When the rebels swept through the village—oh, God, was it only last night?—Teresa had clung to Sarah with terrified, instinctive trust. Frantic with fear herself, Sarah had thrown on Maria's robes in the hope they would protect her and the children. Running out of the clinic, she had sought safety for them all in the darkness of the jungle.

Only they hadn't found safety. And it appeared Teresa had already recognized the fact that her survival might depend on someone other than the woman whose sleeve she was tugging at.

"Will he, Sarita? Will he come back?"

"Yes, yes, I'm sure he will."

Sarah struggled into a sitting position. Only then did she see that Eduard was awake, as well. Unspeaking, he lay propped in the hammock, Ricci curled into a tight, sleeping ball beside him.

At the sight of his solemn face and unfathomable black eyes, Sarah felt again the enormity of the responsibility she'd so rashly assumed. Her dry throat closed as she fought the panic that threatened. How was she going to get them to safety?

She dragged in a deep breath. One step at a time.

"Why don't you go look in that backpack?" she suggested to Teresa. "Maybe there's a comb or a brush in it, and we can make you pretty."

While the girl fussed with the buckle on the knapsack, Sarah ruthlessly suppressed the memory of the mercenary's reaction the last time she'd appropriated one of his personal possessions.

The mercenary. *El gringo.*

Sarah made a moue of distaste as she washed her face with tepid water and a corner of her sleeve, then attacked her mouth with the toothbrush she'd appropriated earlier. If she was going to be stuck with the man until she got herself and the children out of this mess—and it looked like she was, she couldn't go on calling him "the mercenary." She searched for a name that would fit him, one she'd give him herself, since he wouldn't give her his. One that would suit a man too masculine and hard for handsomeness. Too lean and tough for politeness. Too lost to all concepts of right and wrong, she thought, for her to ever trust.

No, Sarah decided with an involuntary shiver. She didn't want to give him a name that reminded her of his disgusting profession. It would be better to come up with one that made him more human, more within her ability to manage. The image of her father's chief of staff flashed into her mind. Perfect.

With Teresa settled between her knees, Sarah went to work on her tangled hair with the black plastic comb the girl had found. She'd finished Teresa's and was attacking her own when the sound of the door swinging open caught her arm in midtug. She angled her head to see the gringo—Creighton, she reminded herself firmly—step inside.

A look of surprise crossed his face when he saw her sitting cross-legged on the folded-up mat, her long white-gold hair draped over one shoulder.

"Here," he said curtly. "Wear these when you're inside the hut."

Sarah arched a brow at his tone and caught the items he tossed at her. Obviously, the man didn't like her appropriating his comb any more than he did his boot. "I think it's better if I stay robed."

"I've got enough problems on my hands right now without you coming down with heatstroke. Put those on and keep them on. But only in this hut. When you go outside, cover yourself up. Especially that hair. Not that it'll help much," he muttered.

While Teresa scrambled to her feet, Sarah shook out the garments and held them up. Her eyes widened at the tattered skirt, in a bright pattern of pinks and greens, and the well-washed cotton blouse.

"Are there other women in camp?"

"Yes."

The terse reply irritated her. It was only a comb, for heaven's sake. "Wouldn't it be better if the children and I bedded down with these other women?" she asked stiffly. "Then we wouldn't have to…impose on you."

He flashed her a sardonic look and started to reply, but Teresa's timid voice interrupted her. "I want to stay with *el gringo*."

"Don't be silly, Teresa. We'll be more comfortable with the other women. Then *el*…then Creighton here wouldn't have to bother with us."

He frowned. "Creighton?"

"You remind me of someone by that name. Since you won't tell me yours—not that I really want to know it, you understand—I'll just call you Creighton."

His upper lip curled in distaste. "Creighton?"

Sarah struggled to her feet, yanking at the heavy skirts that threatened to trip her. "Really, I appreciate what you've done for us, but I think it would be better if you show me where the other women—" She broke off, gasping, as he moved to her side with the swift, silent grace of a jungle cat.

"You don't want to bed down with the other women, Sister Sarah. Trust me."

"I—"

"Trust me."

It took a moment, but Sarah finally got the message in his eyes. "Oh."

"Right. Oh."

After a moment, he tugged off his floppy-brimmed hat and raked a hand through his dark hair. "Look, I need you to just lay low until I figure out what the heck I'm going to do with you, okay? I don't trust any one of those scumbags out there."

"And you're suggesting that I should trust you?" Although she didn't say it, Sarah's tone indicated that she considered him just as much a scumbag as his so-called business associates.

He gave her a nasty smile. "I don't see that you've got a whole lot of choice, Sister Sarah."

Well, that much was true. She turned away, gripping the blouse and the gaudy skirt in both hands.

Jake stared at the fall of blond hair that formed such a startling contrast to the black of her robe. How in hell was he was going to keep the men's hands off her? he wondered with increasing desperation. How did he dare leave her alone in camp long enough to get to the backup radio transmitter that was hidden a couple of kilometers outside camp? He'd raised enough lewd remarks when he went to barter for some clothing with the husband of the vacant, glassy-eyed woman. The men's deep cultural inhibitions about abusing a *religiosa* were straining already.

"I'll be outside," he told her abruptly. "Send one of the children out if you need anything."

When he walked out the door, the tension knotting the muscles in Jake's neck kicked up another notch. Che was coming across the clearing toward the hut, his beefy, red-faced lieutenant at his side.

"So, gringo, you've rested from your night's adventure?"

"As much as I need to," Jake replied evenly. "Why?"

"I go to meet with our backer and arrange another drop." His dark eyes were carefully devoid of any expression. "Do you wish to accompany me?"

Jake felt a quick rush of adrenaline. His mission was to take down the American middleman who was scarfing up drug dollars in exchange for stolen arms smuggled out of the States. The narcs were supposed to take care of the elusive drug lords providing those dollars. But if Jake could get a bead on their location... Cold, sobering reality brought him up short. He couldn't leave the sister alone.

Jake gave a negligent shrug. "I'm not interested in where you get the dollars to pay me. Just that you get them."

He sensed at once that he'd given the right answer. Although Che's expression didn't alter by so much as a flicker of an eyelid, his hands shifted imperceptibly on his belt, to a less rigid grip.

Jake smiled grimly to himself. If he'd started out on the journey with the rebel leader, the chances were pretty good that he wouldn't have finished it.

"I will also discover why the government troops were in our area," Che continued. "Those who sent them will pay for it."

"Good."

If Che didn't find out through his sources, Jake intended to through his. There'd better not be another botched drop, or someone's ass was going to be in a sling, big-time. And it wouldn't be his. He hoped.

"Enrique is in charge in my absence. I'll send word of the new drop date and location as soon as I arrange it. You will go with the men, gringo, to inspect the merchandise before any money changes hands."

"Suspicious bastard, aren't you?" Jake offered with a half smile.

Che allowed a small answering twist of his lips. "Yes, my friend. I am."

As Jake joined the rest of the men squatting in the center of the clearing for the noon meal, a swift, heady feeling of relief coursed through his veins. With Che and half the camp gone, he ought to be able to manage the remaining dozen for a few days. Enrique, pig-eyed brute that he was, sported more brawn than brains.

Now, if Jake could just figure out how to keep the prickly nun and her charges safe without blowing his cover, he might just pull this damned thing off after all.

"I'm telling you, Adam, it's the only way."

Maggie paced the thick carpet in front of her boss's mahogany desk and sent him an impatient look.

Impeccably groomed and wearing a hand-tailored gray suit that had probably cost more than Maggie made in a month, Adam sat back in his black leather chair and listened while she stated her case.

"We haven't heard from Jaguar in almost twenty-four hours. Not since the emergency signal he sent yesterday saying he was in place and had a neutral on board."

"It also said to stand by."

Maggie swung to a halt in front of his desk. "That was before we got a positive ID on the remains. Now we know that Sarah Chandler is the neutral with Jake. What's more, we've had confirmation that three kids disappeared the night of the raid. Jake's got his hands full, if they're all with him."

"He's handled more difficult situations."

"True, but we've got a wild card in this situation that none of us anticipated—Senator Chandler. He's liable to mount his own rescue operation if we don't do something soon."

When Adam didn't respond, Maggie pressed her point.

"Remember how he chartered his own plane and flew into Somalia to negotiate the release of the downed chopper pilot last year? The one who just happened to be the son of one of his constituents?''

"I remember,'' Adam replied coolly. ''Somalia wasn't our operation.''

"No, but Cartoza is. Chandler could get Jake killed if he blunders in down there.''

"So you want to go in instead and work the extraction, if possible?''

The fact that Adam didn't reject her plan out of hand told Maggie that he'd been considering alternative courses of action, too. Still, she'd have to talk fast to convince him to send her in instead of another agent. She knew he was reluctant to relieve her as Jake's control.

The relationship between field agent and controller was critical to any mission. The tie between them grew so intense, the ability to communicate instantly so vital, that the partnership transcended that of mere co-workers. It became a nexus, a bonding such as soldiers experienced in combat. But in this instance Maggie's instincts told her she could help Jake more on-scene than in the OMEGA control center.

"I won't break the communications loop. Samuels will relay Jake's transmissions to me real-time. And Cowboy can take over as controller for us both. He's recovered from his last mission, and knows almost as much about the area as any of us after his years as an attaché. Besides,'' she added, ''he owes me one.''

"I take it you're referring to the incident at Six-Shooters?''

Maggie glanced at Adam in mingled surprise and exasperation. ''How did you know about that? That was personal, between Cowboy and me.''

He merely quirked a brow.

"Okay, so you have your own sources.''

She should've guessed Adam would hear how she'd rescued the handsome, easygoing Cowboy a few months back from the tough-as-nails EPA attorney who'd sunk her claws into him and refused to let go. Her disguise for that little private operation had been perfect. Not even Cowboy, as good as he was in the field, had recognized the streetwalker with the frizzy blond hair and thigh-high black plastic boots who'd sidled up to him in D.C.'s version of a country-western bar. Maggie's husky whisper that he didn't have to worry anymore, she'd been treated at the clinic for that little inconvenience, had made him sputter into his beer. It had made the attorney gasp, snatch up her purse and sail out.

The quick, irrepressible grin that was Maggie's alone flitted across her face. Among the dozen or so OMEGA agents, she was the acknowledged master when it came to impersonations. And the most outrageous. She'd perfected a chameleonlike ability to adopt the smallest nuances of any environment. That, combined with her ear for the rhythm and cadences of a local dialect, had gotten her in—and out!—of the most unlikely, impenetrable target areas. And she knew just the ticket to get her into Cartoza.

"If you agree that Cowboy can take over as controller, I have the perfect cover," she announced. "I'll go in as one of the sisters of Our Lady of Sorrows."

She caught the quick, involuntary glance Adam sent skimming down her figure. So her brilliant turquoise above-the-knee knit tunic with the picture of the latest addition to the Washington Zoo on the front wasn't exactly nunlike? So her tight black leggings hugged her calves? Adam knew that she could go from flashy to demure in the blink of an eye, or vice versa. She much preferred vice versa, Maggie acknowledged with an inner grin.

"I must admit, the idea of seeing you in a nun's habit is an intriguing prospect," Adam admitted, his blue eyes gleaming.

She leaned forward and placed both palms on his desk. "It's perfect, Adam. The sisters move freely in the country, and their chapter house in Cartoza's capital is less than twenty minutes by helicopter from Jake's last known location. Assuming he hasn't moved, and assuming the senator's daughter is still with him, I can get to the target area as soon as he calls for an extraction."

"And if he doesn't?"

"Then I'll do some intelligence gathering of my own among the locals, and at least be prepared if Senator Chandler decides to play his own hand."

"Jake hasn't called for backup," he reminded her, playing devil's advocate. "He might not appreciate you jumping into his operation."

She worried her lower lip a moment. "I know. But I just have this—"

"Prickling sensation at the base of your spine," Adam finished dryly. He rose and flicked down the cuffs of his icy blue silk shirt. "All right, Maggie. Go down to Cartoza. I think I can hold off Senator Chandler at this end for a while."

The cool assurance in Adam's voice convinced Maggie that he could hold off a half-dozen Senator Chandlers. For as long as he wished. Not for the first time, she wondered just where and how Adam Ridgeway had developed his air of authority.

In his public life, he was the son of a wealthy Boston philanthropist, had served a brief stint in the navy after college, and then settled down to the serious pleasures of an international jet-setter. His friendship with and *very* hefty campaign contribution to the dynamic young congressman who had become President had led to Adam's appointment as special envoy.

During his jet-setting years, however, Adam had also led a private, secret double life. The agents at OMEGA knew that over the years he'd provided the government with vital information that only someone who frequented the big-money world of casinos, Greek shipping magnates and international art auctions would have access to. But none of them knew exactly how he'd collected the bullet wound that scarred the flesh of his upper chest. Or how he'd gained his sharp, incisive knowledge of field operations, a knowledge that made them trust him implicitly with the lives they regularly put on the line.

Someday, Maggie thought, she just might find out.

Right now, however, she had a mission to prepare for.

Flashing her boss a quick grin, Maggie whirled and left his office.

Adam's private secretary paused in the act of arranging a bouquet of daffodils in the crystal vase set on her delicate Louis XV desk. "Well, did you get the go-ahead?"

Maggie gave Elizabeth a thumbs-up. The gray-haired woman had worked for the special envoy since the position was created and was a favorite with the OMEGA agents. Multilingual, well-groomed and unfailingly polite, Elizabeth also qualified each year as an expert marksman with the 9 mm Sig Sauer Model P225 handgun she kept in a drawer at immediate hand level. Specially loaded with Glazer Teflon bullets, the weapon was devastatingly accurate at close quarters and would do serious damage to anyone unwise enough to try to force his way past the security screens on the first floor. Even the specialists who regularly tested OMEGA's state-of-the-art security systems joked that they wouldn't want to test Elizabeth.

She gave Maggie the motherly smile that so endeared her to the occasionally cynical and hard-bitten agents. "I'm glad to hear someone's going in, dear. I'll admit I've been worried about Jaguar. Although now I'll just worry about you, as well."

Maggie's eyes twinkled. "You always worry, no matter who goes in. You can rest easy this time, though. I'll be in and out of there before you know it. I'm guessing this little operation will be over within twenty-four hours—two or three days at the most."

Chapter 5

"Aaaarrrooo—ooo—gaaahhh!"

The distant, raucous roar brought Jake to instant awareness. He lay still in the predawn darkness as eerie, deep-throated answering calls echoed through the surrounding hills. A troop of howler monkeys were staking out their feeding area for the day, their deep bass wails warning other troops away from their territory.

Listening to the dominant male who lead the gravelly chorus, Jake felt a decided kinship with the shaggy-maned, bearded animal. He'd done everything but howl himself in the past twenty-four hours to keep the other men in camp away from his territory.

The big, pig-eyed lieutenant had wanted to put the blue-eyed *médica* to work on the fungal diseases and chafed skin common to men who traveled through the wet jungles. Jake had managed to convince him that the complaints could wait. She wouldn't be much use to anyone, as exhausted as she was. He'd won her a day, two at the most, he figured.

Not that Sister Sarah seemed to appreciate his efforts on her behalf.

After two days in this sweatbox, anyone else would've lost some of their starch. Not her. Although she'd exchanged her habit for the baggy cotton clothes he'd procured for her, she was as stiff-backed and prickly as ever. It still rankled when he remembered how she'd snatched the little three year old away last night. The boy had tugged on Jake's pant leg, asking if he really shooted people. Those damned beryl eyes of hers had flashed with scorn as she shushed the child and told him not to bother Señor Creighton.

Creighton, for crissakes.

Jake would have stalked out of the hut then, but a rumble of hoarse laughter outside had told him the men had decided to take advantage of Che's absence to hit the tequila. He wasn't particularly interested in watching the games they'd soon indulge in, nor did he dare leave the sister unprotected long enough to slip into the jungle and retrieve his backup transmitter. He'd have to try tonight. Tomorrow at the latest. Maggie wouldn't, couldn't, give him much longer than that.

Twenty-four more hours, Jake told himself. Forty-eight at the most. That was all he had. With luck, that was all he'd need. Che ought to have the new drop set up by then. As soon as Jake got word—and managed to retrieve his backup transmitter!—he'd tell Maggie to have an extraction team stand by. They'd swoop in and pick up the sister and the children the minute Jake led the patrol out of camp en route to the drop site. The extraction teams OMEGA used were good, a composite of elite special forces from the U.S. and the host country. The team would execute the entire rescue in radio silence, using silenced weapons and a swift, harmless gas that effectively precluded resistance. No one outside the immediate area would have any idea of what was going down. By the time Jake was a mile down the trail, the little nun beside him would be safely on her way back to her convent.

The thought made him frown in the darkness.

He lifted the net tent and rolled off the thin, lumpy mat.

Dawn would come shortly, with its usual sudden swiftness. He might as well see about breakfast for his little extended family.

An hour later, Jake dropped a battered frying pan onto the crate that did double duty as a table.

"Here, I fried up some bananas."

An aroma of cinnamon and glazed sugar drifted across the already hot and humid air. The big cooking bananas, sliced lengthwise and fried to a crisp, would make a filling, nutritious breakfast.

Sister Sarah glanced up in surprise, and Jake struggled to contain his involuntary start. Even after a day and a night in the woman's company, he still wasn't used to the sight of her scrubbed, delicate face without the white wimple and black veil framing it. Or to the long blond hair she'd pulled back and tied with a narrow strip torn from the hem of her habit. Jake had never thought of himself as particularly conservative, but at this moment he wasn't sure he agreed with Pope Who-ever's Vatican Council. Hair like that ought to be worn short, he decided irritably. Short and straight, in a style that didn't add several degrees of attraction to an already stunning face.

"I'll take the boys outside after they eat," he announced, in a tone that warned her not to object. He was in no mood for arguments after his long, hot, nearly sleepless night. And he sure as blazes wasn't about to offer up his boot again. The transmitter might be beyond repair, but rubber boots could save the life of someone tramping through the soggy, rotting vegetation that layered the rain-forest floor.

The primitive latrine Jake had rigged would suffice for her and the little girl, but the boys could darn well use the stream. Besides, they needed exercise. *He* needed exercise. He felt restless and edgy and caged. He wasn't used to sharing his quarters with a woman whose every move seemed to snag his gaze and whose breath fluttered softly in the darkness. Nor with three kids, two of whom, at least, appeared to be recovering from the terror of the raid. He turned away to dig out some water-purifier tablets for the canteens he'd just refilled.

Sarah bristled at the gringo's—at Creighton's—curt tone, but decided not to challenge his assumption of authority over the boys. Actually, it sent a spurt of secret relief rushing through her. After a day and a night with three small children, she was feeling an accumulation of stress that had nothing to do with their uncertain position in the rebel camp. Didn't kids *ever* run out of energy? Or questions?

Struggling to her feet in the overlarge, if blessedly cool, cotton skirt she'd donned yesterday, Sarah moved toward the makeshift table. The mercenary stepped back, but not quite far enough. Her bare arm brushed his. The feel of his warm, taut flesh, liberally sprinkled with wiry dark hair, made Sarah suck in a quick breath. She sent him a wide, startled look.

"Jesus!" he muttered, shifting his eyes back to the canteens.

"Please don't use the Lord's name in vain around the children," she admonished tartly.

His answer was a scowl.

Unsure what had put him in such a foul mood this morning, but sharing his sentiments, Sarah set out the battered tin plates and spoons their reluctant host had provided for them yesterday.

"Come on, children, you need to eat."

While the three youngsters gathered around the crate, Sarah scooped the bananas out of the frying pan. Her taste buds tingled at the delicious aroma. Breaking off an end of one banana, she popped it into her mouth. "Mmm…these are good."

Teresa's accusing black eyes stopped her in midswallow. Oh, hell. She'd forgotten again. Sarah gulped down the sweet, glutinous mass.

"I was just testing them, Teresa. In case they were too hot for you to eat. But they're okay. You can say grace now."

The little traitor shook her head, then smiled shyly up at the tall man standing beside her. "*You* say it, Señor Creighton."

Sarah wasn't sure which she enjoyed more—the pained

expression that crossed his lean, unshaven face whenever one of them referred to him by that name, or his startled look at the thought of leading a prayer. Good, she thought with malicious satisfaction. Let him struggle with the words for a change. She'd stretched her own skimpy knowledge of Catholic prayers, gleaned from Maria in the past two weeks, about as far as they would go.

He cleared his throat, then said gruffly, "Thanks Lord. Let's eat."

His fervent efficiency won grins of approval from the smaller children. Even Eduard managed a smile.

Raising a brow, Sarah passed him a plate. "Is that the best you can do?"

"I'm a little out of practice," he admitted, showing a flash of strong white teeth against his dark stubble.

"It's time you got back into practice," she pontificated, throwing herself into her role. "You have a lot to ask forgiveness for."

The sardonic look that made his eyes shade from misty gray to dark flint passed over his face. "More than you know, Sister Sarah."

They didn't speak during the short meal, except to answer Teresa and Ricci's seemingly endless stream of questions.

Yes, Sarah was aware that Teresa's back tooth was loose.

Yes, the sun streaming in through the broken shutters made a pattern just like a big striped iguana on the dirt floor.

No, Ricci shouldn't add the insect he'd crunched between his fingers with such delight to his mashed bananas.

"C'mon, big guy." The mercenary scooped Ricci up under one arm. "Let's go outside and see if we can find you bigger game. You too, Eduard."

Sarah breathed a sigh of relief as the door shut behind two of her charges. And to think she had laughingly suggested to André one rainy, love-filled afternoon that they make lots of children. Lots of little miniature Frenchmen, with their father's heart-stopping smile and gallant Maurice Chevalier charm.

At the memory, the pain that lingered just below the surface of her consciousness seeped into her heart. Why hadn't she guessed from the way André kissed aside her attempt to picture their future, that he didn't want children? Not with Sarah, anyway. Why hadn't she realized he had no intention of leaving the four he already had, or their mother? How could she have been so stupid? So incredibly gauche? How could she ever forgive herself for making another man's wife try to take her own life?

"Sarita, will you comb my hair?"

Sarah nodded, swallowing to relieve her tight throat. She sat on the now-cleared crate and tucked Teresa between her knees. She'd managed to put a measure of her pain behind her when a soft knock sounded on the door.

Sarah snatched Teresa to her chest. She stared at the door, her heart pounding in painful thumps.

The gringo—Creighton—wouldn't knock. Nor would the boys.

Another soft thump of knuckles sounded against the wood.

Moistening her lips, Sarah called out, "Yes? Who is it? *Quién es?*"

The wooden door slowly inched open. A heavyset woman with thick black braids and a dull expression in her brown eyes stood on the stoop.

"What do you want? *Qué quiere?*"

Her eyes on the little girl, the woman held out a small bundle. *"Para la niña,"* she mumbled.

"For Teresa?"

Sarah scrambled to her feet, trying not to trip over her overlarge pink-and-green skirt. Now she knew who it belonged to. Her unexpected visitor wore a similar one, although its purple-and-blue hues were considerably more faded. Moreover, her stained blouse showed ragged, poorly stitched rips. With a flash of insight, Sarah realized the gringo must have bought or bartered for this woman's best outfit. Maybe her only other outfit.

And now she was offering something for Teresa. Perhaps

a clean shift to replace the sweat-stained one the child wore. Or, better yet, some underpants. Sarah had washed the youngsters' underwear last night. The items refused to dry in the humid, muggy heat. Even chubby, smiling little Ricci had protested at putting the damp things on again.

Sarah gave the little girl a gentle push. "Go ahead, honey. Take it."

Teresa hesitated, then stepped forward. She lifted the bundle out of the woman's hand and scuttled back to Sarah's side. Her nimble fingers made short work of the string wrapped around it.

"Oooh! Look, Sarita! Look!"

Eyes shining in delight, Teresa shook out a dress in bright red cotton. Ruffles embroidered with colorful flowers and birds decorated the neckline and the full skirt. A sash of sunshine yellow looped around the waist, its long, dangling ends also embroidered in gay colors.

Teresa took a few dancing steps around the hut, the dress held up against her thin body. Excitement and the unguarded joy of a little girl shone in her face.

Sarah smiled and turned to thank the silent woman. For a moment she thought she saw a flicker of...of something in the woman's eyes as they rested on Teresa, but as soon as Sarah spoke they immediately became flat and dull.

"It's beautiful. Thank you. *Muchas gracias, señora.*"

The woman stood silent.

Teresa overcame her shyness and went forward, chattering in rapid-fire Spanish. She put out a small and rather grubby hand and laid it on the woman's arm.

Sarah's keen eye caught the convulsive way the woman's fingers folded over Teresa's, as if she wanted to impress the feel of the girl's small hand in her flesh. Then she whirled and was gone.

Teresa shrugged off her sudden departure with the cheerful unconcern of youth. "I will wear this dress now," she announced, prancing around the hut. "To show Señor Creighton how pretty I am."

Señor Creighton again!

"You'll be a lot prettier if you let me wash you first."

Teresa's wide smile faltered at the bite in Sarah's voice. Ashamed of herself, Sarah gathered the girl into her arms.

"I'm sorry, *niña*. It's…it's the heat."

The little girl sniffed.

"Come," Sarah coaxed, "slip out of that old dress, while I get the canteen and a cloth of some sort. I'll wash you, then we'll see if we can find something pretty to tie in your hair, okay?"

Showing her gap-toothed smile once more, the little girl complied. Sarah dug through the backpack she now had no compunctions about raiding and pulled out a pair of the white cotton briefs. With a small smile, she reached for a canteen.

She soon had the girl as clean as possible under the circumstances. The red dress was a little loose on Teresa's small body, so Sarah wrapped the sash twice around her waist and tied it with a big bow. The girl played with the flounces on the full skirt while Sarah worked the comb through her thick black hair, then parted one section of the crown and tied it with a strip torn from the mosquito netting to form a jaunty ponytail.

"Okay, sweetie," Sarah told her, patting her fanny. "You're done. You look very pretty."

Her hands holding out the sides of her skirt, Teresa twirled around once or twice.

"Okay, Sarita," she said after a moment, unconsciously imitating Sarah's slang. "Now you. Your hair needs the comb, also."

It needed a whole lot more than a comb, Sarah thought ruefully. Her lips twisted in a wry smile as she imagined her hairdresser's reaction if he were to see her now. Jonathan would no doubt take it as a personal affront that she'd let the shining mane he labored over with such devotion get into this condition.

She reached up and untied the strip of cloth binding her hair. Wincing, she began to work the comb through the sweat-tangled mess. At last the pointed plastic teeth glided smoothly. Sarah reached up and slid both hands behind her neck, then lifted the heavy weight high up on her head. She arched her back in a slow, luxurious stretch.

The door to the hut crashed open, freezing Sarah in mid-stretch. Shirtless, his broad chest streaked with blood, the mercenary strode in. He held Eduard's thin body high in his arms. Ricci stumbled in behind them, his lips puckered and trembling.

Openmouthed, Sarah stared at them. Creighton's eyes narrowed as he took in her uplifted arms and less-than-nunlike pose, but he didn't slow his stride.

"Shut the damn door," he growled. "Then come over here. Eduard sliced open his arm."

"What?" Sarah let her hair fall and jumped up. Slapping her palm against the door, she rushed to the man's side. "How? How did he cut himself?"

He laid the boy gently in the hammock. "The machete slipped."

"You allowed a child to play with a machete! A *machete?*" Sarah's voice rose incredulously as she shoved him aside.

"He wasn't playing. He was clearing some overgrowth from the stream behind the hut. The damned vines tripped him up."

Sarah gasped at the bright red that stained the khaki shirt wrapped around Eduard's forearm.

"I don't think he sliced through any muscle. The cut's deep, though. You'll have to suture it."

He turned away, missing Sarah's sudden stricken expression. The hand she'd reached out toward the bloodstained khaki shirt trembled violently.

"I have some disinfectant powder in my backpack," he called over his shoulder. "But no sewing kit. I'll have to see if I can round up a needle and some thick thread for you to stitch it with."

Sarah gulped down the lump lodged in her throat. She'd probably only threaded a needle once or twice in her entire life. She'd certainly never sutured anything or anyone. Nor had Sister Maria in the two short weeks Sarah assisted her in the clinic. Sarah had watched her set a broken leg, administer a good number of inoculations and sit up two days and nights tending a new mother stricken with postpartum fever. But the nursing sister hadn't stitched anything.

Sarah met Eduard's wide, unblinking stare and bit down on her lower lip, hard. There was no way she was going to fumble around and inflict unnecessary pain on this child. A man like the gringo, whose life depended on his resourcefulness, would have far more skill at stitching wounds than she did. Regardless of the consequences, she had to tell him that she wasn't a medical sister.

Sarah turned around, only to blink as he shoved a plastic bottle into her hands.

"Here, dust him down while I go find a needle." He spun on his heel and was gone before she could force out the admission trembling on her lips.

Unwrapping the bloody shirt with shaky fingers, Sarah gasped at the sight of the long slash running almost the entire the length of Eduard's forearm. Another inch or two more, and he would've sliced through the veins at his wrist. Bright red blood welled up from the laceration and trickled down his arm to splash against his chest.

"Madre de Dios," Teresa whispered, standing on tiptoe beside Sarah to peer at the wound.

"Does Eduardo die, Sarita?" Ricci's wobbling, childish treble galvanized Sarah into action.

"No. No, of course he won't die. Teresa, get me that wash rag we just used. Be sure to wring it out in clean water first."

She wrestled with the top to the plastic bottle of disinfectant powder. The blasted thing was childproof, of course. She finally got it open, then set the cap back on loosely while she dabbed at the seeping blood with the damp briefs. To her untutored eyes, the edges of the wound gaped hideously, exposing a layer of glistening muscle underneath. She pressed the edges together with trembling fingers, holding them with one hand while she dusted the whole area with the other.

Blood welled sluggishly through her spread fingers, smearing the power. Jaws tight, Sarah wiped it away, clamped the wound together again, then sprinkled more dust. Sweat beaded on her brow and trickled down her cheek. Sarah leaned back, afraid it might drip into the wound, yet kept her tight hold on Eduard's arm. The awkward position made her back strain.

It seemed like hours before the gringo returned.

"Where have you been?" Sarah snapped.

"The only needle in the entire camp is so rusty I wouldn't use it on my boot." He flashed her a sardonic look. "Of course, you have different standards when it comes to the care and maintenance of boots."

Sarah started to tell him indignantly that this was no time to start with his selfish possessiveness again, but he forestalled her.

"You'll have to do it the native way."

"What native way?"

He lifted his hand, and for the first time Sarah noticed the short length of bamboolike stalk he held. Both ends were stuffed tight with leaves.

"You'll have to use ants."

"Ants? Are you crazy?"

His eyes narrowed. "How long have you been down here, anyway?"

"Not...not long."

"Not long enough, obviously. When you've spent as much time in the jungle as I have, you'll learn not to dismiss native customs with such contempt."

"But...ants?"

"The Maya used soldier ants more than two thousand years ago to close wounds. Lots of folks around here still follow their example. A buddy of mine says African tribes do the same with driver ants. Now, do you think you can set aside your modern medical prejudices long enough to hold the edges of the skin together while I work?''

Sarah shot him a venomous look, forgetting her decision of a few moments before to confess all and throw herself on this man's mercy. It appeared that her lack of medical knowledge was totally irrelevant, anyway.

"There's no need for sarcasm." She bit the words out, her hands still clamped around the boy's arm. "My concern is for Eduard. I *have* been down here long enough to know that those ants you're talking about sting. Badly. They can kill small animals, and even the occasional human."

His gray eyes slanted toward the silent boy. "Eduard's man enough to handle the sting. Aren't you?"

The boy met his steady look and nodded slowly.

What was this? Sarah wondered, astounded. Some kind of macho male bonding? Since she didn't have any better option to offer, however, she kept her mouth shut and watched the tall, sweaty, shirtless man next to her.

He pulled the leafy plug out of one end of the tube and tapped it on his palm. Sarah's eyes widened at the sight of the huge ant that fell out. It was as big as one of her native North Carolina's crickets. And far more fearsome.

"Here, plug this back up." He shoved the tube into Teresa's hands and turned to Eduard. "Ready?"

The boy nodded once more.

Grasping the ant between his thumb and forefinger, the gringo held its head against Eduard's flesh, on either side of the cut. The big, sickle-shaped mandibles bit into the skin. When the jaws clamped shut, they drew the flesh together. Eduard jerked, but made no sound.

Leaving the head in place, the mercenary pinched off the ant's body and tossed it aside. He reached for the tube once more and swiftly, competently, repeated the procedure. Sarah moved her hands up Eduard's arm as he worked, clamping the skin together while man and insect closed it. Within moments, a neat track of black ''sutures'' traced up Eduard's wound.

Sarah straightened her aching back. She stared down at the wan, sweating boy, her heart aching for him. She'd been bitten by a soldier ant only once since her arrival in Cartoza, but she remembered how long and how fiercely it had stung.

"When the bleeding stops completely, we'll pat mud around the bites to draw out some of the sting."

Sarah looked up at the man beside her. "More ancient Mayan remedies?"

His cheeks creased. "No, this one's from Field Manual 90-5. The army's handy-dandy guide to jungle operations."

Sarah glanced over at the crates stenciled with U.S. markings. "How convenient. The weapons you and your friends steal come complete with a set of manuals."

She regretted the tart words almost as soon as they were out. They sounded petty after what he'd just done for Eduard. Then she reminded herself that Eduard wouldn't be here in the first place if it wasn't for this steel-eyed mercenary. She had to remember that the man frowning down at her sold his technical knowledge for cold cash to murdering rebels. Lifting her chin, she returned his scowl.

Jake fought the urge to tell her that he wouldn't need to steal the manual. He knew it by heart. Every word. Hell, he'd written most of it. He used to teach it, along with his hard-earned survival skills, at the army's special forces school. A lifetime ago. Before he'd lost his wife to his career, then his career to his own impatience with the inflexibility of a peacetime army. Before OMEGA had lured him into the dark, dangerous, lonely world of clandestine operations.

Did he dare trust her? Should he tell her now that he wasn't the man she thought he was? Jake opened his mouth, then clamped it shut. No, it was safer for her, for the children, for all of them, if he didn't. Not yet.

Jake knew he couldn't keep her confined in this little hut much longer. She needed out—for her own health, if not that of the men who grumbled about their various aches and pains. He'd have enough on his hands trying to minimize Sister Sarah's impact on the gorillas out there without worrying whether she might inadvertently let slip that Jake wasn't the man they thought he was.

When he'd confirmed the date of the drop and set up the extraction, Jake would tell her what to expect. Until then, he'd just have to put up with her scorn, even if it did sting every bit as bad as any ant bite he'd ever experienced. The sister needed to go back to the convent and get a few more lessons in forgiveness for her fellow man, he thought.

And she damn well needed to get back in that black habit.

Jake's jaw tightened as his gaze dropped to the swell of creamy flesh showing above the loosened neckline of her blouse. The image that had greeted him when he carried Eduard into the hut flashed into his mind.

Sister Sarah, with her arms raised to hold the fall of blond hair off her neck.

Her neck arched, as if in invitation.

Her blouse molded around high, firm breasts that Jake had no business noticing.

Sweat popped out on his brow. He edged past her, grabbed one of the tin plates and stalked toward the door.

"I'll go get the mud."

Chapter 6

By midmorning, the primitive sutures and soothing mud had done their job. The swelling from the ant stings had disappeared, the cut remained closed, and Sarah felt competent enough to wrap Eduard's arm in a strip of light gauze bandage she'd found in the bountiful knapsack.

When the boy fell into a light doze, the gringo tugged on his wrinkled spare shirt and left the little hut—to check on the status of his so-called business activities, Sarah supposed.

By noon, Eduard showed little effect from his injury, other than his bandaged arm. The younger children, who'd remained quiet and subdued until now, began to get restive. Sarah tried her best to divide her attention between the three of them, but found herself running out of stories and energy and patience. When the gringo returned some time later to check on them, she greeted him with something very close to relief.

One dark brow arched, but he refrained from commenting on her change of attitude. "How's your patient?" he asked, ducking his head to step closer to the hammock.

"Your patient, you mean," she said with a small, frazzled smile. "He's doing fine."

"Good enough for me to take him outside?"

"*Sí.*"

They both swung around at the soft affirmative, startled to hear Eduard speak.

He didn't say anything more. He just swung his thin legs over the edge of the hammock and sat up, his injured arm cradled in the makeshift sling Sarah had fashioned from a strip torn from the mosquito netting. Sarah started to protest, but Eduard looked at her with a silent plea.

"He has to make the pee-pee," Ricci informed them, with a three-year-old's utter lack of reticence.

The gringo laughed and strode over to help the boy out of the hammock. "Then maybe we'd better take a trip before lunch. Come on, Squirt. You too."

Sarah bit her lip, marveling at the careful yet assured way he handled Eduard. Ricci trailed happily out the door after them.

"Me, also," Teresa chirped. Red skirts swirling, she jumped up and ran out before Sarah could stop her.

Oh, well, let him handle her for a while. He certainly seemed capable of it, Sarah thought wearily. Sinking down on the handy crate, she stared at her grubby hands. Although she'd washed as best she could, mud rimmed her nails. She flipped her hands over once or twice, examining them. The long, polished tips she used to spend so much time and money on were gone, as was the smooth, tanned skin. A spasm of regret for her former life shot through her. Sarah clenched her hands into fists.

She leaned her head back against the wall of the hut and closed her eyes, wishing herself away from this place, away from the children who were more responsibility than she'd ever dreamed they could be. Away from the man who overnight seemed to have become the center of her universe.

He was unlike any of the men she'd ever known, Sarah thought resentfully. So different from the suave, urbane men she'd charmed and flirted with. And he was a universe away from the laughing Frenchman she'd fallen in love with.

Eyes closed, Sarah waited for the familiar pain that came with any memory of André. A ripple of hurt eddied through her, but it lacked the intensity of the waves that had swamped her in past weeks. And André's image seemed less sharp, less vivid, than before.

Instead, a different image imprinted itself in precise detail on the inside of Sarah's lids. Hard-eyed. Lean-hipped. Broad chest bare under the unbuttoned edges of the wrinkled khaki shirt. In her mind's eye, Sarah noted the swirls of black hair scattered lightly across the gringo's pectorals. The soft black pelt narrowed to a thin line as it angled down his chest and traced its way over a flat stomach, then disappeared into his waistband. A sudden, insidious desire to run her fingertip along that line of dark hair snaked through Sarah.

When she realized where her thoughts and her mental image had taken her, Sarah's eyes flew open. Startled, she sat bolt upright on the crate. Good Lord! She had to be more stressed than she realized. She couldn't feel anything remotely resembling physical attraction for a man like him. This liquid heat curling low in her stomach had nothing to do with him. Nothing! She was just tired. Just stressed by all she'd been through. Or maybe she was feeling something like the hostage dependency syndrome that formed a frequent topic of conversation at the dinner parties she'd hosted or attended. Among the Washington elite, international terrorism and diplomatic kidnappings were a very real concern. The State Department even offered courses on dealing with captors to senior officials traveling abroad.

That was all that was between her and this mercenary, she reasoned, a sort of sick dependency relationship. Circumstance had thrown her into his company. Some lingering shreds of conscience had led him to offer what protection he could to a fellow countryman. But Sarah couldn't let herself forget why he was here. She couldn't let herself become emotionally dependent on him. She couldn't, *wouldn't*, allow herself to feel any attraction for him.

She didn't even like him! He was scruffy, and unshaven, and as dangerous as any of the men he associated with, and…and she had no idea what his life was like outside this jungle. For all she knew, he had a wife and a houseful of kids tucked away in New Jersey. Which might explain why he was so good with Teresa and Ricci and Eduard.

The thought sent a rush of mingled pain and determination through Sarah. She'd made a fool of herself once, and hurt a lot of people in the process, herself included. She wouldn't do it again.

Nor, she decided with a rush of determination as she glanced around the hut, would she sit here any longer like some weak, gutless wimp, totally dependent on a man she couldn't allow herself to trust. She was Sarah Chandler, she reminded herself. Daughter of one of the most powerful men in Washington. A personality of some force in her own right for many years. Her reputation might be a bit tarnished these days, and her self-esteem a little dented, but, dammit, she wasn't stupid, and she wasn't going to wallow in her misery any longer. She'd done that once, with disastrous results. Once she'd tried to find an antidote to her shame and hurt in alcohol. Once she'd lost control of herself to the point that she'd plowed her Mercedes into the side of a D.C. metro transit bus. Not again. Never again.

Surging to her feet, Sarah marched over to the stack of clothing, hers and Teresa's, folded neatly atop one of the crates. Within moments, she'd shed her borrowed clothes and the suffocating black robe enfolded her from head to toe. She tied the limp strings of the wimple at the base of her neck, making sure no tendrils of hair escaped it or the black veil. Drawing in a deep breath, she headed for the door.

The reminder that the men outside would expect her to exercise her supposed medical skills made her pause with one hand on the warped wooden door. After her near panic with Eduard, however, Sarah had had time to reflect. She realized

that there couldn't be any serious injuries or maladies await-
ing her treatment in the camp. If there were, she would have
been forced to attend to them before now. Two weeks with
Maria had taught her how to administer penicillin, if necessary, and treat minor jungle ills. Assuming that they even had
any medical supplies in camp. After the fiasco with the needle,
Sarah wondered.

As soon as she stepped outside, she felt an immediate sense
of relief. Air marginally cooler than that inside the hut swirled
through the clearing. The camouflage net strung across the
camp like some huge, rippling parachute provided a measure
of shade. She waited while her vision adjusted after the dimness of the shack, then peered around the littered clearing.
Debris from the abandoned, tumbledown huts lay interspersed
with empty tins and crates the rebels had discarded. The pack-
horses cropped desultorily beside the stream. Sarah caught a
flash of red in the bright, dappled sunlight and lifted her skirts
to head for Teresa.

The black-robed figure was halfway across the clearing before Jake saw her. Surprised and furious that she would dis-
obey his order to stay inside, he jumped up and strode to meet
her. Before she could get a word out of her mouth, he grasped
her arm and spun her around.

"What do you think you're doing? Get back in the hut."

She pulled her arm free. "No."

"No?" He stared at her, clearly taken aback. "What do
you mean, no?"

"No."

"Look here, Sister Sarah—"

"No, you look. I'm tired of not being able to breathe in
that stifling shack. I'm tired of being afraid to face these men.
And I'm particularly tired of the way you say that."

Jake reared back, astounded at the sudden attack. "The way
I say what?"

"The way you say 'Sister Sarah.' In that half-mocking,
half-patronizing tone."

He glanced from Sarah to the hut and back to Sarah again,

trying to figure out just what the hell had happened in the fifteen minutes or so since he'd left her alone.

"I can't stay inside any longer," she told him, her eyes luminous in their intensity. "I have to get out. I have to move around. I won't allow myself to be more of a prisoner than I am."

"Let's just review our options here," Jake growled. "I could damn well drag you back to the hut." In fact, he thought, it would give him a good deal of satisfaction at this moment to pick little *Sister Sarah* up, carry her back inside, and dump her on her keister.

"You could," she acknowledged, her gaze locked with his.

He jerked his chin toward the children squatting by the stream. "Or I suppose you think I could just stand guard over you and the kids, like some medieval knight protecting his lady."

One delicately arched brow told him just how little she considered him a knight in shining armor.

"Or I could let you live with the consequences of your sudden spurt of independence, which is…" Out of the corner of one eye, Jake caught sight of the beefy, pig-faced lieutenant strolling across the clearing toward them. "Which is what I'll have to do. We just ran out of options, lady."

Jake slanted her a quick look, relieved to see that she at least had the sense to wipe the determined expression from her face and dull the impact of her vivid eyes.

The man called Enrique stopped beside them. Hooking his hands in his belt, he rocked back on his heels and gave the sister a narrow, appraising glance. "So, gringo, your little *religiosa* has decided to make an appearance?"

"The heat in the shack grew too much for her," Jake replied with a shrug. "She needs air."

"Or perhaps occupation for her hands, eh?"

Jake saw her swallow quickly, then firm her lips. "Perhaps," he agreed, accepting the inevitable.

The lieutenant lifted a hand to scratch his chest. "When the men get back from patrol, I will tell them to bring their complaints to her. Myself, I'm healthy as a horse. Although…'' His big paw stilled its absent movement. ''Maybe I'll find a pain somewhere that needs attention, eh?''

''I'd suggest you stay healthy until Che gets back,'' Jake drawled. ''He left you in charge of the camp, remember? And me in charge of the woman.''

Enrique didn't miss the unsubtle reminder. He eyed the man opposite him lazily, as if debating whether or not to challenge him. Jake didn't alter his own easy stance, but the hairs on the back of his neck prickled. His .45 was nestled in the holster attached to his web belt. He'd left his automatic rifle propped against the wall inside the hut, however. He wouldn't make that mistake again.

''Have you heard from him?'' Jake asked casually. ''Che said he'd radio in as soon as he arranged a new drop.''

''No, but we should hear from him soon. Unless the *patrón* was not there when he arrived. Then Che must wait until he returned.''

Jake's mouth twisted. For too many years, the great landowners had oppressed the people of this region, paying them slave wages for backbreaking labor on their coffee and banana plantations. Now a new generation of powerful barons had gained financial dominance—the drug lords who operated the processing plants hidden in Cartoza's deep, protected valleys. They were slowly gaining a stranglehold over the economic fabric of the country that was more pervasive, more devastating, than that of the old landowners. Even Che, a man dedicated to overthrowing the current government in favor of a people's democracy, depended on a *''patrón''* for funding. So much for the revolutionary's political purity, Jake thought cynically.

''Let me know when you hear from him. I'll be around.''

''So will I, gringo,'' the man replied, his eyes on the nun. Pig-face would take some watching. Close watching.

Jake shepherded the sister back toward the children. ''I think we need to review a few of the ground rules here, Sister

Sar—'' He stopped himself, remembering her objection to the way he said her name.

She waved an impatient hand. "Oh, just call me Sarah. It's…it's permitted in most orders now, you know."

"No, I didn't know."

Jake frowned, not at all sure he wanted to drop her title. He hadn't realized that he'd been so patronizing when he used it, but at least it had kept a nice, neat barrier between them. Sarah sounded far too…human.

"Why don't you just join the kids by the stream?" he suggested curtly, uncomfortable with this business of names. "I'll go see if I can find something other than beans for lunch."

He recrossed the clearing some time later, juggling two cans of tuna fish that had cost him an infrared starlight rifle scope. The scope's loss wasn't critical, since Jake had another that slid onto the special grooves in the barrel of his .45. With a little modification to the mounting, it could be fitted to the automatic rifle, as well. Still, he was running through his equipment at almost as fast a clip as Sis—as Sarah was running through his personal possessions.

He tossed a can in the air, then almost missed catching it as he halted in midstride. Eyes narrowed, Jake searched the shadowed spot beside the stream where he'd left his charges. They weren't there.

Spinning on his heel, he strode to the hut and yanked open the door. Even before his eyes adjusted to the gloom of the interior, Jake knew they weren't inside. No little girl's giggles echoed in the silence. No little boy demanded that Sarita take him in her lap. Tossing the cans aside, Jake grabbed his automatic rifle. In a movement so swift and instinctive it took less than three seconds, he pressed the magazine release, checked that the clip carried a full compliment, then snapped it back in place. Jaw clenched, he headed back out the door.

He hadn't heard any screams. There hadn't been shouts. Any muted laughter or disturbance among the men. A swift, gut-wrenching fear rose in him that Sarah had decided to carry her unexpected streak of independence to the extreme. Despite his warnings, she might have taken the children and tried to slip out of camp. It would be easy enough. The rebels didn't mount much of a guard. They didn't need to. One of the skills Jake had "sold" them was how to arm the ultrasensitive intrusion detection devices that now ringed the camp's perimeter. The motion sensors concealed tiny built-in computers that differentiated between sizes and shapes and body heat. Small animals wouldn't set the sensors off, but humans would. Even humans as slender and slight as Sarah....

A cold sweat chilled Jake's body. If detonated, those devices wouldn't leave a whole lot of Sarah and the children for the jungle scavengers to feast on. He cursed silently, savagely. He shouldn't have left them alone. Even for a second. He shouldn't have—

"Señor Creighton! Señor Creighton!"

At the sound of Teresa's high-pitched shriek, Jake dropped into a crouch and whirled. The scampering girl stumbled to a halt a few paces away, her mouth dropping at the sight of the gun leveled at her. A short distance behind her, three other faces registered varying degrees of surprise and shock.

Jake's breath hissed out. He raised the barrel skyward and straightened slowly. His eyes blazed at Sarah, searing her small, delicate face, her incredible eyes, her high cheeks and full, pink lips, into his mind, to replace the image that had knotted his stomach just moments before.

"Where the—?" He bit off the blistering words he would've used with any other person in similar circumstances and tried again, spacing each furious syllable for maximum emphasis. "Where...in...the ...*hell*...have...you...been?"

She blinked, clearly taken aback at his vehemence. "We've been with Eleanora. At her lean-to."

"With Eleanora. At her lean-to. Who in the *hell* is Eleanora?"

"Oh, for Pete's sake. What's gotten into you?"

Jake rubbed his hand down his mouth and chin, feeling the rasp of bristles against his palm. He couldn't tell her what had gotten into him. Not yet. The stomach-twisting, heart-pounding fear he felt for her had been too raw, too intense. Too far outside the range of emotions he'd allowed himself to experience for too many years. Jake wasn't quite sure how his emotions, not to mention his life and his mission, had seemed to spin out of control from the moment he parted those damned palmetto bushes and found her crouched behind them.

"I take it Eleanora is the woman who gave Teresa her red dress?" he managed, in a more moderate tone. "The one whose husband sold me those clothes for you?"

It was a pretty safe guess. The only other female in camp was Che's comrade cum mistress, who was with him on his little trek to the *patrón*'s hacienda right now. So much, he thought, for keeping Sarah and the kids away from the camp's other female residents.

Sarah nodded. "She offered to share her lunch with us. It was delicious. Some kind of fresh meat I didn't recognize, with nuts and rice, all mixed together."

Jake had a pretty good idea what the meat was. Except for wild pigs and small, bear-like kinkajous, few mammals inhabited the wet floor of the rain forest. Eleanora had probably cooked up a nice lizard or snake casserole. Before he could tell Sarah so, however, Teresa stepped forward to tug on Jake's pant leg.

"Look, Señor Creighton." Her face regained the excitement it had held before the momentary fright the gun had given her. "Eleanora gave me a dress for the doll you made for me. Look. Look!"

Jake hunkered down and looked. The mango root he'd found beside the stream earlier this morning and carved into a somewhat squash-faced baby now sported a frilly little skirt and kerchief. After duly admiring the root's new wardrobe, Jake straightened. Teresa and Ricci scampered off. Eduard followed more slowly.

Sarah tilted her head, eyeing him thoughtfully. "It was kind of you to make Teresa that doll."

"Yeah, well, it's just a root."

"You're very good with the children." She hesitated. "Do you have a family waiting for you at home? A daughter Teresa's age, perhaps?"

Jake thought of the series of empty, echoing apartments, sparsely filled with rented furniture, that he'd called home since his divorce so many years ago. He hadn't needed or wanted anything more, hadn't had time for anything more.

"No, there's no one waiting," he answered with a shrug. "And it's easy to be good with these kids. They expect so little of life that they're grateful for whatever crumbs fall their way."

She nibbled on her lower lip for a minute, processing the bits of information he'd given her. "You're a man of many talents, Señor Creighton."

"Look," he said with a tight smile, "if I'm going to call you Sarah, you have to stop laying that Señor Creighton bit on me."

"Then what shall I call you...other than gringo?"

"Try Jack."

"Jack." She rolled it around on her tongue experimentally. "Jack. It suits you. Is that your real name?"

His smile eased into a grin. "No, but it's close enough."

"Someday I'm going to find out just who you are."

She'd said it lightly, in jest, but the words seemed to hang between them. A troubled expression crossed her expressive face, as though she'd belatedly realized that knowing too much about him might not be too wise. A man on the wrong side of the law in at least two countries wouldn't want many people walking around who knew his identity.

"Why don't you show me what medical supplies the camp has on hand?" she said quietly, turning away. "And tell me what I can expect to encounter when the patrol returns."

All in all, Sarah thought later that night, she'd handled her first face-to-face encounter with the scruffy band of guerrillas pretty well. She'd kept her head down, her eyes on her work, and her conversation to a minimum. Jack had augmented her sketchy Spanish, translating for her when she couldn't fully grasp the explanation of the symptoms. Luckily, she hadn't been presented with any scabrous sores or debilitating injuries. She didn't have anything more serious than a severe case of warm-water foot immersion to deal with.

Despite its innocuous name, warm-water foot immersion was a potentially dangerous disease. It occurred frequently in areas with a lot of streams or creeks to cross. Sarah had been briefed on it during the first aid course she took as part of her Peace Corps training. Since so much of Cartoza was covered by soggy rain forest, Sister Maria had been particularly knowledgeable about the condition. If left untreated, it was painful and could eventually lead to permanent crippling. But if the sufferer's white, wrinkled, bleeding feet were kept dry and dusted with powder regularly, the condition would soon clear up. Sarah passed her instructions through Jack to her patient, a thin, stoop-shouldered rebel named Xavier, who seemed more interested in her blue eyes than her medical skills.

Now, after sharing another meal with Eleanora, Sarah had cleansed Eduard's cut, rebandaged it, and settled her charges for the night. Shielded by the stack of crates, she'd changed out of the sweaty habit and once more wore the loose cotton blouse and skirt. She sat on her bedroll, knees drawn up, and plucked at the bright pink-and-green material of her skirt.

"Did you see the bruises on Eleanora's arms?" she asked quietly.

Jack's hand stilled momentarily on the shiny nickel-plated revolver he was cleaning. His eyes were shadowed as he sent her a glance across the dim hut, which was lit only by the tiny flame dancing over the Sterno can beside him.

"I saw them," he said.

Sarah crossed her arms on her knees and rested her chin on them. "I don't think that evil little man she's with is really her husband. She doesn't speak much, except to Teresa, but from something she let slip, I think her father sold her, *sold her,* to him when she was just thirteen or fourteen."

"From your work with the church, you must know that it happens a lot down here, especially in the interior. Crops fail, a family has too many children to feed—"

"Knowing about it doesn't make it any more acceptable!"

He refused to be drawn into that argument.

"Eleanora seems so desperate to touch Teresa." Sarah nibbled on her lower lip for a moment. "I think she must have lost a child of her own."

Setting the pistol aside, Jack leaned forward and regarded her intently. "Listen to me, lady. You've got enough problems of your own right now without taking on Eleanora's. We both do."

Sarah lifted her chin from her knees. "Maybe it's time we talked about those problems. I know mine, but I'm not sure I understand yours, or where you're coming from. Why are you protecting me and the children? What's in it for you, Jack?"

She hadn't meant to sound accusing or disdainful, but the contempt she couldn't suppress crept into her voice. He stared at her for a moment, then shrugged and retreated behind the shuttered screen of his eyes.

"Maybe you didn't understand the little discussion Che and I had when we hauled you into camp. The government forces are putting enough pressure on his little band of cutthroats as it is. If I'd allowed the trigger-happy bastards to kill you the night of the raid, the public outcry over a nun's murder would have tripled the intensity of the air patrols. I wasn't eager to have the *federales* descend on this camp, guns blazing, until I'd hightailed it out of here."

Sarah's heart turned over in her chest. "Just when do you plan to do that—hightail it out of here?"

"When my business is done."

"What happens to me and the children when you leave?"

Across the dim, shadowed interior their eyes locked. Silence dragged out between them until Sarah felt it in every pore, every nerve.

"I don't know yet," he finally replied. "You'll just have to trust me."

"Trust you…" She stared at him, unspeaking, for moments longer. Then she turned away and reached for the rolled-up mosquito net. It fell between them, a filmy curtain that shut out his face and shut Sarah in with her doubts and fears.

Jake slid the .45 back into its holster, his throat tight. He wanted to tell her. Christ, his gut ached with the need to tell her. But he didn't dare. Not yet. As he doused the Sterno "candle" and slid into the bedroll beside hers, however, Jake swore that he'd erase that faint, lingering contempt in her eyes if it was the last thing he ever did.

He lay awake in the darkness, one arm crooked under his head, wondering just why it was so important to him.

The children's steady breathing joined the chorus of night songs from the jungle outside. Sarah shifted on her pallet, her hips twisting this way and that as she sought a comfortable position. After a while, her soft, breathy sighs told Jake she'd slipped into slumber.

She was some restless sleeper.

He smiled in the darkness as she mumbled incoherently into the bedroll and twitched her hips once more. But the smile froze on his face when Sarah flopped over on her back. She flung out an arm, touching him as she had the first night in the hut. Only this time her hand didn't just rest on his arm. This time she clutched at him in an unconscious, reflexive reaction to the contact, then followed the touch of her hand with a snuggle. There was no other word for it. She twisted across the space between their bedrolls and snuggled up against his side. Her breast pressed against the wall of his chest. Her cheek rubbed against his shoulder, seeking a comfortable position.

Common sense told Jake to slide his shoulder out from under her head and turn his back to her. Or at least nudge Sarah back over onto her own thin mattress. He didn't do either, however. Instead, he lay still, feeling the wash of her breath against his neck. Hearing the little smacking noise she made as she settled once more into sleep. Reminding himself that she was off-limits. The scent of her surrounded him, all sun-warmed, musky female.

Despite every reminder, despite every stern warning to control himself, Jake felt his senses flicker, then ignite. His groin tightened, slowly, painfully. It took every ounce of discipline he possessed, but Jake resisted the fierce need to curl his arm about her shoulder and press her even more firmly against him. He lay still and unmoving, cursing the tattered remnants of a conscience that wouldn't allow him to roll over and cover her soft body with his own.

He was still wide awake when a booted foot slammed against the door to the hut.

"Hey, gringo!"

Jake had rolled out from under the net and was on his feet before the second kick banged against the wood.

"Che wants to speak with you!" Enrique shouted unsteadily through the door. "Hey, *americano!*"

A third kick sent the door crashing back on its hinges. Enrique stumbled inside, his flashlight waving wildly. Its sharp, powerful beam caught the startled, frightened faces of the children clutching at their hammock edges. It swept over the bedrolls, then jerked back to pin Sarah in its piercing glare. Her silvery blond hair tumbled over her shoulders as she sat up and raised a hand to shield her eyes. Jake stifled a groan at the sight of her high, firm breasts clearly silhouetted against the thin cotton blouse.

Enrique didn't make any attempt to stifle his reaction. He gaped, openmouthed, for several seconds. Then a slow, hoarse chuckle sounded deep in his throat. "So this is why you've not joined us to drink tequila and exchange war stories these past nights, gringo. Your *médica* has been tending to your aches privately, eh?"

His thick, slurred phrasing told Jake there wasn't a hope in hell of them talking their way out of this.

"I, too, have such an ache, gringo." Enrique held the flashlight on Sarah with one hand while he fumbled at his belt buckle with the other. "You go talk to Che, and I will see that my pain is treated, eh?"

Jake had only one option.

He took Enrique down.

Chapter 7

A single, swift chop to the neck, and Enrique's knees buckled. Before he hit the dirt, Jake bent and caught the big man's weight across his shoulders. It happened so fast, so quietly, that the only evidence of any struggle was the flashlight bouncing on the dirt floor.

"Get that," Jake grunted, staggering back a step under the weight of the unconscious man.

Sarah scrambled to the end of the bedroll and caught the spinning metal cylinder. Her hands shaking wildly, she directed the beam at Jake. He winced and turned his head away from the blinding light.

"Point it at the ground, for God's sake, then hand it to me."

When she'd complied, he tried to give her and the children assurances he was far from feeling himself. "Don't worry, we're going to bluff our way through this."

"Bluff?" The word came out in a strangled squeak. "How?"

"I'm guessing Che wants to talk to me because this dumb

son of a b—because Pig-face here is too drunk to understand the specifics on the drop. Che's probably furious with him and wouldn't object too strenuously if I put him out of action for a while." Jake smiled grimly. "You may get the chance to practice a few of your medical skills on this goon when he wakes up. *If* he wakes up."

Sarah's blunt-tipped fingers dug into his arm as he swung away. "Be...be careful."

"I always am. But it probably wouldn't hurt if you say a couple of prayers in the next few minutes."

In fact, Jake thought, it wouldn't hurt if she said a whole basketful of them. Using the flashlight to guide him, he made his way across the clearing to the shack Che had designated as his headquarters, kicked open the door and strode inside. Half a dozen startled faces turned at his entrance. With a twist of his shoulders, Jake dumped Enrique's inert bulk on the floor. His compatriots gaped at the sprawled body. Ignoring them, Jake crossed to a rack of portable communications equipment arrayed on a rickety table.

"Get Che for me," Jake rapped out to the man seated on a stool before the radio. "Now."

"He's...he's standing by."

With a jerk of his head, Jake motioned for the man to vacate his seat. Picking up the hand-held mike, he pressed the transmit button. "This is the gringo. What have you got?"

"Arrangements have been made for another shipment. Our supplier will deliver it personally. He was most unhappy that the last shipment was diverted. There will be no mistakes with this one."

Che's voice bore the sharp edge of anger and frustration. Poor bastard, Jake thought cynically. He had to choose between a lieutenant he couldn't rely on and an *americano* he despised.

"It will arrive at approximately 1100 hours on the twenty-seventh," the rebel announced.

The twenty-seventh! Jake swore viciously under his breath. That was three days from today. He had to make it through three more days in this camp. Three more days of keeping Sarah and the kids safe. Two more nights of lying beside her.

"Give me the coordinates."

"Enrique has them," Che said coldly.

"Enrique may not survive the night," Jake drawled. "He's starting to annoy me, big-time."

Che drew in a swift, sharp breath, audible even over the radio. "Enrique will survive long enough to lead you to the drop site. After you show us how to operate the missiles, I don't care which one of you puts a bullet in the other's head."

"That's what I like about you, pal. You're such a warm, caring son of a bitch. So tell me, what did you find out about the *federale* presence in our sector?"

Jake smiled to himself at the frustration that almost sizzled through the receiver. "It appears it was an unannounced exercise. A stupid scheduling mistake by some staff officer at the headquarters. The *patrón* is most displeased."

"Just tell him to make sure it doesn't happen on the twenty-seventh. One more screwup and even your *patrón* won't be able to afford my fees."

The radio went dead. Jake tossed the mike onto the tabletop and swung around on the stool to survey the occupants of the room. They stared back at him with varying degrees of anger, wariness and interest on their faces. Pig-face lay sprawled in the dirt before them, like one of the huge, hoglike tapirs he resembled.

"Is that tequila?" Jake asked, nodding to the cloudy bottle standing on the table amid a litter of grease-stained cards and half-full glasses.

"*Sí*," one of the men answered cautiously.

Jake rose and stepped over Enrique's bulk. "Pour me a drink. It may be a while before your friend here wakes up and we settle matters between us."

A thin, slumping man who'd been one of Sarah's patients picked up the bottle. He sloshed tequila into a dirty glass, shoved it toward Jake, then jerked his chin toward Enrique. "Why do you fight with that one?"

"His ugliness annoys me."

A ripple of laughter greeted the sardonic response. By the time Enrique began grunting and twitching, the men at the table didn't make any effort to hide their amusement at his graceless return to consciousness. Jake concealed his satisfaction behind an impassive face. He'd spent half his life leading men. He knew that few soldiers would respect or follow someone who'd been made to look ridiculous in their eyes. And the picture Enrique presented when he finally sat up, slack-faced and drooling spittle, inspired very little respect.

"So, Enrique," Xavier called out, "the gringo says your face offends him. I can see why."

The bellows of laughter that accompanied this sally sent a wave of mottled red across the face under discussion. "Perhaps you won't laugh so much when I tell you that I saw the little *religiosa* in his bed," Enrique snarled. "While we make do with Pablo's slut of a wife, this one has been plowing between those tender white thighs."

The sideways glances the men sent Jake contained surprise, suspicion and a faint hint of disapproval, followed swiftly by hot, avid interest.

Jake didn't entertain much hope of convincing the big, red-faced man that he'd been hallucinating, but he figured it was worth the try. "You're a pig, Enrique. And you're drunk. You let your filthy mind run away with you. You frightened the woman and disgusted me."

Enrique lumbered to his feet. "I know what I saw. You thought to keep her to yourself, eh, gringo? No more. After tonight, we all share her. Except you, of course. Tonight you die."

He fumbled for the pistol in his holster.

Jake didn't alter his loose-limbed sprawl. One hand toyed with the tequila glass, the other rested negligently in his pants pocket.

"You cannot kill him, Enrique," a short, frowning rebel protested. "Che has said he must be at the drop site in three days."

In a few succinct words, Enrique dismissed his leader. He pulled out a big-framed .45 with a silver replica of the Mayan sun calendar on its decorated grip. Chairs tumbled over backward as the men scrambled out of the line of fire.

"And do you also expect your *patrón* to perform that particular unnatural act?" Jake inquired lazily. "He will be no more pleased than Che if you make him waste the money he's laying out for the shipment."

The casual observation brought even the drunken lieutenant up short. Enrique knew as well as Jake that the drug lords would be far more relentless and exacting in their retribution toward one who crossed them than Che would ever be. The guerrilla leader wouldn't hesitate to put a bullet through an enemy's forehead. The drug lords' henchmen would make him beg for it.

Enrique hesitated, the .45 wavering in his big paw. After a long, tense moment, he jammed it back in its tooled leather holster. "Maybe I won't shoot you, after all. Maybe I will just cut off your *cojones*."

"You can try, my snout-nosed friend. You can try."

Jake loosened his grip on the weapon in his pocket. The palm-size .22 carried five hollow-point rounds, any one of which would've put Enrique down. Jake wouldn't need them now. Tossing down a last swallow of tequila, he rose.

A feral light sprang into the lieutenant's eyes at the sight of the easy target. His hand moved toward the belt hooked over the back of a nearby chair.

Jake's razor-sharp machete sliced through the air. Its lethal, specially balanced blade pinned the leather belt to the chairback and toppled the chair over with the force of the throw.

"No knives," Jake told the startled lieutenant. "No guns. Let's settle this in a way that will give satisfaction to us both."

A slow grin spread across Enrique's red face. "You're right, gringo. I will much enjoy feeling my fists smash into your face. Almost as much as I will enjoy your woman squirming and thrashing beneath me."

Jake could have ended the farce that followed at any time, but he took a savage pleasure in reducing Enrique to a staggering, gurgling, bloody hulk. His rational mind argued that he needed to destroy the last shreds of confidence the other men placed in the lieutenant's authority. A primitive, wholly male instinct, however, wanted to make sure Enrique understood what the consequences would be if he touched Sarah.

Jake didn't escape totally unscathed himself. For all Enrique's bulk and drunken state, he packed the power of a bull behind his hammerlike fists. When the big man lay sprawled on the dirt floor once again, Jake hooked a foot around a chair leg and dragged it to the table.

"Now, my friends," he panted, dragging the back of his hand across his bleeding lip, "let's finish that tequila."

Jake closed his eyes as clear liquid fire slid down his throat and curled in his belly. He sagged back against his chair, enjoying the heat, the feeling of satisfaction, even the pain that throbbed in his chin.

He should go back to the hut. Sarah would be wide-eyed and trembling with anxiety, he knew. He also knew that there was no way he could soothe her fears and stretch out beside her right now. Not with his blood pounding in his veins and the remembered feel of her body next to his battling with the last remnants of his conscience.

Sarah sat in rigid, unmoving silence. The flickering light of the Sterno lamp surrounded her and the children in a small circle of gloom. They huddled against her, clinging to the black robe she'd hastily pulled on. It had saved them once before. With a sick, wrenching fear, Sarah hoped it wouldn't have to save them again.

When no shots or screams sounded for what seemed like hours, the children's fear slowly eased. Sarah's, however, mounted with each passing moment. Where was he? she wondered with increasing desperation. What would she do if he didn't return? Oh, God, he had to return. She squeezed her eyes shut and repeated for the hundredth time the prayers he'd suggested.

Only gradually did Sarah realize that more than just self-preservation motivated her fervent prayers. It wasn't the lean, unshaven mercenary she wanted to see step through that door. She wanted to see Jack. Or, better yet, the Señor Creighton Teresa idolized. The man who'd carved a doll out of a mango root and tucked a delighted, squealing three year old under his arm. The man who coaxed even the still, silent Eduard to speak. The man who made Sarah's breath catch when he creased his cheeks in that damned crooked smile of his.

The man who finally returned, however, wasn't any of the ones Sarah had prayed for. She gave a glad cry of welcome when she saw his shadowy but unmistakable form silhouetted in the door, then gasped when he stepped into the little circle of light. Brownish dried blood covered most of his face and spattered his bare chest. Even in the dim sputter of the tiny flame she could see the dark bruise that covered one side of his jaw.

At her startled gasp, he attempted what must have been meant as a reassuring smile but ended up as a grimace of pain. He staggered a bit as he put a hand up to his jaw.

"Oh, my God!" She pushed herself out of the children's grasp and flew across the hut to take his arm. "Move, children. Let him sit down on the crate. Teresa, get me the cloth we use to wash with. Eduard, you find the disinfectant. The little bottle of liquid antiseptic, not the dry powder we used on you."

"It looks worse than it is," Jack muttered as she helped him ease down. "Most of the blood belongs, uh, belonged to Pig-face."

"Did he die?" Ricci asked, wide-eyed and tremulous.

Sarah bit her lip as she took the canteen and the white cotton briefs from Teresa. That a three year old should have such a fixation with death tore at her heart.

The gringo tried again. This time he managed more grin

than grimace. "No, Squirt, he didn't die. But he'll probably wish he had when he wakes up."

"Good!" Eduard's low response made up in ferocity what it lacked in volume.

Jack's head swung toward the boy. "You didn't like old Pig-face, either, huh?"

"For pity's sake," Sarah said, turning his chin back to examine it. "Hold still."

With a rush of relief, she saw that he'd been right when he said most of the blood wasn't his. Aside from several swelling bruises, she discovered only one laceration, along his jawline.

"Tilt your head back so I can clean this," Sarah ordered, hoping against hope that she wouldn't have to perform an antoptomy.

He propped his head back against the wall. Eyes closed, he allowed her to tend him. She wiped the last of the dried blood from the underside of his chin, then took the bottle of antiseptic Eduard handed her.

"Ouch!"

Sarah blinked. Somehow she hadn't thought this tough-as-unchewed-leather mercenary would be so sensitive to pain. Gentling her touch, she dabbed at his chin once more.

"That stings."

The plaintive complaint sounded so much like that of a little boy that Sarah couldn't help smiling. She moved closer to his side and slipped one arm around his neck. Cradling his head against her shoulder as she would Eduard's or Ricci's, she swabbed his cuts.

But the body pressed against hers wasn't Eduard's or Ricci's. It was long and sleekly muscled and musky with the scent of a man. Sarah felt a stir of awareness at the feel of him leaning into her. Her swift, instinctive reaction quickly gave way to another emotion, however. An unexpected tenderness welled up in her heart. For so many days now, she'd drawn from this man's strength. For so many nights, she'd fallen asleep knowing he was beside her. That he would now wrap an arm around her hips and lean into her for support filled her with soft, sweet warmth.

She was so bemused by the feeling that it was some moments before she realized his head had turned a few degrees, until his cheek rested on the slope of her breast. And that his arm had slowly tightened, drawing her even closer into the heat of his body. It took a moment more before she registered the fact that the hand on her hip no longer just rested there. Through the heavy fabric of her robe, his fingers kneaded the swell of rounded flesh.

"What are you doing?" Sarah gasped, pushing herself out of his hold.

"I…" A wave of confusion crossed his face for a moment, to be replaced almost immediately by a scowl. His arm dropped. "Damn, it was the tequila."

Sarah was so disturbed by the sensations his touch had aroused that she didn't even chastise him for his inappropriate language.

"Tequila? Have you been drinking?"

"A little." He met her incredulous stare, then shrugged. "Hell, a lot."

Sarah's mouth sagged open, then closed to a thin, ominous line. "You mean we've been sitting here in the dark, frantic with worry, and you've…you've been swilling tequila with that rabble out there?"

At her accusing tone, a tinge of red rose in his cheeks. "Look, I was just cementing my relationship with the boys. So they wouldn't come looking for Sister Sarah to tend their 'aches,' as well."

Sarah stood rigid while a slow, fiery fury flowed through her veins. He'd been drinking, while she sat here terrified, praying her heart out for him! He'd been schmoozing with his cretinous pals while she blocked out every despicable aspect of his character and painted him as a cross between Santa Claus and an unshaven Pierce Brosnan! He'd stumbled in, covered with blood, and made Sarah's heart leap in fear. She'd cradled him to her breast like some hurt child. Now he

had the nerve to sit there, his head tilted up at her belliger-
ently, and scowl at her as though the whole thing had been
her fault.

Acting on pure impulse, Sarah tipped her hand and poured
the entire bottle of disinfectant over his cut.

"Jesus H. Christ!"

This time Sarah would have chastised him, if she hadn't
been so startled by his reaction. His drinking hadn't dulled
his reflexes, she discovered. With the deadly speed of a bush-
master, he uncoiled his long body and sprang up. A hard hand
grabbed her outstretched wrist and twisted it up behind her.

Off balance, Sarah stumbled against his bare chest. The
soft, springy pelt she'd fantasized about brushed her cheek.
She tried to push herself away with the flat of her palm. He
held her easily with one hand, which only added to Sarah's
pounding, white hot anger.

"You want to explain that little bit of medical malpractice,
Sister Sarah?"

"Figure it out for yourself, gringo."

She realized her mistake as soon as the words were out.
There wasn't anything even remotely nunlike in the way she
challenged him, eyes flashing, fury radiating from every inch
of the body he held pressed against his own.

His eyes narrowed. In the dim light, Sarah couldn't see their
expression, but she felt his body stiffen against hers. The hand
holding her wrist behind her back tightened, and her breasts
were crushed against a solid, unyielding wall of hard, male
flesh.

They stared at each other, unspeaking, until a small whimper shattered the tension arcing between them.

"Please, Señor Creighton, you and Sarita, you must not
fight."

Teresa's tearful voice brought them back to the reality of
a small, airless hut and three frightened children. The hold on
Sarah's wrist loosened, then fell away. She stepped back and
drew in a long, shuddering breath.

"I'm...I'm sorry," she stuttered.

His eyes were guarded, curiously so after his blazing anger of moments before.

"I was petrified, sitting here in the dark, not knowing what was happening. I...I said every prayer I knew for you." She stumbled through the apology, not really sorry, but shaken enough by what had just occurred that she felt the need to reestablish their previous relationship.

His jaw worked for a moment. "Well, I suppose I have to thank you for your spiritual intervention, but I'll damn sure let you know when I want any more of your medical attention. Now let's see if we can get some sleep for what's left of the night."

The children managed to drift back into quiet slumber, but they were the only ones. Jake lay still and tense in the darkness, waiting for dawn to slice through the cracks in the tin roof with its characteristic suddenness. He could tell from Sarah's lack of movement that she wasn't sleep. She lay with her back turned stubbornly to him, too far away to touch, too close for him to ignore the prickling sensation her mere presence caused within him.

He knew the knife-edged tension that kept him awake was the culmination of the night's events. The brawl with Enrique. The knowledge that the drop was set and Jake could finally contact OMEGA. The fiery tequila. The feel of Sarah's hips cradled in his arm.

The desire that had been curling in Jake's belly since the moment she'd snuggled up to him all those hours ago suddenly jackknifed. He gritted his teeth, straining to keep a leash on his rampaging libido. Drawing up one knee to ease the coiled ache, he cursed himself and her in the darkness.

Didn't she know better than to hold his head against her breast like that while she swabbed his cuts? Didn't she know that every time she even brushed his arm, fire streaked all along his nerves? Couldn't she sense how it twisted his gut every time she feathered her fingers through her hair?

For all that she wore a nun's habit, wasn't she still woman

enough to recognize the effect she had on a man when she flashed those magnificent, fury-filled eyes up at him? At that moment, Jake had come so close to forgetting who she was and where they were that it scared the hell out of him.

His jaw clenching, Jake played and replayed that strange confrontation in his mind.

He'd dealt with enough people in his time to know that no human being ever really fit a stereotype. The toughest first sergeant he'd ever worked with had had an almost pathological fear of heights. The sweet, honey-haired second-grade teacher he'd dated for a while after his divorce had kept a library of porno flicks just the other side of kinky. Maggie Sinclair, with her long legs, sparkling brown eyes and infectious grin, could put a bullet through the center of a target forty-four out of forty-five times.

So it didn't bother Jake that Sarah wasn't exactly a younger version of Mother Teresa. He could accept that she sported a fall of silvery-blond hair under the black veil. He understood that she was only human, like when she alternated between quiet competence and frazzled weariness with the children. He knew that the fear and strain of waiting for him tonight had toppled many of the barriers between them, causing her to blaze up at him like any outraged female confronting an errant male.

Still, that confrontation bothered him. And he didn't know why.

Jake's mouth settled into a tight line. Maybe it was his own internal alert mechanism that had activated this indefinable tension that shimmered right below his skin's surface. Maybe his body was signaling that he'd gotten too close to this operation, too emotionally involved with Sarah. He needed to back off, to avoid any repetition of the fierce, primal protectiveness he'd felt when Enrique threatened her. He sure as hell needed to avoid any more physical contact with her. From here on, he had to concentrate more on his mission and less on this woman who intrigued, irritated and aroused him in equal measures.

That was it, Jake decided. He had to get this operation moving forward again. As soon as he could slip out of camp, later today, he'd reclaim his backup transmitter and reestablish contact with his OMEGA control. Now that he knew the approximate time of the drop, he could work out the details of the extraction and strike with Maggie Sinclair.

Some of Jake's tension eased at the thought of Maggie. Once again he thanked his lucky stars she was the controller for this operation. Not that the others weren't good—damn good. But Maggie and that sixth sense of hers were in a separate category altogether. Of course, her uncanny instincts were probably going bananas right now. No doubt she'd worn a track in the tile floor of the control center with her pacing over the lack of contact with Jaguar.

Jake wiped away the trickle of sweat that signaled the imminent arrival of another hot, humid dawn, then grinned wryly in the dark. At least Maggie was doing her worrying and pacing in air-conditioned comfort.

Chapter 8

Maggie couldn't remember the last time she'd been so hot!

It was still early morning, just an hour past dawn, and yet her heavy black robes were already sticking to her back. She sat on the sticky vinyl seat of the bus taking her into Cartoza's capital and fanned the air with one hand. The sleeve of her habit flapped energetically but stirred up a lot more dust than breeze. Despite the heat and the crowd packed belly to belly in the wheezing, huffing bus, however, Maggie felt a familiar drum of excitement beating in her veins.

She was back in the field!

After an intense session with Cowboy to get him up to speed and a hurried outfitting by the OMEGA uniform specialists, she'd left Washington just after midnight. An air force jet had flown her to her insertion point at a base in neighboring Costa Rica. From there she'd boarded a commercial flight into Cartoza's only airport, thus establishing her cover as a newly arrived medical sister.

And now she was back in the field!

So what if sweat rolled down her ribs? So what if her stiff

black habit scratched and the white wimple got in her way every time she unthinkingly tried to rake a hand through her hair? Maggie would've endured far worse—and had in the past—to feel the intensity and awareness of everything around her that came only with being in the middle of an operation.

Settling her small brown suitcase more comfortably across her knees, she made sure the blue steel Smith & Wesson .22 automatic pistol tucked in her sleeve didn't show, and sat back to enjoy the ride into the capital. She'd stay at the sisters' chapter house today, until she heard from Jake. Or until outside pressure or circumstance made her decide to go in for Sarah Chandler.

As the bus bounced over the rutted road that led out of the airport, chickens squawked, babies cried, and deafening music blared from a loudspeaker. The old woman next to Maggie smiled at the din, then held up a gnarled, arthritic hand to display the rosary beads she clutched. It didn't take Maggie long to realize that the old woman wasn't saying her rosary just to pass the time. She was probably praying fervently that she survived the trip. Maggie herself muttered a few prayers as the bus careered along the narrow, twisting road that led from the airport into the capital. On one side, lush vegetation in more shades of green than Maggie had ever seen climbed up the steep hillsides. On the other was a sheer two-hundred-foot vertical drop to the sparkling blue-green Atlantic. Sure that the bus would sail off the road at every turn, Maggie tried to focus on the bright flashes of brilliantly colored flowers on the right and ignore the empty stretch of air on the left.

When the bus turned inland and approached the tumble of shacks that formed the city's suburbs, she breathed a sigh of relief. Almost immediately, Maggie realized that she'd relaxed too soon. Cartoza's capital clung to the steep slopes of the Teleran foothills like barnacles on a ship's keel. Huffing and groaning, the bus crept up one almost perpendicular street, then plunged down the next, in wild defiance of any and all traffic laws. Pedestrians shouted curses and jumped out of the

way, horns blared, and thick exhaust fumes from poorly re-
fined fuel added to the collection of odors trapped in the bus.

When she wasn't bracing herself against the seat in front
of her, arms stiff and eyes squeezed shut in anticipation of
her imminent demise, Maggie caught glimpses of adobe-
covered buildings plastered with posters advertising everything from Diet Pepsi to the topless dancers at Café La Boom
Boom. After countless stops to let off and take on passengers,
the bus finally puffed to a halt before a pair of tall wooden
doors set in a pink adobe wall.

"El convento!" the driver bellowed back over his shoulder.

"Thank the Lord," Maggie muttered, easing her way past
the old woman.

A firm tug on the bell rope soon gained her access to a
shaded, flowering courtyard. After paying her respects to the
senior sister, she was shown to a small, sparsely furnished
room kept in readiness for transients. As soon as the door
shut behind her escort, Maggie sank down on the bed, tugged
off her veil and raked a hand through her thick mane.

Seconds later, she pulled up the antenna on her hand-held
secure-transmission satellite communications device. The
transmitter-receiver, called a transceiver for short, was small
and thin, not much bigger than a lady's compact. It switched
from transmit to receive mode at the slightest touch of a finger.

"Nothing from Jaguar yet," Cowboy relayed, his voice as
clear as if he were calling from across town instead of bouncing a signal off a low-orbiting satellite.

Maggie knew that she would've been contacted instantly if
Jake had called in, but she still couldn't help feeling a stab
of disappointment. That, combined with fatigue and the accumulated tension of the operation, made her sag for a moment. It was probably just as well she wasn't jumping right
into action, she reflected. She wouldn't be much good to Jake
if she let her instincts become dulled.

"Roger," Maggie replied, acknowledging Cowboy's transmission. "I'm going to grab a few hours' sleep, then reconnoiter."

"I'll hold the fort," he replied.

Slipping out of the black robe, Maggie placed her gun on the handy night table and stretched out on the cot in her underwear. True to her cover, she wore plain, unadorned white cotton panties and bra, which the uniform specialists had assured her were *not* easy to find in D.C. on such short notice. The thick adobe walls gave the small room a cool, dim cast. Within moments, she was asleep.

Half an hour later, a raucous, booming bellow sent her leaping from the bed, .22 in hand. She dropped into a crouch, weapon held straight out, then swung it in an arc across the width of the room. A second bellow thundered through the walls.

The sound of scurrying feet outside drew Maggie toward the door. Opening it a cautious crack, she saw several sisters hurrying down the hall. A young, olive-skinned novice in a gray dress stopped at her signal.

"Excuse me. Is that a fire alarm?"

"It's the bell for midmorning prayers," the young woman explained. She glanced pointedly at Maggie's underwear and uncovered hair. "You have only five minutes before you must be in place."

"Mmm..." Maggie thought she just might skip midmorning prayers in favor of her first few hours' sleep in almost two days.

"Of course," the novice said earnestly, "if you miss these prayers, just listen for the bell after next. It calls one to a special half hour of contemplation and prayer before lunch."

Maggie stared at her in gathering consternation. "You mean the bell rings like that all morning long?"

"Oh, yes, Sister," the young woman assured her. "All day long. Every thirty minutes, from five-o'clock wake-up to ten o'clock last prayers. It is, perhaps, a trifle loud, but one gets used to it."

Not in this lifetime, Maggie thought. She closed the door and leaned against it. Jake had better call in, and soon!

"Xavier and I are going into the jungle to check the intrusion-detection devices."

Sarah's hands stilled as she stared up at Jack's shadowed face. The black plastic comb hovered over her dull, limp hair.

"Xavier?"

"The man whose feet you treated." His mouth twisted in a mocking smile. "He's supposed to be my assistant."

"How long will you be gone?"

"Not long. Here, take this."

She glanced at the small, toy-size gun he held out to her and repressed a shudder. She hated guns, and the violence they caused. Her mother had been killed in a hunting accident when Sarah was just a baby. The senator hadn't allowed a gun anywhere in the house since. Sarah had never touched one in her life. Lowering her hands, she clasped them tight in her lap. The sharp teeth of the comb bit into her palm.

"I...I don't..."

His mouth tightened at her reluctance to take the weapon. "Look, Sister, I'm not asking you to violate some deep-seated religious principles here. You don't have to shoot to kill. If anyone comes into the shack, just aim the thing straight up in the air and pull the trigger. I'll be back before the echo dies away."

"Couldn't we just go with you?"

"I can't take you out of here just yet," he said sharply. "I told you, I've got some business to conduct in a few days."

"I wouldn't dream of asking you to put our welfare ahead of your *business*," Sarah retorted, acid dripping from her voice. "I just want you to take me and the children a little way upstream."

"And leave you alone? To try and make it out on your own? Don't be stupid. One misstep and you'd all be monkey bait."

Sarah glared up at him. "I wasn't thinking of escape. I

wouldn't risk the children's lives by trying to find my own way through your booby traps. I just thought that I could bathe them while you did your…your business."

The undisguised scorn in her voice tightened the skin across his cheeks. He closed his fingers around the gun.

"They need a bath," Sarah insisted. *She* needed a bath, too. Badly. But she'd settle for dangling her feet in some cool water and splashing what she could over her face and arms.

Sarah set her jaw as she waited for his response. His shuttered gray eyes gave no clue to what he thought. He'd been so withdrawn this morning, so reserved. Ever since they'd rolled back the mosquito netting and gone about the business of seeing to the children's needs, Sarah had sensed a change in him. She wasn't sure exactly when she'd become so attuned to this man's moods, but she knew that something had changed between them last night. Irrevocably.

Maybe he was still suffering from all that tequila he'd downed, Sarah thought irritably. Or maybe he was still angry about the way she'd poured that disinfectant on him. Or maybe he was finding the prospect of protecting her and the children more of a strain on his patience and his admittedly tattered conscience than he'd bargained for.

Too bad.

Sarah wasn't any happier about being stuck in this camp than he apparently was, but until she figured out a way to get herself and the children back to civilization, she wasn't letting Mr. Mercenary off the hook. He was stuck with them. And they were stuck with him.

"All right," he answered finally. "There's a pool about a kilometer from here. Far enough away to give you some privacy, but still well within the perimeter defenses."

Sarah scrambled to her feet before he could change his mind. "Good! I'll gather a few things while you go get the children. They're with Eleanora."

One dark brow rose cynically as she headed for the backpack she now considered her own. He didn't comment, however, and stepped out the door.

The prospect of being out of the hut and the oppressive camp for even an hour lifted Sarah's spirits. Her unease over Jack's strange quietness vanished as she dug through the pockets of the backpack for the few remaining toiletry items.

She felt like a child being given a special treat, like an adventurer setting off on an exciting journey instead of just trudging a half or so mile upstream. Sarah smiled, remembering the vacations she'd taken with her father at five-star resorts. The junkets provided by lobbyists who were currying his favor. The yearly trips to Europe to buy clothes and enjoy the hospitality of the ambassadors and diplomats she'd entertained in D.C. None of those jaunts had thrilled her as much as the prospect of this little excursion.

She threw on the black robe and rolled her few supplies up in the cotton blouse. The blouse was so big and baggy on her, she could wear it while she was bathing the children and still be covered from neck to knees.

Hearing Teresa's childish giggles, Sarah pulled open the door and watched the little procession cross the clearing. Ricci was perched on Jack's shoulders, his black hair covered by the floppy-brimmed camouflage hat. Silent, unsmiling Eduard walked beside them. Teresa danced along in her bright red dress, holding on to her precious doll with one hand and Eleanora with the other. Bringing up the rear was the thin, stoop-shouldered guerrilla whose bleeding feet Sarah had treated yesterday. He grinned and pointed to his boots with the tip of his rifle.

The cavalcade came to a halt. Jack nodded toward the heavyset, expressionless woman beside him. "She says she can help you with the children."

Sarah flashed Eleanora a wide, grateful smile. As much as the children tugged at her heartstrings, they still overwhelmed her at times. She'd gained a whole new appreciation of motherhood in the past few days. The younger children's constant demands for her attention, their swift mood swings from happy to tearful, the utter lack of privacy, even to go to the bathroom, had added to the stress of her ever-present uncertainty and fear.

"I managed to round up some soap," Jack added, handing her a much-used bar.

Sarah grabbed it with an involuntary cry of delight. She didn't want to know what he'd had to barter or promise for it. It was one thing for him to sell his knowledge of stolen weapons for cash, she admitted to herself with rueful honesty. It was another thing altogether when he sold it to benefit her or the children.

From the way his lips twisted cynically, Sarah guessed that he'd noticed this apparent inconsistency in her rigid contempt for his business dealings. Shrugging, she tucked the soap inside her bundle.

"Okay, troops," he said dryly, "fall in. Stay behind me on the path once we leave the clearing, understand?"

"*Sí, Señor Creighton,*" Teresa trilled.

Jack rolled his eyes, then led the way out of camp.

When Sarah saw the small pool, she gasped in surprised delight. Until this moment, she'd never realized that the jungle could be so incredibly beautiful and seductive.

A ribbon of water tumbled down one of the steep hills that surrounded the camp and collected at the bottom to form a silvery, glistening basin. Feathery ferns the height of small trees formed a lush green backdrop for the pool. A single beam of sunshine sliced through the dense canopy overhead, illuminating the brilliant scarlet and yellow trumpet flowers that basked in its light.

"The pool's shallow enough for the kids to wade in," Jack said, drawing her wide-eyed gaze away from the delightful scene.

"What about snakes and such? Is it safe?"

"A safe as anything is in the jungle," he replied with a shrug, "but I'll check it out for you."

He slid his machete from the leather scabbard and spoke a

few words to the rebel, who nodded and moved toward the far side of the pool.

"While Xavier and I are gone," Jake said in a quick undertone, "Eduard will stand guard. Just to make sure no one else has decided to follow along and drop in on your little party uninvited."

Sarah bit her lip and glanced down at the eight-year-old. Eduard needed to bathe, as well, but she knew he would resist if she tried to coax him in. He was such a quiet, contained little boy. He didn't seem to want cuddling or attention, as the younger ones did, and he shied away from allowing Sarah to help him with any personal needs.

"We men will take a turn later, when you're done," Jack said deliberately.

Eduard sent him a grateful man-to-man look.

"But…"

"Don't worry, I won't let his arm get wet. I've spent enough time in the jungle to know as much about blood flukes as you do."

He knew a whole lot more than she did, Sarah thought ruefully as she watched him walk toward the pool. About blood flukes—whatever those were—and about the jungle and young boys. In his own quiet way, Eduard seemed to have developed a severe case of hero worship. More of that male bonding, Sarah supposed.

She shook her head, wondering at the contradictions in the man. Over the past few days, she had found herself by turns disgusted by him and grateful to him. She'd laid awake at night, aware of his uncompromising masculinity but unwilling to acknowledge its effect on her. He cold-bloodedly dealt in death, and yet…

And yet he'd provided her what safety he could in this precarious situation. Moreover, he was so kind to the children, in his brusque way. Teresa preened like a little banty rooster in her bright dress whenever she caught his eyes. She refused to go to sleep unless the root he'd carved for her was tucked into the hammock with her. Little Ricci followed him about with the eagerness of a happy puppy.

Sarah frowned as she watched the object of her thoughts hunker down on a flat rock and slap the water gently with a stick to see what creatures, if any, he disturbed. Why should it surprise her that she couldn't reconcile the complexities in his nature? For all her much-touted charm and skill at playing the Washington social game, she'd failed miserably to understand what drove the one other man who'd swept into her life with such devastating impact.

Now there was a contrast, Sarah thought dryly. André, with his impeccable manners and skilled lovemaking. And this…this soldier of fortune, with his hard gray eyes and his soiled khaki shirt stretched across his broad back. The rolled-up sleeves displayed the tanned, muscled arms that had wrapped around her with such lack of gentleness last night. Sarah shivered, remembering the feel of his body pressed against hers.

"Sarita! Can we go in now?"

"Can I make the pee-pee in the water, Sarita?"

Sarah glanced down at the two children dancing around her, one thin and wiry, the other stubby and plump. "Why don't you make the pee-pee before you get in the pool?" she suggested with a smile.

"Can we go in now? It is safe," Teresa insisted, tugging on her sleeve.

The mercenary rose, confirming Teresa's opinion. "The water's clean. Just don't leave the clearing. Xavier and I will be close enough to hear you if you scream, but far enough to give you privacy. Thirty minutes long enough?"

"Thirty minutes is fine."

He tipped two fingers to the floppy brim of his hat, then started back around the pool to join Xavier.

"Now, Sarita? Now?" Both children tugged on her sleeves now as they hopped from one foot to the other in their eagerness.

Smiling at their antics, Sarah glanced up and caught Elean-

ora's eye. For a brief, unguarded moment, the other woman
shared her enjoyment of the youngsters' unrestrained eagerness. Almost as quickly as it had appeared, however, the flash
of awareness in Eleanora's eyes faded and her features took
on their habitual vacant flatness.

"Okay, okay," Sarah said, laughing. "Let me get changed,
then Eleanora and I will take you in."

She edged behind a screen of ferns to shed her black robe
and the panties she intended to wash. As she pulled on the
baggy blouse, she pondered what she now guessed was a deliberate shield erected by Eleanora. Sarah bit her lip, imagining what it was that the older woman retreated from behind
that dull passivity. Jack's warning that she had enough problems of her own without adding Eleanora's to them sounded
in Sarah's mind. She wanted to heed his warning. She *needed*
to heed it. But when she knelt beside the older woman to
undress the wiggling, squirming children, Sarah knew the
warning had come too late. Just what she could do about
Eleanora's plight eluded her at this precise moment. But she
would have to think of something.

The children waded into the pool, shrieking at the cold and
jumping up and down. Their small hands beat the water and
sent silvery spray flying everywhere. Laughing, Sarah sat
down on the flat rock beside Eleanora. She rucked the hem
of the long blouse up over her knees, dangled her feet in the
water and let the children splash and play. Within seconds,
the two women were almost as soaked as the youngsters.

The cool water felt wonderful. Sarah longed to slip off the
rock and join the kids. Her fingers clenched around the soap.
Maybe after they'd cleansed the children, she'd slip into the
pool, blouse and all, and wash her hair.

Out of the corner of her eye, Sarah caught a blur of khaki.
She looked up to see Jack emerge from the jungle on the far
side of the pool. He stopped abruptly, his body slowly tensing
as he stared at her. Even from this distance, Sarah could see
how his skin stretched tight across his cheekbones and his
eyes devoured her.

Her heart slamming up against her ribs, she glanced down and saw how the wet blouse clung to her breasts and thighs. The soaked cotton molded her, shaped her, revealed her.

Sarah's first instinct was as old as time. A feminine response to the danger she sensed in the man stripping her with his eyes. She lifted her arms, intending to shield herself. Then a second urge—as old as, and even more powerful than, the first—gripped her. The woman in her responded to his hunger, and an answering need shivered down her spine.

She'd been ashamed for so long. Of her complicity in another woman's tragic attempt to end her life. Of her inability to deal with the relentless media in Washington, who'd hounded her every move. Of her own ineptness during these weeks in Cartoza. Jack's hot male look stripped away her shame and doubt and fear. What was left was basic. Elemental. Cleansing in its raw power. Whatever else she might or might not be, whatever strengths or inadequacies she possessed, Sarah Chandler was a woman.

Her arms dropped to her sides. Slowly she straightened her shoulders.

Jake held himself rigidly still. A bead of sweat rolled down his cheek. Hard and aching, he fought the urge to stalk around the pool, haul her up, and carry her into the jungle. More than he'd ever wanted anything in his life, Jake wanted to see her on a bed of green springy ferns, her white legs spread and a woman's smile of welcome in her luminous blue-green eyes. He ached to lose himself in the damp valley between her thighs.

She couldn't know, he thought savagely. She couldn't know how that wet shirt clung to her skin. She couldn't know what the sight of her beautiful body did to a man. She couldn't have any idea of the searing lust that blazed in his belly.

Or could she?

The vague, unspecified tension that had kept him awake most of the night sharpened into a sudden, gut-wrenching doubt. He stared at Sarah a moment longer, then forced himself to turn away. He moved slowly, as if the smallest step pained him—which it did.

"Here," he said brusquely, handing Eduard the canteen he'd forgotten to leave with him earlier. "The pool water is probably safe, but there's no need to take chances."

He left the clearing without looking at Sarah again. He didn't have to. Her image hovered in front of him as he re-traced his steps down the trail and rejoined Xavier. With each step, suspicion curled in Jake's mind like a damp, pervasive mist. Just what exactly did he know about Sister Sarah Josepha?

Suppressing the aching male need that had gripped him the moment he saw her wrapped in that wet blouse, Jake forced himself to step back and assess the situation. Methodically, ruthlessly, he reviewed every moment since he'd parted those damn palmettos and seen her white, terrified face staring back at him. Had he missed something vital, something he should have seen?

He'd shrugged off her stumbling Spanish with the expla-nation that she was new to the area, not long in country. That made sense. The dialect used here in the mountains was dif-ficult even for Cartoza's coastal city dwellers to understand, let alone outsiders.

He'd understood when she gritted her teeth and treated the minor ills of the men in the camp with a superficial skill. They'd murdered her friends, after all. He didn't expect her to show a tender, caring bedside manner.

He'd ascribed her sometimes gentle, sometimes exasperated care of the children to the natural stress of their situation. She'd cleansed them, fed them, heard their prayers with a determination he could only call dedication.

No, Sister Sarah hadn't given Jake any reason to think she wasn't the frightened nun he thought her to be.

Until last night. Last night, when she'd blazed with fury and challenged him, woman to man.

And today, when her eyes had met his across the silvery green surface of the pool. When she had responded to the raw hunger that must have shown on his face by straightening her shoulders.

At the vivid image of Sarah's small, rounded breasts thrusting up against the wet cotton, the ruthless agent and the fierce, hungry male in Jake merged once more, painfully. Swearing viciously, he concentrated on placing one foot in front of the other.

A hundred meters down the trail, he stopped in his tracks.

Ahead of him, Xavier froze and dropped into a crouch. "What is it, gringo?" he whispered, pivoting on the balls of his feet.

"I thought I heard something," Jake answered quietly. He jerked his chin toward the left. "In there."

Xavier swung the barrel of his weapon toward the area Jake had indicated.

"Don't fire!" Jake ordered. "You'll detonate the charges."

The man's thin shoulders slumped even more as he swallowed and stared, wide-eyed, at the dense undergrowth.

"Do you want me to check it," Jake asked, "or will you do it yourself?"

Xavier glanced from Jake to the jungle, then back to Jake. "You do it, gringo. I will cover you."

Jake eased his machete out of its scabbard. "Give me ten minutes. If I'm not back by then, get the woman and children back to camp, pronto."

The rebel's fingers tightened on his weapon. *"Sí!"*

Ten minutes was all Jake needed. It would take him two minutes to reach the huge strangler fig where he'd stashed his backup transceiver. Even less to update his OMEGA control on the operation. And that would leave him plenty of time to pump Maggie for details about Sister Sarah Josepha.

Jake knew Maggie wouldn't have wasted these past few days. By now, she would've uncovered every existing detail about the nun's life. How much Sarah had weighed at birth. The exact date she'd had her wisdom teeth extracted. And, Jake was sure, she'd have an explanation for why a woman with Sarah's delicate beauty and plucky courage had chosen to become a nun. Jake wanted to hear the explanation. Badly.

Jaws clenched, he reached into the dark cavity formed by the roots put down by the strangler fig from its perch on a high branch of the host tree.

"OMEGA control, this is Jaguar."

"Howdy, Jaguar. This is Cowboy. Good to hear from you, pal."

Jake's brow furrowed. He'd recognized Cowboy's distinctive Wyoming twang even before the agent identified himself. Tall, rangy, and seemingly easygoing, Cowboy disguised a razor-sharp mind with a sleepy smile and tanned, weathered skin. Jake had worked with the former air force fighter jock on a couple of operations and thoroughly respected him. Still, it was disconcerting to change controls in midoperation.

"Where's Chameleon?"

"She's on-scene, close enough to spit. Stand by while I patch you through."

Maggie was here? In Cartoza? The knowledge that she would lead the extraction team to pick up Sarah and the children sent a shaft of relief shooting through Jake.

"Chameleon here. Glad you finally decided to check in, Jaguar. What took you so long?"

"My transmitter experienced a slight...technical malfunction. I had to wait a few days until it was safe to recover the backup unit."

"Anything you want me to relay to the lab?" Cowboy inquired. "They'll go nuts when they hear their equipment failed."

As Jake recapped the problem with the boot, Maggie's laughter echoed Cowboy's.

"They're going to love that," she said, still chuckling. "Now they'll have to come up with a seal that's waterproof and piddleproof. I'm glad to have confirmation that the children are with you, though. The Cartozan authorities only had a sketchy ID on the kids and weren't sure they were with the woman when she was taken. How's she holding up, by the way?''

Jake's muscles tensed. ''As well as can be expected,'' he replied evenly.

''Good. Given her background, I was afraid you'd have your hands full.''

Chapter 9

Still shaken by the intensity of what had passed between her and Jack, Sarah sat cross-legged on the flat rock. She barely heard the children's splashing pursuit of an orange-colored frog or Eleanor's murmured response to their gleeful shouts. All she could think of was the way she'd responded to the raw hunger she saw in the mercenary's eyes.

She couldn't want him, she told herself fiercely. She *couldn't!*

Her fingernails dug into the bar of soap she clutched as she tried to convince herself once more that what she felt for him sprang from hostage-dependency syndrome. From the emotional upheavals she'd been through. From sheer proximity!

She couldn't be on fire for a man who refused to take her and the children to safety because he still had some blood money to earn. She couldn't want to feel his mouth against hers, his legs entwined with hers.

She *couldn't!*

Oh, God, she could! She did!

Sarah gave a silent groan and buried her face in her hands,

overwhelmed by the all-consuming desire that coiled in her stomach.

What was wrong with her? Hadn't she learned anything from her busy, brittle, empty life? She'd been courted and flattered and stroked by men of charm. Men of power and wealth. But none of the men who'd said they loved her—not even the one she had loved so desperately in return—could make her pulse hammer and her thighs clench together in a spasm of desire with just a look. How could this one man wake instincts in her she'd thought well buried? He was grimy and hard and made his living in a way she despised. He…

"Sometimes it's best for a woman not to fight what happens."

The soft murmur pierced Sarah's swirling, chaotic thoughts. She lifted her head sharply and turned to find Eleanora watching her. To her surprise, she saw that the woman's brown eyes had lost their dull flatness and held a deep, soul-shattering awareness.

"He is much a man, the gringo. At least if he takes you to his bed, you will find pleasure in it."

Sarah gaped at Eleanora, translating and retranslating the older woman's words in her mind. "He…he won't take me to his bed," she answered in halting Spanish. "He thinks I'm a… I mean, he respects that I'm a sister."

Something incredibly close to amusement flickered across Eleanora's face. "We are all sisters," she said softly. "Here, give it to me."

"Huh?" Sarah struggled stupidly with the other woman's thick mountain accent and her own astonishment.

"The soap. Give me the soap. I will wash your hair for you. Then we will wash the children, yes?"

Dazed, Sarah passed her the yellowed bar of soap. At Eleanora's nod, she slipped off the rock and sank to her knees in the shallow basin. Miraculously cool water eddied around her thighs.

Sarah sat back on her heels, then slowly bent forward and dunked her head under the surface. She was too confused to sort out the emotions whirling through her right now. She decided not to think, not to try to understand anything that had happened in the past few minutes. She'd just remove her layers of sweat and dust, one by one. She'd let Eleanora wash her hair. She'd play with the children. That was about all she could handle at this particular moment.

Sarah sensed rather than saw Jack's return a half hour later. One minute she was sitting quietly on the flat rock, her knees tucked under her chin, her hair clean and damp under the veil that covered it once more. The next moment the skin on the back of her neck began to prickle.

Sarah didn't move for a long moment, alarmed but not unduly frightened by the odd sensation. When it didn't go away, she swiveled slowly on the rock, trying to discover its source.

At first she didn't see anything that would account for it. Two squeaky-clean children sat on the bank and made cakes out of wet, soggy fern leaves with Eleanora's quiet assistance. Eduard dozed, his back against a tree trunk and his still-bandaged arm cradled against his chest.

Sarah swiveled a few more degrees.

For the second time in less than an hour, she met Jack's eyes across the width of the pool. Only this time they didn't glitter with a searing masculine desire that called to the woman in her. This time they held a deadly rage that made Sarah's throat go dry. She stared at him, stunned by his anger.

A shadow moved behind him, and then Xavier appeared at his shoulder. Jack's expression became so swiftly, so carefully, blank that for a moment Sarah thought she'd imagined the cold fury in his eyes.

"Eduard," he called softly.

The boy sat up, rubbing a hand over his face. *"Sí?"*

"Xavier will take you and Eleanora and the children back to camp."

Both Sarah and the slope-shouldered rebel stared at him in surprise.

"I will stay with the *religiosa* while she gathers the white fungus that she needs for treating fevers,'' he said, in a low, deliberate tone that rasped along Sarah's nerve endings. She didn't understand why just the sound of his voice should suddenly make her so nervous.

The guerrilla glanced from her to Jack, then shrugged and walked toward the boy. Sarah knew that the men weren't quite sure about her relationship with the mercenary, but no one had challenged him or tried to molest her since the big, beefy lieutenant. After catching a glimpse of his face, Sarah wasn't surprised.

''Go with Xavier, Eduard.''

The boy rose, clearly not happy at leaving them.

''Now.''

The absolute authority in the single syllable convinced Eduard. He walked over to Eleanora, who stood watching the scene with the children. Lifting Ricci onto his hip, Eduard turned without another word and started back down the trail. Eleanora hesitated, then took Teresa's hand and followed silently.

The small sounds they made as they left seemed unnaturally loud to Sarah. Teresa's protest that she hadn't finished making her cake echoed hollowly. Ricci's sleepy murmur seemed to reverberate in Sarah's ears. The flap of a toucanette's wings as it soared off the branch Eleanora brushed against sounded like a rattle of distant thunder.

Then there was only stillness.

And Jack.

He watched her with the silent intensity of a predator that had spotted its prey. Just as silently, he began to move toward her. His lean, taut body radiated an aura of barely leashed power.

The nervous tension that had collected along Sarah's nerve endings seemed to explode in tiny, stinging pinpricks. She tried to think of something to say to break the tense silence between them, but no words came.

Never taking his eyes from her face, he circled the edge of the pool. Slowly, deliberately, he stalked her.

With each step, Sarah felt the fluttering of some primitive inner fear. She wet her lips nervously, not understanding either his menacing approach or her reaction to it. The sunlight reflected from the pool cast his face in hard, uncompromising planes and angles. His eyes glittered with a fierce light that seemed to sear her skin wherever it touched. A maleness so raw, so potent, emanated from him that Sarah reacted instinctively.

She whirled and tried to flee.

Before she'd taken three steps, his fingers closed over her wrist and spun her around. She struggled against his hold, panting with fear and some indescribable, undefinable emotion.

"Jack, what—what is it?"

The noise he made far back in his throat sent ripples of sensation down Sarah's spine. Without speaking, he pulled her slowly toward him.

Sarah battled his hold, like a frightened creature staked out at the end of a rope. She resisted his pull with all her strength, but knew even before his other arm wrapped around her waist that it was hopeless.

Still without saying a word, he hauled her up against him. His arm tightened, banding her, molding her. His free hand reached up and tore the veil away. Sarah gasped and flung her head back.

"Jack, for God's sake…"

"Oh, no," he snarled. "This is for my sake."

The hand tangled in the fall of her hair. Wrapping a length of it around his fist, he held her steady while his mouth took hers.

There was no other way to describe it. Sarah had kissed and been kissed by her share of boys and men in her time. She been made love to by a skilled, considerate Frenchman. But she'd never felt so *taken* before. This was a kiss meant to dominate, to subdue, to possess. And it did.

Thoroughly alarmed now and deeply ashamed of the liquid heat that rose inside her, Sarah wedged both hands against his chest. Using all her strength, she managed to lever her upper body a few inches away. She was bent backward over his arm and her hips were thrust intimately up against his, but at least she could see his eyes. What she saw in them made her heart trip.

"What are you doing?" she panted. "Have you lost the last shred of decency you possessed? I'm a nun! A—a bride of Christ!"

A sharp, slicing derision hardened his eyes to tempered steel. "Some bride," he sneered. "No, don't bother to protest. I know all about you, *Sister Sarah.*"

"Wh-what do you know?"

"I know that three months ago you were caught in bed with a French diplomat. A very married French diplomat."

Sarah felt the blood drain from her face.

"I know that the wife who'd come to Washington to surprise him ended up being very surprised herself. She subsequently tried to OD on sleeping pills."

Sarah fought to force some sound out of her closed throat. "Jack, how did—?"

Relentlessly he ignored her feeble whisper. "I also know that the son of a bitch returned to France with his wife. At which point the spoiled, pampered little socialite he'd been screwing felt so sorry for herself she went on a bender and slammed her Mercedes into a busload of Girl Scouts who were touring the capital."

For a bleak, endless moment, Sarah felt as though she were back in Washington. She cringed as she relived those moments of devastating shame when she'd realized that André had never told his wife he wanted a divorce, as he'd led her to believe. When his young wife's shocked, stunned face had burned itself into her conscience forever.

She could see again her father's pain as he'd come to the darkened bedroom she'd retreated to, bringing her the news that Madame Foutier was in Georgetown Medical Center's emergency room and had linked Sarah to her hysterical, sobbing suicide attempt.

She saw the flash of cameras, heard the shouts of the reporters who'd dogged her every step for weeks, until she'd refused to leave the house. Until, finally, alcohol had brought a stupid, foolish bravado that made her say to hell with them.

She gave a little moan as she heard the sickening sound of metal crunching and glass shattering.

His arm tightened around her waist, bringing her up on her toes, until her face was within inches of his. "You want to tell me I'm mistaken, *Sister Sarah?* You want to deny that was your picture plastered across the front page of the *Washington Post?*"

She wanted desperately to deny it. Staring up at his hard, chiseled face, she would have given her soul to deny it. Instead, she could only press her lips together and, to her shame, make a little whimpering sound far back in her throat.

"Oh, no," he growled. "Don't get all white-faced and piteous on me. Not now. Not when we've got something to settle between us."

He loosened the fist that had tangled in her hair and released her. Sarah stumbled back a pace or two, her legs unsteady and her heart aching. She sucked in a long, ragged breath, then let it out again in a rush. Swallowing, she gaped as Jack began to unbutton his shirt. He shrugged out of it and tossed it onto the springy mat of ferns at his feet. His hands moved to the buckle that held the web belt slung low on his hips.

"Wh-what are you doing?"

The belt thudded down on top of the shirt. "What does it look like?" He lifted a foot and planted it against a rock, bending to untie the laces.

Sarah stared at his dark head, stunned. Her lips worked, but she couldn't force any word out.

One boot, then the other, followed the belt. He peeled off thick white socks and straightened.

Sarah couldn't breathe as she watched his hands work the fastening at his waist. A thousand tumultuous emotions surged through her—astonishment, incredulity, heart-hammering disbelief. But not fear. One small corner of her psyche noted that fact, and her rational mind grabbed it with both hands.

"You won't rape me," she said, in a small, breathy voice. "Not after these past days together. I don't know much about you, but I know that much. You won't rape me."

His hands paused on the zipper. One corner of his lip lifted in a smile that made shivers race along Sarah's nerve endings. "No, I won't rape you. I won't have to."

That stiffened her spine a little. She lifted her chin a small notch. "Listen, Mr. Macho Mercenary, you may think…"

"Save it, *Sister Sarah.* I've done all the listening to you I'm going to do."

"Stop calling me that!"

"I felt your heart thumping against my cheek when you held me last night." His voice low and harsh, he stepped toward her. "I saw the look that flashed into your eyes when I held you."

Sarah stepped back.

He took another forward. "I saw the way you displayed yourself to me a little while ago."

Heat surged into her face. She clenched her fists and refused to move another inch.

"I didn't know what it meant then, *Sister Sarah,* that little display of yours. Those tender little touches. Like a fool, a blind, stupid fool, I assumed your actions were those of a woman who didn't know what she was doing to me. A woman who didn't realize that her slightest touch made my nerves sizzle. That one look from those eyes of yours tied my gut into knots."

Sarah's stomach did a little twist of its own at his admission. "Jack…"

The single word hung on the air between them. He stopped a heartbeat away from her, his face stark, his mouth grim, waiting for her to say more. When she didn't, something flared in his eyes that Sarah couldn't even begin to interpret.

"I held myself on so short a leash these past days I was almost doubled over with it," he said slowly, "and all the time you were playing with me. Well, Sarah Chandler, it's time to stop playing.''

Sarah held her breath.

"Put your arms around me."

The soft, steely command surprised her. And aroused her as nothing else could have. She'd known deep within her heart that he wouldn't force her, but only this hard-edged mercenary would stand there and expect her to initiate her own seduction.

No, it wouldn't be a seduction. With a deep, visceral sureness, Sarah knew that if she touched him, the small, steady fire he seemed to have sparked within her would leap into flame and consume her. Consume them both.

In that moment, she felt the need to strip away all pretense between them. She wouldn't lie to him anymore.

She wet her lips and gave the only answer she could. "I...I don't know if I want this, Jack."

A muscle twitched in one side of his jaw. "Put your arms around me and find out."

For what seemed like an eternity, Sarah didn't move. She tried to deny the desire that arced between them like summer lightning slicing through a hot, sultry night. She tried to tell herself that she despised this man, this hard, unyielding man who called to the primitive and elemental in her.

But she refused to lie to herself any longer. Or to him. Swallowing, she lifted a trembling hand. Her fingers grazed the warm, rounded muscle of his chest. Her other hand lifted to join the first. Flattening her palms, she slid them upward. The light dusting of chest hair teased her fingertips. The strong column of his neck shaped her hands.

Sarah gave a little sigh of surrender and stepped forward. Her breasts brushed his chest, their nipples peaking with the rasp of the scratchy black robe. The flame flickering deep within her gathered heat and intensity. Wrapping her arms tighter around his neck, she brought his mouth down to hers.

Any vague idea that he would hold back and make her pay for the way she'd supposedly teased him vanished immediately. At the touch of their lips, Jack's arms banded her waist once more. He shifted his stance and brought her into hard, intimate contact with his hips. Through the fullness of her robe, Sarah felt his rigid member leap against her stomach, even as his mouth slanted more fully over hers. His lips took her touch and gave it back, magnified a hundredfold. Firm, warm, slick, they fueled Sarah's own need.

Straining, she arched against him. His hand slid down to cup her breast. He mounded it in his palm, shaping it, kneading it through the rough fabric that covered it. His handling added to the friction that made her taut nipple ache.

Leaving one arm curled around his neck and her lips molded to his, Sarah ran her other hand over his shoulders, his arm, his ribs. His skin burned under her fingers. She stroked and kneaded it with the same intense, exploratory touch he gave her breast. When her hand slid down and encountered the waistband of his pants, Sarah went crazy with the need to get rid of all barriers between them.

She pushed herself out of his arms. They stood for a moment, their breath harsh and ragged on the air, their eyes hot and wild. Then Sarah's hands lifted to the top fastening of her habit.

"No, let me." His hands brushed hers aside. A slow, sardonic grin twisted his lips. "You have no idea how many times I've fantasized about doing this."

Sarah bit her lip to still the quivers that raced through her as he unfastened the hooks, one by one, then pushed the heavy weight off her shoulders. It slipped down her arms, caught for a moment on the stiff peaks of her nipples, then slithered over her hips. She stood before him, clad only in her still-damp bikini briefs.

He swallowed, raking her with his eyes. "You mean that's all you've been wearing under that robe?"

Sarah felt pinpoints of fire everywhere his gaze lingered. "This is what I was was wearing under my sleep shirt the night of the raid. I...I didn't have time to do anything except yank off the shirt and pull on the habit."

"I'm sure glad I didn't know that. I lost enough sleep trying not to think about what was under those folds of material as it was.''

Sarah gave a strangled laugh and stepped toward him. "I've lost a little sleep myself the past few nights.''

She reached out and traced a finger down the line of soft, springy hair. His stomach muscles jumped under her touch.

"You've no idea how much I've fantasized about this,'' she whispered.

The small sound broke the last of Jack's restraints. With a smothered groan, he pulled her to him. Mouths hard against each other, they sank to their knees. His weight tumbled Sarah over onto her back, then crushed her into the bed of ferns. Within moments, they'd shed the last of his clothes.

Sarah matched him kiss for kiss, stroke for stroke. When his knee pried her legs apart and his hand tangled in the curls at the juncture of her thighs, she arched upward, seeking his touch. Hot, slick wetness eased the way for the fingers he slid into her. Sarah moaned as he stroked and primed her. Her hand closed around his satiny shaft, priming him, as well.

Jake felt her caress and willed himself not to explode in her hand. He'd never felt a need so great, or such a savage desire to possess a woman. No, not any woman. This woman. Sarah.

He raised himself up on one elbow and stared down into her flushed face. If he'd allowed his fantasies full rein, if he hadn't always jerked himself up short whenever the insidious need for Sarah spiraled in his groin, he would have imagined taking her here, like this. With her shining, spun-gold hair spread out against the lush green of the ferns. Her eyes wide, and shimmering with the same incredible blue-green as the pool. Her lips red and swollen. Her skin flushed with need. For all her delicate beauty, Sarah responded with a primal, elemental directness to his touch. The sight of her sent a shaft of fierce male satisfaction shooting through him.

Although… Jake had spent half his life in the jungle. It occurred to him that he'd never seen anything as beautiful or as pagan as the woman who stared up at him.

That was his last rational thought. Suddenly fiercely impatient, Sarah curled both arms around his neck and brought him down to her. Jake needed no further prompting. Spreading her legs farther, he reached down to position himself, then thrust forward.

Sarah arched her neck and gasped at the intrusion. Within seconds, her tight sheath had fit itself to him, and she gave herself up to the slow pace Jake set. His deliberate approach didn't last long. Her muscles gripped him, almost shredding the last of his control. He gritted his teeth and reached down between their sweat-slick bodies. His hand found the small, hard bud at her center.

Moments, or maybe hours, later, Sarah felt her climax coming. She groaned, arching under him. A slow, dark wave swept up her belly, then receded. Another followed, and then another, until they washed over her in a sudden rush of pure, shattering sensation.

Before the spasms of pleasure subsided, Jack's weight crushed down on her. He shoved his fingers through the hair on either side of her head, held her steady while his mouth plundered hers, and thrust into her. Seconds, or maybe years, later, he followed her over the edge.

Chapter 10

Sarah had never experienced such shattering intimacy. Nor, she admitted in startled surprise, such a swift transition from all-consuming passion to intense, immediate alertness.

The dark head that had been buried in the juncture of her neck and shoulder lifted suddenly. Eyes narrowed, Jack stared at the narrow path from the camp. Before Sarah could gather her uneven breath to ask what was the matter, he'd rolled off her, scooped up his pants, and pulled them on.

"Get dressed."

The low command and the smooth, efficient way Jack slid the .45 out of its holster had Sarah scrabbling for her clothes. She pulled them on with fumbling fingers, then snatched up her veil.

"What is it?"

"I'm not sure. Get behind me and keep quiet."

Her heart pounding, Sarah complied. She didn't much care for Jack's peremptory habit of ordering people around, but in this instance she decided not to take issue with it.

A faint rustle sounded in the undergrowth. The smooth,

broad back in front of her stiffened. Sarah could see every ridge in his spine, the delineation of every hard, roped muscle under his skin.

"Señor Creighton?"

The muscles twitched. Jack sent Sarah a disgusted look over his shoulder, then called a response, "*Sí,* Eduard."

The boy hurried into view, his young face scrunched into worried lines. He stuttered a few quick sentences in idiomatic Spanish. Sarah caught Eleanora's name, and Teresa's. She pushed past Jack and ran across the clearing.

"What is it, Eduard? What's happening?"

"It is trouble. Eleanora's man, he hit her face because she didn't do the rice and the beans for him."

"*What?*"

"She bleeds, and Teresa cries. Ricci cries, also. I put them in the hut and came for you."

Although he spoke to Sarah, his eyes sought approval from the man standing behind her.

"You did good," Jack told the boy, laying a hand on his thin shoulder before turning to Sarah. "Get your gear."

She didn't need his quiet order this time. She was already running to the bush where she'd spread the wet cotton blouse to dry. She snatched it and was back beside the waiting pair within minutes.

"Eduard thinks Eleanora's nose may be broken," Jack told her as they hurried toward camp. "If so, you'll have to pack it until the swelling goes down."

Sarah threw him a stricken look.

His mouth twisted. "Just how much medical expertise do you have, *Sister?*"

Her hands fisted on the wet blouse. "I worked in a clinic for two weeks with Sister Maria, the nun whose clothes these are. Were."

"Two weeks! Christ!"

"She was a good teacher," Sarah snapped. "I managed well enough yesterday, if you recall, when I treated your so-called soldiers of the revolution."

Jack shook his head in disgust. "Right. One case of heat exhaustion and another of foot immersion. Good thing they didn't bring back one of their *compadres* with a nice bullet wound in the gut for you to test your skills on." He glanced at the boy ahead. "Could you have sutured Eduard's arm?"

Sarah hated to admit her own inadequacy, but she was past the point of pretense. "No, not with a needle, or with ants. Nor would I have tried. I wouldn't have done that to Eduard. I was going to tell you then, but..."

"Yeah, sure."

"Honestly."

"So why didn't you?"

"Because you handled the situation yourself," she retorted, "and because I didn't trust you."

He slanted her a quick look.

Sarah saw the unspoken question in his eyes, and knew the answer immediately. She still didn't trust him. Even now, after she'd lost herself in his arms. After the shattering union of their bodies. She wanted him, but she didn't trust him. The realization stunned her. And shamed her.

Something of what she was feeling must have shown on her face. His eyes narrowed, and the skin across his cheeks seemed to tighten. A bend in the trail brought them within sight of the camp, however, and he bit off whatever he'd intended to say. Instead, his mouth firmed and he said only, "We'll talk about it later. And about what happened at the pool."

Sarah swept past him. "No, we won't. We won't talk about that. We won't discuss it. We won't mention it, ever again."

She was too confused, too overwhelmed, by what had just happened to talk about it. She needed time to sort through her incredible, explosive response to this man. She needed time and space and privacy. None of which she was likely to get, Sarah thought glumly.

She waited impatiently while he sent Eduard back to the hut to stay with the children. Passing the boy her wet blouse, Sarah gave him what she hoped was a reassuring smile, then walked beside Jake to the lean-to Eleanora shared with the man who claimed her.

They saw him first, a short, wiry little bantam with mean eyes, a scraggly brown mustache, and an evil-looking knife strapped to his thigh. He sat on an upturned crate just outside the lean-to, with the disassembled pieces of the automatic rifle he'd been cleaning scattered on a rubber poncho in front of him.

"Let me do the talking," Jake warned softly.

"All right. Just get him to let me take a look at... Good God!"

Sarah stopped abruptly, her mouth dropping in shock. Eleanora huddled in a corner of the lean-to. Her battered, bloody face was almost unrecognizable.

"I'll handle..."

Paying no heed to Jake's murmured words, Sarah stomped forward.

"You pig!" she snarled at the little man who stood and blocked her entry. "You stupid, sniveling, slimy pig."

Stifling a curse, Jake considered his options.

He could let the guerrilla handle his adversary, or vice versa.

He could haul Sarah away before she attracted a crowd and gave every man in camp a glimpse of her magnificent fury.

Or he could... Oh, hell. He couldn't. Jake knew there was no way he could walk away from Eleanora's wounded face. Or from Sarah.

She threw an imperious look over her shoulder, summoning him to her side. "You tell this little bastard that I'm taking Eleanora back to our hut. He's not to touch her or speak to her or even come near her without my permission."

Jake's translation was far more succinct. "The *religiosa* will see to your woman's hurts."

The man's eyes shifted from him to the bristling figure in black. "The woman has no need of this one's attentions."

"She's of no use to you like that. Nor to anyone else,"

Jake added casually. "No one will want her, looking like that. You'll make no money off her until she's healed."

As he'd anticipated, an appeal to the little man's greed had more effect than any appeal to his nonexistent humanity could have. A speculative gleam entered his black eyes.

"You think so, gringo?"

Jake knew this was going to cost him. Big-time. He gave a small nod, signaling his acceptance of the deal. "I think so."

The guerrilla didn't bother to turn around. "Go with the *religiosa,* woman," he called over his shoulder. "Maybe if she works on you long enough she can make you pretty, eh?"

Eleanora rose slowly, like an old woman, using one hand to pull herself up. Jake's stomach knotted at the sight of the red, swelling bruises that were already starting to discolor, but he'd been in enough brawls to see that she had no smashed or broken bones.

Sarah ran forward and wrapped an arm around the older woman's waist. Without a word to either man, she led Eleanora back to the storage hut. Jake watched them make their way across the clearing, then turned back to face the wiry, mustached little man.

The rebel reached behind the crate and pulled out a half-full bottle. "So, gringo, sit down, sit down. Have some tequila."

The bottle's contents sloshed as he gestured toward the automatic rifle lying in pieces on the poncho. "You must give me your expert opinion on this weapon of mine. It's a Russian model, shipped to Cuba before the capitalists undermined the Soviet economy and they stopped producing altogether. It's ancient, eh? Not fast and efficient, like the one you carry."

Jake stifled a sigh and hooked a boot around another crate to drag it forward. He suspected it was going to be a long afternoon.

And an even longer night.

Listening with half an ear as Eleanora's "husband" began bartering for her, Jake knew that the cramped little hut was about to acquire another occupant. Sarah would no doubt bed the injured woman down next to her, leaving Jake to make room for himself somewhere else. A sharp disappointment lanced through him. He didn't like the prospect of sleeping where he couldn't see the outline of Sarah's pale, high-cheekboned face in the dim light or hear the breathy little smacking noise she made when she settled into sleep or fold her soft body into his. After his one taste of her body's honeyed sweetness, Jake found himself craving it, like a man given a thimbleful of water to slack a raging thirst.

Frowning, Jake reached for the tequila bottle. He suddenly realized that he'd crossed some invisible line in the past few hours, a line he'd never allowed himself to step over before. Always before, he'd been able to resist any personal involvement while in the field. Not that it had been easy.

During any operation, OMEGA's agents lived on the edge. Every emotion was magnified, every reaction could lead to either success or quick death—if they were lucky. Jake knew from textbook studies and from long experience that danger was debilitating in some instances, a powerful aphrodisiac in others. People clung to each other in desperate situations, seeking to affirm life in the face of death. Sometimes that transitory need solidified into a stronger emotion.

One of his fellow agents had almost compromised his mission and his life by falling hard for a laboratory researcher suspected of selling the latest information on genetic engineering to a well-armed and particularly vicious neo-Nazi group. As it turned out, the woman had stumbled onto her lab's suspicious research accidentally, but the agent had gone through twenty stages of hell before he discovered that.

As Jake had with Sarah. He'd desired her, and he'd been so disgusted with himself because of that desire that he tied himself into knots. When he found out she wasn't really a nun, he'd allowed his tight control to slip. Slipped, hell. It had shredded completely. Which wasn't exactly smart for a man who wanted not only to walk out of this jungle alive, but to make sure one woman and three children made it out, as well. Two women, he corrected with an inner grimace. Somehow he suspected Sarah wouldn't leave the compound without Eleanora.

Jake took another swig of the tequila as the little weasel across from him shook his head despairingly over the much-dented stock of his aged weapon. Jake grunted noncommittally, making a mental note to inform Maggie that she might have an additional neutral to extract when she led the team in.

Thank God Sinclair was in the field! She wouldn't blink an eye if she learned she had to extract the entire Cartozan World Cup soccer team from this little camp perched halfway up a mountain. Jake would have to find a few moments to slip away and contact Maggie tomorrow. He didn't dare leave the women alone in camp, though. Maybe he'd take them back to the pool. Have another damn picnic!

Despite his disgust at the way he'd lost control, Jake couldn't prevent the sudden tightening in his groin as he thought of Sarah beside the pool. Her shining hair bright against the green ferns. Her small, delicate body open and welcoming. His hand clenched around the neck of the bottle.

It was going to be a long afternoon.

And an even longer night.

For the first time, Jake began to think beyond this mission. Beyond the moment Maggie plucked Sarah and the children from this little compound.

"You will be back before the evening meal, Sister?"

Maggie smiled to herself. If the evening meal was anything like the noon one, she would certainly not be back. She needed more than a small bowl of rice and beans to sustain her high energy levels.

"No, Sister," she told the earnest young postulant who'd escorted her to the gate. "If I'm to travel into the interior tomorrow or the next day, I have many arrangements to make and people to see."

That much was true, anyway.

"I'm surprised the mother house sent you to make these arrangements yourself. Usually such matters are taken care of before a new sister arrives to take over a mission."

"This is a rather special mission."

"Oh. I see."

A sudden boom made Maggie jump.

The young sister didn't even blink. "There's the call to afternoon meditation. Go with God."

Maggie returned the benediction, shut the wooden gate behind her and set off down the dirt road. She sighed with relief as the echoes of the thundering bell died away. It still amazed her that a community of women didn't choose a more melodious sound to mark their hours. A bell that chimed, perhaps, or tinkled, or pinged. Not one that shook the rafters with its booming clamor every thirty minutes. The realization that she had to endure the sound for two more days was enough to put a momentary dent in Maggie's soaring spirits.

As she plodded along, however, her hands tucked in her sleeve and her black skirts swishing, Maggie soon put all thoughts of the bell behind her. The excitement that had bubbled in her veins ever since Jake had made contact with her an hour ago brought a gleam to her coffee-brown eyes.

The operation was still viable. Jaguar had confirmed that a new shipment of heat-seeking missiles would be delivered to an unspecified location on the twenty-seventh, two days from now. He would accompany the party that went to the drop site, while Maggie herself hit the camp. Jake had briefed her on the precise layout of all buildings and where he'd have the woman and the children positioned.

The gleam in Maggie's eyes deepened as she remembered Jake's terse rundown of the situation in the camp. He'd confirmed that Sarah Chandler was safe, that she'd donned the dead nun's robes as cover the night of the raid to protect herself and the three children. According to Jake, the disguise had kept her from being molested. So far. At that moment, however, he'd sounded as though he wanted to strangle the woman himself.

He probably did. After five days in Sarah Chandler's company, Jake no doubt couldn't wait to see the last of the socialite. Maggie grinned, wondering just what the other woman made of the terse, hard-eyed mercenary. Jake wasn't exactly sociable, even when he wasn't in the field. In this undercover role, he must terrify the poor woman.

Although... Maggie had to admit Sarah Chandler had shown real courage and ingenuity in carrying off her disguise this long. The media had painted her as weak-willed and shallow, but Maggie knew that no one was that one dimensional. Maybe, just maybe, there was more to Sarah Chandler than anyone realized. After all, she was Senator Chandler's daughter.

Maggie's grin deepened as she pictured Adam Ridgeway facing down the big, bluff senator, who never appeared in public without an unlit cigar clamped in one corner of his mouth. That would be a confrontation worth seeing. Unleashed, unrestrained energy versus absolute control. Raw power colliding with unshakable authority. Maggie put her money on Adam, hands down.

Still, she thought, if she had to choose between witnessing a spectacular demonstration of two civilized, sophisticated males locking horns like bull elks or walking down a dusty road in a colorful, sweltering tropical city, she'd choose to be here. Cartoza's capital—called confusingly enough, Cartoza City—teemed with life.

City dwellers shouted as they alternately zoomed their vehicles for a few yards, then braked to a screeching halt a few inches from the pedestrians clogging the streets. People, taxis, buses, trucks, donkeys and one or two pigs streamed in or out of the city. Traffic was snarled hopelessly around the plaza that housed the colorful open-air market, Cartoza's center of commerce.

Concentrating on her role, Maggie settled her face into calm, quiet lines and shrank within herself. Someone with her height would stand out in a crowd unless she made herself inconspicuous. Head bowed, shoulders slightly slumped, hands folded over the .22 tucked into her sleeve, she entered the throng of people swarming through the market. She had a couple of days before the drop. She intended to use them.

By the time she joined the women who invited her to share their evening meal at a rickety table set in a patch of shade cast by a market stall, Maggie had gathered a cache of informational nuggets. Cartoza was a small country, barely a hundred miles from the Pacific to the Atlantic coast. Everyone was related to everyone else in some remote way. And everyone knew what happened in the interior, although few talked about it openly to outsiders.

Of course, the sisters of Our Lady of Sorrows weren't really outsiders. The nuns understood how difficult it was for a woman to stretch a little bit of milk among five children. Their work brought them into contact with the grinding poverty of the working people.

"One does what one must, Sister," a tired, once-pretty young woman said, scrupulously dividing her dish of paella to give Maggie half.

Maggie ate slowly, listening while the women described the hardships since the guerrillas had begun battling government troops, with the peasants caught between.

"The *federales*, they make it so hard on us," another woman said with a sigh. "They set up roadblocks. They stop our trucks. They search everything for chemicals. We were four hours getting home from market last week."

The mention of chemicals set Maggie's pulse tripping. She knew that cocaine-processing plants needed a steady supply of hydrochloric acid, sulfuric acid and ether to leach the coca leaves and extract a paste that could be shaped into bricks for shipping to refineries. She also knew that a good percentage of the population in many Latin American countries had become economically dependent on coca production. There weren't any programs like welfare or unemployment or food stamps in these countries. People starved to death every day. As a result, many peasants worked the coca fields or tried desperately to make a living by smuggling chemicals to the plants hidden deep in the interior. It wasn't a matter of right or wrong. It was a matter of survival.

Jake's initial reports had confirmed the report that a drug lord had set up a processing plant in Cartoza's interior. The same lord supplied the funds to arm the rebels, thus keeping the government too busy to mount a major search for his plant. Although this part of the operation was outside OMEGA's area of responsibility, Maggie couldn't let slip the chance to gather any useful information. Washing down the paella that had suddenly lodged in her throat with tepid orangeade, she turned a gentle, inquiring look on the woman who'd just spoken.

"It took you four hours to get home, *señora?* You must have traveled far."

"No, Sister, it was those pesky *federales,* I tell you. They set up a checkpoint on the only road into the mountains. Traffic was backed up for two or three miles. They searched everyone, everything. Everyone had to get off the bus in front of us and open every bundle. Then the searchers found some gallon containers under a load of manure on the truck ahead of us." She shook her head. "As soon as the police would unload a container, the husband would flap his arms and argue while the wife snatched it up, ran around to the other side and shoved it back on the truck."

The younger woman chuckled. "My sister-in-law's cousin tried sitting on a container last month. The woman weighs well over two hundred pounds. The *federales* didn't find that container."

She caught herself and threw an embarrassed glance at Maggie. "She does not do that often, Sister. But her baby was sick and needed medicines."

Maggie couldn't condemn these women for their obvious acceptance of the illegal trade. They were caught in a system perpetuated by her own country's insatiable appetite for a deadly, destructive drug. But neither could she condone their support. So she simply nodded and tried to steer the conversation toward the destination of these chemical containers.

Two hours later, Maggie waited for the reverberations of the lights-out bell to stop bouncing off the walls of her small room at the convent, then punched the code for OMEGA control into her satellite transceiver. As soon as Cowboy came on-line, Maggie pressed the transmit button with her thumb.

"Tell Thunder that I have something he might be interested in."

"He's downstairs. Want to talk to him?"

"Yes."

"Hang tight. I'll call him."

Maggie propped one foot up on the chair beside the narrow bed, hunched a shoulder and pressed the transceiver to her ear. She'd guessed that Adam—code name Thunder—would still be at OMEGA headquarters. There was only two hours' time difference between Cartoza's capital and D.C. It wasn't yet eight o'clock in the evening there. Adam was probably just getting ready to attend some diplomatic dinner or political fund-raiser—no doubt with that sleek, ultraelegant redhead who usually accompanied him to such functions. The one pictured hanging on Adam's arm in a glossy magazine that had featured a story about Washington's most eligible bachelors. The one in the yellow silk sheath that contained less than a yard of material, probably cost more than Maggie had taken home last month, and left no doubt in anyone's mind that underwear was a quaint, if outmoded, custom of the middle classes.

Maggie glanced down at her white, unadorned underwear and grinned.

"Thunder here." Adam's low, steady voice came over the receiver. "What do you have?"

Maggie summarized her conversation with the women. "It's all coming together," she concluded, trying hard to keep the excitement out of her voice. "Once we extract the neutrals and Jaguar springs the trap on the middleman, we should go for these druggies.''

"No. Under no circumstances.''

Maggie frowned at the denial. "I think I can pin down their location in the next day or so.''

"I can't authorize extending the operation.''

Adam paused, and Maggie waited for the explanation she knew would follow. For all his cool authority, Adam wasn't arbitrary. Most of the time.

"Despite Senator Chandler's cooperation, rumors are starting to circulate about the raid and the fact that his daughter was serving in the area. It's only a matter of time until one of the wire services picks up the story and plasters her picture across the front page again. That flimsy disguise Jaguar told us about won't last. Your mission is to get her out of there in one piece.''

"I've got the extraction laid on,'' Maggie reminded him. "A joint U.S. and Cartozan force, in unmarked helicopters, will be ready to move the moment Jaguar signals.''

"Good. Concentrate on the extraction, not on the drug lords,'' Adam reiterated in his precise way. He hesitated. "We'll pass your information on to the appropriate narcotics agencies. Good work, Chameleon.''

"Thanks,'' Maggie responded dryly.

She signed off a few moments later. Tucking the transceiver under her pillow, next to her .22, she stretched out on the narrow bed.

Maggie was a professional. She understood the importance of focusing on the operation she was responsible for and letting others handle theirs. She knew that Adam would ensure the information she uncovered was passed to people who would use it.

Still, she couldn't rid herself of the conviction that a little more digging, a few more casual contacts, and she'd have the location and maybe the name of the man who was supplying Jake's band of guerillas.

She nibbled on her lower lip, wide awake and staring up into the darkness.

It was going to be a long night.

Chapter 11

Sarah rolled over on her side and wiggled, trying to find a little padding in the thin bedroll to cushion her hips. She sighed, wondering if this long night would ever end.

She'd spent what was left of the daylight hours caring for Eleanora. The woman had refused to speak, refused to even look at Sarah as she bathed her face and dabbed it with antiseptic.

Jack had come back to the hut briefly. He'd stayed only long enough to kneel in front of Eleanora and press her cheekbones with a gentle finger. They weren't broken, he'd informed Sarah. He wouldn't be able to tell about the nose until the swelling went down, but then, there wasn't much they could do about it even if it was broken. Then he'd grabbed his automatic rifle and left.

When he returned a little while ago, minus the weapon, Sarah had already fed the children and Eleanora and had them bedded down. He'd frowned at Sarah across the hut, as if wanting to have that talk he'd promised, but a small moan from Eleanora had broken the shimmering tension between them.

Now Sarah lay restless and on edge, her ear tuned to the labored breathing of the woman beside her, but every other sense achingly aware of the man who'd rigged a hammock in the far corner of the shack.

She'd had so little time to think, so little time to let herself recall what had happened this afternoon beside the pool. Now she found that she couldn't think about it without wanting to creep across the quiet hut and touch Jack lightly on the arm to awaken him. Everything in her wanted to lead him out into the dark privacy of the night. The realization that she desired him, that she ached for him with an intensity she'd never known, filled her with confusion and kept sleep at bay.

A sobbing whimper wrenched Sarah from her self-absorption. Teresa twitched in her hammock, caught in the throes of a bad dream. Sarah rolled over and started to rise, then hesitated as a dark shadow moved toward the girl.

"Hush, *niña,* it's okay," Jack whispered. "Don't be afraid."

His low, calming voice sent waves of longing rippling along Sarah's nerves. She would've given anything she possessed, which admittedly wasn't much at that particular moment, to hear him whisper like that to her. To have him hold her gently and soothe away her fears.

She watched, breath suspended, while he stooped to pick up something from the floor. Sarah couldn't see the object, but she knew instinctively it was the root, in its frilly dress. Jack tucked the doll in Teresa's arm, then melted back into the darkness.

Oh, God, Sarah groaned to herself as she eased back down onto the bedroll. Why did the blasted, infuriating man have to be so damned contradictory? Why couldn't he be totally evil, so she could hate him? Or totally good, so she could love him?

Her thought came zinging back to mock her. She couldn't love Jack if he was a plaster saint. She couldn't love him if he didn't possess the hard, biting edge that made him so different, so unlike any other man she'd ever known.

She loved him just the way he was.

Sarah's stomach lurched, and she flung up an arm to cover her eyes. She'd done some stupid, useless things in her life, and this ranked right up there among the worst of them. For all her so-called sophistication, for all her determination not to become emotionally dependent on this man, she'd merged more than her body with him this afternoon. Somehow, sometime during those searing, soaring moments, she'd merged her soul.

What in the world was she going to do about it?

What *could* she do about it?

She groaned again, not quite as silently this time, and flopped over to bury her face in the bedroll.

The sharp tang of cosmolene, the grease used for packing and shipping weapons, permeated the still morning air outside the hut. Jake wiped the last residue of grease from a blue steel barrel, frowning slightly. He'd dug through several crates to find something halfway acceptable as a replacement for his bartered rifle.

"I need to talk to you."

He glanced up at the sound of Sarah's voice. She stood in the doorway of the shack, one foot tapping under the skirts of that damn black robe.

"So talk," he said, resting the barrel across his knees.

Her gaze flicked to the children playing in the shade a few feet away. "Not here. We need to speak privately. About... about yesterday."

He sent her a mocking look. "I thought you didn't want to discuss yesterday. Ever."

"Yes, well, I've had some time to think, to come to a few decisions. I didn't get much rest last night."

"No kidding. Do you always toss and turn in bed like that? You keep a man awake all night just listening to you."

As soon as the words were out of his mouth, Jake could've

kicked himself. Who was he kidding? Any man who shared a bed with Sarah wouldn't want to get much sleep. His hormones shot into overdrive at the vivid image that leaped into his mind, an image of a small, curved body sprawled across a wide, rumpled bed.

A flush stained her face. "I didn't realize I was such a restless sleeper. No one's ever mentioned it before."

"No one, Miss Chandler?"

His soft, taunting drawl surprised Jake as much as it did Sarah. He cursed himself when she drew back, hurt reflected in her expressive eyes.

Dammit, what was the matter with him this morning? Jake's hand tightened on the gun barrel as he realized exactly what had triggered his mocking response. Old-fashioned, gut-level jealousy. A destructive emotion he hadn't known he was capable of, and sure as hell didn't like acknowledging.

With brutal honesty, Jake forced himself to admit he'd spent the long hours of the night struggling to reconcile the Sarah he knew with the one whose picture had been plastered across the dailies for so many weeks. The woman the press had crucified had been made to look shallow, selfish, immoral. The woman he knew was no saint, but her courage and determination to care for the children had tugged at Jake's heart. It had taken him a while to accept that whatever she'd been or done before had shaped her into the remarkable woman she now was. But that was as far as he'd gotten.

Sarah, however, tackled the issue head-on. She came to stand before him, planted both hands on her hips and sent him a steely look.

"That's another thing I want to talk to you about. How you discovered who I am. And how my identity figures into this little…situation we have."

"Situation?"

Jake didn't much care for her choice of words. He wasn't exactly sure what was between them or where it was going, but he'd describe it differently.

Not *affair*. It was too intense to call an affair.

Not *relationship*. That was too pansy.

"Situation," she replied firmly, then ran out of patience. "Are you going to get off that crate and take a walk with me, or do I have to do something totally unnunlike and knock you on your backside?"

Jake stared at the diminutive figure before him. Whatever had kept Sarah tossing and turning, whatever decision she'd come to in the dark hours of the night, had put a fierce spark of determination in her eyes. He stared at her, impressed in spite of himself.

There probably weren't two women in the world more dissimilar than Sarah Chandler and Maggie Sinclair in appearance, background, or current employment, but at that moment he could have sworn they were sisters. Maggie was the only woman who'd ever taken Jake down during the defensive-maneuvers training he conducted for OMEGA agents. Right now, Sarah could probably toss him on his head—and would definitely enjoy doing it.

The fierce protectiveness that had colored Jake's feelings for Sarah since the night of the raid shifted, altering subtly in shape and substance. Jake hadn't planned to tell her about the extraction until just before he left camp tomorrow. He'd hoped to minimize her worry and fear and lessen the chance that she might inadvertently let something slip. But, seeing the determination in her eyes, he knew it was time.

Jake set the gun barrel aside and wiped his hands on the stiff khaki shirt he'd been using as a rag, the one so stained with Eduard's blood that it was good for nothing else, and rose.

"You're right. We need to talk. Is Eleanora well enough to walk to the pool?"

She nodded. "I think so. She doesn't speak, but she got up and insisted on dressing herself this morning."

"I'll go let Pig-face know I'm taking you out of camp for a little while." Jake thought rapidly. "I'll tell him you need to gather some fiddlewood bark to soak and use on Eleanora's face."

Sarah slanted him a wry look. "More prehistoric medicine?"

He grinned down at her, feeling the tension that had sprung up between them ease. "Indian shamans in the Amazon rain forest still use the bark in a sort of herbal bath to cure sores caused by tropical parasites. I doubt if it would have any real usefulness on bruises, but I'm betting that Pig-face won't know that."

He didn't.

The big man grunted, not happy at being awakened this early to be informed of Jake's plans. The animosity between the two men hadn't lessened since the night the lieutenant had stumbled into the little hut, but he'd kept his distance since then. Still, Jake knew it was only a matter of time until Enrique erupted.

Twenty minutes later, he left the smaller children splashing happily in the pool, Eleanora sitting silently on the rock, and Eduard on guard.

"We'll only go a little way down this trail," Jake told the boy. "You just have to call out, and I'll be back within seconds."

The boy nodded.

"Wait for us here. We may be a while. Sarah and I have much to discuss, but we'll hear you if you need us."

Jake led the way down the narrow, twisting trail. After the first bend, they were out of sight, but not out of earshot. He could hear Ricci shrieking as Teresa splashed him, and Teresa's answering cry when the boy dunked her precious doll. Using his machete, Jake hacked the twisting vines from a toppled tree trunk, then whacked the wood once or twice with the flat of his blade to dislodge any occupants.

Nothing more threatening than a small ctenosaur emerged, its scaly, blue-banded skin and spiny back quivering in outrage. The lizard, which Jake knew could grow to the size of a small dog, bobbed its head up and down as a signal that the tree trunk was private territory. Jake smiled at Sarah's involuntary "Ugh," and nudged the creature on its waddling way with the toe of his boot.

Holding her skirts up with both hands to make sure nothing slithered underneath them, Sarah approached the trunk. She settled herself gingerly, then reached behind her neck to untie the strings of the veil.

Jake stabbed the machete into the dirt beside the tree to keep it close at hand and propped a foot up on the impromptu bench. Leaning easily on arms crossed over his knee, he watched while Sarah loosened the tie that held her hair. Her fingers raked through it, lifting the soft, fine curtain of pale silk off her neck. Sighing, she unhooked the top few buttons of her habit and flapped the material against her heated skin.

"When and if I get back to civilization, I don't think I'll ever wear black again," she murmured.

Jake, who had entertained more than one fantasy about Sarah's small, deliciously curved body in a black lace garter belt and little else, smiled ruefully to himself.

"You'll get back," he told her quietly.

She stopped fanning the material and tilted her head to look up at him. "Will I?"

"I'm doing my best to make it happen."

Jake hesitated, then took the first step in what he knew would be a difficult explanation. There was so much he wasn't cleared to tell her—about OMEGA, about the mission, about himself.

"I contacted someone yesterday who'll arrange to take you out of here," he told her slowly.

Her fingers curled around the fabric, scrunching it in her fist. "You contacted someone yesterday?" She wet her lips. "Was that before or after you recognized me?"

He shrugged. "Let's just say my contact confirmed the doubts I had about Sister Sarah."

"And from the description you gave him, he recognized Sarah Chandler."

The bitterness in her voice made Jake frown.

"It couldn't have been that difficult," she continued when

he didn't respond. "I suppose the press has already picked up the story of the raid. My picture is no doubt splashed all over the dailies again."

She shivered. It was a quick, involuntary shake, so much like that of a small, trapped animal that Jake's jaw tightened.

"There aren't any news stories. Not yet."

"Never mind. I guess it doesn't really matter how you recognized me. What matters is what you're going to do about it." She rose and faced him, nose to nose. "Just tell me how much this is costing my father."

"Your father?"

"My father. How much are you and this contact of yours charging him to arrange this little escape of mine?"

Jake straightened. "What the hell are you talking about?"

Her chin jutted out. "It didn't take you long to cash in on the prize that was right under your nose, did it? You wouldn't let the welfare of a nun and three children interfere with your business deals, but you can arrange something overnight for a senator's daughter."

"Oh, for crissakes!"

"So how much did you ask for, gringo? You can tell me. I'd like to know what you think a senator's daughter is worth."

"I'm not ransoming you, dammit."

"Keep your voice down!" she hissed. "I don't want the children running down here until you and I get a few things settled between us."

"It sounds to me like you've already got everything settled in your mind."

Jake told himself that he shouldn't blame her for leaping to conclusions. Hell, he'd done everything in his power to make her think he was a conscienceless expatriate who'd sell his country for a few dollars. But somehow the fact that he'd succeeded so well didn't give him one iota of satisfaction.

She drew in a deep breath, as though steeling herself for some unpleasant task. Jake sensed that he was about to learn what had kept her—and him—awake so long into the night.

"I don't want you to do it, Jack. I don't want you to black-mail my father. I don't want you to sell yourself to the scum you're working with. I have some money of my own. Not a lot, but enough to stake you until you find some...some other line of work."

Jake's eyes narrowed. A sudden, incredible suspicion curled in his belly and wound its way up to his heart. "What makes you think I want some other line of work? What if I told you I make a good living at what I do?"

"Look at you!" she exclaimed, flinging out her arms in exasperation. "You call this living? You haven't shaved in three days, your shirt looks like something that...that lizard wouldn't even wear. Obviously you haven't had a good whiff of yourself from downwind, and...and..."

"And?" he prompted, his pulse pounding a slow, heavy rhythm.

"And you act about as civilized as some jungle creature," she finished in a huff. Then she sighed, and put a hand on his arm. "All the money in the world isn't going to make up for what this place and these people you work with are doing to you, Jack."

Jake stared down at the small, fine-boned hand. He remembered suddenly that that was the first glimpse of Sarah he'd had in the daylight, that morning after the raid—her work-roughened fingers trembling as she lifted a black sleeve to wipe her face.

He remembered, also, how that same hand had touched him yesterday. How it had speared through the hair on his chest. Slid up to his neck. Pulled his head down for her kiss. The pounding rhythm of his blood grew more intense.

He smiled down at her, wanting to hear just how she'd decided to reform him. "You didn't have any complaints about my uncivilized actions yesterday."

She sucked in a quick breath and snatched her hand away. "Okay, so I didn't exactly scream in maidenly outrage when you touched me. So I, uh..."

"So you went up in flames, and took me with you." A

grin tugged at Jake's lips. "I've been in the arms business a long time, Sarah, but I've never seen or felt a detonation quite like that one."

Flushing, she turned away. "Let's not get too technical here."

Jake laughed and slid his arm around her waist, drawing her back against his chest. "It was good between us, Sarah. More than good. I couldn't sleep last night, either, thinking about it."

She laid her head back against his shoulder, sighing. "I don't know how or why I let that happen between us. I'm confused by it. I'm confused by you, and by my responses to you. I only know that I can't run away from it, like I've run away from everything in my life."

She twisted in his arms and placed her palms on his chest. "Let me help you, Jack. Don't extort money from my father. Don't do whatever it is these men want you to do with that arms shipment. Have this contact of yours arrange to pull you out of here at the same time he pulls me and the kids and Eleanora out."

Jake smiled. He'd known she would consider it a package deal. Her and the kids and Eleanora.

"I can't do that," he told her gently. "I can't leave with you."

"Why not?"

"I have a job to do here." He firmed his hold when she would have pushed herself away. "No, not the one you think. I'm here on government business."

"Right," she said bitterly. "You and Ollie North."

"Sarah, listen to me...."

"No, you listen to me. My father heads the Senate Intelligence Subcommittee on Latin-American Affairs, remember? I know darn well that no government agency would be selling arms to this scruffy little band of guerrillas, not when official U.S. policy is to support the Cartozan government."

"We're not selling. We're trying to stop the sale. I've been undercover with this group for almost three weeks now."

Sarah's face registered first disbelief, then skepticism.

Jake kept his voice low and deliberate, trying to convince her. "My mission is to take out the middle link in the international chain that trades stolen U.S. arms for drug dollars. I intend to do that tomorrow night, when he makes his drop."

"My God!" she breathed, staring up at him. "You're... you're serious?"

This, time when she pushed away from him, he let her go. Jake felt a wrench at the dazed expression in her eyes.

"I'm deadly serious. You know how shaky this country is. If we don't stop the arms flow, fast, Cartoza will probably see the same wave of political assassinations and drug wars that have torn Peru and Colombia apart."

"You...you really are under cover? With the CIA?"

"Close enough."

Jake felt a curious sense of relief to have it out at last. He waited for some confirmation, some sigh of relief, or a welcome laugh.

"You *bastard!*"

Jake was so surprised by her explosive fury that he didn't even see the punch coming.

In any other circumstance, a blow from Sarah's small fist wouldn't have even dented stomach muscles that were conditioned to take karate kicks and powerhouse punches. But she hit him with just enough unexpected speed and force to send him stumbling backward.

His heel thumped against the fallen tree trunk, and his momentum carried him the rest of the way over. Jake landed on his duff on the dense, springy layer of vegetation, his breath whooshing out of his lungs.

Chest heaving, fiery blue-green sparks shooting from her eyes, Sarah clambered over the log.

"You rat! You despicable, chauvinistic, arrogant rat!"

Jake levered himself up. "What in the—?"

Her foot planted itself square on his chest and shoved him back down. "How dare you! How dare you let me think you were the scum of the earth!"

"Sarah…"

"Don't *Sarah* me. You made me ache with wanting you, and I loathed myself for it!"

"Well, I wasn't exactly thrilled to find myself lusting after a nun."

"And that's another thing. Where did you get off being so angry over *my* disguise? I can't believe all the bristling male indignation you displayed yesterday. The way you stalked me. The way you made *me* feel guilty about *your* unbridled lust!"

"Unbridled lust?" Despite himself, Jake felt his shoulders shake.

"Don't you dare laugh!" She spit the words out. "If you do, I swear, I'll…I'll…"

She looked around wildly. Jake saw her glance fall on the machete stuck in the dirt beside the tree trunk.

"Oh, no," he warned. His hand snaked out and caught her ankle, just in case. She kicked her foot, trying to break his hold.

"How could you make love to me yesterday and not tell me the truth?"

Jake hung on to her flailing leg while he scooted back and pushed himself into a sitting position. "Look, I'm sorry about yesterday."

"You should be!"

"It was a mistake," Jake admitted.

She halted in midkick. "What do you mean, it was a mistake?"

"I should never have allowed myself to lose control like that. It was stupid and dangerous."

"Stupid and dangerous," she repeated blankly, taking a little hop to maintain her balance. "Making love to me was stupid and dangerous?"

"In the middle of a mission, yes. I won't let it happen again, at least not until we get out of here."

"*You* won't let it happen again?" She closed her eyes. "Let go of my leg."

Jake decided he'd better hang on until he figured just what was putting that choked quality in her voice.

Sarah opened her eyes and pinned him with a scathing look. "You know, Mr. Gringo-Creighton-Jack-whatever-your-name-is, I'm beginning to think I liked you better as a sleaze. At least I had hopes of reforming you then. This new you might just turn out to be hopeless."

At that moment, with his butt planted in a bed of jungle vegetation, his stomach throbbing and his fist wrapped around the ankle of the woman hovering over him like a vengeful angel, Jake knew he loved her.

This Sarah wasn't the heartless socialite the media had crucified. She wasn't the spoiled daughter of a powerful senator who protected her at every turn. Whatever she might have been before, this woman with the jewellike eyes and the straggling hair was magnificent.

In the time Jake had known her, she'd spent every waking moment caring for three kids who had no claim on her. She'd championed a battered, helpless woman. She'd given herself to a mercenary, with an open, searing passion that still stunned him, then set out with Sarah-like determination to reform him.

Jake would just have to convince her that the real him was far from hopeless. Admittedly, he might have one or two rough edges that needed filing down. When he got them all out of Cartoza, he intended to give her plenty of opportunity to work on them. Right now, however, he needed to soothe her ruffled feathers.

"You may prefer me in my undercover persona, Miss Sarah-Josepha-Sarita Chandler, but I much prefer knowing you're not a nun."

Grinning, he gave her ankle a little yank, pulled her off balance and tumbled her down on top of him.

Chapter 12

Sarah's bottom landed with a solid *whump* on Jake's stomach. He was prepared for the blow this time, however, and barely registered her weight as he rolled over, taking her with him. Before she could do much more than utter a few sputtering protests, he pinned her against the verdant earth.

Holding her easily with one leg thrown over hers and an arm across her waist, Jake waited patiently for her halfhearted struggles to still. When they did, he lifted a hand to smooth away the strands of pale blond hair that had twisted across her cheek.

"Don't write me off as hopeless just yet, Sarah. I must have one or two salvageable traits."

She glared up at him. "I haven't seen any."

"Is that so?" He brushed the back of a knuckle along her chin. "What about the fact that I'm a great cook? Are you forgetting those bananas and cold beans you scarfed up?"

Folding her lips together, Sarah declined to respond.

"And I carve a pretty decent mango root, if I do say so myself."

That won a grudging response. "Well, it wasn't bad."

He smiled down at her. "When we get out of here, you'll have all the time in the world to find some sterling character traits among my less admirable tendencies."

She frowned up at him for a moment or two longer, but then the fight went out of her in a long, huffy sigh.

"When we get out of here," she repeated slowly, as if testing the feel of the words, the concept of some time and some place after these days in the humid jungle and the squalid little hut. "Jack, I... What *is* your name, anyway?"

Jake smiled down at her. "Does it really matter?"

Sarah searched his eyes. Their gray depths held lingering laughter, a rueful tenderness, and something deeper, something that made her heart suddenly slam against her ribs. The doubts and uncertainties that had haunted her for so long melted away. Whatever else she'd done wrong in the past, however poor her judgment had been, she knew she wasn't mistaken about what she saw in his eyes and felt in her own.

"No," she said, after a long, breathless moment. "It doesn't really matter."

Jake told himself he couldn't kiss her. He warned himself that if he bent his head and covered those soft lips with his, he might not be able to stop there. The tendons in his neck corded with the effort of holding back.

Sarah took the matter out of his hands. Curling an arm around his shoulders, she pulled him down.

The touch of her mouth on his sent slow, sweet tendrils of desire spiraling through Jake's chest. He let himself savor them for as long as he dared, then raised his head. He drew in a harsh, ragged breath.

"Sarah, let's just consider the options for a moment."

She planted a line of little kisses along the underside of his chin. "You consider them."

"This is too dangerous. I can't let myself lose control again like I did yesterday."

"So stay in control," she murmured against his skin. "If you can."

"The kids are just a shout away. They might— Hey!"

She laved the little bite she'd given him with her tongue. "You told Eduard to call if there's trouble. He'll call."

"You could get pregnant."

She went still under him, then laid her head back on the springy grass. For once Jake couldn't decipher the expression in her luminous eyes.

"I could," she acknowledged at last. "If I'm lucky."

Jake almost lost it then. He hadn't thought in terms of a family for years. Since his divorce, he'd immersed himself in his work, in OMEGA, in teaching newer, less experienced agents the skills they needed to survive in the dark worlds they inhabited. But the idea of Sarah swelling with his child stirred some long-buried, atavistic need. For the first time, he realized that his feelings for her went beyond desire, beyond the tentative, hazy emotion he'd identified as love earlier. He wanted to mate with her in the most elemental, essential way. He wanted to merge his body and his life with hers. But first, he reminded himself savagely, he needed to make sure they had lives to merge.

Disentangling the arm she had wrapped around his neck, Jake sat up. He ignored her reproachful look and drew her up beside him.

"We don't have much time," he said quietly. "We need to talk about tomorrow."

Sarah wasn't ready. She didn't want to shatter the sweet, sensual moment with the fear his words engendered, but she knew she had no choice. She'd run away from her fears too many times in the past. She couldn't, wouldn't, run away from these.

"Yes, we do," she agreed.

"When I leave for the drop site, my contact will…"

"When you leave?" She swallowed. "Sorry, just a small panic attack. Go on."

He raked a hand through his dark hair. "I've been through this a thousand times in my mind. I don't like it any more than you do, but it's the safest extraction I can arrange for you and the kids.''

"And Eleanora," Sarah added. "I'll talk to her as soon as you tell me it's safe, but I know she'll want to go with us.''

"And Eleanora," Jake said. "Look, Sarah, the choices were simple. The first was to risk an assault on the camp while the men were still there. I could've held them off until the team landed, but it would've meant a heavy firefight.''

She thought of the arsenal of deadly weapons that each man carried and suppressed a shudder.

"The second choice was to get you away from camp and try an extraction through the jungle canopy.''

Sarah tilted her head back to look up at the dense, leafy roof. So little sunlight penetrated that she couldn't see through it to the sky. She estimated that the overhead carpet must be three hundred feet above the ground.

"What you're seeing is only the first layer, the canopy," Jake told her. "Above that is the emergent layer, where the crowns of the tallest trees stick out. The chopper would have to hover above that, which is dangerous in itself. This hot, sticky humidity increases density altitude and reduces the rotor blade's lift. Which makes it doubly dangerous to try to hoist anyone through that thick, impenetrable screen. I've seen it tried several times. I've seen it done. Once.''

She swallowed. "So what's the third choice?''

"The third choice is for me to take all but a few of the men out of camp to reduce the opposition. My contact will lead the extraction team in moments after we depart.''

"He better be good," Sarah mumbled.

A smile lightened the shadows in Jack's eyes. "She's the best. I trained her myself.''

Sarah told herself that the spurt of jealousy that shot through her was childish and unreasoning. There was too much at stake here to let personal feelings interfere.

"Tell me exactly what will happen," she said evenly.

She was glad he didn't insult her intelligence by minimizing the risks. Rubbing her damp palms down her thighs, Sarah memorized every detail, every brief instruction.

Jack had her repeat the procedure in her own words, then run through it one more time.

When she had it down to his satisfaction, he eased back against the log and drew up one knee. His dark brows knit, as if he were examining the plan yet again, looking for holes.

Sarah let the silence between them spin out like a gossamer web, until it surrounded them in a silken cocoon, shutting out the sounds of the birds in the trees overhead and the faint echo of childish laughter. For this moment, at least, there was just her and this man whose name she didn't need to know.

He looked so hard, she thought, studying the angles of his face. So self-contained and withdrawn. His flinty eyes were distant behind their screen of black lashes. Driven by a need to bring him back to her, Sarah reached out to touch him.

She froze with her hand half-out, startled by the flash of color that flew past. A huge bird swooped down on what looked like a wild avocado plant a few feet away and plucked a fat ripe fruit with its bill.

"What is it?" Sarah whispered, mesmerized by its long, streaming emerald tail feathers and brilliant red breast.

"It's a quetzal," Jack murmured. "Pretty rare around here."

"I've never seen anything like it."

He smiled at her awed expression as the bird tilted its head back, puffed out its shimmering ruby chest and swallowed the fruit whole.

"Indian legend says its breast wasn't always red."

She slanted him a quick, amused look. "More prehistoric lore?"

"No, this tale's more modern. Supposedly the Spaniards who invaded this area in the 1500s attacked a Mayan chief. The quetzal swooped down and landed on the dying man's chest, either to protect him or to mourn him. When it flew away again, its breast was colored with the chieftain's blood."

Sarah glanced back at the exotic creature, feeling her pleasure in its exotic beauty slowly fade. When it took off with a flap of emerald wings, she sat still for a long moment. Then she reached up and began to work the fastenings on her robe.

Jake eyed her lazily, reluctant to see this interlude of quiet between them end. She was right, though. They needed to get back to the kids. Back to camp. Jake straightened, only to realize that she wasn't hooking the few fastenings she'd undone earlier to fan herself. She was unhooking the remaining ones.

"What are you doing?"

She pulled another hook open. "I'm taking this off. Then I'm going to make love to you."

"We talked about this earlier," Jake said gently. "I can't let myself lose control like that again. Much as I want you, I can't cross that line again—not until I get you out of here."

"What makes you think the decision is yours alone to make?" She jiggled her shoulders. The black gown slid down her arms and pooled around her hips.

Lord, she was beautiful, Jake admitted ruefully. He'd never seen anyone so small and perfectly proportioned. All gold and tan and white in places he damn well shouldn't be staring at.

"Sarah, this isn't smart."

"No," she replied, leaning forward to brush the edges of his shirt aside and lay her palms against his heart. "But it's necessary. Maybe not for you, but for me. I need you, Jack. I need you to hold me and kiss me and know that, whatever happens tomorrow, we had this time together."

He felt the soft touch of her fingertips against his bare skin and drew in a ragged breath. "I don't think I can just hold you."

Her lips curved in a slow, wicked grin. "Why don't you put your arms around me and find out?"

Maybe it *was* time for him to find another line of work, Jake thought. He couldn't ever remember making a conscious decision to put his own desire ahead of operational needs before. The thought worried him for the few seconds it took to reach out and pull Sarah into his lap.

She nestled against him, her arms wrapped around his waist, her head tucked under his chin. He breathed in the sun-warmed scent of her hair. Her skin was damp with the humidity of the jungle and incredibly soft against his.

Jake rested his chin on the top of her head, content for the moment just to absorb the tactile sensations Sarah's mere touch generated. Content, that is, until her hands began to move on his back. With feather-light strokes, she explored his skin, his spine. Her hips shifted, and the lazy sensuality of the moment suddenly sharpened. He felt himself hardening against the rounded curve of her bottom.

She straightened, leaning a little bit away from him. Her eyes gleamed up at him, as shimmering and brilliant as any of the birds that swooped through the canopy.

"Well, I guess that settles that," she declared solemnly. "Holding is definitely not an option for us."

Jake groaned and bent his head.

Sarah responded by wrapping her arms around his neck and kissing him with all the warm eagerness that characterized her. Her lips opened under his. She tasted and explored his mouth with a hunger that matched his. Her breasts pressed against his chest, their small, round centers peaking against his flesh.

This time, when they shed their clothes and rolled onto the green, springy carpet of ferns, their loving wasn't hard and fast and furious. This time it was slow and indescribably sweet. At least at first.

Sarah herself set the pace. Smiling, she pushed Jake onto his back. She stretched out at his side and explored him, tasting, touching, teasing with her hands and mouth. Her hair formed a silvery puddle on his stomach as she left a trail of kisses from his navel to his chin, then back down again. Her fingers speared through the light mat of hair on his chest, twisting it and tugging lightly.

Jake lay with one knee bent, the woman he now considered his own cradled at his side. He closed his eyes, savoring the feel of her body pressed to his and wondering at the crazy junction of time and circumstance that had brought them to this place and this moment.

"Are you going to sleep?"

He opened one eye to see Sarah propped on her elbow, staring down at him with a rueful smile.

"No, ma'am. I'm just lying here thinking about that nun who whacked me over the head all those years ago."

"The one with the umbrella?"

"Mmm...."

She pursed her lips. "I'm not sure I want to hear why you're thinking of her at this particular moment."

He grinned and reached up to twist a strand of her hair around one finger. "If she hadn't scared the bejesus out of me, I might not have been so intimidated by your little disguise for so long."

"And?"

He tugged gently on her hair, bringing her face closer to his. "And I might not have been so angry when I discovered that the woman who'd been twisting me in knots wasn't little Sister Sarah Josepha after all."

"And?"

He brushed his lips across hers. "And I might not have forced the issue between us yesterday."

"No," she whispered against his mouth, "but I might have. In fact, if you hadn't forced it, I probably would've done exactly what I'm going to do now."

Jake's stomach muscles jumped as her seeking fingers slid through the thick hair at his groin and closed around his shaft.

"Now you just close your eyes again," Sarah murmured in between tiny, wet kisses, "and let me give you something else to think about besides being whacked with an umbrella."

She definitely did that. Within moments, she had him rigid and aching and straining against her hold. Her mouth teased and nipped at him with the same erotic impact as her hands. As much as he ached to roll her over into the thick green carpet, Jake held back, giving her the time she wanted, needed. Every muscle quivered with the effort. When his low, strangled growl gave evidence that he couldn't restrain himself any longer, she took him into her body, her hips straddling his and her back arching as she met his slow, driving thrusts with a strength that stunned him.

Jake saw his hands, dark against the pale skin of her breasts. He heard her breathless, panting cries as her passion deepened. He felt her moist heat surround him, clench him. When she braced her hands on his shoulders and brought her mouth to his, Jake drank in her dark, sweet taste.

Sarah was right, Jake thought—while he could still think at all. Whatever happened tomorrow, they'd have this. They'd always have this.

Slowly, reluctantly, they rejoined the universe they'd left behind for a moment out of time. Jake brought Sarah up into his arms for a last touch of his lips against hers, then turned away to reach for their clothes.

She clutched at his shoulders, achingly reluctant to allow even a breath of space between their sweat-slicked bodies.

"Jack, I...I want you to know that everything you heard or read about me was true."

He stopped her with a brush of his thumb over the soft skin of her lips. "We both have things in our past that are best forgotten."

She took his hand in both of hers, needing to tell him what was in her heart. "I was stupid and self-centered and uncaring who I hurt, before. I...I thought I was in love. But now...now I'm just beginning to understand what the word means."

His thumb shaped her lower lip. "When we get out of here, Sarah Josepha, we're going to take a long, slow, cool shower in the biggest, most decadent hotel room money can buy. We're going to make wild, sweet love on a bed with clean sheets. And then we're going to do some serious talking about the future."

Not five minutes later, the future reached out to grab them by the throat.

They'd collected the children and Eleanora and were only a few hundred meters from the camp when the sharp crack of a gunshot set the parrots overhead squawking. The dense undergrowth shielded the camp from view, but there was no mistaking the source of the sound.

"Get down!" Jake ordered instantly. Eleanora dropped like a sack of ballast, tugging Teresa down with her. Sarah grabbed Eduard's good arm and pulled him down with her and Ricci. Tucking the toddler under the shelter of her body, she wrapped a protective arm across Eduard's thin shoulders.

Jake strained to hear above the noise of the birds. No other sound reached him from camp. He straightened slowly, rapidly assessing the possibilities. One of the men could've shot a viper. Or amused himself by taking a potshot at one of the monkeys that occasionally darted into camp to snatch at shiny objects in the debris. Or an argument between a couple of the rebels could've taken a personal, ugly twist. It had happened before.

He turned and crouched beside Sarah. "I don't think it's anything to panic over. I'm going in. Stay here until I signal for you."

He pulled the palm-size pistol from his boot. She hesitated, swallowing hard, then reached out a shaky hand and took it.

"It's ready to fire," Jake warned softly. "If I'm not back in five minutes, take the children back to the pool. I'll call in what help I can and try to hold off the others as long as possible."

"Jack, I—" She broke off, unable to articulate her thoughts. Her eyes expressed them for her.

"Me too," Jake answered, smiling. Ruffling Eduard's hair, he rose and moved down the trail with the silent, swift tread of a hunter.

Che met him at the edge of the clearing, his pistol drawn and a cold, flat rage in his eyes. A half-dozen men were strung out behind him, their expressions nervous. Jake caught the stoop-shouldered Xavier's frowning look. Clearly the leader's unexpected return had shaken the camp.

For several tense moments, they faced each other. Jake's finger curled around the trigger.

At last the rebel leader broke the crackling tension. "I was just coming to look for you."

Jake let his eyes drift to the leader's drawn gun. "Did you think I'd gone somewhere? Without getting paid?"

Che straightened slowly, contempt replacing some of the rage in his eyes. "That was what Enrique said, when he tried to justify letting you go into the jungle with only the women."

"You still don't trust me?" Jake asked mockingly.

"I don't trust anyone who's not dedicated to the revolution," the rebel said flatly. "Nor do I tolerate those who disregard my orders."

Jake knew then what had caused the single pistol shot. He wouldn't have to worry about Pig-face any longer.

Che uncocked his weapon and slid it into its holster. "Where is the woman?"

Jake lowered the barrel of his own weapon. "Where I left her."

The other man eyed him for a long moment. "You've taken your responsibility for her welfare most seriously, gringo."

"You put it on my neck, remember?"

"Call her in. We're abandoning this camp. We leave immediately."

Jake's stomach clenched. "Why?"

"The *patrón* has sources in the city. They tell him people, unknown people, have been asking questions. Too many questions. He is not nervous, you understand, but cautious. He's bringing in the shipment we've been waiting for tonight...."

Tonight, not tomorrow! Beads of sweat collected in the hollow between Jake's shoulder blades.

"After tonight, we will have what we need to bring this decadent government to its knees." The intense fanaticism that characterized the leader vibrated in his voice. "After tonight, we will not need this camp. We will take the revolution out of these hills and into the city."

And take the heat off the *patrón*'s little operation, Jake thought in gut-twisting disgust.

"Call in the woman," Che said impatiently.

Jake slung his weapon over his shoulder. "Why not let her go?" he suggested casually. "She and the children will only slow us on the march. She has served her purpose here."

"I would as soon put a bullet in her head. The church she serves is nothing but a tool of the corrupt government that suppresses our people. But the *patrón* has said to bring her."

"Bring her where?"

"You have no need to know our destination, only that your job with us ends tonight."

It was going to end, all right. One way or another.

"Come, collect the woman and your gear. You will take the point. I have need of a man who's good with his eyes and his weapon out in front."

In other words, Jake thought grimly, Che intended to put the gringo where he could watch him every minute. With Xavier dogging his footsteps, Jake went to collect Sarah and the others, his mind racing with possible options.

Chapter 13

"OMEGA control, this is Chameleon."

Maggie tucked the tiny transceiver between her shoulder and her ear and leaned against the rest room wall. While she waited for Cowboy to respond, she glanced around the dingy room.

As unisex bathrooms went, this one contained all the essentials. A grimy, once-white stool with an old-fashioned overhead flush unit. A urinal hanging crookedly on one wall. A rusted faucet set over an equally rusted sink. A sliver of mirror nailed above the tap. Maggie caught sight of herself in the mirror and grimaced. She fit right in with the rest of the clientele in this raunchy café, but she was ready to wipe off the half pound of green eye shadow that weighted her lids, slip out the back door to retrieve her discreetly concealed habit and make her way back to the relative quiet of the convent. Even the raucous chapter house bell was melodious compared to the disco music booming off the walls of the Café El Caribe.

"This is Cowboy, Chameleon. What's happening? We

thought you'd— What's that noise?'' His voice sharpened. "Are you under assault?"

"Not me, just my ears," Maggie responded quickly. "I'm at the local night spot."

"Let me guess," Cowboy drawled. "You're soliciting contributions from the patrons for the sisters' welfare fund?"

Maggie glanced down at the skintight glowing-pink tube of slinky fabric that hugged her from well below her collarbone to well above her knees. "Let's just say I'm soliciting…information. Heard anything from Jaguar in the last few hours?"

"No, nothing."

She nibbled on her well-glossed lower lip. Everything was set for tomorrow. She really didn't need Jake's confirmation. Still, Maggie would like to talk to him one last time before going in.

"Did you pick up anything interesting at that end?" Cowboy asked.

"Very. I've been sharing a table for the last half hour with a runner."

"One of the big guys?"

"No, just a mule. A small-time carrier trying to earn enough for a stake for herself in Hollywood."

"Aren't they all?"

Maggie frowned, thinking of the young wives and mothers she'd talked to yesterday. They were simply trying to feed their families.

"No, not all the ones down here, anyway. But this one is definitely in it for the thrills, as well as the money. She makes a run to the States every month or so, ferrying about ten kilos each time. She's also a personal friend—a *very* personal friend—of the man the folks around here call the *patrón*."

Cowboy's low whistle was audible even over the boom of disco. "The same *patrón* who's funding the arms for Jaguar's little band?"

"Right the first time. She mentioned that she paid him a visit a couple of nights ago. Bragged about a chopper flying her in. She also let drop that our friend Che was visiting at the same time."

Maggie hesitated, still not sure of the import of her next tidbit of information. "She said that Che mentioned a nun his band had taken, and that the *patrón* was very interested in her."

"Interested how?"

"I'm not sure. I'm going to follow this up, though. I have this funny feeling…"

Cowboy groaned. "You and your feelings."

"Look, I have to go. I've tied up this rest room long enough. Tell the chief—"

She broke off as the door handle rattled. "Gotta go, Cowboy. Talk at you later."

Flipping the tiny, flat transceiver shut, Maggie hitched up her short skirt and clipped it to the garter belt she'd filched at the same time as the stockings and the high spiked heels. She shimmied her hips to smooth the tight fabric down over them and grinned, remembering the ridiculous ease with which she'd acquired her new wardrobe.

She'd made the rounds of the tawdry shops this afternoon with the young novice to hand out pamphlets describing a free clinic the sisters were offering next week. While the earnest young novice explained the various treatments, Maggie had collected her present outfit, bit by bit. She'd tucked the items under her robe and left notes where the shopkeepers could find them directing them to present a bill to the U.S. consulate. Maggie grinned, imagining the expression on some State Department rep's face when he had to issue a voucher for a black lace garter belt and net stockings.

The door handle rattled once more.

"Just a minute," she called, taking a quick peek in the mirror. She poked her fingers a few times in the mass of hair she'd pulled to one side and teased mercilessly, fluffing it even more. She applied another layer of scarlet lipstick and dusted more green on her lids. Satisfied that even Adam would have had to look twice to recognize her under her layers of paint, Maggie opened the door.

Waves of pulsing music hit her with hurricane force. She stopped on the threshold, wincing, and waited for her eyes to adjust to the flashing lights that cut through an otherwise murky darkness. She saw with disgust that the woman she'd been subtly pumping had left the club.

"It's all yours," she shouted to the figure lounging beside the door. She started to step forward, but found her way blocked by an arm planted across the door jamb.

Maggie glanced down at the white-sleeved arm. Arching one brow, she followed its line to a solid, broad-shouldered body. The shoulders strained against a tailored white linen sports coat. Maggie noted the gold medallion gleaming at the open neck of the shirt. A square, faintly shadowed chin. A luxuriant black mustache. Gleaming brown eyes.

It was only after the tall, dark-haired figure stepped out of the shadows that Maggie saw how the collection of individual features all added up to the most handsome man she'd ever seen. No, not handsome. This guy was drop-dead gorgeous. She managed to keep her mouth from sagging—barely. He was Omar Sharif and Julio Iglesias and Emilio Estevez all rolled into one.

He was also, she discovered, smiling at her in a way that raised the hairs on her arms.

"You want something, my friend?" she asked coolly

The dark mustache lifted, showing white, even teeth. "Perhaps."

His deliberate move forward crowded Maggie's space too much for her liking. She took a quick couple of steps backward, deciding that she needed some distance between her and this hunk.

He stepped into the dingy rest room and closed the door, cutting the noise down from mind-bending to merely ear-splitting. Leaning his shoulders back against the door, he folded his arms over his chest. Maggie saw the flash of a gold Rolex on his wrist.

She didn't make the mistake of thinking this was some wealthy aristocrat out cruising Cartoza's only night spot. Until he showed his hand, however, she would play her role. She gave him a slow half smile. "So, my friend, what is it you want?"

His dark eyes lingered on her mouth for a moment, then traced a slow, casual path down her body. Maggie willed herself not to stiffen, not to react in any way. In his own good time, he brought his gaze back to her face.

"Maybe I wish a few moments of your company."

She flicked a quick glance around the dingy bathroom. The small disparaging smile on her face said she didn't think much of his choice of a trysting place. Maggie used the few seconds to catalog possible escape routes. There weren't any. The rest room had no window. No other door. No crack in the graffiti-covered plaster walls.

"Or maybe I just want to know why you ask so many questions," he said lazily. He jerked his chin toward the outer room. "Our little friend out there says you have an interest in the interior."

Maggie shrugged. "I was just making small talk."

"A particular interest."

She took her lower lip between her teeth, hesitating. "All right, I admit I am interested. I'm new here, you understand. Just down from Mexico. I have need of funds."

When he didn't answer, she pouted and turned to survey herself in the piece of mirror. Running one finger along the line of her darkened brow, Maggie watched him in the cracked glass.

"I understand there is money to be made," she said to his reflection. "Much money. You will tell your *patrón* I am interested, yes?"

He smiled and levered his shoulders off the door.

"Perhaps you can tell him yourself. You will come with me, I think."

At that moment, Maggie would've given everything she possessed to be primary agent on this mission. If it was her operation, she could've followed this promising lead and walked out of the Café El Caribe with this man she suspected was one of the *patrón's* lieutenants. But she was Jaguar's backup. She was here, as Adam had so succinctly pointed out, to work Sarah Chandler's extraction.

She sighed with real regret. "No, I think not."

He had quick reflexes, Maggie had to give him that. He blocked her first blow with an upflung arm. That gave her just the opening she needed for a swift, sharp jab to the solar plexus. He bent over in an involuntary reaction, his breath rushing out in a startled grunt. Maggie finished him with a chop to the back of the neck. He crumpled to the cement floor without a sound.

She stared down at his sprawled figure, regretting the waste of such magnificent malehood. Too bad the men she met in this job were either first class weirdoes or all-around scumbags. She dropped to one knee and quickly, expertly searched him.

The lethal little Benelli she found in a holster tucked under his arm didn't surprise her, but the small leather case she extracted from a hidden pocket did. When she flipped it open, Maggie's eyes narrowed.

He came awake with a little jerk of one leg. Maggie leaned her shoulders comfortably against the wall and watched with interest as his muscular thigh bunched, then drew up, until his knee was bent and an expensive alligator boot was planted firmly on the floor. He propped himself up on one elbow and shook his head. He must have caught sight of her orange-and-pink-striped shoes out of one corner of his eye. His head tilted, studying the shoe for a moment. Then he rose to his feet with an athletic grace and dusted off the seat of his linen slacks.

Maggie had had plenty of opportunity to study him while he lay sprawled on the less-than-clean cement floor. She discovered, however, that a handsome, unconscious man, and one whose eyes held a reluctant gleam of admiration for a worthy adversary, were two different creatures altogether. She held the Benelli easily in her left hand, hoping she wouldn't have to use it, and flipped open the leather case with the other.

"So, Colonel, do you care to tell me why the chief of security for Cartoza was going to take me to the one called the *patrón*?"

His mustache lifted. "I wasn't. I was going to...shall we say, convince you to take *me* to *him*."

"What makes you think I know his location?"

"My men listened via a remote device the whole time the little songbird poured her heart out to you. Unfortunately, the noise levels drowned out all but a few words. Those were enough, however, for me to pay a little visit to my favorite night spot to check out the latest arrival."

"You come here often? The chief of security?"

"Often enough." He saw the skepticism in her eyes and shrugged. "This is a small country. Everyone knows who I am. I don't hide from the men who seek to destroy our government. It is better to let them see me, and know that they are watched."

He was either incredibly brave or had reasons not to worry about the political assassinations that regularly rocked this part of the world. Maggie's face remained bland, but the Benelli never wavered.

"You're Chameleon, I take it." His eyes flickered down her miniskirted length once more. "I understood you were good, but I didn't realize how good. Or how attractive."

He wasn't exactly dog food himself, Maggie thought with an inner smile.

"You're wise not to trust me," he continued smoothly. "Check with your headquarters. They will verify what I say, who I am."

"I know who you are," she admitted at last. "Luis Barbedo Esteban. Educated here and at Oxford. Colonel, Cartozan army. Former instructor in counterterrorist tactics at the Inter-American Defense College in Washington. Appointed by the president as chief of security two years ago."

"You don't seem particularly impressed," he commented, his white teeth gleaming.

"Oh, I am. I'm also impressed by your off-duty uniform. You appear to have expensive tastes, Colonel. Or was that watch you're wearing a gift from a grateful citizen?"

"Actually, it was a gift from the president. Yours, not mine."

Maggie notched a brow.

"For a slight service I rendered him some years ago," Esteban said with a shrug. "He was a private citizen at the time."

"That was you? You're the one who swam two miles out to the boat where he was being held hostage? You took the terrorists out, single-handed?"

The incident had occurred long before Maggie was recruited by OMEGA, but a few of the older heads still cited it as a textbook example of surprise and brains triumphing over armed brawn.

The colonel grinned. "Your president managed to assist quite ably with one or two."

Well, hell! Adam had stated in no uncertain terms during the mission prebrief that Colonel Esteban was to be trusted, but he'd left out a couple of rather pertinent details about the man. Maggie's mouth twisted at the thought of what her boss would say when he learned that she'd dropped the colonel and held him at gun point in a sleazy little nightclub.

She lowered the Benelli, thumbing the safety before she handed it to him. "I hope the men who'll be with me on the extraction team tomorrow night will have the same skill as you and my president."

"Perhaps I will find it necessary to accompany the team myself," Esteban murmured, holstering his weapon.

"Perhaps you should."

He buttoned his coat and lifted his broad shoulders once or twice to settle the linen smoothly over the holster. With the simple action, he seemed to assumed a different persona. Harder, more precise, more authoritarian.

"Tell me what you learned from the woman you were speaking with."

Maggie arched a brow.

He caught her look and moderated both his voice and his stance. "I know my country's interior. I was raised in the mountains. Perhaps I can recognize some hint of where she went to visit this friend of hers, identify some feature."

Knowing that someone could pound on the rest room door at any moment, Maggie ran through every detail quickly, precisely.

"Are you sure she said this *patrón*'s hacienda was only fifteen minutes by helicopter?"

"I'm sure. Does that help?"

"It would help more if I knew the exact airspeed and wind direction at the time of the flight," he answered with a grin, "but it narrows the search area considerably."

"Perhaps we can narrow it even more. There are three major roads leading out of Cartoza City into the interior. My source—Juana's sister-in-law's cousin, you understand—says the road heading north is the shortest way to get chemicals such as hydrochloric acid and ether to their destination."

Surprise etched his aristocratic features. "You have been busy, haven't you?"

"It's my job."

"You do it well, Chameleon."

"Thanks," Maggie said, tipping two fingers to her brow. "Glad to be of service, Colonel. Now, if there's nothing else, we'd better free up this room before someone wonders just exactly what's going on in here."

He gave a leer that was only half feigned. "They won't wonder."

Maggie tossed a smile over her shoulder and opened the door. She winced as fresh waves of music assaulted her ears. She hadn't taken two steps before the colonel grabbed her arm and hauled her back. Maggie found herself wedged between the hard concrete wall and a body that was every bit as unyielding.

"Do not fight me," he ordered swiftly, then covered her mouth with his.

In the curious way the human brain has, Maggie's processed a half-dozen sensory perceptions all at once. She felt his belt buckle press against her stomach. She tasted the golden hint of rum on his breath. She saw his dark head slant to take her mouth more fully. And she heard the faint thud of footsteps passing.

"Who was that?" Maggie whispered against his mouth when she could breathe again. Barely.

"I don't know," he murmured, brushing his lips across hers.

"But…why…this?"

"Because…I've been wanting…'this'…since the first moment I saw you."

He muffled her indignant little huff with another kiss, feather-light this time, but just as devastating as the first. From the tensile strength of the body pressed against hers, Maggie knew that she wouldn't take him down as easily as she had before. Assuming she wanted to. She was still debating the issue when he raised his head and smiled down at her.

"Until tomorrow."

"Until tomorrow."

Breathless, she watched him make his leisurely way through the crowd in the club. Several of the patrons sent curious looks at Maggie, still lounging against the door jamb. She sighed. She wouldn't get much out of them now, not after they'd seen her in the arms of Cartoza's chief of security.

She sauntered toward the end of the crowded bar, waiting for the right moment to melt into the shadows and slip out the door. She flicked a quick glance up at the clock embedded in neon palm trees above the bar. Not even eight o'clock. She thought of the convent bell and shuddered. This could turn out to be another long night.

In fact, it turned out to be far shorter than Maggie anticipated. She was only halfway back to the convent house when a discreet ping signaled an incoming transmission. She ducked into a nearby alley and whipped the transceiver out of her side pocket.

"Hold on, Chameleon. Jaguar's on the line."

Maggie's fingers curled around the tiny instrument.

"I've only got a few seconds." Jake's disembodied whisper vibrated with tension. "We've been on the march most of the day. Che hasn't let me out of his sight until now. He won't say where we're going, only that the drop has been moved up to tonight. Sarah and the children are with us, and a woman named Eleanora, who will be extracted, as well."

Great, Maggie thought. Just great. Two women. Three kids. Unknown location. Unspecified time. Uncertain size of opposition. She reassessed the size of her team and of the strike team that Jake would call in at the drop site. If he made it to the drop site.

"I've got the GPS unit on," Jake continued, low and fast, referring to the Global Positioning Satellite compass built into his digital watch. The GPS could pinpoint a location anywhere in the world to within a few square meters, as the tank commanders who used it in the vast, featureless deserts of Iraq during Desert Storm had discovered. With GPS, Maggie would be able to track Jake's exact location, and try to anticipate where he was heading.

"Be ready to come in on my call. I'll give you more detail when I can. Out."

Five minutes later, Maggie gave a heartfelt prayer of thanks and shed her scratchy habit for the last time. Pulling a pair of dark slacks and a black cotton turtleneck from the small cardboard suitcase she'd carried into the country, she dressed hurriedly and slipped out the convent gates for the last time. She climbed into the Jeep she'd had Cowboy summon via his channels and sped through the night to the army's heavily guarded airfield outside town.

Despite the black-and-green camouflage paint on his face and the stark, utilitarian fatigues that had replaced his white linen suit, Maggie recognized the tall man who strode forward to meet her immediately.

"You look much different," he said, eyeing her scrubbed face and tumbled hair.

"So do you, big guy. Have you got the gear I requested?"

"It's all here."

"Then let's go."

Chapter 14

"Are you all right?"

Jake pointed the powerful beam of the flashlight at the ground, but enough peripheral light filtered upward to illuminate Sarah's pale, strained face.

"I'm all right," she answered stiffly, leaning her shoulders against the withers of the patient packhorse that carried the two smaller children. Eduard stood beside her, silent and watchful. Eleanora's solid figure loomed in the darkness just behind them.

Jake bit back a curse, wishing he could offer the little group some words of encouragement, but Che and the woman he shared the revolution and his bed with weren't three yards away. One or the other of them had been at Sarah's side throughout the long, exhausting day. The woman had even gone with Sarah and Eleanora into the bushes the few times the rebel leader allowed a stop so that they could rest and attend to personal needs.

Jake himself had been under close watch, as well. He'd

managed to take a few unguarded moments to send his hurried transmission to Maggie an hour ago, but not much else.

The children, however, were not watched quite as closely. Eduard had varied his pace, sometimes walking silently beside Jake, sometimes falling back to lay a reassuring hand on the bewildered Ricci's stubby leg. Occasionally he'd marched beside Sarah. Using the boy as an intermediary, Jake had made what plans he could with her. This would be their last stop, he guessed. It was time to implement those plans.

Under the watchful eyes of the leader, Jake studied Sarah's face. "You don't look all right. You look like something the jungle scavengers would pass by."

Her chin lifted. "Thanks. That's just what I needed to hear right now."

He gave an exasperated grunt. "Look, I've put my neck on the line for you about as long as I intend to. I don't have the time or the energy to deal with a fainting female. You've got to keep up."

"I'll keep up."

Jake flashed the powerful beam into her face, causing Sarah to flinch back against the horse and throw up an arm to shield her eyes. He swung the beam down again, shaking his head in disgust.

"Drink some water, dammit. From the look of your face, you're half a step away from dehydration."

"I don't have any. I gave it all to the children."

"Christ!"

He unhooked the canteen that hung from his web belt and shoved it at her. Jake heard Teresa's little sob of fright at the roughness in his voice and hardened his heart.

"Here," he snarled. "Take it."

Sarah's fingers trembled as she took the canteen and fumbled with the cap.

"You just unscrew it," Jake said caustically. "Two turns to the left. Think you can manage that?"

She flashed him a look of scorn that was visible even in the dim light. "I can manage it."

Deliberately she wiped the mouth of the canteen with a corner of her sleeve. The folds of the dark habit fell over her fingers and covered the small, flat box that Jake had passed her with the canteen.

As he watched Sarah tilt her head and drink greedily, Jake felt a sharp, lancing pride in her courage. He'd shared some desperate moments with a wide spectrum of people in his lifetime. Some of them had crumpled under the stress of fear and imminent death, but many had found resources within themselves they didn't know they possessed to challenge it with. Sarah definitely fell into the latter category. He wanted, he *needed* to tell her so.

Jake pulled off his floppy hat and raked a hand through his sweat-dampened hair. "Look, I'm sorry I snapped at you. I'm a little uptight knowing I'll finally be able to get my business done and get out of this steam bath."

She wiped the canteen's mouth once more and passed it to the children, saying nothing.

"You've done okay, Sister," Jake offered, putting his hat on again. "In fact, I know of only one other woman who would've stood up as well as you have. Maybe you'll get a chance to know her someday."

Oh, she would, Sarah thought with a tight, inner smile. She would definitely get to know this partner/contact/special friend of Jack's. In fact, that was one of her top priorities after they got out of this nightmare. She wanted to check this woman out and make sure she understood that Jack had some new priorities in his life now. Sarah had already begun planning her campaign to smooth out those rough edges he'd mentioned. And she was a master at laying out campaign plans. She'd spent half her life helping her father in his bids for reelection. Jack didn't know it yet, but he was going to have to make a few major career decisions in the very near future.

If there was a future.

Sarah managed a shaky smile. "Maybe I will. Get to know her, I mean."

"We'll see what we can work out." He sent her a look of

silent command. "Just do as I tell you, and we'll both get through the next few hours."

"Enough of this." Che stepped out of the darkness. "We must move."

Jake wrenched his attention away from Sarah. Turning slowly, he faced the rebel leader. "Isn't it about time you tell me just where the hell we're moving to?"

"You will collect your fee by the time the night is over. That's all you need to know."

"Wrong. The last time I went to a drop with your trigger-happy little band, the site was almost overrun with *federales*. What guarantees do I have that I'm not walking into the same kind of situation tonight?"

"This site is well protected."

"Yeah? Who says?"

"The *patrón*." Che gave a thin smile when he saw Jake's narrowed eyes. "We go to his headquarters, you see. Your countryman, the one who brings the missiles, is as anxious as you to collect his money. There is an airstrip at the hacienda he will use to off-load, and then perhaps take on a different cargo."

Jake's mind whirled with the implications. Instead of an isolated airstrip hacked out of the jungle, they were heading for one that would be well defended. He had to get word to Maggie. There was no way he was going to let Sarah walk into what he knew would be a self-contained fortress.

"Come," the rebel leader said impatiently. "It's not far now."

Jake lifted his weapon, his eyes on Sarah.

Her gaze flickered to Che, and then to Jake's face. "I'm glad we're almost there," she said calmly. "I'm ready for this to be over."

Jake smiled at her. "So am I, Sister Sarah, so am I."

His hungry gaze raked her face once more, and then he laid a casual hand on Eduard's thin shoulder. "Come on, kid. Let's get this show on the road."

* * *

Maggie had experienced some real thrills in her life, even before joining OMEGA. One of her earliest memories was of sneaking away from her mother to watch her father's crew bring in a well. She'd been standing only a few feet away from the rig when the earth began to rumble and black liquid leaped into the air. She'd clapped her hands in delight. Her father had shouted something she learned the meaning of only years later and dashed across the burning desert sands to snatch her up. Afterward he'd shown her how she could've been weighted down and drowned by the viscous liquid, but at the time she'd thought it was a great adventure.

As adventures went, however, skimming along at ninety knots a mere twenty-five feet above the impenetrable jungle canopy had that little escapade beat hands down. The pilot had explained that they'd fly a contour pattern until they reached the target area, then drop down to nap of the earth. From that point on, they'd slink in at a death-defying five to ten knots, with their skids brushing the top of the trees, leaving just enough clearance above the branches for the rotor blades. Their only safety systems would be their night-vision goggles and the pilot's skill. Maggie tried not to think about nap of the earth. This contour stuff was bad enough.

Lifting off her goggles for a moment, she wiped the perspiration from around her eyes. She stole a glance at the figure beside her. If Colonel Esteban was nervous about dodging around treetops in the black of night at ninety knots, he sure didn't show it. He flashed her a smile that won an answering grin and a thumbs-up from Maggie.

She settled the goggles over her eyes again and peered out the helicopter's side hatch into the hazy green sea below. The magnification of the lenses was so powerful that the copilot had bragged he could read a name tag on a soldier's chest. At night. From the air. Maggie didn't want to read any name tags. She just wanted some sight, some signal from Jaguar.

He was down there, only a few minutes' flight time away. The copilot was tracking his coordinates and relaying position updates to Maggie. In between his reports, an air surveillance officer in the Big Bird aircraft orbiting high above the Caribbean was providing regular updates on the approaching suspect smuggler. He was a half hour out and closing fast. The strike team that would take him down was on his tail, also sending Maggie periodic updates via a secure ultra-high-frequency data link.

Cowboy was tracking everything at the control center, as well. Maggie knew she could call him for confirmation if she missed anything, but she doubted she would. Things happened too fast, decisions would have to be made in split seconds. She'd have to coordinate the two prongs of this operation with the information she processed in her own, internal computers.

It would sure help matters, though, if Jake would let her know just how he planned to deploy his little ground cadre when he reached his destination.

She got her wish some ten minutes later.

Maggie jerked upright in her web seat as a thin, frightened voice came over the secure voice link. The first words were so garbled she didn't catch them.

"Retransmit your ID," she rapped out. "Over."

"Is there anyone there?"

"Repeat your last transmission. Over."

"Can anyone hear me? Please," the frightened voice sobbed. "Please, someone hear me."

Maggie groaned into the mike. It was one of Jake's kids. He was pushing the transmit button, but either didn't know or had forgotten to release it so that he could receive.

"If you are there, please listen. I have not much time. My friend, Señor Creighton, he talks with the one called Che while I am in the jungle."

Señor Creighton? Maggie shook her head. It had to be Jake. Only he could set the transceiver to this frequency. Her mouth went dry as she thought of the courage it must have taken for this child to slip into the dark, impenetrable jungle on his own.

"He says to tell you we go to the hacienda of the *patrón*," the boy whispered. "It is not far, he thinks."

Maggie's heart jumped into her throat. Jake and company were on their way to the drug lord's hideaway!

Their operation didn't have just two prongs. It now had three, all of which were about to slam together with the force of three freight trains colliding. The extraction of the senator's daughter. The takedown of the middleman, the link to the United States that the president wanted to sever. And the elimination of the big man, the one who supplied the money. If Maggie had been any less of a professional, she would've shouted her excitement. Instead, she listened intently while the boy stumbled on.

"Señor Creighton says to tell you we will separate when we arrive there. Sarita…the woman Sarah…she has the st… str…"

The strobe! She had the strobe, Maggie thought exultantly. Smaller and flatter than a cigarette package, the strobe packed enough power to fire a pulsing halogen light that could be seen for miles.

"She use this light to signal our location. Señor Creighton will create a noise…"

A diversion, Maggie interpreted.

"He has red pins to tell you where he is."

What he had were .38 caliber pin-gun flares, no bigger than a cigarette. One twist of the spring mechanism and they shot out a flare that would light up the target area like a string of high-powered Christmas lights.

"I must go. Please, please, you must help us."

A faint, flat hum came over the earphones.

Wetting her lips, Maggie turned to the man beside her. "Did you hear?"

"Every word." Excitement threaded the colonel's smooth voice. He spread an aerial map across his lap and drew a rough vector with a grease pencil borrowed from the copilot. "This is where your Jaguar is now, according to the GPS signals. And this is the location of a plantation house owned by one of Cartoza's most influential businessmen, an exporter of tropical fruit."

He pointed to a wide, flat valley surrounded on all sides by steep hills. Maggie saw at once the thin, straggling line that led from the plantation to the capital city. A road. A road that would transport produce out. And bring chemicals in.

"Maybe this businessman grows more than fruit."

Esteban's white teeth gleamed as his mustache lifted in a slow, dangerous smile. "I think perhaps he does. I sent a man in undercover to infiltrate his operation a few weeks ago, but he met with an unfortunate accident. It will give me great pleasure to take this *bastardo* down. I thank you for this one."

Maggie grinned. "Anytime, Colonel."

"So, my Chameleon, we will direct the strike team to the plantation and have them waiting when our friends arrive, will we not?"

Maggie's grin faded. This was the crucial moment. The irrevocable decision point that came in almost every operation. Normally the field agent made the call about when and where to direct the strike team, regardless of whether that consisted of a single sharpshooter, a civilian SWAT team, or, as in this case, a combined military and civilian force from two nations.

Jake had passed every scrap of information he had to Maggie, which was all he could do at this point. The decision was now hers.

She nodded to Esteban. "Send them to the plantation."

Sarah knew they were only minutes away from their destination. She sensed it by the ripple of preparation in the men strung out ahead and behind her. By the low murmurs and coarse jokes they exchanged. By the sharp admonishment Eleanora's "husband" gave her to move her carcass.

She wondered vaguely why she wasn't more afraid. She couldn't work up enough moisture in her throat to swallow. By contrast, her palms were so damp she wiped them continually on the sides of her habit. But the physical manifestations of fear didn't penetrate to her inner self.

Her entire being was focused on the dim silhouettes moving

ahead of her, intermittently illuminated by the flashlights they carried. Every few steps she'd catch a glimpse of Jack. He wasn't hard to distinguish from the other shadowy shapes. If she hadn't been able to pick out the broad shoulders that strained against his disreputable khaki shirt, she would have recognized him from the way he moved. With a silent, self-contained coordination. A smooth, easy grace that belied his size.

The memory of their afternoon by the glistening, silvered pool flashed into Sarah's mind. Jack had circled the water with the same deadly grace, stalking her like some kind of predator that had spotted its prey. She hadn't been afraid then, either, Sarah remembered.

She should have been, but she hadn't.

She should be now, but she wasn't. She'd passed beyond fear to that curious state where every sense is heightened, every emotion suspended, every faculty focused on one thing and one thing only.

She ran over the simple instructions Jack had passed to her, repeating them over and over in her mind like a litany.

By the time they halted at the edge of a vast clearing, she was as ready as she'd ever be.

Her heart began to thump against her ribs as her eyes swept the scene. For a moment, Sarah thought they'd stumbled by mistake onto a movie set. Spotlights mounted on high towers bathed the clearing in light and illuminated the cluster of buildings that occupied it. Set square in the middle was a tile-roofed two-story house, surrounded by an arched veranda on the upper floor. Gauzy curtains fluttered at the open windows upstairs, while light spilled out of the patio doors on the ground floor. Sarah caught the brief, intermittent flare of insects grilled by the bug lights that guarded the windows and, incredibly, the sound of chamber music floating from one of the downstairs rooms.

Only someone with supreme self-confidence would leave his home open to the night, Sarah thought, her gaze sweeping the neat, orderly complex once more. Only someone of indomitable strength could force the jungle back and bend it to his will.

The music rose to a polite crescendo. A cello led the chorus, followed by a trill of violins. Sarah felt an eerie sense of displacement. She was standing on the edge of a tropical rain forest, surrounded by men who carried their automatic rifles with the ease and nonchalance with which the men of her world carried their briefcases, listening to a sonata that she'd last heard performed by an ensemble at the Kennedy Center.

The strange sensation heightened, until Sarah clutched at Ricci's leg to anchor herself in reality. She tore her eyes from the surreal scene before her and searched the dim figures at the edge of the clearing. Jack stood out among them, tall, solid, a dark shape barely visible in the wash of the lights from the hacienda. He faced the far end of the clearing, his body taut and stiff. Sarah followed his line of sight and saw what he'd come for. What he'd risked his life for.

There, at the end of a grassy runway, sat a medium-size plane, propellers still whirling. Portable spotlights ringed it, washing it in a bright, incandescent light. Sarah couldn't tell the make, and wouldn't have recognized it in any case. But even from this distance she recognized the U.S. markings on the crates being unloaded by a scruffy-looking crew.

Slowly, her arms feeling as though they were weighted with lead, Sarah reached up and lifted Ricci from the packhorse. She wrapped her arms around his small body, pressing his face against her shoulder. He trembled against her but made no sound.

Eleanora moved up to lift Teresa down. The girl burrowed into the woman's legs, clutching her skirt with one hand and the root doll with her other. Eduard stood stiff and silent beside them.

Sarah searched the other woman's bruised, swollen face in the dim light, wondering if she had any hint of what was to come, wishing desperately she could explain it. Eleanora met her look and gave a slow, silent nod.

The stillness of the moment was broken when one of the men from the rear guard edged past their small, still group, anxious for a better view of the clearing. A second followed, then a third. The plane and its rich haul drew them like a magnet, as Jack had hoped it would. Over the pounding of her heart, Sarah heard their excited murmurs.

Their eyes were locked on the prize they'd waited for.

Hers were on Jack.

Che and the woman in fatigues stepped into the clearing.

Jack took one step with them. Two.

The other men followed.

Jack half turned, searching the dimness for her face.

Sarah tightened her arms around Ricci and pressed his head more firmly into her shoulder. She watched Jack lift his hand, slowly, deliberately…then freeze as a new sound cut through the night.

He whirled to meet this unexpected threat, as did the men around him. The snicker and click of bolts being drawn back competed with the rhythmic pounding of a horse's hooves.

"It is the *patrón!*" someone called.

A white stallion danced to a halt.

"You are late, Che," a cultured voice called out. The speaker didn't use the mountain dialect, but instead a pure, flowing Spanish that Sarah had no trouble following. "Did you bring the woman?"

"Yes, as you instructed. She is back there, with the pack-horses."

The rider shifted in his saddle. Sarah heard the creak of leather. The thud of a hoof dropping against the hard-packed earth.

"Welcome to my humble *estancia*, Miss Chandler," the rider said in clear, unaccented English. "I've been anticipating your arrival with great eagerness."

Chapter 15

Sarah stood frozen for an endless moment, her arms wrapped around Ricci. If Jack gave the signal, she didn't see it.

Her stunned gaze was riveted on the horseman. A thousand conflicting, chaotic thoughts chased through her mind. Out of them all, only one emerged to impress itself on her numbed consciousness. She and Jack and the children hadn't been brought here because of a rescheduled drop. Nor because the rebels had decided to abandon camp. They'd been brought here because this criminal had somehow learned her identity.

The fear that Sarah had held at bay earlier swamped through her. Her stomach knotted as she watched the horseman swing off his mount with a lithe, easy confidence. He was a short man, she noted, and rather heavy, yet fluid in his movements. He drew the reins over the stallion's head and patted its muzzle with absent affection.

"I met your father once, some years ago," he said conversationally, moving toward Sarah. "A most forceful and invigorating man. Very strong in his opinions. When you're rested and recovered from your ordeal, you must tell me how best to deal with him.''

Jack stepped forward to block the man's path. "Nobody's going to be telling—"

"I'll handle this."

Ever afterward, Sarah would wonder at the cool authority in her voice. It stopped Jack in his tracks. He spun on his heel, staring through the dark shadows. Before he could say anything, the *patrón* signaled his approval.

"Very wise, Miss Chandler."

"What the hell is going on here?"

Jake's low growl raised the hairs on the back of Sarah's neck. "Isn't it obvious?" she said, only the faintest tremor in her voice. "You have your business to conduct, and so, apparently, does this gentleman."

"Very perceptive, my dear. You are indeed your father's daughter."

Sarah didn't acknowledge the compliment, if it was one. "Take Ricci, Eduard."

A thin, small shadow materialized at her side. Her hands shaking, Sarah passed the child to Eduard. At the same time, she pressed the small, flat box Jake had given her under the older boy's elbow.

Her low murmur was for Eduard's ears alone. "Just turn the top. To the left. Understand?"

"*Sí.*"

"Sarita?" Ricci's childish treble quavered. "Do we die, Sarita?"

Sarah closed her eyes, swallowing. "No, of course not. You stay here with Eduard and Teresa and Eleanora until I see what is to be done."

"I want to go with Señor Creighton." Teresa tugged against Eleanora's hand, a hiccup of fear in her voice.

"No!" Tension sharpened Sarah's reply. "You will stay here! Señor Creighton has...has business to conduct. You will be in the way."

"Creighton?" Amusement tinted the *patrón*'s voice. "Is that what he told you his name was?"

"That's what she calls him," Che volunteered with a sneer, coming forward to join the other two men. All three turned to watch Sarah approach.

She stepped out of the jungle shadows and walked toward them. Light from the spotlights across the clearing caught the skirts of her robe and moved higher with each step, until it fell across her face. Seeing the *patrón*'s narrowed, speculative eyes on her, Sarah reached up to tug off the veil.

The short, heavyset man drew in an appreciative breath. "The pictures in the newspapers didn't do you justice, my dear."

She forced a small shrug. "They weren't taken at my best moment."

"Nor does that habit particularly become you," he murmured.

At the man's soft, almost caressing tone, a sick feeling curled in Sarah's stomach. She sensed, rather than saw, Jack stiffening beside her.

Sarah ignored Jack, concentrating on the man she faced. She recognized his type. Urbane, cultured, confident of himself and his power. She'd dealt with men like him all her life. Summoning the slow half smile she'd so often used to good effect with lecherous ambassadors and interested politicians, she plucked at the black skirts.

"The habit served its purpose. I must confess it is rather uncomfortable, however."

She reached up to unhook the top fastening. Then the second. She fanned her heated skin with the fold of material. The *patrón*'s eyes narrowed on the patch of flesh she bared to the glare of the spotlights.

"I apologize that you had to endure such discomfort for so long," he murmured. "My sources were a bit slow in passing me the information I sought about the medical sister my friend Che held in his camp."

Sarah lifted one shoulder. "The camp is behind us now.

Perhaps you have something at the hacienda that I might change into.''

"Perhaps I do." He gave a little bow. "Please, allow me to escort you."

Sarah didn't move. "First we must settle the issue of the children. They were taken with me in the raid. They're tired and frightened. I would ask your—'' She choked a bit. "I would ask your word that you will send them back to their village with the woman, Eleanora.''

He flicked a glance at Eleanora and the three youngsters and gave a dismissive shrug. "I have no interest in the children or the woman.''

Sarah nodded and started forward.

Jack caught her wrist, swinging her around. "What the hell do you think you're doing?''

"I'm going with him.''

"Just like that? You're going with him?''

She searched his eyes, pleading with him to understand. "It's best for the children, and for—''

"And for Miss Sarah Chandler.'' Jack sneered. "Do you think I'm going to let you just walk away? After all I did for you?''

"I'm grateful, truly grateful. But—''

He gave a vicious oath. Twisting her arm behind her waist, he brought her slamming up against his chest. "Want to know what you can do with your gratitude, lady?''

Jack's explosive violence startled Sarah. For a moment, she feared he didn't understand her motives. Didn't realize that she couldn't jeopardize the children for her own safety. She couldn't add to the risks he himself already faced.

At that moment, she felt him slip the small, palm-size gun into the hand twisted behind her back. For the space of a heartbeat, Sarah sagged against him, relieved that he understood, afraid to leave the safety of his arms. She wanted so much to wrap her free arm around his neck, to burrow into his strength and let him shield her.

The old Sarah might have done just that.

This Sarah had learned that she had strengths within herself she hadn't been aware of before. If she'd learned nothing else in these past days, it was that she could no longer hide.

Summoning her will, Sarah wrenched free and faced him, her fists buried in the folds of her skirts.

"All right, gringo. If my gratitude isn't sufficient, then perhaps you'll accept some more tangible form of thanks. I'm sure the *patrón* will give you a bonus for taking care of us, as an advance on what he'll receive from my father. Will you not?"

The man nodded politely, his eyes on Sarah's face. "Certainly, my dear. You will have to tell me, of course, just what specific…services…he performed for you, and what you think they're worth. Come, let us go to the hacienda and discuss this more comfortably."

Sarah threw a last look over her shoulder at the children, swept her gaze past Jack's tight, rigid features, then turned and started across the clearing without another word. Covered by the heavy folds of her skirt, her finger curled around the trigger of the small gun.

Holding his horse's reins, the *patrón* fell into step beside her.

The steady plopping of the animal's hooves thundered in Sarah's ears. She strained to hear some other sound, some movement behind her.

Jake watched her walk away, a slight figure in black, identifiable only by the silvery-gold hair that tumbled around her shoulders. He turned slowly, one thumb hooked in his belt. He would have reassessed his options, but Sarah had just preempted them all.

Che wore a tight, satisfied expression on his face, as though the the sight of the woman walking away from Jake pleased him enormously. Which it probably did, the bastard.

"So, gringo," he said with a sneer, "let us now turn to the business at hand."

"Yes," Jake responded. "Let us turn to the business at hand."

His finger tapped a single coded signal on the metal gusset next to his buckle.

When it came, the attack took Sarah by surprise, even though she was expecting it. Halfway across the clearing she heard a low, steady *whump-whump-whump*. Suddenly the treetops rattled, as though a violent wind had just blown in. The man beside her froze, then spun in the direction of the sound. Sarah swung around, as well, gasping at the sight that greeted her.

Like a giant moth rising from the jungle canopy, a huge, black-painted helicopter lifted out of the trees and hovered over the clearing. Powerful spotlights switched on, and what Sarah later learned was a million footcandles of brilliant white light lit the entire area.

Sarah brought the little pistol up. "I wouldn't do that if I were you!"

The heavyset man paused with one foot in the stirrup and a hand on the saddle horn. Squinting against the glare, Sarah saw rage seize his features.

"You will not shoot." He sneered. "Your hand is shaking so badly you would not hit me if you did. You hold that as though you've never fired a weapon before."

Sarah wrapped her second hand around the first. "I haven't," she admitted. "I've never touched a gun before in my life, and I'm extremely nervous about this."

In the wash of bright light, Sarah couldn't tell if the man paled, but he did take an involuntary step backward, his eyes wide and fixed on her trembling hand. She heard the first shouts from the compound, and a sudden rattle of gunfire.

"Get down," she ordered. "On your face."

A sudden explosion rocked the earth back, far down the grassy runway. The horse, already skittish, danced sideways a few steps, threw up its head to avoid the piercing light, then galloped away. The *patrón* swore savagely and started toward her.

"Get down!" Sarah shouted. "Get down, or I'll…"

She wasn't sure what she'd do. She didn't have to make the decision, however. The *patrón* was only a few yards away when a figure launched itself from behind her and took him down in a flying tackle. Sarah sobbed in relief as Jack's fist slammed into the man's face. Before she could say a word, he reached behind her, grabbed a handful of her skirts and yanked her down. Sarah fell beside him just as a brilliant red flare soared into the sky, marking their place.

Red, she thought dazedly, her face pressed to the earth. As red as the quetzal's breast, stained by the blood of the dying Mayan chief.

It seemed to Sarah as though the red flare must have been a signal. The noise all around her suddenly intensified a thousandfold. A sudden whizzing sound split the night overhead. Rockets were launched from the helicopter, leaving bright trails as they arced overhead. Small explosions detonated all around the cluster of buildings. The hiss of escaping gas was added to the shouts and gunfire exploding all around.

Her ear pressed to the earth, Sarah felt the reverberations of footsteps thudding toward them. Her fingers tightened around the little pistol.

"Jaguar! Have you got her?"

Sarah assimilated the sound of the woman's voice and the name she used for Jack in the same second. She twisted her head and collected a confused picture of a tall, long-legged woman in black, with paint smeared across her face and a lethal-looking weapon in her hands. Incredibly, she was grinning at Sarah.

"I've got her," Jack replied, scrambling to his feet. "What about the kids?"

"They're already in the chopper. The strobe guided us right to them."

The tight, choking tension that had gripped Jake by the throat eased enough for him to swallow. He reached down and hauled Sarah to her feet. Her knees shook so badly that she sagged in his hold and would have crumpled to the ground.

Jake swore, then bent and scooped her over his shoulder. He wrapped one arm around her legs, keeping his other hand free for the weapon he snatched up from the ground.

"Take care of this guy. I'll put Sarah in the chopper, then join you. We've got work to do."

He raced to the helicopter, bent low, protecting Sarah's body with his own. When he reached the side hatch, he tossed her inside. She scrambled to her knees, hampered by her skirts and the three year old who launched himself at her and wrapped both arms around her neck.

"Jack!"

"Stay here! Don't try any more of your damned cowboy tactics. If you move, if you so much as stick your hand out the door, I swear I'll—"

A rattle of gunfire nearby cut him off. He whirled and ran to Maggie's side.

It was over in minutes.

The gas canisters the assault helicopter had fired into the compound soon stilled all but a weak resistance. A burst of fire from the 50 mm cannons bristling from its nose shredded most of the tail on the smuggler's aircraft and halted its desperate attempt to take off. The combined force of elite Cartozan and U.S. rangers moved through the compound, subduing the dazed, coughing defenders and collecting an arsenal of weapons that would have supplied a small army.

"So, Chameleon, I will leave you now."

Maggie turned at the sound of Colonel Esteban's voice. "Let me guess," she said, grinning. "You've had a chat with one of the prisoners and managed to discover the exact coordinates of the processing plant nearby."

His black mustache lifted. "I have. The rest of my force will arrive within moments. You may see the explosion from here when the chemicals go up."

"I'd give anything to go with you!"

He grinned. "So come."

Maggie shoved a hand through her hair. She was tempted.

Lord, she was tempted. The thought of facing Adam held her back. She was going to have enough difficulty explaining to him how her simple extraction mission had expanded so dramatically.

"I'd better not," she said ruefully. "I'll stay here and help clean up."

He stepped forward and curled a finger under her chin. Maggie swallowed—hard!—at the impact of his stunning masculinity at such close quarters.

His thumb brushed her lips. "Perhaps we will work together again sometime, my Chameleon."

"Perhaps we will," she answered, more than a little breathless.

His thumb traced her lips once more, and then he was gone. Maggie watched him climb aboard a Cartozan helicopter. Stifling a small sigh, she went to back to work.

The prisoners—including Jake's middleman, a coldly furious *patrón*, and a superficially wounded Che—were herded aboard waiting choppers.

Gleeful at the rich haul, Maggie greeted Jake with a sweep of one hand. "Do you believe this?"

Fully expecting Jake's usual quiet words of praise after a successful mission, Maggie gaped when he stalked past her toward the open hatch of the helo.

"Jaguar! Wait, what—?"

He reached inside, grabbed a fistful of black skirt and hauled the pseudosister out the open side hatch. She tumbled down into his arms, apparently not at all averse to his rough treatment. The three children scrambled out after her, followed by a heavyset woman.

Maggie watched in astonishment as Sarah Chandler wrapped her hands around Jake's neck and smiled up at him. Her eyes were luminous in the glare of the searchlights, and shining with an emotion that sent a spear of envy through Maggie's heart. She dismissed it immediately. If anyone deserved to win a look like that from a woman, it was Jake. Self-contained, quiet, controlled Jake. A man who had put his duty and his dedication to OMEGA ahead of his own life for so many years.

It occurred to Maggie that she wouldn't have thought a woman with Sarah Chandler's background would tumble into love with someone like Jake. But there wasn't any doubt from the expression on her face that that was exactly what she'd done. Of course, what Maggie had seen tonight made her realize that the senator's daughter was one heck of a lot tougher than her fragile, delicate appearance suggested.

Jake didn't seem to be appeased by the glowing look in Sarah's remarkable eyes. His dark brows were drawn into a slash, and he glared down at her.

"If you ever—*ever*—do anything as harebrained and idiotic as that again, I swear I'll…I'll…"

Maggie, the three children and assorted strike team members all waited with interest to hear what exactly he would do.

So did Sarah. When he appeared unable to articulate his precise intentions, she laughed up at him.

"What you need to do, Mr. Gringo-Creighton-Jack-Jaguar, is consider your options. You can stand here and sputter at me. You can put me down. Or you can kiss me."

Jake gave a strangled groan and bent his dark head.

Maggie folded her arms across her chest and rocked back on her heels, thoroughly fascinated by this new, previously hidden facet of Jaguar's personality. She'd worked with him for two years, seen him operate in every conceivable situation. Except this one. Evidently he was as thorough and as skilled in his lovemaking as he was in everything else, she thought in amusement, wondering when either of them was going to come up for air.

The little girl beside Maggie watched in smug complacency, a strange-looking doll tucked under her chin.

"Sarita is not the *religiosa,* you understand," she explained earnestly. "She just wears the robes. She and Señor Creighton are going to be married. By a padre. A *real* padre."

"I have to make the pee-pee," the smallest child announced.

The helicopter ride back to Cartoza City was considerably less hair-raising than the one that had brought Maggie out. She held the squirming little three year old in her lap. Once assured that they weren't going to die, he squealed in delight every time the aircraft banked, and bounced on her thighs. Maggie noted with some interest that although the little girl clung to Jake like a limpet, he managed to hang on to Sarah's hand, as well.

One of Colonel Esteban's aides met them at the military airstrip outside the city. He came screeching up in a Jeep loaded with an assortment of supplies and a dapper little man in a neat, dark suit and discreet red tie. Maggie jumped out, waiting while Jake unloaded the children. She smiled as the precise, prissy little man wiped a handkerchief across his damp, balding forehead, folded it in neat squares, then tucked it into his breast pocket, leaving an exact half inch showing.

When Jake lifted Sarah out of the chopper, he stepped forward.

"I can't tell you how relieved I am to see you safe, Miss Chandler."

Sarah swung around, her mouth dropping in surprise. "What on earth are you doing here?"

The man minced forward. There was no other word to describe it, Maggie decided. He definitely minced.

"I came at your father's behest, of course." He folded his lips in a thin, prim smile. "I was prepared to go into the jungle to search for you, but these gentlemen assured me their colonel would bring you back safely. In fact, they forcibly restrained me." His nose wrinkled. "In a rather disgusting cell."

Sarah stepped forward to lay a hand on the man's shoulder. "Thank you for coming for me, Creighton."

Jake gave a strangled choke.

Sarah ignored him and smiled down at the balding little

man. "I know from past experience that you would've whisked me out from under those guerrilla's noses with the same efficiency you use when you extract my father from the political messes he's forever creating."

He preened under her generous and quite sincere praise.

Maggie had to admire Sarah Chandler's style. She was good. Damn good. She exuded an aura of charm and elegance, despite the ragged black robe that hung shapelessly around her and her limp, straggling hair. Maggie hid a grin. Jake was *not* going to know what hit him when Miss Chandler got back to Washington and was once more in her own element.

Then again, she thought as Jake stepped forward and slid a proprietary arm around Sarah's waist, maybe he already had a pretty good idea.

"A jet is waiting for you," the aide informed them, then waved toward the Jeep. "My colonel told me you may wish some fresh clothing and food for the journey. He also sent some gifts for you. And something for the one called Chameleon."

He reached into the back seat and pulled out a cardboard box. Maggie took it with a smile of thanks, then jumped when the box moved in her hands.

The aide turned to address Sarah. "We have a padre standing by at headquarters to take the children. He will see they are cared for until they find homes. The colonel said to tell you he himself will ensure that the woman finds a place to live and good employment."

Sarah nodded numbly. She turned, her throat closing at the sight of Teresa standing beside Jack, the root doll dangling from one hand. Eduard, still, silent, brave Eduard, stood at his other side. Eleanora held Ricci in her arms, her face impassive.

"I…" She wet her lips and tried again. "I…"

"We have to go, Miss Chandler," Creighton—the *real* Creighton—said kindly, clearly understanding her distress. "I've arranged for an air-force jet to take us back to Washington. Your father is most anxious to have you home."

"Do not worry, they will be well cared for," the aide assured her.

Sarah ignored both men. Her eyes met Jack's across a few feet of concrete runway. "I can't do it. I can't leave them."

"Miss Chandler!"

She stepped around Creighton. Two steps brought her to within a heartbeat of the tall, lean mercenary.

"I love you, Jack. I love you more than I ever dreamed it was possible to love in any lifetime. But I can't leave them here."

He reached for her. "Sarah, I don't want—"

She grasped his arms, her eyes pleading, needing this settled before she walked into his hold. Once there, she knew, she'd never want to leave.

"I know we haven't had time to talk about the future, our future. You're so self-sufficient, so independent, I don't even know if you want me in your life."

"Just try getting out of it," he growled.

Her fingers dug into his arm. "Can't you make room for all of us? We've been through so much together. We're a family. We...we need each other."

He slid his hands around her waist, drawing her up against him. "Sarah, listen to me. I love you, too. I don't want to leave the children or Eleanora behind, either. I have no *intention* of leaving them behind. And there's plenty of room in my life for all of you."

He tightened his hold. "In fact, I didn't realize how empty it was until I met you and your assorted charges, Sarita Sarah Josepha."

Sarah stared up into his shadowed eyes, wondering how she'd ever thought them cold and hard. At this moment, they gleamed with a warmth and a love that Sarah knew was reflected in her own eyes.

A small hand tugged at her much-tried black robe. "There is a padre here," Teresa reminded them both solemnly. "I heard the man with the Jeep say so. If he is a *real* padre, he can make us a *real* family."

"Yes," Sarah said slowly, "he can." She turned back to Jack, a question in her eyes.

"Miss Chandler, really." Creighton materialized behind Teresa, his mouth pursed disapprovingly. "This is all highly irregular."

"Go get him," Jake ordered quietly, his eyes never leaving Sarah's face.

"I beg your pardon?"

"Go get the padre."

"Now see here, Senator Chandler would hardly approve. I suggest you—"

"Move it, Creighton. Now!"

Sarah bit her lip as the little man huffed off and clambered into the Jeep. It roared away into the darkness, leaving them wrapped in silence for a moment.

"You know," Sarah said softly, "this means you'll finally have to blow your cover. You're going to have a tough enough time convincing the padre to perform a marriage for someone wearing a nun's habit. Somehow I don't think he'll consent to do it if you give your name as Mr. Gringo Jaguar."

His lips twitched. "No, I guess not."

She leaned back in his arms. "Well?"

"Jake?"

"Jake what?"

"Jake MacKenzie."

She shook her head. "Not good enough. I want the whole thing. Exactly as it appears on your birth certificate. The one you had before it was no doubt altered by this agency you work for."

He grinned down at her. "You sure you're ready for this?"

"I'm ready for anything."

"Stonewall Jackson Duncan MacKenzie."

"Oh, my," she said faintly.

Jake nodded, his eyes gleaming with laughter. "My father was a great admirer of men of action."

She answered with a smile of her own. "So am I, my darling. So am I."

Chapter 16

An afternoon breeze rustled the branches of the oak trees that lined the quiet side street just off Massachusetts Avenue. A small family of tourists wandered down the brick sidewalk, obviously lost. The sandy-haired mother consulted her tour guide, then peered at the discreet bronze plaque beside the door of one of the elegant town houses. She shook her head. The father grimaced, hitching his heavy camera bag higher on his shoulder. Taking one of the towheaded youngsters by the hand, he turned around and headed back toward the main avenue. The mother and the two other protesting children followed.

Maggie watched from the town house's second-story window as the family trudged past. The children looked cranky and bored, the father exasperated and the mother tired. Right now she would have exchanged places with any one of them.

"The special envoy will see you now."

She swiveled around and returned Elizabeth's smile. Jake rose from one of the high wing-backed chairs placed on either side of an exquisite and extremely rare Queen Anne table.

Maggie, no expert in antiques, knew it was Queen Anne because the knowledgeable, gray-haired Elizabeth had told her so. She could discern for herself the beauty in the rectangular thumb-molded marble top and delicately carved walnut legs.

"I've cleared his calendar for the next two hours," Elizabeth said, giving Jake and Maggie a kind, grandmotherly look. "The security folks downstairs have been alerted to seal this floor until I signal."

"Two hours, huh?" Maggie shoved a hand through the neat, shining mass of her chestnut hair.

Elizabeth nodded sympathetically. "He requested it."

Maggie threw Jake a quick, wry glance. "Why do I suddenly wish I had stayed in Cartoza for an extended vacation?"

He laughed and opened the door that led to Adam's inner office. "Come on, it can't be too bad. We survived the postmission debrief last night."

"You know he never lets loose in front of the other team members. In fact," Maggie added gloomily, "he never lets loose at all."

She preceded Jake down the short corridor between the inner and outer doors, paying no attention to the lights that pulsed discreetly as she passed. Had they not recognized her, any one of those sensors could have activated a lethal variety of devices that the security people euphemistically, if accurately, termed "stoppers." Although the second floor was open to the public who came to see the special envoy, the security systems made sure that the public was well screened.

As always, the sight of Adam upped Maggie's awareness quotient by several degrees. She frowned, wondering why. While Jake accepted Adam's offer of coffee and poured himself a cup, Maggie studied her boss.

He certainly looked distinguished enough in his expertly tailored navy suit and white shirt, but he wasn't as handsome as Colonel Luis Esteban. Or rather he was handsome in a different way. Where Esteban's classic male-model perfection could stop a woman in her tracks at fifty yards, Adam Ridgeway's attraction stemmed not so much from his lean, dark looks as from his aura of cool, unshakable authority. He was a man in charge. Of himself and of the agents he directed.

Maggie settled comfortably in her chair, knowing that she had a darned good chance of shaking him out of his customary control in the next two hours.

Adam sat on the edge of his mahogany desk, one knee bent as he scanned the papers in a plain manila folder. Shutting the folder, he laid it aside.

"All right, Jake. Let's start with you. I've reread the summaries of the debrief you gave us last night, but there are some key points I'd like cleared up."

Maggie steepled her fingers while Jake and Adam worked through his phase of the operation, from the initial botched drop to the takedown of the white-faced, stuttering businessman who had just happened to be delivering a shipment of stolen U.S. arms to a Cartozan drug lord. She caught Adam's brief smile as Jake recounted the "equipment failure" that had led to his periods of noncommunication. Adam nodded once or twice, listening intently while Jake answered each question in precise technical terms.

Maggie's admiration for her fellow agent, already profound, deepened as he unemotionally detailed his own decisions during the operation—including the very emotional one to step over that invisible line separating an operative from those he dealt with in the field. Her admiration for Sarah Chandler also increased with every passing moment.

Maggie wasn't fooled by the flat, expressionless tone Jake used when he described Sarah's actions during the days they'd been together. Maggie had worked with him long enough to hear what he tried so hard to suppress. Besides, she'd been part of the appreciative audience that witnessed that spectacular kiss beside the helicopter. A tiny thread of envy wiggled through her veins once more. Someday, she thought, she just might find what Jake seemed to have found with Sarah Chandler.

"Maggie?"

Maggie blinked, surprised to realize that Jake had finished and both men were looking at her expectantly.

Adam listened without interrupting while she ran through her part of the operation. When she finished, he stared at her thoughtfully for a moment.

"I think you may have left out one or two details."

"If I did, they're irrelevant," Maggie stated calmly.

"Perhaps to you, but I'd like just a bit more information."

"What is it you need to know?" Maggie was every bit as cool and professional as Adam when it came to her job.

He reached behind him and lifted the manila folder. Flipping it open, he examined the top document. "Could you explain this interagency memo the State Department forwarded? It requests that we reimburse them for payment, made through diplomatic channels, for a black lace garter belt and, ah, two-inch pink-and-orange spiked heels. Among other things. The bill comes to three hundred dollars."

"Three hundred dollars!" Maggie screeched. "Surely those dunderheaded bureaucrats didn't pay that. Don't they know they're supposed to haggle? The shopkeepers probably weren't expecting a tenth of that."

"Yes, well, it appears the United States government doesn't haggle when presented with a bill through diplomatic channels."

"Well it had better learn how, if I'm going to be operating in the field. I appropriated those clothes as part of the disguise that got me into the Café El Caribe. Where," she added pointedly, "I contacted Colonel Esteban."

"Ah, yes. Luis."

"Do you know him?"

"We've met," Adam said noncommittally. He pulled out another document. "This is an official intergovernmental communiqué. On the advice of his chief of security, the president of Cartoza has requested that a certain agent, code name Chameleon, be detailed to a special inter-American task force he's forming. Our president has asked for my recommendation as to whether you can be spared. For an indefinite period of time.''

Maggie felt her breath catch somewhere in midchest. She knew that Adam would support the request if she wanted it. Did she want it? She met Adam's eyes, telegraphing a silent message.

He slipped the document into the folder. ''I can't spare you.''

Maggie sagged in relief, only to discover she'd relaxed too soon.

Adam pulled yet another document out of the damned folder, this one a faxed memo of some kind.

''Customs is rather upset with us. It seems one of their new, rather inexperienced agents tried to process an international flight that landed at Andrews Air Force Base last night. When he attempted to confiscate a certain…'' Adam referred to the fax. ''When he tried to confiscate a certain *agamidae iguanid*, an agent assigned to this organization told him in rather forceful terms to back off.''

''It…it was a gift,'' Maggie explained, biting down on her lower lip.

Adam's brows rose as he referred to the faxed page. ''A rather repulsive-looking one.''

''It's all in the eye of the beholder,'' Maggie responded, grinning. ''Actually, I'm told these lizards make great house pets. They grow to about the size of a small dog, and can snatch a fly off the wall with their tongues from halfway across a room.''

''Just don't ask me to baby-sit the thing for you when you're in the field,'' Jake said, laughing.

Adam wasn't quite as amused.

Maggie pushed her shoulder-length fall of brown hair behind one ear. ''The lizard changes colors, Adam. It can blend into any environment. Like me.''

''I see. That explains it, then.'' He slipped the fax inside the folders. ''What it doesn't explain, however, is why an agent whom I directed to focus on one specific aspect of her

mission managed to expand that mission to include an extraction, a takedown, and a major drug bust.''

Maggie shrugged. ''I couldn't let that tripleheader pass,
Adam.''

''She brought in three for the price of one,'' Jake put in
quietly. ''That's what makes Maggie one of your best,
Chief.''

Adam nodded. ''I'm not disputing—''

The phone on Adam's desk chimed discreetly. He arched
a dark brow, clearly not pleased at the interruption after having left specific instructions. He lifted the receiver.

Saved by the bell, Maggie thought in relief.

''Yes, Mrs. Wells?''

Adam listened for a moment, then nodded. ''Send them
in.''

Maggie and Jake glanced at each other in surprise.

OMEGA's director stood and fastened the monogrammed
button of his navy suit. His blue eyes glinted. ''We'll finish
later, Chameleon. Right now, it seems Jaguar has more pressing business to attend to.''

Maggie and Jake both turned as the inner door opened and
Sarah Chandler swept in, followed by what seemed to be half
the population of Washington D.C. The children filed in after
her, followed by Eleanora in a flowered, lace-trimmed dress.
Maggie's favorite, the chubby little Ricci, squealed a rough
approximation of ''Cammie'' and toddled over to her side.
She scooped him up, duly admiring his purple-and-green Barney shirt. Although she cuddled the boy until he laughingly
protested, Maggie's attention was on the big, bluff senator and
his fussy, oh-so-efficient chief of staff.

Sarah's father had been at the airport to meet them yesterday, weak with relief at getting his daughter back and ready
to whisk her away. Maggie had felt as though she had a front-
row seat at ringside when Sarah calmly explained that she had
a prior engagement. She'd just discovered that her husband
had exactly three hours before he had to report to his headquarters to debrief his mission. If that was all the honeymoon

she was going to get, Sarah didn't intend to waste a minute of it.

And, to judge from the radiant expression on her face today, she hadn't.

If ever there was a woman who looked less like the bedraggled nun Jake had thrown over his shoulder and tossed into the helicopter, it was this one. Poised, confident, stunning in a royal blue suit that hugged her slender figure and deepened her eyes to an astonishing blue-green, she walked over to Jake's side. Her shining silvery-gold hair was swept up in a French twist that revealed the sapphires winking in her earring.

"Sorry to intrude like this, Ridgeway," the senator boomed. "But we have an appointment with the head of Immigration in a half hour. The damn fool insists Sarah and Jake have to sign two reams of documents in front of witnesses and half a dozen notaries. I've got to take a look at this refugee processing procedure," he muttered. "Make a note of that, Creighton."

"Yes, sir."

Maggie hid a grin. She had no doubt that the Immigration Department's procedures were going to be on the Senate agenda next week.

"Actually," Sarah interjected, "we need to make a stop before we go to Immigration."

"What now?" the Senator boomed. "We've hit every department store and toy store between here and Bethesda."

"Yes, but…"

"I have a new doll," Teresa put in with a gap-toothed grin. "But I don't like it as much as the one Señor Creight—" She stopped, a look of confusion crossing her face.

"Señor Jake," Sarah reminded her.

Her lips pursed. "I will call him Papa," she announced, then sent an anxious look at the tall, quiet man.

Jake hunkered down before her, his gray eyes alight with pleasure. "That's fine with me, *niña.*"

The senator's huff broke the silence that gripped the office.

He chomped on his cigar, shifting it from one corner of his mouth to the other. "Well, let's get this caucus underway."

Reluctantly Maggie let Ricci slip out of her arms. He waddled across the room, stopped to show Adam his Barney shirt, then reached up to be lifted into Eleanora's arms.

"Here, let me, *señora*." Creighton stepped forward and lifted the child into his arms. To Maggie's surprise, the chief of staff didn't even blink when Ricci tugged his paisley handkerchief out of his pocket and flapped it experimentally.

"It is not *señora*."

Everyone in the room turned to stare at Eleanora.

Her dark eyes held a shy smile as they met Creighton's. "I am not married."

"Really?" He smoothed his free hand over his shiny forehead. "Well, you must let me show you some of Washington's sights. There's an exhibit of pre-Columbian art at the Smithsonian you may be interested in."

He hefted Ricci higher on his hip, took Eleanora's arm and escorted her out of the office.

Sarah wasn't the only one whose mouth dropped in astonishment.

Senator Chandler gaped.

"I'll be damned," Jake murmured.

Even Adam snorted.

Maggie laughed outright. She just might have to recalculate the final success ratio on this operation. It appeared there might have been more takes than she'd originally thought.

She bid repeated affectionate goodbyes to the children, then sighed as the door closed behind the lively group. Sudden, undisturbed silence descended, wrapping her and Adam in a quiet cocoon.

"Listen to this," she said, indicating the quiet room with a wave of one hand. "I don't think Jake's going to hear anything like this ever again. Think he'll be able to handle it?"

"He'll manage."

Maggie turned at the sound of Adam's cool voice. "Still

torqued about my little adventures in Cartoza? That's 'upset' in oil-field lingo,'' she added helpfully.

His blue eyes rested on her face. "I rarely get upset, and have yet to get torqued."

Someday, Maggie thought. Someday.

"You pulled this one off, Maggie, but I don't want any more tripleheaders. I can't afford to lose any of my agents. Particularly a stubborn, independent one with a built-in sixth sense as accurate as radar—who always manages to get the job done in her own inimitable style."

Maggie offered her version of a salute. It brought a pained expression to Adam's face. "Aye, aye, Chief. I promise, I'll be the perfect model of a docile, well-behaved secret agent."

She strolled to the door, tossing him a cheeky grin over one shoulder. "Until the next time I go in the field."

* * * * *

THE COWBOY
AND THE COSSACK

To Cary and Lori and David,
who've added such richness and
warmth to my life—with all my love!

Prologue

"*There is only you.*"

The low voice, made harsh by the rasp of pain, tore at Alexandra's soul. She leaned over the recumbent figure. "*Don't ask this of me.*"

Gnarled fingers tightened around hers. "*I must.*"

"*No. I'm not the one to lead these people.*"

"*You're of my blood, the only one of my blood I can entrust them to. They are your people, too.*"

"*But I'm not of their world.*"

In the dimness of the shadow-filled tent, she saw bitterness flare in the golden eyes staring up at her. A hawk's eyes, mesmerizing even in the thin, ravaged face. Fierce, proud eyes that proved Alexandra's lineage more surely than the goatskin scrolls used to record the tribe's births. And the deaths. So many deaths.

"*Don't fool yourself,*" the old man went on, his voice grating. "*Although your father, damn his soul, took you away,*" *the steppes are in your heart.''* Hatred long held and little lessened by imminent death gave strength to the clawlike hold on her hand. For a moment, the fierce Cossack chieftain of Alexandra's youth glared up at her.

''Grandfather...'' she whispered.

His burst of emotion faded. He fell back against the woven blanket, gasping. A ripple of frightened murmurs undulated the circle of women surrounding the aged warrior, tearing Alex from her personal, private battle with the old man. She glanced up and saw the stark fear on their faces.

He was right, she thought in despair. There was no one else. Certainly no one in this huddle of black-clad widows and young girls. Nor among the crippled old men, as war-scarred and ancient as her grandfather, who sat cross-legged on the far side of the smoldering peat fire. They were so old, these men, and so few. Alex felt a stab of pain for her lost uncles and cousins, men she vaguely remembered from her youth. Bearded, muscled warriors who'd flown across the windswept steppes on their shaggy mounts, at one with their horses. They were gone now. All that remained were these women. A few children. The old men. And her.

''We...we wrested back our land when the Soviet bear fell,'' her grandfather gasped. ''We cannot lose it to the wolves who would devour it now that I...that I...''

A low rattle sounded, deep in his throat. One of the women moaned and buried her face in her hands, rocking back and forth.

''Prom—promise me!'' he gasped, clutching at Alex's hand. His lips curled back in a rictus of effort. ''Promise me you'll hold against—aaah!''

''Grandfather!''

The golden eyes glazed, then rolled back in their sockets. Alex sat back on her heels, ignoring the ache in her fingers from his agonizing hold, unmindful of the fact that she hadn't eaten or slept in two days of hard traveling to reach his side. She wanted to scream at him not to leave her, not to desert these people who needed him so desperately. She wanted to run out of the smothering black tent and fly back to Philadelphia, to her own world and all that was familiar. But she did none of these things. With the stoicism he himself had taught her, Alexandra watched her grandfather die.

Later, she stood alone under the star-studded sky. The distant sound of women keening vied with the ever-present whistle of the wind across the steppes. Low in the distant sky, the aurora borealis shimmered like an ancient dowager's diamond necklace.

Slowly, Alex lifted her hand. Unclenching her fingers, she stared at the two objects her grandfather had passed to her. A silver bridle bit, used by a fourteenth-century Cossack chieftain, the host's most sacred relic of their past. And a small, palm-size black box, a piece of twentieth-century technology that would ensure her people's future—or spell their doom.

Curling her fist around the two objects, she lifted her face to the velvet sky.

Chapter 1

On a quiet side street just off Massachusetts Avenue, in the heart of Washington's embassy district, hazy September sunlight glinted on the tall windows of an elegant Federal-style town house. Casual passersby who took the time to read the discreet bronze plaque beside the front door would learn that the tree-shaded building housed the offices of the president's special envoy. That wouldn't tell them much.

Most Washington insiders believed the special envoy's position was another of those meaningless but important-sounding titles established a few administrations ago to reward some wealthy campaign contributor. Only a handful of senior cabinet officials were aware that the special envoy performed a function other than his well-publicized, if mostly ceremonial, duties.

From a specially shielded high-tech control center on the third floor of the town house, he directed a covert agency. An agency whose initials comprised the last letter of the Greek alphabet, OMEGA. An agency that, as its name implied, was activated as a last resort—when other, more established organizations such as the CIA, the FBI, the State Department or the military couldn't respond for legal or political reasons.

OMEGA's director alone had the authority to send its agents into the field. He was about to do so now.

"Karistan?"

Perched on one corner of a mahogany conference table, Special Agent Maggie Sinclair swung a burgundy suede boot back and forth. Brows several shades darker than her glossy, shoulder-length brown hair drew together in a puzzled frown. She threw a questioning glance at the other agent who'd been called in with her.

Sprawled with his usual loose-limbed ease in a wingback chair, Nate Sloan shrugged. "Never heard of the place, unless it's where those fancy rugs come from. You know, the thick, fuzzy kind you can't even walk across without getting your spurs all tangled up in." His hazel eyes gleamed behind a screen of sun-tipped lashes. "That happened to Wily Willie once, with the most embarrassin' results."

Maggie swallowed the impulse to ask just what those results were. No one at OMEGA had ever met Wily Willie Sloan, but Nate's irreverent tales about the man who'd raised him had made the old reprobate a living legend.

She'd have to get the details of this particular incident later, though. The call summoning her and Nate to the director's office had contained a secret code word that signaled the highest national urgency. She turned her attention back to the dark-haired man seated behind a massive mahogany desk.

"Karistan is a new nation," Adam Ridgeway informed them in the cool, precise voice, which carried only a trace of his Boston origins. "Less than two months old, as a matter of fact, although its people have been struggling to regain their independence for centuries."

He pressed a hidden button, and the wood panels behind his desk slid apart noiselessly to reveal a floor to ceiling opaque screen. Within seconds, a detailed global map painted across the screen, its land masses and seas depicted in vivid, breathtaking colors. Several more clicks of the button reduced the area depicted to the juncture of Europe and Russia. Adam nodded toward a tiny, irregular shape outlined in brilliant orange.

"That's Karistan. I'm not surprised you haven't heard of it. Neither the State Department nor the media took any special note when it emerged as a separate entity a few months ago. Part of the country is barren, mountainous terrain, the rest is high, desolate steppe. It's sparsely populated by a nomadic people, has no industry other than cattle, and possesses no natural resources of any value."

"It has something we want, though," Maggie commented shrewdly.

"We think it does," Adam admitted. "The president is hoping it does."

She leaned forward, tucking a thick fall of hair behind one ear. The tingling excitement that always gripped her at the start of a mission began to fizz in her veins. Adam's next words upped that fizz factor considerably.

"The borders of the new nation run right through a missile field."

"Missile?" Maggie asked, frowning. "Like in nukes?"

Adam nodded. "SS-18s, to be exact."

Nate Sloan's slow drawl broke the ensuing silence.

"Best I recall, the Soviets scheduled the SS-18s for dismantling under the Strategic Arms Reduction Treaty. They're pretty ancient."

"Ancient and unstable," Adam confirmed. "Which is why the Soviets offered them up so readily under the treaty. Many of the SS-18 missiles have already been dismantled."

"But not the ones in Karistan."

"Not the ones in Karistan. When the U.S.S.R. fell apart, the resulting instability in that area derailed all efforts to implement the treaty. Only recently did things settle down enough for a UN inspection team to visit the site."

Adam paused, then glanced at each of them in turn. "A U.S. scientist was on the team. What he saw worried him enough for him to pay a personal and very secret visit to the Security Council as soon as he got home."

Here it comes, Maggie thought, her every sense sharpening. She hunched forward, unconsciously digging her nails into the edge of the conference table.

"According to this scientist, the device that cycles the warhead's arming codes is missing."

Nate whistled, low and long.

"Exactly," Adam responded, his voice even. "Whoever holds this decoder can arm the warheads. Supposedly, the missiles can't be launched without central verification, but with the former Soviet missile command in shambles, no one knows for sure."

For a few moments, a strange silence snaked through the director's office, like a finger of damp fog creeping and curling its way across the room. Maggie felt goose bumps prickle along her arms. It was as though some insidious presence from the fifties had drifted in—a nebulous ghost of the doomsday era, when the massive buildup of nuclear weapons had dominated international politics and school children had practiced crouching under their desks during nuclear-survival drills. She swallowed, recalling how she'd recently chuckled her way through a replay of the old movie *Dr. Strangelove,* starring Peter Sellers. She didn't find it quite so amusing now.

Crossing her arms, Maggie rubbed her hands up and down her silky sleeves. "So the agent you're sending into the field is supposed to find this missing device? This decoder?"

"As quickly as possible. Intelligence believes it's in the possession of either the Karistanis or their neighbors in Balminsk. The two peoples have been feuding for centuries. They're currently holding to a shaky cease-fire, but it could shatter at any moment. There's no telling what might happen if either side felt threatened by the other."

"Great," Maggie muttered, her gaze drawn to the postage-stamp-size nation outlined in orange.

"Which is why OMEGA's going in. Immediately."

Her attention snapped back to the director. Since both she

and Nate had been called in, Maggie knew one of them would man the control center at the headquarters while the other was in the field. Although the controller's position was vital during an operation, she, like the dozen or so other handpicked OMEGA agents, far preferred being in the middle of the action.

Nibbling on her lower lip, she rapidly assessed her strengths and weaknesses for this particular mission. On the minus side, her technical knowledge of nuclear missiles was limited to the fact that they were long and pointy. She'd be the first to admit she didn't know plutonium from Pluto.

But she enjoyed an advantage in the field that none of the other OMEGA agents could lay claim to—an incredible gift for languages. Having traveled with her Oklahoma "tool pusher" father to oil-rich sites all over the world, she could chatter away in any one of four languages before she learned to read or write.

With formal study, that number had grown considerably, and her natural ability had become her profession. Until two years ago, she'd chaired the foreign language department of a small midwestern college. A broken engagement, a growing restlessness and a late-night phone call from a strange little man her father had once helped escape from a Middle Eastern sheikhdom had culminated in her recruitment by OMEGA.

Given Karistan's location, Maggie suspected its dialect was a mixture of Russian, Ukrainian and possibly Romanian. She could communicate at the basic level in any of those languages. With a day of intensive audio-lingual immersion, she could do better than just communicate. Her speech patterns, idioms and intonation would let her pass for a native.

Adam's deep voice interrupted her swift catalog of her skills. "The mission is a bit more complex than just finding the decoder. The old Karistani headman, the one who allowed in the UN team, died a few weeks ago. The president wants us to deliver a gift to the new ruler, something he hopes will cement relations and get the nuclear-reduction efforts back on track."

"What kind of gift?" Nate asked. "Something along the lines of a blank check written on the U.S. Treasury?"

"Not exactly. The Karistanis are descendants of the Cossacks who used to roam the steppes. They're fiercely proud, and stubbornly independent. They fought a bitter war for their country, and now guard it fiercely. The new ruler flatly refused the economic aid package the State Department put together, saying it had too many strings attached. Which it did," Adam added dryly.

He paused, glancing down at the notepad beside his phone. "This time the president is sending something more personal. We're to deliver a horse called Three Bars Red. He's a—"

"Whooo-eee!"

Nate's exultant whoop made Maggie jump.

Adam gave a small smile, as if he'd expected just such a reaction from a man whose background had earned him the OMEGA code name Cowboy. A former air force test pilot with skin weathered to a deep and seemingly permanent bronze by his native Wyoming's sun, Nate had won a rodeo scholarship to UW at seventeen, and still worked a small spread north of Cheyenne when he wasn't in the field for OMEGA.

"Three Bars Red's a short-backed, deep-barreled chestnut who happens to possess some of the greatest genes in American quarter horse history," Nate exclaimed, no trace of a drawl in his voice now. "He's a 'dogger right off the range. Only did fair to middling on the money circuit but darned if he didn't surprise himself and everyone else by siring two triple As and eight Superiors."

As Cowboy rattled off more incomprehensible details about this creature named Three Bars Red, Maggie realized that her extensive repertoire of languages had one or two serious gaps. Somehow, she'd missed acquiring horsese, at least the version Nate was speaking.

"I'm not sure of the exact count," he continued, raking a hand through his short, sun-streaked blond hair, "but I know over two hundred of Ole Red's offspring have won racing and performance Register of Merits.''

Maggie's mouth sagged. "Two hundred?"

"It may be closer to three hundred by now. I haven't read up on him in a while.''

"Three hundred?" she echoed weakly. "This horse has sired three *hundred* offspring?"

"He's produced three hundred *winners*," Nate said with a grin. "And a whole bunch more who haven't placed that high in the money.''

"Which is why the president convinced his owner to part with him in the interests of national defense," Adam interjected, his blue eyes gleaming at Maggie's stunned expression. "Our chief executive is as enthusiastic about the animal as Nate appears to be.''

Cowboy's grin took on a lopsided curve. "Well, hell! If I'd known he was so horse-savvy, I might have voted for the guy. Sending Ole Red to Karistan is one smart move. A quarter horse is the perfect complement to the tough little mounts they have in that part of the world. He'll breed some size and speed into their lines. I hope the new headman appreciates the gift he's getting.''

"I'm sure she does.''

Nate arched a brow. "She?"

"She. The granddaughter of the old headman, and now leader of the tribe, or host, as they call it. Alexandra Jordan. Interestingly enough, she carries dual citizenship. Her mother was Russian, her father a U.S. citizen who—''

This time it was Maggie who gave a startled yelp. "*That* Alexandra Jordan?"

"Do you know her?"

"I know *of* her. She's one of the hottest fashion designers on either side of the Atlantic right now. As a matter of fact, this belt is one of her designs.''

Planting the toe of one of her suede boots in the plush carpet, Maggie performed a graceful pirouette. The movement showed off the exotic combination of tassels, colored yarn and gold-toned bits of metal encircling the waist of her matching calf-length suede skirt.

"These are genuine horsetail," she explained, fingering one of the tassels. "They're Alexandra Jordan's signature. She uses them in most of her designs. Now that I know about her Cossack heritage, I can understand why. Isn't this belt gorgeous? It's the only item I could afford from her fall collection."

The two men exchanged a quick glance. Suave, diplomatic Adam merely smiled, but Nate snorted.

Maggie pursed her lips, debating whether to ignore these two fashion Philistines or set them straight about the Russian-born designer's impact on the international scene.

Nate gave her a placating grin. "Maggie, sweetheart, you can't expect a cowhand to appreciate the subtleties of a fashion statement made by something that rightfully belongs on the back end of a horse. Besides, that little doodad could be dangerous."

At her skeptical look, he raised a palm. "It's true. Wily Willie once got bucked backward off an ornery, stiff-legged buckskin. He took a hunk of the bronc's tail with him when he went flying, then decided to weave it into a hatband. As sort of a trophy, you understand, since he was out of the money on that ride."

Despite herself, Maggie couldn't resist asking. "And?"

"And the other horses got wind of it whenever Willie strolled by. After being kicked halfway across Saturday by a mare in season who, ah…mistook him for an uninvited suitor, Willie was forced to burn that hatband. And his best black Resistol with it."

"I'll try to avoid mares in season when I'm wearing this belt," Maggie promised dryly.

Nate winked at her, then turned his attention to the director again. "So who's going in, Adam?"

"And when?" she added.

"You both are. Immediately. Because of the remoteness of the area and the lack of any organized host-country resources to draw on, you'll back each other up in the field. Nate will deliver the president's gift to the new Karistani ruler, and Maggie...'' Adam's blue eyes rested on her face for a moment. ''You'll go into neighboring Balminsk.''

Maggie was still trying to understand exactly why that brief glance should make her skin tingle when the director rose, tucking the end of his crimson-and-blue-striped Harvard tie into his navy blazer.

''David Jensen's flying in from San Diego to act as controller. He should be here in a couple of hours.''

''Doc?''

Maggie felt a spear of relief that the cool, methodical engineer would be calling the shots at HQ during this operation. His steady head and brilliant analytical capabilities had proved perfect complements to her own gut-level instincts in the past.

''Your mission briefings start immediately, and will run around the clock. An air force transport is en route to pick up Three Bars Red, and will touch down here at 0600 tomorrow to take Nate on board. Maggie, you have an extra day before you join the team.''

''Team?''

''The UN is pulling together another group of experts to continue the inspections. You'll go into Balminsk undercover with them. Experts from the Nuclear Regulatory Agency and the Pentagon are standing by to brief you.''

Maggie swallowed an involuntary groan. She understood the urgency of the mission, and was far too dedicated to protest. But she couldn't help feeling a flicker of regret that she'd be spending her time in the field with a clutch of scientists instead of the brilliant international designer whose work she so admired.

The next ten hours passed in a blur of mission briefings and intense planning sessions.

The initial area familiarization that Maggie and Nate received focused on topography, climate, the turbulent history of the nomadic peoples who inhabited the target area, and the disorder that had resulted from the disintegration of the Soviet political system.

Maggie hunched forward, chin propped in one hand, brown eyes intent on the flashing screen. Her pointed questions sent the briefer digging through his stack of classified documents more than once. Nate sprawled in his leather chair, his hands linked across his stomach, saying little, but Maggie knew he absorbed every word. The only time he stirred was when a head-and-shoulders shot of Karistan's new ruler flashed up on the briefing screen.

"This is a blowup of Alexandra Jordan's latest passport photo," the briefer intoned. "We've computer-imaged the photo to match her coloring, but it doesn't really do her justice."

"Looks damn good to me," Nate murmured.

"They all look good to you," Maggie replied, laughing.

Not taking his eyes from the screen, he slanted her an unrepentant grin. "True."

With his easy smile, rangy body and weathered Marlboroman handsomeness, Nate never lacked for feminine companionship. Despite the very attractive and very determined women who pursued him, however, Cowboy made it a point to keep his relationships light and unencumbered. As he reminded Maggie whenever she teased him about his slipperiness, in his line of business a man had to keep his saddlebags packed and his pistol primed.

Once or twice Maggie had caught herself wondering if his refusal to allow any serious relationship to develop had something to do with the disastrous mission a few years ago that had left a beautiful Irish terrorist dead and Nate with a bullet through his right lung. No one except Adam Ridgeway knew the full details of what had happened that cold, foggy morning in Belfast, but ever since, no woman had seemed to spark more than a passing interest in Cowboy's eyes.

Which made his intense scrutiny of the face on the screen all the more interesting.

Studying Alexandra Jordan's image, Maggie had to admit

that she appeared to be the kind of woman who would prime any man's pistol. Her features were striking, rather than beautiful, dominated by slanting, wide-spaced golden eyes and high cheekbones Maggie would have killed for. A thin, aristocratic nose and a full mouth added even more character. Long hair flowed from a slightly off-center widow's peak and tumbled over her shoulders in a cloud of dark sable.

All that and talent, too, Maggie thought, repressing a sigh. Some things in life just weren't fair.

"Alexandra Danilova Jordan," the briefer intoned, in his clipped, didactic manner. "'Danilova' is a patronymic meaning 'daughter of Daniel,' as I'm sure you're aware. Born twenty-nine years ago in what is now Karistan. Father an economist with World Bank. Mother a student at the Kiev Agricultural Institute when she met Daniel Jordan."

The thin, balding researcher referred to the notes clutched in his hand. Maggie knew he'd had only a few hours to put together this briefing, but if there was any facet of Alexandra Jordan's life or personality that would impact this mission, he would've dug it up. The OMEGA agents didn't refer to him privately as the Mole without cause. Of course, the man's narrow face and long nose might have had something to do with his nickname.

"Ms. Jordan spent a good part of her youth on the steppes, although her father insisted she attend school in the States. Evidently this decision severely strained relations between Daniel Jordan and the old Karistani chieftain, to the point that the headman…"

The Mole frowned and squinted at his notes. "To the point that the headman once threatened to skin his son-in-law alive. Ms. Jordan herself held the chieftain off. With a rifle."

"Well, well…" Nate murmured. "Sounds like a woman after Wily Willie's heart."

When David Jensen arrived a short time later, the pace of the mission preparation intensified even more. With his engineer's passion for detail, Doc helped put together a contingency plan based on the situation in Karistan as it was currently known. True to his reputation within OMEGA as a problem-solver, he swiftly worked up the emergency codes for the operation and defined a series of possible parameters for mission termination.

Around midnight, the chief of the special devices lab arrived with the equipment Maggie and Nate would take to the field. After checking out an assortment of high-tech wizardry, the agents sat through another round of briefings. Just before dawn, the last briefer fed his notes into the shredder and left. Nate packed his personal gear, kept in readiness in the crew room lockers, and had a final consultation with Doc.

The long night of intense concentration showed in Maggie's tired smile as she walked him to the control center's security checkpoint.

"See you on the steppes, Cowboy."

The tanned skin at the corners of Nate's eyes crinkled. "Will I recognize you when I see you?"

"*I* probably won't even recognize me."

Maggie had earned her code name, Chameleon, by her ability to alter her appearance for whatever role the mission required. This skill, combined with her linguistic talents, had enabled her to penetrate areas no other agent could get into— or out of—alive. Still, she couldn't help eyeing Nate's well-worn boots, snug jeans and faded denim jacket with a touch of envy. She doubted her own working uniform would be nearly as comfortable.

"I can just imagine what the field dress unit has come up with for a scientist traveling to a remote, isolated site. Clunky, uncomfortable, and Dull City!"

"Maybe you can talk them into including some of Alexandra Jordan's horsetail jobbies in your kit," Nate replied with a grin. "Just to liven it up a bit."

"Right."

"I'd wear some myself, just to get on the woman's good side, you understand, but the champion stud I'm delivering from the president might mistake me for the competition and try to take me out.''

"I suspect that if you show up in Karistan wearing tassels, Alexandra Jordan will take you out herself.''

"Might be interesting if she tried.'' Nate's grin softened into a smile of genuine affection. "It's going to be wild out there. And dangerous. Be careful, Chameleon.''

"You too, Cowboy.''

Settling a black Denver Broncos ball cap over his blond head, he swung his gear bag over one shoulder and pressed a hand to a concealed wall sensor. After the few seconds it took to process his palm print, the heavy, titanium-shielded oak door hummed open. Fluorescent lights illuminated a flight of stairs that led to the lower floors and a secret, underground exit.

Nate tipped two fingers to the brim of his ball cap. "Be talkin' to you, sweetheart.''

When the door slid shut behind his tall, broad-shouldered form, Maggie brushed off her weariness. Squaring her shoulders, she headed for the room where the field dress experts waited. She had a few ideas of her own about her disguise for this particular mission.

Chapter 2

Nate was driven to Andrews Air Force Base, just outside Washington, D.C. After showing a pass that gave him unescorted entry to the flight line, he walked across the concrete parking apron to the specially outfitted jet transport and met his charge for the first time.

Three Bars Red was everything Nate had expected, and then some. A compact, muscular animal, with a strong neck set on powerful, sloping shoulders, a deep chest and massive rounded hindquarters, he stood about fifteen and a half hands. Liquid brown eyes showed a range-smart intelligence in their depths as they returned Nate's assessing look. After a long moment, the reddish brown chestnut chuffed softly and allowed the agent to approach.

Nate ran a palm down the animal's sleek neck. "Well, old boy, you ready to go meet some of those pretty little Karistani fillies?"

At that particular moment, Ole Red seemed more interested in immediate gratification than in the promise of future delights. He nosed the slight bulge in Nate's shirt pocket, then clomped hairy lips over both the pocket and the pack of chewing gum it contained.

Nate stepped back, grinning. "Like sugar, do you?"

"Like it?" The handler who'd flown in with Red grunted. "He's a guldurned addict. You can't leave a lunch bucket or a jacket around the barns, or he'll be in it, digging for sweets."

Nate took in the innocent expression on Ole Red's face. "Guess I'd better lay in a supply of candy bars before we leave."

"Just make sure you don't set them down within sniffing distance," the man advised, "or you'll have twelve hundred pounds of horseflesh in your lap, trying to get to them."

The aircraft's crew chief good-naturedly offered to procure a supply of candy bars, which were duly stored in the aft cargo hold, while Nate conferred with the trainer on Ole Red's more mundane needs. Just moments after the man deplaned, the pilot announced their imminent departure.

The stallion didn't bat an eyelash when the high-pitched whine of the engines escalated into an ear-splitting roar and the big cargo plane rumbled down the runway. Once they were airborne, Nate made sure his charge was comfortable and had plenty of water. Then he stretched out in a rack of web seats, pulled his ball cap down over his eyes and caught up on missed sleep.

After a late-night stop at Ramstein Air Force Base in Germany to refuel and allow their distinguished passenger some exercise, the crew set the transport down the following noon at a small airport in the Ukraine, about fifty miles from the Karistani border. As had been prearranged, a driver waited with a truck and horse van to transport them to the border.

Two hours later, the truck wheezed to a stop at the entrance to the gorge guarding the western access to the new nation. Nate backed Red out of the trailer, smiling at the stud's easygoing nature. Quarter horses were famed for their calm dispositions, but Red had to be the most laid-back stallion Nate had ever worked with. He stood patiently while the foam stockings strapped to his hocks to prevent injury during travel were

removed, then ambled along at an easy pace to work out the
kinks from the long ride. He was rewarded with an unwrapped
candy bar that Nate allowed him to dig out of a back pocket.
Big yellow teeth crunched once, twice, and the candy was
gone.

Red whickered, either in appreciation of the treat or in demand for more, then suddenly lifted his head. His ears swiveled
to the side, then back to the front, trying to distinguish the
sound that had alerted him. He gave a warning snort just as a
mounted figure rode out of the gorge.

"Your guide comes," the driver informed Nate unnecessarily.

"So I see." Hooking his thumbs in his belt, Nate eyed the
approaching rider.

Slumped low in a wooden saddle, his knees raised high by
shortened stirrups, the Karistani looked as though he'd just ridden out of the previous century. Gray-haired and bushy
bearded, he wore a moth-eaten frock coat that brushed his boot
tops and a tall, black sheepskin cap with a red bag and ragged
tassel hanging down the side. An old-fashioned bandolier
crossed his chest in one direction, the strap of a rifle in the
other.

With his creased leather face and I-don't-give-two-hoots-
what-you-think air, he reminded Nate instantly of Wily Willie.
Of course, Willie wouldn't be caught dead with a gold ring in
his left ear, but then, this scraggly bearded horseman probably
wouldn't strut around in a gaudy silver bolo tie set with a chunk
of turquoise the size of an egg, either.

The newcomer reined to a halt some yards away and crossed
his wrists on the wooden tree that served him as a saddle horn.
His rheumy eyes looked Nate over from ball cap to boot tip.
After several long moments, he rasped something in an unfa-
miliar dialect. The driver tried to answer in Russian, then
Ukranian.

The guide turned his head and spit. Disdaining to reply in
either of those languages, he jerked his beard at Nate. "I have
few English. You, horse, come."

With the ease of long practice, Nate outfitted Ole Red with the Western-style tack that had been shipped with the stud. After strapping his gear bag behind the cantle, he slipped the driver a wad of colorful paper money, mounted, and turned Red toward the gorge.

As they stepped onto the ledge hacked out of the cliff's side, Nate felt a stab of relief that he was riding a seasoned trail horse instead of some high-stepping, nose-in-the-air Thoroughbred. The chestnut kept his head down and picked his way cautiously, allowing his rider a good view of what lay ahead.

The view was spectacular, but not one Nate particularly enjoyed. Except for the narrow ledge of stone that served as a precarious track, the gorge was perfectly perpendicular. Wind whistled along its sheer thousand-foot walls, while far below, silvery water rushed and tumbled over a rocky riverbed.

A gut-wrenching half hour later, they scrambled up the last treacherous grade and emerged onto a high, windswept plain. Rugged mountains spiked the skies behind them, but ahead stretched a vast, rolling sea of fescue and feather grass. The knee-high stalks rippled and bowed in the wind, like football fans doing the wave. Karistan's endless stretch of sky didn't have quite the lucid blue quality of Wyoming's, but it was close enough to make Nate feel instantly at home.

"There," the old man announced, pointing north. "We ride." Slumping even lower over his mount's withers, he flicked it with the short whip dangling from his wrist.

After thirty-eight hours of travel and a half hour of sheer, unrelenting tension on that narrow ledge, Nate was content to amble alongside his uncommunicative host. The wind whistled endlessly across the high plains, with a bite that chilled his skin below the rolled-up sleeves of his denim jacket, but he barely noticed. With every plop of Ole Red's hooves, Nate felt the power of the vast, empty steppes.

Aside from some darting prairie squirrels and a high, circling hawk, they encountered few other living creatures and even fewer signs of human habitation. At one point Nate spied a rusted truck of indeterminate vintage, stripped of all remove-

able parts and lying on its side. Later Red picked his way over
the remains of a railroad track that ended abruptly in the middle
of nowhere.

After an hour or so, they rode up a long, sloping rise and
reined in.

"Karistani cattle," the guide said succinctly, jerking his
beard toward the strung-out herd below, tended by a lone rider.

Nate rested a forearm on the pommel and ran a knowing
eye over the shaggy-coated stock. A cross between Hereford
and an indigenous breed, he guessed, with the lean, muscled
hardiness necessary to survive on the open range.

At that moment, a couple of cows broke from the pack and
skittered north. The lone hand jerked his horse around and took
off in pursuit. Almost immediately, a white-faced red steer
darted out of the herd. This one decided to head south—straight
for the edge of a deep ravine.

The guide grunted at about the same moment the powerful
muscles in Red's shoulders rippled under Nate's thighs. He
glanced down to see the stallion eyeing the runaway steer
intently. Red's ears were pricked forward and his nostrils were
flaring, his inbred herding instincts obviously on full alert.

"So you think we ought to stop that dumb slab of beef
before it runs right into the ravine?" Nate gave the stallion's
dusty neck a pat. "Me too, fella."

He unhooked the rope attached to the saddle and worked out
a small loop. "I haven't done this in a while, but what the hell,
let's go get that critter."

Bred originally for quick starts and blinding speed over a
quarter-mile track, a quarter horse can leap from a stand into
a gallop at the kick of a spur. True to his breeding, Red lunged
forward at the touch of his rider's heels, stretched out low, and
charged down the slope.

Nate ignored the guide's startled shout, focusing all his concentration on the animal running hell-bent for disaster.

Ole Red closed the distance none too soon. The ravine
loomed only fifty yards ahead when he raced up behind the
now galloping steer. Nate circled his right arm in the air, his

wrist rotating, then swept it forward. The rope dropped over the right horn and undulated wildly a few precious seconds before settling over the left.

Red held his position just behind the charging steer as Nate leaned half out of the saddle. With a twist of his wrist, he slipped the line down the animal's side and under its belly. Then he reined Red to the right, and the horse took off.

When he hit the end of the line, Three Bars Red showed his stuff. He never flinched, never skittered off course. His massive hindquarters bunching, he leaned into the breast harness with every ounce of power he possessed. At the other end of the rope, the cow's momentum dragged its head down toward its belly. In the blink of an eye, a half ton of beef somersaulted through the air and slammed into the earth.

Fierce satisfaction surged through Nate. It was a neat takedown, one of the best he'd ever made, and far safer for the charging animal than simply roping it and risking a broken neck when it was jerked to a halt.

He dismounted and moved toward the downed steer, planning to signal Red forward and loosen the tension on the rope when it stopped its wild thrashing. Intent on the indignant, bawling animal, he paid no attention to the thunder of hooves behind him.

But there was no way he could ignore the sharp, painful jab of a rifle barrel between his shoulder blades.

"Nyet!"

The single explosive syllable was followed by a low, deadly command that sliced through the steer's bellows. Although he didn't understand the dialect, Nate had no difficulty interpreting the gist of the woman's words.

He raised his arms and turned slowly.

Squinting against the sun's glare, he found the business end of a British Enfield bolt-action rifle pointed right at his throat— and the golden eyes that had so fascinated him during his mission briefings glittering with fury.

* * *

On the screen, Alexandra Jordan had stirred Nate's interest. In the flesh, she rocked him right back on his heels.

Narrowing his eyes, he tried to decide why. An impartial observer might have said she was a tad on the skinny side. Her slender body certainly lacked the comfortable curves Nate usually enjoyed snuggling up against.

But long sable hair, so rich and dark it appeared almost black, whipped against creamy skin tinted to a soft gold by the wind and the sun. Thick lashes framed tawny eyes that reminded Nate forcibly of the mountain cats he'd hunted in his youth. In high leather boots, baggy trousers and a loose white smock belted at the waist, Alexandra Jordan looked as wild and untamed as the steppes themselves.

Wild and untamed and downright inhospitable. The rifle didn't waver as she rapped out a staccato string of phrases.

"Sorry, ma'am," Nate drawled, "I don't par-lay the language."

Her remarkable eyes narrowed to gleaming slits and raked him from head to foot. "You're the American! The one I sent Dimitri to meet!"

Nate lowered his hands and hooked his thumbs on his belt. "That's me, the American."

"You fool! You damned idiot!"

With a smooth, coordinated movement that told Nate she'd done it a few times before, she slid the rifle into a stitch-decorated, tasseled case.

"Don't you know better than to come charging down out of nowhere like that? I thought you were raiding the herd. I was about to put a bullet through you."

"You were about to try," he said genially.

The laconic response made her mouth tighten. "Be careful," she warned. "You're very close to learning how to dance, Cossack-style. If this steer has been lamed, you might yet!"

She swung out of the saddle and stalked toward the downed bovine. Pulling a lethal-looking knife from a sheath inside her boot, she sawed through the taut rope tethering it to Red. The animal scrambled to its feet, gave an indignant bellow, then took off.

"Hey!"

Nate jumped back just as it dashed by, its horns scraping the air inches from his stomach. His jaw squared, he turned back to face the woman.

"Look, lady, you might at least show a little appreciation for the fact that I kept that hunk of untenderized meat from running headfirst into that ravine."

"That ravine is where it's *supposed* to go," she informed him, scorn dripping from every word. "There's water at the bottom."

Nate glanced sideways, just in time to catch the irritated flick of a tail as the shaggy-haired beast stepped into what looked like thin air. Instead of plunging into oblivion, however, he stomped down a steep, hidden incline and disappeared, pound by angry pound. Almost immediately, Nate heard the slow rumble of hooves as the rest of the herd moved to follow.

"Well, I'll be—" He broke off, a rueful grin tugging at his lips.

One dark eyebrow notched upward in a sarcastic query. "Yes?"

Still grinning, Nate tipped a finger to the brim of his ball cap. "Nate Sloan, at your service. Out of Wolf Creek, Wyoming. I run a few head there myself, when I'm not delivering stock for the president of the United States."

All of which was true, and would be verified by even the most diligent inquiry into his background. What wouldn't be verified was any link between Nate Sloan, former AF test pilot turned small-time rancher, and OMEGA.

She glanced over his shoulder at Three Bars Red. "And that, I take it, is the horse I was told about."

"Not just the *horse*," Nate told her, offended on Ole Red's behalf by her slighting tone. "The sire of champions."

He turned and whistled between his teeth. Red ambled forward and plopped his head lazily on Nate's denim-covered shoulder.

As Alexandra eyed the dusty face, with its white blaze and its wiry gray whiskers sprouting from the velvet muzzle, the ghost of a smile softened her face, easing the lines on either side of her mouth.

"This is the sire of champions?"

"World-class," Nate assured her. He rubbed his knuckles along Red's smooth, satiny cheek, while his senses absorbed the impact of that almost-smile. "I've got his papers in my gear bag, but you'll see the real evidence for yourself come spring."

The hint of softness around her mouth disappeared so fast it might never have been. "I may see the evidence," she replied stiffly, "*if* I decide to accept this gift."

Nate's knuckles slowed. "Why wouldn't you accept him?"

Her chin angled. "The people of this area have an old saying, Mr. Sloan. 'When you take a glass of vodka from a stranger, you must offer two in return.' I've made it clear that I'm not prepared to offer anything, to anyone, at this point."

Well, that settled the question of whether Alexandra Jordan might hand over the decoder if asked quietly through diplomatic channels...assuming she had it in her possession, that was.

Tipping the ball cap to the back of his head, Nate leaned against the chestnut's shoulder.

"There aren't any strings attached to this gift," he told her evenly, "except the one you just hacked up with that Texas-size toothpick of yours."

"I'm not a fool, Mr. Sloan. I've learned the hard way that you don't get something for nothing in this world, or any other. Karistan is in too precarious a position right now to—" She broke off at the sound of approaching hooves.

When the guide drew up alongside, she held a brief exchange in the flowing, incomprehensible Karistani dialect. After a few moments, Alexandra gave a small shrug. *"Da, Dimitri."*

She turned back to Nate, her eyes cool. "Dimitri Kirov, my grandfather's lieutenant and now mine, reminds me that it is not the way of the steppes to keep travelers standing in the wind, offering neither food nor shelter.''

If he hadn't been briefed on Alexandra Jordan's cultural diversity, her formal, almost stilted phrasing might have struck Nate as odd, coming from a woman who'd graduated from Temple University's school of design and maintained a condo in Philadelphia when she wasn't holed up in her Manhattan studio. Here on the steppes, Alexandra's Karistani heritage obviously altered both her speech and her attitude toward a fellow American.

"You'll come to our camp and take bread with us," she told him, "until I make up my mind whether to accept this gift."

It was more order than invitation, and a grudging one at that, but it served Nate's purpose.

"Ole Red and I appreciate the generous offer of hospitality, ma'am."

Her golden eyes flashed at the gentle mockery in his voice, but she turned without another word. She headed for her mount, holding herself so rigid she reminded Nate of a skinned-cypress fence pole...until a fresh gust of wind flattened her baggy trousers against her frame.

A bolt of sheer masculine appreciation shot through Cowboy. Damned if the woman didn't have the trimmest, sweetest curving posterior he'd been privileged to observe on any female in a long, long time.

Too bad she didn't have the disposition to go with it, he thought, eyeing that shapely bottom with some regret. He generally made it a point to steer clear of prickly-tempered females. There were enough easy-natured ones to fill his days and occasional nights when he wasn't in the field.

Although... For a fleeting moment, when she eyed Ole Red, Nate had caught a hint of another woman buried under Alexandra Jordan's hard exterior. One who tantalized him with her elusiveness and made him wonder what it would take to coax her out of the shell she'd built around herself.

Shaking his head at his own foolishness, he gathered Red's reins. Although OMEGA agents exercised considerable discretion in the field, Nate was careful not to mix business with pleasure. He'd learned the hard way it could have disastrous results.

As he pulled Red around, he glanced across a few yards of windswept grass to find Dimitri combing two arthritic fingers through his scraggly beard, his cloudy eyes watching Nate intently.

"I stay, cattle. You ride." The aged warrior's chin jerked toward the mounted woman. "With *ataman*."

Ataman. Nate chewed on the word as he rode out. It meant "headman," or so he'd been briefed. Absolute ruler of the host. Although the Karistanis practiced a rough form of democracy based on the old Cossack system of one man, one vote, they left it to their leader's discretion to call for that vote. Thus their "elected" rulers exercised almost unchallenged authority, and had through the centuries, despite the efforts of various czars and dictators to bend them to their will.

Red's longer stride closed the distance easily. As Nate drew alongside the new Karistani leader, he found himself wondering how a woman coped with being the absolute leader of a people descended from the fierce, warlike Cossacks...the legendary raiders who had made travel across the vast plains so hazardous that the Russian czars at last gave up all attempts to subdue them and gradually incorporated them into their ranks. The famed horsemen whose cavalry units had formed the backbone of Catherine the Great's armies. The boisterous warriors who swilled incredible amounts of vodka, performed energetic leg kicks from a low squat, and dazzled visitors and enemies alike with their athletic displays of horsemanship.

Having seen the way Alexandra Jordan handled both the raw-boned gray gelding she rode and that old-fashioned but lethal Enfield rife, Nate didn't make the mistake of underestimating her physical qualifications for her role. But he had more questions than answers about her ability to lead this minuscule country into the twentieth century. Why had she refused all offers of aid? What was causing those worry lines at the corners of her eyes? And where the hell was that decoder?

Nate had the rest of the day and most of tomorrow to find some answers to those questions, before Maggie arrived in the area. He ought to have the situation pretty well scoped by then. Maybe he'd even get lucky and find the decoder right away, saving Maggie at least a part of the long trip.

He slanted the woman beside him another glance.

Then again, maybe he wouldn't.

Alex ignored the man beside her and kept her eyes on the far horizon.

Damn! As if she didn't have enough to worry about without some long-legged, slow-talking *cowboy* from the States charging down out of nowhere, almost scaring the wits out of her with his rodeo stunts! Every time Alex thought about how close she'd come to putting a bullet through him, her heart thudded against her breastbone.

She had to stop jumping at every shadow. Despite the garbled message old Gregor had received a couple days ago over his ancient, wheezing transmitter, there'd been no sign of any raiding party from Balminsk. In two days of hard riding, the patrols she'd led out hadn't found any trace of them. It was just another rumor, another deliberate scare tactic from that wild-eyed bastard to the east.

The old wolf was trying to keep her off-balance, and he was succeeding. He wanted to goad her into some action, some incident that would shatter the shaky cease-fire between Balminsk and Karistan and give the outside world the excuse it was waiting for to intervene. And once the outside powers came in, they would never leave. Karistan's centuries-long battle with the Russians had taught them that.

Even her own country, Alex thought bitterly. Even the U.S. Her hands tightened on the reins as she recalled the conditions the State Department representative had laid out as part of the aid package he presented. If she'd agreed to those conditions, which included immediate dismantling of the missiles on Karistan's border, her tiny country would've lost its only bargaining power in the international arena. It would've become little more than a satellite, totally dependent on the vagaries of U.S. foreign policy to guarantee its future.

The sick feeling that curled in Alex's stomach whenever she thought of those missiles returned. Swallowing, she gripped the reins even tighter to keep her hands from trembling. She still couldn't believe she was responsible for such awesome, destructive power.

Dear God, how had her life changed so dramatically in three short weeks? How had she been transformed overnight from the latest rag queen, as the trade publications had labeled her, to a head of state with absolute powers any dictator might have envied? How was she—?

"This country's a lot like Wyoming," the man beside her commented, his deep voice carrying easily over the rhythmic thud of hooves against soft earth. "It's so big and empty, it makes a man want to rein in and breathe the quiet."

"It's quiet now," Alex replied. But it wouldn't be for long, she thought, if she didn't find a way to walk the tightrope stretching before her.

As if reading her mind, the stranger nodded. "I heard about Karistan's troubles."

"I'm surprised." Alex was careful to keep the bitterness out of her voice. "Most of the press didn't consider my grandfather's struggle for independence front-page material."

His lips curved. "Well, there wasn't much coverage in the *Wolf Creek Gazette,* you understand, but I generally make it a point to do a little scouting before I ride over unfamiliar territory."

Alex frowned, not at all pleased with the way his crooked grin sent a flutter of awareness along her nerve endings. Good Lord, the last thing she needed right now was a distraction, especially one in the form of a broad-shouldered, lean-hipped man! Particularly one with a gleam in his eyes that told her he knew very well his impact on the opposite sex.

She almost groaned aloud, thinking of the problems his presence was going to generate in a camp whose population consisted primarily of ancient, war-scarred veterans, a handful of children, and a clutch of widows and young women. As if she didn't have enough to worry about.

"You want to tell me about it?" His deep voice snagged her attention. "Karistan's struggle for independence, I mean?"

For a crazy moment, Alexandra actually toyed with the idea of opening up, of sharing the staggering burden that was Karistan with someone else. Almost as quickly as the idea arose, she discarded it. The responsibility she carried was hers and hers alone. Even if she'd wanted to, she couldn't risk sharing anything with a man who was delivering a gift that, despite any claim to the contrary, came with obligations she wasn't ready to accept.

"No, Mr. Sloan, I don't care to tell you about it," she replied after a moment. "It's not something you need to be concerned with."

His brown-flecked agate eyes narrowed a bit under the brim of his hat, but he evidently decided not to push the issue.

"Might as well call me Nate," he offered, in that slow, deliberate drawl that was beginning to rasp on Alex's taut nerves. "Seeing as how we're going to be sharing a campfire for a while."

She gave a curt nod and kneed her horse into a loping trot that effectively cut off all conversation.

Drawing in a slow breath, Cowboy tugged his hat lower on his forehead and set Red to the same pace. Alexandra Jordan was one stiff-necked woman.

He suspected he had his work cut out for him if he was going to have anything significant to report to Maggie when she arrived in the area.

Chapter 3

At that moment, Maggie wasn't sure if she was ever going to get to her target area.

She dropped a clunky metal suitcase containing her personal gear and a stack of scientific tomes on the second-floor landing of OMEGA's headquarters and scanned the flickering closed-circuit TV screen overhead. Verifying that the director's outer office was clear, she palmed the sensor.

"Is he in?" she asked the receptionist breathlessly.

Gray-haired Elizabeth Wells glanced up from the Queen Anne-style cabinet she was locking. Her hands stilled, and a look of uncertainty crossed her usually serene features. "Maggie? Is that you?"

Maggie reached up to whip off glasses as round and thick as the bottom of a Coke bottle. Her spontaneous grin slipped into a grimace as her scraped-back hair tugged against her scalp.

"Yes, Elizabeth. Unfortunately."

"Good heavens, dear. I doubt if even your own father would recognize you."

Maggie hitched one hand on a hip in an exaggerated pose. "Amazing what a pair of brogans, a plaid shirt and a plastic pocket pack full of pens can do for a woman's image, isn't it?"

"But...but your face! What did you do to it?"

"A slather of bone white makeup, some gray shadow under my eyes, and a heavy hand with an eyebrow pencil." She waggled thick black brows Groucho Marx would have envied. "Good, huh?"

"Well..." Elizabeth's worried gaze flitted to the dark blemish of the left side of her jaw.

Maggie fingered the kidney-shaped mark, pleased that it had drawn Elizabeth's notice. The unsightly blemish should draw everyone else's attention, as well. Maybe, just maybe, the distraction would give Maggie the half second's edge that sometimes meant the difference between life and death in the field.

"Don't worry," she assured the receptionist. "The guys in Field Dress assured me they didn't use *exactly* the same technique as a tattoo. They have some formula that dissolves the ink under my skin when I get back."

"I hope so, dear," Elizabeth said faintly.

Maggie clumped toward the hallway leading to the director's inner office. "Is the boss in? I need to see him right away."

"You just caught him." The receptionist pressed the hidden electronic signal that alerted Adam Ridgeway to a visit from an OMEGA operative. "He wanted to be sure you were on your way before he left for the ambassador's dinner."

Maggie hurried down the short corridor to the director's inner office, not the least worried that her dramatically altered appearance might trip one of the lethal devices the security folks euphemistically termed "stoppers." The pulsing X-ray and infrared sensors hidden behind the wood-paneled walls didn't rely on anything as unsophisticated as physical identification. Operating at mind-boggling speed, they scanned her body-heat signature, matched it to that in the OMEGA computer, and deactivated the security devices.

Maggie stopped on the threshold to the director's office, searching the dimly lighted room. She caught sight of Adam's lean silhouette in front of the tall, darkening windows, and drew in a sharp breath.

Adam Ridgeway in a business suit or expertly tailored blazer had stopped more than one woman in her tracks on D.C.'s busy streets.

In white tie and tails, he was enough to make Maggie's heart slam sideways against her rib cage and her lungs forget to function.

Damn, she thought as she fought for breath. No man should be allowed to possess such a potent combination of self-assurance and riveting good looks. Not for the first time, she decided that the president couldn't have chosen a more distinguished special envoy than Adam Ridgeway. In his public persona, at least, he epitomized the wealthy, cultured jet-setter dabbling in politics that most of the world believed him to be.

The dozen or so OMEGA agents he directed, however, could attest to the cool, ruthless mind behind the director's impenetrable facade. None of them were privy to the full details of Adam's past activities in service to his country, but they knew enough to trust him with their lives. What was more, he possessed knife-edged instincts, and a legendary discipline during crises.

Only Maggie had been known to shake him out of his rigid control on occasion. She cherished those moments.

Evidently this wasn't one of them. Adam lifted one dark brow in cool, unruffled inquiry. "A last-minute glitch, Chameleon?"

Folding her arms across her plaid-shirted chest, Maggie peered at him over the rims of the thick glasses. "Didn't I disconcert you? Even for a moment?"

After a hesitation so slight she was sure she'd imagined it, his mouth curved in a wry smile. "You disconcert me on a regular and frequent basis."

She would've loved to explore that interesting remark, but a driver was waiting for her downstairs. "Uh, Adam, I have a small problem. The sitter I had lined up for Terence just backed out. Would you keep him while I'm gone?"

"No."

The flat, unequivocal refusal didn't surprise her. "Adam…"

"Save your breath, Maggie. I will not keep that monster from hell. In fact, if he ever crosses my path again, I'll likely strangle him with my bare hands."

She tugged off the glasses. "Oh, for heaven's sakes! What happened last time was as much your fault as his. You shouldn't have left that rare edition on your desk. I told you he likes to eat paper."

"So you did. You failed, however, to mention that he also likes to creep up behind women and poke his head up their skirts."

Maggie concealed a fierce rush of satisfaction at the thought of the dramatic encounter between the scaly, bug-eyed blue-and-orange iguana she'd acquired as a gift from a Central American colonel and Adam's sophisticated sometime companion. By all accounts, Terence had thoroughly shaken the flame-haired congresswoman from Connecticut and sent her rushing from Adam's Georgetown residence. The redhead couldn't know, of course, that the German shepherd-size reptile was as harmless as it was ugly. Nor had Maggie felt the least urge to correct the mistaken impression when she called to apologize.

As much as that incident had secretly delighted Maggie, however, it had drawn her boss's wrath down on her unattractive pet. She tried once again to smooth things over.

"Terence was only feeling playful. He's really—"

"No."

"Please. For me?"

Adam's eyes held hers for a few, fleeting seconds. Maggie

felt her pulse skip once or twice, then jolt into an irregular rhythm.

"I can't," he said at last. "The Swedish ambassador and his wife are staying with me while their official quarters are under repair. Ingrid's a good sport, but I don't think Börg would appreciate your repulsive pet's habit of flicking out his yardlong tongue to plant kisses on unsuspecting victims."

Having been subjected to a number of those startling kisses herself, Maggie conceded defeat.

Adam held himself still as her sigh drifted across the office. Over the years, he'd mastered the art of controlling his emotions. His position required him to weigh risks and make a calculated decision as to whether to put his agents in harm's way. There was little room for personal considerations or emotions in such deadly business.

Yet the distracted look in Maggie's huge brown eyes affected him more than he would admit, even to himself.

"You might try Elizabeth," he suggested after a moment.

"I tried her before I hired the sitter. She still hasn't forgiven Terence for devouring the African water lilies she spent six years cultivating. In fact," Maggie added glumly, "she threatened to shoot him on sight if he ever came within range."

It wasn't an idle threat, Adam knew. The grandmotherly receptionist requalified every year at the expert level on the 9 mm Sig Sauer handgun she kept in her desk drawer. She'd only fired it once other than on the firing range—with lethal results.

Watching Maggie chew the inside of one cheek, Adam refrained from suggesting the obvious solution. She wouldn't appreciate the reminder that lizard meat had a light, tasty succulence when seared over an open fire. Instead, Adam pushed his conscience aside and offered up OMEGA's senior communications technician as a victim.

"Perhaps Joe Sammuels could take care of…it for you. He returned last night from his satellite-communications conference in the U.K."

"He did? Great!" Maggie jammed her glasses back on,

wincing as the handles forced a path through the tight hair at her temples. "Joe owes me, big-time! I kept the twins for a whole week while he and Barb went skiing."

Adam's lips twisted. "He'll repay that debt several times over if he takes in your walking trash compactor."

Behind the thick lenses, Maggie's eyes now sparkled with laughter. "Joe won't mind. He knows how much the twins enjoy taking Terence out for a walk on his leash. They think it's totally rad when everyone freaks out as they stroll by."

"They would."

"I'll go call Joe. I can leave a key to my condo for him with Elizabeth. Thanks, Adam." She started for the door, throwing him a dazzling smile over her shoulder. "See you...whenever."

"Maggie."

The quiet call caught her in midstride. She turned back, lowering her chin to peer at him over the black rims. "Yes?"

"Be careful."

She nodded. "Will do."

A small silence descended between them, rare and strangely intense. Adam broke it with a final instruction.

"Try not to bring home any more exotic gifts from the admirers you seem to collect in the field. Customs just sent the State Department another scathing letter about the unidentified government employee who brought a certain reptile into the country without authorization."

Wisely, Maggie decided to ignore Adam's reference to what had somehow become a heated issue between several high-ranking bureaucrats. Instead, she plucked at the sturdy twill pants bagging her hips and waggled her black eyebrows. "Admirers? In this getup? You've got to be kidding!"

She gave a cheerful wave and was gone.

Adam stood unmoving until the last thump of her boots had faded in the corridor outside his office.

"No," he murmured. "I'm not."

He flicked his tuxedo sleeves down over pristine white cuffs, then patted his breast pocket to make sure it held his onyx pen. The microchip signaling device implanted in the pen's cap emitted no sound, only a slight, intermittent pulse of heat.

Adam never went anywhere without it.

Not when he had agents in the field.

After a quick flight from Washington to Dover Air Force Base in Delaware, Maggie jumped out of the flight-line taxi and lugged her heavy suitcase across the concrete parking apron. The huge silver-skinned stretch C-141 that would transport the UN inspection team crouched on the runway like a mammoth eagle guarding its nest. Its rear doors yawned open to the night.

"Be with you in a minute, ma'am," the loadmaster called from inside the cavernous cargo bay.

Maggie nodded and waited patiently at the side hatch while the harried sergeant directed the placement of the pallets being loaded into the hold. A quick glance at the stenciling on the crates told Maggie that about half contained supplies for the twelve-person UN team, and half were stamped FRAGILE— SCIENTIFIC EQUIPMENT.

Racks of floodlights bathed the plane in a yellow glare and heated the cool September night air. Maggie stood just outside the illuminated area, in the shadow of the wing, content to have a few moments to herself before she met her fellow team members for the first time. Now that she was within minutes of the actual start of her mission, she wanted to savor her tingling sense of anticipation.

The accumulated stress from almost twenty hours of intense mission preparation lay behind her.

The racing adrenaline, mounting tension and cold, wrenching fear that came with every mission waited ahead.

For now, there was only the gathering excitement that arced along her nerves like lightning slicing across a heated summer sky.

She breathed in the cool air, enjoying this interlude of dim, shadowed privacy. In a few minutes, she'd be another person, speak with another voice. For now, though, she—

The attack came with only a split second's warning.

She heard a thud. A startled grunt. The loud rattle of her metal suitcase as it clattered on the concrete.

Maggie whirled, squinting against the floodlights' glare. If the lights hadn't blinded her, she might have had a chance.

Before she could even throw up her hands to shade her eyes, a dark silhouette careened into her.

Maggie and her attacker went down with a crash.

She hit the unyielding concrete with enough force to drive most of the air from her lungs. What little she had left whooshed away when a bony hipbone slammed into her stomach.

An equally bony forehead cracked against hers, adding more black spots to those the blinding lights had produced. Fisting her fingers, Maggie prepared to smash the soft cartilage in the nose hovering just inches above her own.

"Oh, my— Oh, my God! I'm—I'm sorry!"

The horrified exclamation began in something resembling a male bass and ended on a high soprano squeak. Maggie's hand halted in midswing.

Almost instantly, she regretted not taking out the man sprawled across her body. As he tried to push himself up, he inadvertently jammed a knee into a rather sensitive area of her female anatomy.

At her involuntary recoil, he stammered another, even more appalled apology. "Oh! Oh, I'm sorry! I'll just... Let me just..."

He lifted his knee in an attempt to plant it on less intimate ground. He missed, and ground it into Maggie's already aching stomach instead. She stilled his jerky movements with a death grip on his jacket sleeves.

He swallowed noisily as he peered down at her. With the lights glaring from behind his head, Maggie couldn't make out any facial features.

"Are...are you all right?"

"I might be," she said through tight jaws, remembering just in time to clip her words and adopt the slightly nasal tone she'd perfected for this role. "If you'd stop trying to grind my liver into pâté."

"I'm...I'm sorry."

"So you've said. Several times. Look, just lift your knee. Carefully!"

Once freed of his weight, Maggie rolled, catlike, to her feet. Taking a couple of quick breaths to test her aching stomach muscles, she decided she'd live. Barely.

Turning so that the spotlight no longer blinded her, she shoved the glasses dangling from one ear back onto her nose. The black spots faded enough for her to see her attacker's features at last.

The man—no, the boy, she corrected, running a quick searching glance over his anxious face and gangly frame—tugged his zippered jacket down from where it had tangled under his armpits.

"I'm sorry," he repeated miserably. "Your suitcase... I, uh, tripped. I didn't mean to..."

"It's okay," she managed. "I think my digestive system's intact, and I'm getting close to the end of my childbearing years, anyway."

Actually, at thirty-two, she still had plans for several children sometime in the future. She'd only meant to lighten the atmosphere a little, but she saw at once her joke had backfired. The boy's face flamed an even brighter shade of red, and he stammered another string of apologies.

"I'm fine," she interjected, her irritation easing at his obvious mortification. "Really. I was just teasing."

He stared at her doubtfully. "You were?"

"Couldn't you tell?"

"No. No one ever teases me."

Maggie didn't see how this clumsy young man could possibly avoid being the butt of all kinds of jokes. He was all legs and arms, a walking, talking safety hazard. Which made her distinctly nervous on this busy flight line.

"Look, are you supposed to be out here? This is a restricted area."

"I'm...I'm traveling on this plane." He glanced up at the huge silver C-141, frowning. "At least, I think this is the plane. The sergeant who dropped me off here said it was."

Maggie's eyes narrowed, causing a painful tug at her temples. She grimaced, vowing silently to get rid of the tight bun at the back of her neck at the first possible moment, while her mind raced through the descriptions of the various team members she'd been given. None of them correlated with this awkward individual. For a heart-stopping moment, she wondered if her mission had been compromised, if an impostor—other than Maggie herself—was trying to infiltrate the team.

Apparently thinking her grimace had been directed at him, he hastened to reassure her. "Yes, I'm sure this is the right plane. I recognize the crates of equipment being loaded."

"Who *are* you?" she asked, cutting right to the heart of the matter.

"Richard. Richard Worthington."

With the velocity and force of an Oklahoma twister, Maggie's suspicion spiraled. "Richard Worthington?"

He blinked at the sharp challenge in her voice. "Uh, the Second."

The tornado slowed its deadly whirl. Drawing in a deep breath, Maggie studied the young man's worried face. Now that she had some clue to his identity, she thought she detected a faint resemblance to the scientist who would head their team. Not that she could have sworn to it. Even the Mole had been able to produce only sketchy background details and a blurred photo of the brilliant, reclusive physicist. Taken about a year ago, the picture showed a hazy profile almost obliterated by a bushy beard.

"I didn't realize Dr. Worthington had a son," she said slowly. "Or that he was bringing you along on this trip."

"He's not. Er, I'm not. That is, I'm Dr. Worthington."

Right, and she was Wernher von Braun!

Maggie wanted to reject his ridiculous claim instantly, but

the keen mind that had helped her work through some rather improbable situations in the past three years suggested it *could* be possible. This earnest, anxious young man *could* be Dr. Worthington. The Mole had indicated that Worthington had gained international renown at an early age. But this early?

"You don't look like the Dr. Richard Worthington I was told to expect," Maggie challenged, still suspicious.

A bewildered look crossed his face for a moment, then dissolved into a sheepish grin. "Oh, you mean my beard? I just grew it because my mother didn't want—that is, I decided to experiment." Lifting a hand, he rubbed it across his smooth, square chin. "But the silly thing itched too much. I shaved it off for this trip."

Maggie might have questioned his ingenious story if not for two startling details. His reference to his mother caught her attention like a waving flag. The intelligence briefing had disclosed that Dr. Worthington's iron-willed mother guarded the genius she'd given birth to with all the determination of a Valkyrie protecting the gates of Valhalla.

With good reason. At the age of six, her famous child prodigy had been kidnapped and held for ransom. His kidnappers had sent his distracted mother the tip of one small finger as proof of their seriousness. The hand this young man now rubbed across his chin showed a pinkie finger missing a good inch of its tip.

Despite the conclusive evidence, Maggie didn't derive a whole lot of satisfaction from ascertaining that the individual facing her was in fact Dr. Richard Worthington. With a sinking feeling, she realized she was about to take off for the backside of beyond, where she'd proceed to climb down into silos filled with temperamental, possibly unstable, nuclear missiles, alongside a clumsy boy…man…

"Just how old are you?" she asked abruptly.

"Twenty-three."

Twenty-three! Maggie swallowed, hard.

"You're *sure* you're the Dr. Richard Worthington who possesses two doctorates, one in engineering and one in nuclear physics?"

His eyes widened at the hint of desperation in her voice. "Well, actually…"

Wild hope pumped through Maggie's heart.

"Actually, I was just awarded a third. In molecular chemistry. I didn't apply for it," he added, when she gave a small groan. "MIT presented it after I did some research for them in my lab."

"Yes, well…" With a mental shrug, Maggie accepted her fate. "Congratulations."

She'd been in worse situations during her years with OMEGA, she reminded herself. A lot worse. She could handle this one. Pulling her new identity around her like a cloak, she squared her shoulders and held out a hand.

"I'm Megan St. Clare, Dr. Worthington. A last-minute addition to your team."

Maggie had constructed a name and identity for this mission close enough to her own that she could remember them, even under extreme duress. A minor but important point, she'd discovered early in her OMEGA career.

Worthington's fingers folded around hers. "Could you call me Richard? I'm a bit awkward with titles."

Was there anything he wasn't awkward with? "Richard. Right. I believe the UN nuclear facilities chairman faxed you my credentials?"

"Well, yes, he did. Although I must say I was surprised he decided to add a geologist to the team at the last moment."

Maggie could've told him that the chairman had decided—with a little help from the U.S. government—to add a geologist because she'd known she could never pass herself off as an expert on nuclear matters with this group of world-renowned scientists for more than thirty seconds. But she'd absorbed enough knowledge of geological formations from her oil-rigger father to hold her own with anyone who wasn't fully trained in the field.

She started to launch into her carefully rehearsed speech

about the need to assess the soil around the missile site for possible deep-strata permeation of radioactive materials, but Worthington forestalled her with another one of his shy smiles.

"Please don't think I meant to impugn your credentials. This is my first time as part of a UN team...or any other team, for that matter. I'm sure I'll appreciate your input when we arrive on-site."

Maggie stared at him for a long, silent moment. "Your first time?"

A gleam of amusement replaced the uncertainty in his eyes, making him seem more mature. "There weren't all that many physicists clamoring for the job. I'm looking forward to it."

At that particular moment, Maggie couldn't say the same. She stared at him for a long moment, then shrugged. "Well, I suppose we should get this...expedition under way."

She bent to pick up her suitcase, only to knock heads with Worthington as he reached for it at the same moment.

He reached out one hand to steady her and rubbed his forehead with the other. "Oh, no! I'm sorry! Are you hurt, Miss St. Clare? Uh, Dr. St—?"

Maggie snatched her arm out of his grip and blinked away bright-colored stars. "Call ... me ... Megan ... and ... bring... the—"

Just in time, she cut off the colorful, earthy adjective she'd picked up from the rowdy oil riggers she'd grown up with.

"Bring the suitcase," she finished through set jaws.

Stalking to the side hatch, she clambered aboard the cargo plane and forced herself to take a deep, calming breath. Her mission was about to get under way. She couldn't let the fact that she was saddled with a bumbling team leader distract her at this critical point.

She'd just have to turn his inexperience to her own advantage, Maggie decided, buckling herself in beside a gently snoring woman with iron gray hair and a rather startling fuchsia windbreaker folded across her lap. Worthington's clumsiness would center the other team members' attention on him as much as his reputed brilliance. Which would make it easier for her to search for the decoder and slip away when she needed to contact Cowboy.

Maggie glanced down at her digital watch. Calculating the time difference, she estimated that Nate should be arriving at the Karistani camp about now.

Sternly she repressed a fervent wish that she could exchange places with him right now.

Chapter 4

As Nate rode beside Alexandra into the sprawling city of black goathair tents that constituted Karistan's movable capital, he decided that the average age of the male half of the population must hover around sixty. Or higher.

Eyes narrowed, he skimmed the crowd gathering in the camp to greet their leader. It seemed to consist mostly of bent, scarred veterans even more ancient than Dimitri. Only after they'd drawn nearer did Nate see a scattering of children and women among the men.

Most of the women wore ankle-length black robes and dark shawls draped over their heads. A few were in the embroidered blouses and bright, colorful skirts Nate associated with the traditional dress in this part of the world. Whatever their age or dress, however, the women all seemed to greet his arrival with startled surprise and a flurry of whispered comments behind raised hands.

As the riders approached, one of the women stepped out of the crowd and sauntered forward. Although shorter and far more generously endowed than Alexandra, the girl had a dramatic widow's peak and confident air that told Nate the two women had to be related.

Alexandra drew to a halt a few yards from the younger woman and swung out of the saddle. Nate followed suit, hiding his quick stab of amusement as the girl looked him over from head to toe with the thoroughness of a bull rider checking out his draw before he climbed into the chute.

She asked a question that made Alexandra's lips tighten. Flashing the girl a warning look, the older woman indicated Nate with a little nod.

"Out of courtesy to our guest, you must use the English you learned during your year at the university, Katerina. This is Mr. Sloan…"

"Nate," he reminded her lazily.

Alexandra wasn't too pleased with the idea of his getting on a first-name basis with Katerina, if her quick frown was any indication, but she didn't make an issue of it.

"He brings the horse we were told of," she continued, "the one from the president of the United States. He only visits with us for a *short* time."

The well-rounded beauty's brows rose at the unmistakable emphasis. "Do we… Do we…"

She paused, searching what Nate guessed was a limited and long-unused English vocabulary. Triumph sparkled in her dark eyes when she found the words she sought.

"Do we…give him much comfort, my cousin, per-perhaps he will visit longer."

Comfort sounded more like *koom-foot,* and Nate had to struggle a bit with *wheez-it,* but he caught her drift. Seeing as how she tossed in a curving, seductive smile for good measure, he could hardly miss it. His answering grin made Alexandra's sable brows snap into a straight line.

Katerina sashayed forward, ignoring her cousin's frown. "Come, *Amerikanski,* I will—how you say?—take you the camp."

Nate was tempted. Lord, he was tempted. The little baggage had the most inviting eyes and beguiling lips he'd stumbled across in many a day. As accommodating as she appeared to be, he figured it would take him about three minutes, max, to extract whatever she knew of the decoder. Among other things.

Too bad he hadn't yet reached the point of seducing young women to accomplish his mission, he thought with a flicker of regret. Still, he wasn't about to let a potential source like Katerina slip through his fingers entirely.

"That's real friendly of you, miss," he replied, smiling down at her. "Maybe you can, ah, take me the camp later. Right now, I'd better see that Three Bars Red here gets tended to."

Her full lips pursed in a pretty fair imitation of a pout. "The men, they can do this."

"I'm sure they can," Nate replied easily, "but I don't plan to let them. I'm responsible for this animal…until your *ataman* decides if she's going to accept him."

Alexandra's eyes narrowed at his use of her title, but she said nothing. Katerina, on the other hand, didn't bother to hide her displeasure at coming in second to a horse.

"So! Perhaps do I take you the camp later. Perhaps do I not." Tossing her head, she walked off.

Yep, the two women were definitely related, Nate decided.

At her cousin's abrupt departure, Alexandra gestured one of the watching men forward.

"This is Petr Borodín."

The way she pronounced the name, *Pey-tar Bor-o-deen*, with a little drumroll at the end, sounded to Nate like a sort of musical poetry.

"He is a mighty warrior of the steppes who served in two wars," she added.

Nate didn't doubt it for an instant. This bald scarecrow of a man with baggy pouches under his eyes and an empty, pinned-up left sleeve sported three rows of tarnished medals on his thin chest. Among them were the French Croix de Guerre and the World War II medal the U.S. had struck to honor an elite multinational corps of saboteurs. These fearless sappers had destroyed vital enemy supply depots and, incidentally, guided over a hundred downed U.S. airmen to safety.

"Petr will show you where you will stay," Alexandra continued, in the rolling, formal phrases that intrigued Nate so. "And where you may take the horse."

He thought he saw a shadow of a smile in the glance she gave Ole Red, who was watching the proceedings with sleepy-eyed interest. A sudden, inexplicable desire to keep that smile on her face for longer than a tenth of a second curled through Nate.

Surprised by the sensation, he tucked it away for further examination and stood quietly while Alexandra issued quick instructions to this Petr fellow. When she finished, he gave her a nod and gathered Red's reins.

"I've never been in these parts before," he offered as he fell in beside his new guide, testing the man's English and value as a possible information source. "What say we take a ride after I drop off my gear, and you show me the lay of the land?"

"No!"

Alexandra's sharp exclamation halted both men in their tracks. She stepped forward as they swung around, and shot a quick order to the Karistani before facing Nate.

"The steppes can be treacherous, if you don't know them. You mustn't leave this camp, except as I direct."

Nate let his gaze drift over her face. "Guess we'd better talk about that a bit. Much as I wouldn't mind lazing around for a few days, Ole Red here will need exercise."

"You'll stay in camp unless I say otherwise," she snapped. "And even in camp, you will stay with your escort. Our ways are different. You may give offense without knowing it, or…" She circled a hand in the air. "Or go where you're not permitted."

Nate didn't so much as blink, but the pulse in the side of his neck began a slow tattoo. "So you're saying certain parts of the camp are off-limits? You want to be more specific? Just so I don't give offense, you understand."

Her chin lifted at his sarcasm. "To be specific, I suggest you stay away from the women's quarters, and from Katerina."

Now that was hitting just a little below the belt. Nate hadn't exactly invited the girl to swish her skirts at him the way she had. What was more, he fully intended to enter the women's quarters at the first opportunity. At the moment, though, the thought of searching Alexandra's belongings didn't hold nearly as much appeal as the thought of searching Alexandra herself. The unfriendlier the woman got, the more Nate found himself wanting to pierce her hard shell.

"Do you hold all men in such low regard?" he drawled. "Or maybe just me in particular?"

She sent him an icy stare. "That, Mr. Sloan, is none..."

"Nate."

"...of your business. All you need to know is that I'm responsible for what happens in this camp. Everything that happens. For your own safety, I won't have you wandering around unescorted. As long as you're here, you'll respect my wishes in this and in all other matters."

Not quite all, Nate amended silently as she spun on one heel. He had a few wishes of his own to consider. One had to do with a certain decoder. Another, he decided, watching her trim bottom as she walked away, just might have to do with discovering Alexandra Jordan's answer to the second part of his question.

Petr Borodín took his chief's orders to heart and stuck to Nate like cockleburs to a saddle blanket for the rest of the afternoon. After showing the *Amerikanski* to a tent where he could dump his gear, the aged warrior helped unsaddle and curry Red with a skill that belied his lack of one arm. That done, he led the way to the pasturage.

A dozen or so geldings and a shaggy roan that Nate guessed was the band's alpha mare were hobbled in a stretch of prairie at the rear of the camp. Another dozen mares, and several yearlings, grazed around them. Evidently none of the females were in season, since neither Red nor the feisty little stallion tethered some distance away showed much interest in them. They did, however, take immediate exception to each other. For all his gregarious nature and easy disposition, Red recognized the competition when he saw it.

After a prolonged display of flat ears, snaked necks and pawed ground, Nate decided to keep the quarter horse away from the band until Alexandra made up her mind about him. No use letting Red chase off the smaller stallion if he wasn't going to be allowed to claim the mares.

Peter the Great, as Nate christened the veteran—much to his delight when he understood the reference—tethered Red to the side of their tent. Once fed a mixture of prairie grass and the oats Nate had brought along to help him adjust to the change in his diet, the stallion was once again his usual placid self.

Placid, at least, until he got a whiff of the candy bar Nate stuck in his shirt pocket before he scooped a bucket of water from the sluggish stream behind the camp. By the time Red had satisfied his sweet tooth, both man and horse were soaked.

Ducking under the tent flap to change his shirt, Nate surveyed the dim interior. Dust pushed under the sides by the wind drifted on air scented by old boots, musty furs, and a faint, lingering hint of incense. The tent's interior was larger than some of the crew quarters Nate had occupied in the air force, and a good deal cleaner than some of the dives he'd shared while riding the rodeo circuit.

While Nate sat on a low, ingeniously constructed folding cot piled high with rough blankets and a thick, shaggy wolf pelt to strip off his shirt, Peter the Great rummaged through a low chest.

"*Wodka!*" he announced, holding up a bottle half filled with cloudy liquid.

Nate answered the man's gap-toothed grin with one of his own. "Well, now, I don't mind if I do."

A stiff drink would be more than welcome after the chill of his unexpected bath. And, he reasoned, it just might loosen up his appointed guardian enough to allow some serious intelligence-gathering.

Several hours later, Nate leaned back against a high, sheepskin-covered saddle. Smoke from a half-dozen campfires curled into the star-studded sky and competed with the lingering aroma of the beef slathered in garlic that had constituted the main course at the evening meal. In the background, the small portable gas generators that provided the camp with electricity hummed. It was a foreign sound in a night that belonged to flickering fires and a star-filled sky.

Low murmurs and laughter from the men beside Nate told him they were engaged in the age-old pastime of cowboys around the world—sharing exaggerated tales of their prowess in the saddle. Or out of it. He smiled as one mustachioed individual in a yellowed sheepskin hat broke into a deep, raucous belly laugh. Pushing his impatience to the back of his mind, Nate took a cautious sip of vodka.

So he hadn't been able to shake Peter the Great this afternoon, not even for a trip to the communal latrine that served the camp. So Dimitri, when he took over guard duty from his cohort, had shrugged off all but the most casual questions. The afternoon still hadn't been a total loss. In the preceding hours, Nate had memorized the layout of the camp, cataloged in exact detail the Karistani's eclectic collection of weapons, and done an exterior surveillance of the tent Alexandra and the other unattached women slept in.

Nate was turning over in his mind several possible scenarios for gaining access to that tent, some of which involved Alex's cooperation, some of which didn't, when the rustle of heavy skirts stirred the air behind him.

Katerina plopped down beside him, a hand-thrown pottery jug in hand. Nate could tell by the sultry smile on her full lips that she'd decided to forgive him for declining her invitation this afternoon.

"You wish…more *wodka?*"

He glanced down at the tin cup in his hand. It was still full of the throat-searing liquid, which the little minx could see as plain as tar paper. His lips curved as he tipped some of the potent mixture into the dirt and held up his cup.

"Sure."

With a look of pure mischief on her face, Katerina leaned forward to refill his cup. The cloaklike red wrap she'd donned against the night air gaped open, revealing full breasts that spilled just about clear out of her low-necked blouse.

Nate imagined Alex's reaction if she knew her cousin was pressing those generous breasts against his arm right now. He considered the implications of said reaction to his mission. He even reminded himself that Katerina looked to become something of a problem if he didn't rein her in soon. All the while, of course, he enjoyed the view.

Not that he could've avoided it, even if he'd wanted to. Katerina made sure of that. She dipped even lower to set the jug on the ground beside him, and Nate's brow skittered upward.

"Are you…cowboy?" Katerina asked softly.

The hairs on the back of Nate's neck rose. Years of intense survival training and his own iron control kept his muscles from coiling as she leaned even closer.

"Cowboy, like in films I see at university?" she cooed. "Like the men of the steppes?"

Air snuck back into Nate's lungs. "Sort of."

"So do I think." A smug little smile traced her mouth. "You walk, you ride the same. Like all this, you own."

Her sweeping gesture encompassed the vast, rolling prairie, the inky black sky, and the waterfall of stars tumbling out of the heavens. From that gesture, Nate gathered that the men of the steppes swaggered a bit when they walked, and rode as though they and their ponies were alone in the universe. Much like their Wyoming counterparts, he decided with an inner smile.

"Do you have the land, in *Amerika?*"

"A little."

She slid one hand up his arm, then edged it toward his chest. "How much it is, this little?"

Grinning, Nate caught her hand before her fingers slipped inside his denim jacket. "Where I come from, a lady doesn't ask a man the size of his spread. It tends to get him real nervous...or real interested."

Keeping her wrist in a light hold, he rose and pulled her up with him. "Being of the nervous type myself, I'd better walk you back to your campfire."

Clearly, Katerina had no idea what he was talking about, but she didn't seem the least averse to taking a stroll with him. She tucked her hand in his arm and tipped him a look that warned Nate he'd better keep to the well-lighted areas.

"Have you the woman in *Amerika*? The...um...wife?"

On reflection, Nate decided that handling Katerina might just be a bit trickier than he'd anticipated. The girl had the tenacity of a bull terrier and the subtlety of the rodeo clowns who whacked a rampaging bull up side the head to get its attention.

"No, no wife," he answered, then firmly shifted the conversation to what he hoped might eventually lead to little black boxes. "So, what about you? Have you always lived here, on the steppes?"

"Always." The single word held a wealth of emotion. Pride. Bitterness. Frustration. "Except for the year I go to university, always do I live here."

"What university?"

She gave a little shrug. "The institute of technology. In Lvov. My grandfather wished for me to learn the science."

"That so? What kind of science?"

"Pah! You would not believe! Such courses he wished me to take. The...the *mathematik*. The *physik*. I have perhaps the head, but not the heart for such—"

"Katerina!"

At the sharp admonition, the girl whipped her hand free of Nate's arm and spun around. He turned more leisurely, his senses leaping at the sight of the woman who strode toward them.

A long khaki coat covered her from shoulder to boot top. One of her own designs, Nate guessed. Only someone as talented as Maggie said Alexandra Jordan was could've fashioned that particular model. Similar to the long, open-fronted frock coats favored by the men of the camp, the semifitted military-style garment showed off her slender figure to perfection and swirled about her ankles seductively when she walked. With some interest, Nate noted the tassels banded in colored yarn that decorated the yoke of the garment.

Damned if those horsetail thingamabobs weren't starting to strike his fancy.

What didn't strike any fancy, however, was the braided horsetail whip looped about Alexandra's wrist. It cracked ominously against her boot top with each step.

Katerina's lower lip jutted out as her cousin strode toward them. Obviously deciding to take the offensive, she rattled off something in Karistani that earned a sharp retort.

The two women faced each other, one softly rounded and flushed, the other rigid and unyielding in her authority. After a short, terse exchange, Katerina evidently came out the loser. Her eyes snapping, she faced Nate.

"God keep you until the dawn," she muttered. She flounced away, then added defiantly over her shoulder, "I will see you then."

Alexandra's whip snapped several more times against her leather boot, and she gave Nate a look that would've made bear bait out of a less seasoned hand.

"I want to talk to you." She threw a quick glance at the circle of interested faces watching from around the campfire. "Privately."

She whirled and strode toward the far perimeter, only to stop when she noticed he wasn't following.

Having made his point, Nate nodded. "I guess maybe it is time we had a little chat."

* * *

Her mind seething with a jumble of emotions, Alex led the way toward the outskirts of the camp. She didn't understand what it was about this unwanted visitor that had set her teeth on edge from the first moment of their meeting.

He was handsome enough, in his rangy, loose-limbed way, she admitted. If one cared for sun-streaked blond hair, a square jaw, and skin tanned to the sheen of fine oak, that is.

Who was she kidding? she thought testily. Sloan made the models she'd hired last spring for the premiere of her Elegance line of men's evening wear look as though they hadn't gone through puberty yet.

All right, it wasn't his appearance that irritated her, Alex decided with a fresh spurt of annoyance. It was his attitude. His deliberately provocative manner. The way he drew out his words until they grated on her ears. The way his hazel eyes seemed to brim with some lazy private amusement when they looked at her and issued a challenge only she seemed to see.

Alex wasn't used to being challenged.

By anyone.

Even before she assumed leadership of the host, the men of the steppes had always accorded her the deference due the headman's granddaughter. In the business world, her associates had given her respect she'd earned by her success in an industry that regularly devoured its own.

Even the few men in her life with whom she'd developed anything more than a business relationship hadn't affected her equilibrium the way Sloan did. Not one of them had let his gaze slide from her lips to her throat so slowly that she felt her very skin burn in anticipation of its touch. None had drawn out each move, each touch, each murmured word, until she wanted to scream...

Alex pulled herself up short, not quite believing the direction her mind had taken. She was getting as bad as Katerina, she thought grimly, her worry coming full circle.

She halted abruptly beside the wood-framed trailer that was used to transport the tents. Its high sides afforded a modicum

of privacy in a city without walls. Wasting no time on prelim-
inaries, Alex plunged to the heart of the matter.

"Look, Mr.— Look, Nate. You're only going to be here
for a short time. I don't want you to encourage Katerina."

Sloan leaned an arm against the side of the wagon and le
his shadowed gaze drift over her face. "Seems like you've
got a long list of things you don't want me to do while I'm
here, *ataman*."

"And that's another item to add to the list," Alex snapped
"I don't want you to call me by that title. It's one the elders
gave me, but I've not yet earned."

His head cocked. "That so?"

"That's so."

"And just what do you have to do to earn it…Alexandra?"

He drew her name out in that deep, slow way of his, unti
it assumed a consistency similar to the thick, creamy yogur
the women made from mare's milk. The suspicion that he did
it deliberately tightened Alexandra's mouth.

"That's not something that concerns you. What *should* concern you, however, is the fact that many of the people of thi
country cling to the old ways." She tilted her head, eyeing
him through the screen of her lashes. "Do you have any ide
how Cossacks of old dealt with those who transgressed thei
laws?"

His eyes glinted in the moonlight. "No, but I suspect I'm
about to find out."

She held up her short braided whip. "This is called a
nagaika. The horsemen of the steppes use this instead of spur
to control their mounts. They also use it to strip the flesh from
anyone who dishonors a woman of the host."

He didn't appear overly impressed. "Aren't you getting
your feathers all ruffled up unnecessarily? Where I come
from, a man doesn't exactly dishonor a woman by taking her
for a stroll through a crowded camp."

"You're not where you come from," she reminded him
emphasizing her words with a crack of the whip. "You're in
Karistan. I told you, our ways are different."

He glanced down at the braided flail. When his eyes met hers again, they held a glint she couldn't quite interpret.

"Not that different, sweetheart."

Before she could protest this rapid progression from a respectful title to casual familiarity, he straightened and took a step forward.

"Now, maybe if I'd invited your cousin to stroll out here in the darkness the way you invited me, Alexandra, you might've had reason to be suspicious."

The low, husky quality of his voice took Alex by surprise. Good Lord, surely the man didn't think she'd brought him out here for any other reason than to...

"And maybe if I'd let that pie-plate moon stir my blood," he continued, closing the distance, "you might've had cause to flick that little horsetail flyswatter of yours against your boots."

His voice retained its easy, mocking modulation, but as he moved toward her Alex was suddenly and disturbingly aware of the breadth of his shoulders and the leashed power in his long body.

"But you wouldn't have had any real cause to be concerned..."

Her breath caught as he planted both hands on wood planking, caging her in the circle of his arms.

"Sloan! What—?"

"...unless I'd done something like this."

Sheer astonishment held her immobile as he brushed his mouth across hers, once, twice.

For a moment, when he loomed over her, Alex had felt a flutter of trepidation, as though she'd wakened a sleeping beast she wasn't sure she could control. But the soft, unthreatening touch of his lips told her how ridiculous that fear was. Imperceptibly she relaxed her rigid stance.

As if he'd been waiting for just such a reaction, he slanted his head and deepened the kiss. Wrapping one arm about her waist, he pulled her up against his unyielding body.

Stunned at the swift, confident move, Alexandra yielded her

lips to a skilled assault. Disconcerted, unable to move, she clutched at his tough denim jacket.

A deep, hidden part of her leaped in response to his rough possession. The part of her with roots fed by women of the steppes, women who celebrated victories with their men in wild abandon. For a fleeting moment, Alexandra tested his strength, tasted his lips, and took a swift, fierce satisfaction in the uncompromising masculinity of the body pressed against hers.

It was only after he raised his head and she drew in a slow, unsteady breath that Alex realized he'd proved his point.

If he'd brought Katerina out here under the dark skies and ignited her senses like that, she certainly would've had cause to worry. More cause to worry.

Gathering the shreds of her dignity, she met his shadowed gaze. "If you touch me again without my permission," she said quietly, "I'll use this whip you dismiss so contemptuously."

He stared at her for a long moment, and then his mouth twisted into a rueful grin. "If I do, and if you did, you'd be in the right of it."

The apology—if it was one—surprised her. Alex frowned up at him, as confused by the way her heart refused to cease its wild pumping as by the way he lifted one hand to rub his thumb gently along her brow.

"Oh, hell, I didn't mean to put that crease back in your forehead," he murmured, half under his breath. "Wily Willie would have my hide for that."

"Who?" she asked, pulling back from his touch, confused by her reaction to this man.

"Wily Willie Sloan. He always warned me never to put a frown on a pretty girl's face—especially one as handy with a gun or a knife as you are. I figured he knew what he was talking about, since I once saw the sweetest, most demure little strawberry blonde west of the Mississippi pepper his backside with buckshot for doing what I just did."

Alex shook her head. "Is this...is this your father you're talking about?"

Sloan's grin widened. "Well, he never actually admitted to it. Except once when I was about six, and got a little too close to an edgy jenny mule. She darn near kicked me into the next county. Willie dusted me off and bragged that I must have inherited my hardheadedness from him, but he was pretty drunk at the time, so I didn't put any stock in it."

Alex stared at him, her mind whirling. She didn't understand how Sloan had managed to defuse what only a few moments ago had been an explosive situation. For her, at least. But the shattering tension between them had somehow softened, mellowed.

It was that damned grin, she thought with a wave of self-disgust. The gleam in his eyes as he spun his tales of this Willie character.

"Look, I—"

She broke off as a scream shattered the night.

Without thought, without hesitation, Alex whirled.

Her booted feet flew across the stubble as she raced toward the sound of muffled shouts. Cursing herself for having left her rifle at her tent, she bent down on the run and drew her knife from the leather sheath strapped just inside her boot top.

Sloan appeared beside her, as swift as she was, and far more silent. Alex barely spared him a glance, but she caught the glint of moonlight on the gun in his hand. She'd assumed he was armed. Anyone who traveled to such a remote part of the world without protection was a fool, and she was fast coming to the realization that, whatever else he was, Sloan was no fool.

As another high-pitched shriek sounded, Alex dodged through the rows of tents. She gathered a following of grim-faced armed men as she ran. No one spoke, no one questioned. As silent as death, the warriors of the steppes raced toward the unknown danger.

Chapter 5

Alex dodged the dark shape of a tent, then skidded to a halt. Her heart pounding, she stared at the chaotic scene before her.

Half the ropes mooring the tent she shared with Katerina and the other unmarried women had been pulled loose. The heavy goathide had partially collapsed, and was now draped over several thrashing figures of indistinct shape and size.

As she watched, a muffled shriek sounded from under the smothering material, and the pole supporting the peaked roof was knocked aside. The entire structure tumbled down. Various articles of clothing, several brass cooking pots and the white fur pelt that ordinarily covered her bed lay exposed to the night as those trapped inside dragged the heavy black hide this way and that.

Her knife held low for a slashing attack, Alex stalked toward the heaving mass. She sensed, rather than saw, Dimitri and Sloan a half pace behind her, while the others fanned out to encircle the collapsed structure. Whoever battled within would not escape.

At that moment, an edge of the hide lifted and a dark shape tumbled out.

"Katerina!" Alex bent and grasped her cousin's arm, helping her to rise. "Are you all right?"

The young woman lifted a shaky hand and shoved her hair out of her eyes. "Y-yes," she gasped.

"What happened?"

"That...that beast...came into the tent."

"Beast!" Releasing Katerina's arm, Alex whirled. "Give me your rifle!"

Without a word, Dimitri passed her the weapon. Holding the Enfield at waist level, she spun back to face the tent and snapped the bolt.

"No, cousin!" Katerina screeched.

At the same instant, a dark figure stepped in front of her and grabbed the rifle barrel. In a swift, powerful movement, Sloan pushed it toward the sky.

"I'm not sure what you think is under that tent, but the—"

"Release my rifle."

"But the shape looks a bit familiar. I'd appreciate you not putting a bullet through it just yet."

"Release my weapon."

The command was low, intense and deadly. After a long, silent moment, Sloan complied. To Alex's consternation, he also turned and strode toward the tent, his broad shoulders blocking her line of fire. When he stooped and heaved the hide upward, she gripped the rifle in tight hands and moved forward.

It would serve the fool right if she let him be savaged by whatever was trapped beneath the hide, Alex thought furiously. He couldn't know about the wolves that roamed the steppes, or the vicious wild dogs that could bring down even full-grown cattle.

It wasn't a wolf or a dog that finally emerged from under the edge of the hide, however. Her mouth sagging, Alex stared at the apparition before her.

"Dammit, Red!" Sloan snarled. "What the hell did you get into?"

Goathair, Alex thought wildly. He'd gotten into the long, fleecy angora hair one of her aunts spun into mohair yarns. Huge clumps of the stuff decorated the chestnut's face, while more long, fuzzy strands hung from his chin. What looked like Katerina's best silk blouse was draped over one twitching ear, and the copper pot Ivana used to collect wild honey was stuck on his muzzle.

With a low, colorful curse, Sloan stepped through the scattered debris toward his charge.

Chuffing softly, the stud tossed his head up, then from side to side. At first Alex thought he was trying to shake the copper pot loose, but she soon realized he was draining the last of Ivana's honey and licking the inside of the vessel.

"You lop-eared hunk of crow bait, get your head down."

Sloan yanked at the rope dangling from the animal's halter, then flung up an arm as Red obeyed his terse command. The copper pot whacked against his upraised forearm.

"Christ!" he muttered.

Alex bit down on her lower lip.

Treating Three Bars Red to a version of his ancestry that Alex suspected didn't appear anywhere in his papers, Sloan worked the honey pot off the stallion's muzzle. Once free, Red licked his lips to catch the last drops of honey. He also caught a mouthful of fuzzy angora hair, which he promptly spit out.

Swearing once more, Sloan swiped at the sticky glob decorating his jacket front.

Alex's teeth clamped down harder on her lip.

The honey pot empty, Three Bars Red had no objection to departing the scene of his crime. Responding to the jerk on his halter, he picked his way through the scattered debris with all the aplomb of a gentleman out for an evening stroll.

Nate led his charge toward the waiting woman, his jaws tight. In the dim light, he couldn't see the look in Alexandra's eyes, but he had a pretty good idea of what must be running through her mind. His supposed attentions to Katerina a while earlier had earned him a casual threat of being skinned alive. He could just imagine what this disaster might warrant.

Grimly he eyed the men ranged on either side of their leader. He wondered if he'd have to knock a few heads together to keep Ole Red—and perhaps himself—from joining the ranks of the geldings.

"You—" Alexandra cut off whatever she was going to say.

"Yeah?" Nate growled. "I what?"

"You—" She swallowed. "You have goat's hair hanging from your chin."

Glowering, he ran his free hand across his chin. It came away with a sticky mass attached.

Alex gave a hiccuping little gasp.

When Nate tried to shake the mess from his fingers, the gasp became a gurgle, then spilled over into helpless giggles.

Nate stopped in midshake, transfixed by the sight of Alexandra with the lines smoothed from her brow. Her generous mouth curved in a delighted smile, and her eyes sparkled in the dim light. This vibrant, laughing woman was all that he'd sensed she'd be, and then some.

Desire, heavy and swift, stirred in his belly. Not the casual, rippling kind of desire that streaks through a man when the woman he's taken an interest in unexpectedly pleasures him with a certain look, or a smile, or a come-hither hitch of her shoulder. This was a gut-twisting, wrenching sort of need that Nate had absolutely no business feeling for a woman who was his target.

For the second time in less than an hour, the urge to kiss Alex gripped Nate. This time, he rigidly controlled it.

"Take this…" She flapped one hand in his general direction. "Take this marauder away. Then you can come back and help repair the damage he's done."

As he led the animal back through the camp, any lingering exasperation Nate might have felt over the stallion's antics vanished. With a wry grin, he realized that Ole Red had accomplished two of the objectives he himself had been wrestling with all evening.

He'd handed Nate the perfect excuse to go nosing around Alexandra's tent.

And he'd brought a smile to her face that just about blinded them both with its candlepower.

Of course, Nate reflected, he'd accomplished the third objective on his own. He'd discovered that Alexandra wasn't averse to all men. In fact, for a few moments out there beside the wagon, he'd gotten the feeling maybe she wasn't even as averse to him as she let on.

Tying the halter lead more securely to a tent rope, Nate pulled a wad of fleecy hair from above Red's left eye.

"I guess we both got a taste of something sweet tonight, fella. I'm afraid it's gonna have to last us awhile."

Leaving Red to think about that, Nate rejoined the crew gathered at the scene of the disaster.

It took less than fifteen minutes to raise the heavy black goathide tent.

The women untangled the ropes and stakes with smooth efficiency, while Sloan and several Karistani men rolled out the hide and raised the poles.

Since Alex had spent most of her summers riding the steppes beside her grandfather, she was less skilled in these domestic matters. The thick, oiled ropes felt awkward and uncooperative in her fingers, the stakes shaky. One of her aunts by marriage, a gentle, doe-eyed woman closer to Alex's own age than to the tall, mustached man she'd married and subsequently buried some years ago, edged her aside. Giving Alex a small smile, Anya secured the anchoring line with competent hands.

"Your mother always claimed you were better with the horses than with the tents and cook fires," she said, in her soft, pretty voice.

Alex sat back on her heels. "So she did."

The older woman glanced sideways as she gave the rope a

final twist. "It was a matter of much pride to her that your grandfather favored you. And much worry."

"I know."

Her aunt's words echoed in Alex's mind a short time later, as she knelt among her scattered possessions. She righted a small bird cage-shaped chest, her heart aching at the painful memories it brought. Her mother had laughed and hidden little treasures for a young, curious Alex in the chest's many small drawers. It seemed so long ago, so many tears ago, that Alex had last heard her mother laugh.

Even now, five years after Elena Jordan's death, Alex still carried the scars left by the complex relationship between the hawk-eyed chieftain and the daughter who'd defied him to wed where she would. For as long as Alex could remember, the three people she'd loved most in the world had been pulled in opposite directions. Her grandfather by tradition and his responsibilities. Her mother by her love for the outsider she'd married. Her father by his refusal to believe guns were the solution to Karistan's problems.

During her visits to Karistan, Elena had pleaded with the old chieftain to understand that violence and bloodshed were not her husband's way. Daniel Jordan was an economist, a man of learning, wise in the ways of the outside world. Although he chose words over weapons, he wasn't the weak half man the headman believed him to be. In disgust, the Karistani chieftain had tolerated the outsider only for his daughter's sake.

The tension between the two strong-willed people had grown with each passing year, however, until at last Elena had stopped returning to the steppes altogether. She'd sent Alex back each summer, refusing to deny her her heritage.

Ultimately, her grandfather's unceasing hostility toward Daniel Jordan had driven Alexandra away, as well. Fiercely loyal to the man whose gentleness had often been her refuge, Alex had sprung to her father's defense whenever the chieftain's hatred spilled over into some vitriolic remark. The summer she turned seventeen, the *ataman* had made one scathing comment too many. The final quarrel between them had shaken the entire camp with its fury. That had been the last summer Alexandra had spent on the steppes.

She'd been back only once since. After her parents' deaths. After the fall of the Soviet Union, when reports of the violence between Karistan and Balminsk had begun to filter out to the rest of the world.

She'd been appalled at the devastation she found during that brief visit. And hurt as she'd never been hurt before. Her grandfather had told her brutally that she was of no use to him unless she wrung all trace of Daniel Jordan from her soul and stayed to fight by his side. She must choose, once and for all, between her two worlds.

Alexandra had refused to deny the father she loved, and the hawk-eyed chieftain had turned away in silent fury.

He hadn't spoken to her when she left, or during the years that followed. He must have known she'd funneled every penny of profit she earned from her designs into Karistan through Dimitri, but the headman had never acknowledged it. He hadn't relented, hadn't ever forgiven her for not choosing him over her father's memory.

In the end, he'd taken the choice out of her hands.

She was here. And she was *ataman*. Now she carried the burden he had shouldered for so long.

"This yours?"

Alex glanced up to see the American standing over her, a gold satin bra trimmed with ecru lace in his hand and a wicked gleam in his eyes. She pushed the painful memories aside and reached for the filmy undergarment.

"It is."

"I thought so. From the color," he added, when she flashed him a quick look. "It's the same as your eyes—sort of halfway between honey and hardtack."

Alexandra snatched the lacy confection from his hand. "Thank you...I think!"

What was it with this man? Despite her best efforts to keep him in his place, Sloan simply wouldn't stay there. In the short hours since he'd arrived, he and his grin and his blasted horse had literally turned the camp upside down. Stuffing the bra into one of the mother-of-pearl boxes, Alex tried again to assert her authority.

"I told you a half hour ago, we don't need your help any longer. We'll take care of the rest."

"Now, that wouldn't be right, Alexandra, seeing as how Ole Red caused this havoc in the first place."

He rolled her name in his slow, teasing way that caused Alex to grit her teeth and Katerina to send him a sharp look. Across the width of the tent, the younger woman's eyes narrowed with suspicion and instant jealousy.

Alex suppressed a sigh. Things were bad enough between her and her cousin without this man's presence exacerbating them further. An ancient Cossack saying, one passed from mother to daughter over the centuries, rose in her mind. Men were ever the burden women must bear in life—one could not live with them, nor cook them in oil rendered from yak grease, as they generally deserved.

Unaware of the fate she contemplated for him, Sloan hunkered down beside her and picked up one of the odd-shaped drawers. "Do all these little jobbers go in that chest?"

"Yes, but I'll put them away."

Ignoring her protest, he angled the box to fit into an empty slot. In the process, he also spilled its entire contents. Childhood trinkets, her mother's hand-carved ebony comb, her pens and the few sketches Alex had found time to do since returning to Karistan tumbled out onto the patterned carpet.

His big hands shuffled through the loose papers, adding to their general disorder and Alex's exasperation. Tilting them up to the light provided by the overhead bulb, he studied the top sketch.

Alex glanced at the drawing. It showed her cousin standing at the edge of the steppes, her head thrown back and her hair whipping in the wind. She wore the traditional calf-length skirt and belted tunic of Karistan, to which Alex had added rows of piping in an intricate, exotic motif. Both the skirt and the tunic shirt were smoother, sleeker versions of the traditional dress, and allowed the ease of movement and tailored comfort the women who could afford Alex's designs preferred.

The overall effect was one of East meeting West. A blending of cultures and continents. A harmony that Alex could express in her designs, but had yet to find in herself.

When Sloan gave a low, appreciative murmur, however, Alex was sure he wasn't admiring her design or her cousin. Irritation spurted through her, and something else that she refused to identify. She tugged the sketches out of his hand.

"I'll put those away. Go join the men!"

He quirked an eyebrow at her tone, then pivoted on one heel and swept the tent with an assessing glance. When he swung back to face her, his knee brushed against her thigh with a sudden, startling intimacy.

"It's still the far side of disaster in here. Sure you don't want me to—?"

"No! Yes! I'm sure." Alex edged her leg away from his. "Just go."

He rose, dusting his hands on his jeans, then stared down at her for a moment. "God keep you until the dawn, Alexandra Danilova Jordan."

She blinked, surprised at how comforting the traditional blessing sounded in his deep voice.

"And...and you."

The tent's flap had barely dropped behind his broadshouldered silhouette before Katerina made her way across the tent.

"How is it the *Amerikanski* calls you by name? You don't permit the men of our host to do so!"

Alex crammed the last of her belongings into the chest and rose. She was too tired for another bout with her cousin, but from long experience she knew Katerina wouldn't be put off when she wore that surly expression.

"It's not that I don't permit them to call me by name. They choose not to, out of respect." As they always did when she spoke Karistani, her dialogue and thoughts alike took on a more formal, stylized structure.

"So he does not respect you, this countryman of yours?" Katerina's upper lip curled. "Just what did you do after you sent me back to my tent like a child tonight, that caused him to lose respect for you?"

"Cousin!"

Katerina placed both hands on her full hips. "What, *Alexandra?*"

Alex bit back a sharp rebuke. As much as the younger woman had strained her patience these past weeks, she disliked arguing with her in front of the others.

"We will not discuss the matter now."

"Yes, we will."

"Katerina, I don't wish us to argue like this, in front of the others."

The women watching the scene from the far end of the tent stirred. Ivana of the honey pot set down the skirts she'd been folding. "We'll go, *ataman.*"

Alex shook her head. "No, there's no need."

Her face pale against the black kerchief covering her hair, the young widow glanced at the others. Evidently, what Ivana saw in their faces gave her the courage to speak.

"There is need. You must talk with Katerina. Listen to her. She…she echoes many of our thoughts."

A familiar sense of frustration rose in Alexandra's chest as the other women filed out. She was their leader, yet they would not confide in her. She was of their blood, yet different from them in so many ways.

Suppressing the feeling with an effort of will, she faced her cousin. From the set, angry expression on Katerina's face, Alex knew she'd have to take the first step to heal the breach.

"I'm sorry if I embarrassed you tonight. I should have used more tact."

"Yes, you should have."

"And you, my cousin, perhaps you should have shown more restraint."

"More restraint?" Katerina's voice rose. "More restraint?"

"You were draped over Sloan like a blanket," Alex reminded her. "Such forwardness is not our way."

A long-held bitterness flared in her cousin's dark eyes. "What do you know of our ways? What can you possibly know? You've passed your life in America, enjoying your pretty clothes and your fancy apartment and your lovers."

"Katerina!"

"It's true. You may have spent long-ago summers on the steppes, but you're not really one of us. You weren't here in the winters, when the cattle froze and we ate the flesh of horses to survive. You weren't here during the years of war, when our men died, one after another."

Stunned by the vicious attack, Alex could only stare at her.

"And even when you were young," Katerina rushed on, as though a dam had broken inside her, "our grandfather set you apart. You rode, while the rest of us walked. You sat with him and listened to his tales of forgotten glory while we labored at the cooking pots. He petted and protected you even then."

Alex's pride wouldn't allow her to point out that grueling fourteen-hour days in the saddle hardly constituted petting and protecting. "I but followed his will," she answered through stiff lips.

"Just as you followed his will when you assumed leadership of this host, *Alexandra?* You, a woman! An outsider!"

"I'm of his blood, as are you."

"Yet he chose you over me."

Now they came down to it…the hurt that had festered between them for weeks.

"Yes, he chose me. I didn't want this, Katerina! You know I never intended to stay when I came back. But I gave my promise."

The girl bent forward, her eyes glittering. "Do you know why our grandfather called you back, cousin? Do you?"

Her heart twisting at the irony, Alex nodded. "Yes, I do.

As much as he hated my other life, he came to realize it gave me knowledge of the outside world. Knowledge necessary to deal with the vultures he knew would descend on Karistan with his death.''

"So you may think!" Katerina retorted. "So you may tell yourself! But it was not your knowledge of the outside world that made him choose you. It was your hardness! Your coldness!"

"What are you saying?"

"Do you think our grandfather mourned your absence all these years? Pah! He reveled in it. He boasted that it proved you as strong and proud as he himself. So proud you couldn't refuse the title when he passed it to you. So strong you would never be swayed by your heart, like the other women of this host."

Alex reeled backward, wanting desperately to deny the stinging charges. Yet in a dark, secret corner of her mind she knew Katerina was right. Her grandfather had possessed a strength of will that was both his blessing and his curse.

As it was hers.

The two women faced each other, one breathing fast and hard with the force of her anger, the other rigid and unmoving. Then, slowly, like rainwater seeping into the steppes after a pelting storm, the bitterness drained from Katerina's face.

"Don't you see, cousin? Our grandfather gave you leadership of the host because you alone have the strength to hold Karistan together, as I...as the others...could not. Only you would ensure that our people don't scatter to the winds."

Under her embroidered blouse, Katerina's shoulders slumped. "But perhaps only by scattering, by leaving this bloodstained land, will we find peace."

Her heart aching at the bleakness on her cousin's face, Alex reached out to grasp her hand.

"Katrushka..." she began, using the pet name of their childhood in a desperate attempt to bridge the gap between them. "You must give me time. A little time."

"Too much time has been lost already. Too much blood

spilled, and too many tears shed." The younger woman sighed. "Only the old ones are left now, 'Zandra, and the women. We...the women...we talk of leaving. Of going to the lowlands."

"You can't leave. Not yet."

"Don't you understand? We want husbands, men to warm our beds and our hearts. Children to bring us joy. We won't find them here."

Alex gripped her fingers. "You mustn't leave here. This is your home. Just give me a little time. I...I have a plan. Not one I can speak of yet, because it may not work. But someone comes, someone who can help us, if we just hold out a little longer."

The two women searched each other's eyes.

"I'm sorry," Katerina said at last. "I but add to your burdens. I don't mean to, cousin."

Alex forced a small smile. "I know."

"I...I shouldn't have become so angry when you took me to task tonight."

"And I shouldn't have taken you to task so clumsily."

Katerina hesitated, then gave Alex's hand a little squeeze. "I know you think me overbold, 'Zandra, but I'm not like you. None of us here are. We don't think as you do. We believe a woman is not a woman unless she has a man to warm her bed."

Well, she was right there, Alex thought. In that, at least, she and her cousin were worlds apart.

"I... We... We want a man," Katerina said simply. "Someone like this *Amerikanski.*"

"What?" Alex jerked her hand free.

"Someone young and strong, with laughter in his eyes instead of hate. Someone whose blood runs hot on a cold night and whose arms were made to hold a woman."

"Katerina!"

"Why do you sound so shocked? He's much a man, this one. Any woman would be happy to take him to her bed."

"For heaven's sake, he's only been in camp for a few

hours! You know nothing about him. He could be an...an ax murderer! Or have a wife and six children waiting for him in America.''

If he did, Alex thought, remembering their searing kiss, she pitied the woman.

Some of the lingering hurt between the two women faded as Katerina flipped her hair to one side and essayed a small, brave grin. ''Pah! Do you think I waste my time? I learned all I need to know of him in less time than it takes to thread the needle. He has no wife, although many pursue him, I would guess. One has only to see the gleam in his eyes to know he has the way with women.''

He had that. He certainly had that, Alex agreed silently.

''He's an outsider,'' she protested aloud.

''He may be an outsider, but he has the wind and the open skies in his blood. He owns only a small piece of land in America, not enough to hold him, or he would not wander as he does, delivering horses to strange countries.''

Surprised at her cousin's shrewd character assessment, Alex stared at her.

''He's like the men of the steppes used to be,'' Katerina finished on a dreamy note. ''Strong and well muscled. He would give a woman tall, healthy children. Smiling daughters and hearty sons.''

The guilt, worry and resentment that had been building within Alex since the night of her grandfather's death threatened to spill over.

''Perhaps we should consider putting the man instead of the horse to stud,'' she snapped.

''Perhaps we should,'' Katerina agreed, laughing.

Alex shook her head. This was all too much. ''I...I need to think!''

Now that she'd said her piece, Katerina's earlier animosity was gone. ''Go. Take the air, and do your thinking. I'll finish here and brew us some tea. Go!''

Grabbing the coat she'd tossed down earlier, Alex lifted the tent flap. Once outside, she sucked in deep, rasping gulps of the cold night air.

With all her heart, she longed to saddle her gelding and head north for the ice cave her grandfather had shown her as a child. It had been her special place, her retreat whenever they clashed over his unceasing hostility toward her father. Since her return, it had become the only place she could really be alone in a land with few walls and little privacy. The only place she could find the quiet to sort through the worries that weighed on her.

But she didn't dare ride out at night unescorted. Not with the ever-present threat of raiders from Balminsk. Not with Nate Sloan in camp. She couldn't take the chance that he might stumble over something he wouldn't understand.

Damn it all to hell!

Simmering with frustration and confusion, Alex threw her cloak over her shoulders and stalked to the outskirts of the camp.

What in the world was she doing here?

Why had she abandoned her business, her scattering of friends, her on-again-off-again fiancé, to come back to Karistan?

Why, after all those years of unrelenting silence, had she answered her grandfather's stark three-word message?

"I die," the telegram had read. "Come."

So she had come. And been forced into the leadership of a people she barely knew anymore. She'd promised, and on the steppes, a promise made was a promise kept.

Although she felt trapped by this unfamiliar role, there was no one to pass it to. Katerina herself admitted she didn't have the strength; nor did the other women still left of her grandfather's line. Although one of her aunts was an artist of great skill, and another cousin a gifted healer who'd studied at the Kiev Medical Institute, the women of Karistan hadn't been trained for leadership. Nor did they want it.

With a small groan, Alex tried to come to grips with what they did want.

Her mind whirling, she tucked her chin into the folds of her coat. Gradually, the ordinary, familiar sounds of the camp settling down for the night penetrated her chaotic thoughts.

A man's low, gruff laugh.

The whinny of a horse in the distance.

The plink of a three-stringed balalaika picking out an ancient melody.

Alex tilted her head, straining to catch the faint, lilting notes. Like the wipe of a cool cloth across fever-burned skin, the music of the steppes eased the tight band around her heart.

Soothed by the haunting tune, she shrugged off her doubts and feelings of inadequacy. Whatever the reasons her grandfather had had for summoning her, she was here. Whether she wanted it or not, she carried the burden of this small country until she could pass it to someone else and get on with her life.

As the balalaika poured its liquid, silvery notes into the night, Alex felt a gathering sense of purpose.

She had to hold off the wolf from Balminsk.

She had to keep her disintegrating host together.

For a few more days. A week at most. Just until the man she'd sent for arrived and told her whether she could barter death for life.

Drawing in a deep, resolute breath, Alex turned and strode back to the tent. When she entered, Ivana and the other women threw her tentative looks. Katerina came forward with a peace offering and a determined smile.

Alex accepted the steaming mug of tea. "Thank you, Katrushka. Now we must talk. All of us."

In the tent he shared with Dimitri and the others, Nate declined another glass of vodka and weaved his way through the scattered cots toward his own. After the long day and even longer evening, he was ready to pull off his boots and crawl into his bedroll.

One scuffed boot hit the faded carpet covering the earthen floor with a dull thud. Nate was tugging off the other when the sound of music drifted over the murmur of the other men. Resting his forearms across a bent leg, Nate tilted his head to catch the faint, distant tune.

Whoever was plucking at that sweet-sounding guitar could sure make it sing. The haunting notes seemed to capture the vastness of the steppes. Their loneliness. Their mystery.

When the song ended, Nate shook his head at his fancifulness and slipped his automatic under the folded sheepskin that served as a pillow. As he emptied his pockets, an old Case pocketknife with a worn handle clattered down beside a handful of oddly shaped coins.

Nate fingered the handle, imagining how surprised Wily Willie would be to know that the knife he'd won in a poker game all those years ago and given to Nate as a belated birthday gift now housed one of the world's most sophisticated metal detectors. So sophisticated that it would register the wire used to solder transistors to circuit boards. More specifically, the solder used on the circuits in the small black box that cycled the arming codes for 18 nuclear warheads. The wizards in OMEGA's special devices unit had rigged the pocketknife to vibrate silently if it was within twenty yards of the decoder Nate sought.

Hefting the knife in one hand, he scowled down at it. He wished the blasted thing had begun to vibrate in the women's tent tonight. Somehow his need to find the decoder had escalated subtly in the past ten hours. That black box was a major factor in the lines etched beside Alexandra's golden eyes, Nate was convinced.

Now that he'd caught a glimpse of those glorious eyes free of worry and sparkling with laughter, he couldn't seem to shake the need to keep them that way.

Chapter 6

"You wanted to speak with me, *ataman*."

"Yes, Dimitri. Will you take tea?"

When the gray beard bobbed in assent, Alex picked up a hammered tin mug and half filled it with steaming green tea from the samovar that was always kept heated just outside the women's tent. Adding thick, creamy milk from a small pitcher, and four heaping teaspoons of coarse sugar, Alex handed the mug to Dimitri. He cradled it in arthritic hands for a moment, letting the soothing heat counteract the chill of the early-morning air.

"Did the sentries note any unusual activity last night?" she asked when he'd taken a sip of the rich, warming brew.

Amusement flickered in his cloudy eyes. "Other than the attack on the honey pot?"

"Other than that."

He peered at her through the steam spiraling from the mug. "There were no riders, if that's what you ask. No new tracks."

"That relieves me, Dimitri."

"Me, also, *ataman*."

"Nevertheless, I wish you to choose four of our best men to ride with me this afternoon," she instructed. "I would check our borders."

"It is done."

There were many aspects of life on the steppes that made Alex grit her teeth. The lack of privacy. The constant wind. The impermanence of a way of life built around grazing herds. This unquestioning obedience from subordinates, however, was one facet that definitely appealed to her. If only the dedicated but temperamental genius responsible for translating her designs into market-test garments was as cooperative as Dimitri, Alex thought wryly. She'd be spared the dramatic scenes that punctuated the last frantic weeks before a new line debuted. There'd be no bolts of fabric thrown across fitting rooms, no mannequins in tears, no strident demands to know just what in God's name Alex had been thinking of when she draped a bodice in such an impossible line!

Perhaps when she flew back to the States, she could convince Dimitri to come with her and impose some order on the chaos of her small but flourishing firm…assuming she had a firm left after she'd dumped the latest batch of designs in her assistant's hands and taken off as she had.

Deliberately Alex forced all thought of her other world from her mind. She wouldn't be flying anywhere, not for a while. Not until Karistan's future was assured. Which brought her to the point of her conversation with her lieutenant.

"There is another matter I would speak to you about," she said.

Weak early-morning sunlight glinted on the gold hoop in Dimitri's left ear as he cocked his head, waiting for her to continue.

"This man, Sloan, and the gift he brings. I've…I've given both much thought."

"That does not surprise me."

At her quick look, Dimitri shrugged. "Gregor saw you with him last night."

"Yes, well, I... That is, Katerina and the other women..."

"Yes, *ataman?*"

Alex squared her shoulders. She alone could take responsibility for this decision.

"I've decided we should accept the president's gift."

Nate chewed slowly, savoring the coarse bread covered with creamy, pungent cheese. As breakfasts went, this one was filling and tasty, but he would've traded just about anything he owned at that moment for a cup of black coffee. Controlling an instinctive grimace, he washed the bread down with a swallow of heavily sweetened tea.

Beside him, Peter the Great argued amiably with a sunken, hollow-cheeked man who looked like he'd last seen action in the Crimean War. While they bantered back and forth, Nate stole a quick look at his watch.

Two hours until his first scheduled contact with Maggie. She should be in Balminsk right about now. He was anxious to hear her assessment of the situation there, to see if it tallied with the bits of information he'd gleaned about its vitriolic, reactionary leader from the Karistanis.

He'd have to give his one-armed guardian the slip for a few moments to contact Maggie. Peter the Great hadn't relaxed his vigilance, but Nate knew his way around well enough now to put some tents between himself and the aged warrior when he was ready to.

At a sudden stirring among the men, he glanced over his shoulder and spied Alexandra crossing the open space in the center of camp. The sight of her caused his fingers to curl around the tin mug. He'd spent more hours last night than he wanted to admit imagining her long, slender body in that satin bra and not a whole lot more. But even his most vivid mental images didn't convey the vitality and sheer, stunning presence of the woman who walked toward him.

In her black boots and those baggy britches that shaped themselves to her hips with every shift in the contrary wind, she would have caught Nate's eye even if she wasn't wearing

a belted tunic in the brightest shade of red he'd ever seen.
Rows of gold frog fastenings marched down its front, reminding him of an eighteenth-century hussar's uniform. More
gold embroidery embellished the cuffs, giving the illusion of
an officer's rank.

Come to think of it, he decided with an inner grin, it wasn't
an illusion.

Like a general at the head of her troops, Alex led a contin-
gent of the camp's women. She was flanked on either side by
Katerina, bright-eyed and pink-cheeked in the crisp air, and a
pale, honey-haired widow Nate had heard referred to as Ivana.
More women streamed along behind her, as well as a gathering trail of curious camp residents. Dimitri followed more
slowly, his lined face impassive.

Tossing the rest of his tea to the ground, Nate set the tin
mug aside and rose. Ole Red must have done more damage
to the women's tent last night than he'd estimated to generate
a turnout like this. Wondering just what he'd have to do to
smooth over Karistani-American relations, he hooked his
thumbs in his belt.

He didn't wonder long.

After a polite greeting and the hope that he'd slept well,
Alexandra plunged right to the heart of things.

"I've given the matter that brought you to Karistan a great
deal of thought."

"That so?"

"Yes, that's so. I…I have decided to accept the president's
offer of a stud."

Nate wasn't sure exactly why, but the way she announced
her decision didn't exactly overwhelm him on Ole Red's behalf. Maybe it was the strange, indecipherable glint in her
eyes. Or the curious air that hung over the small crowd,
watching and intent. Shrugging, he acknowledged her decision.

"You won't be sorry. He's one of the best in the business."

The glint in her eyes deepened, darkening them to a burnished bronze. "That remains to be seen. There are conditions, however."

"What kind of conditions?"

"He must prove himself."

"That shouldn't be difficult. Just turn him loose with the females."

Katerina gave a smothered laugh. Her dark eyes dancing, she treated the other women to what Nate guessed was an explicit translation of his words, since it drew a round of giggles. Alex quieted them with a wave of one hand.

"I meant that he must prove himself on the steppes. Show he has endurance and heart for this rugged land."

Nate could understand that. He wouldn't acquire a horse without seeing it put through its paces, either.

"Fair enough."

"We ride out this afternoon," she told him. "The ride will be long and grueling."

"Ole Red and I will manage to keep up somehow," he drawled. Relieved that one part of his mission, at least, was under control, Nate allowed himself a grin. "Trust me. Three Bars Red won't disappoint you. Or the fillies, when you put him to stud."

Drawing in a long, slow breath, Alex met his gaze with a steady one of her own. "I'm not talking about Three Bars Red, Sloan."

"Evidently I missed something vital in this little conversation. Just who *are* we talking about?"

"You."

Nate narrowed his eyes. "You want to run that one by me one more time?" he asked slowly, deliberately.

"It's very simple. The president was right, although he didn't know it. Karistan needs new blood. New life. But not…" She wet her lips. "Not just among our horses."

His first thought was that it was a joke. That Alex and the other women were paying him back, in spades, for the havoc Red had wrought last night.

His second, as he took in the determined lift to Alex's chin, and Katerina's eager expression, was that Maggie was never going to believe this.

As the dilapidated truck she was riding in hit another rut, Maggie braced both hands against the dash. She felt her bottom part company with the hard leather seat, then slam down again. Suppressing a groan, she glared at the driver.

"If you don't slow down," she warned him in swift, idiomatic Russian, "your mother will soon have a daughter instead of a son."

Shaking his head in admiration, the brawny driver grinned at her. "How is it that you speak our language with such mastery?"

"I watched the Goodwill Games on TV. Hey, keep at least one eye on the road!"

Whipping the steering wheel around to avoid a pothole the size of the Grand Canyon, the driver sent the truck bouncing over a nest of rocks at the edge of the track. He spun back onto the road without once letting up on the gas pedal.

Maggie grabbed the dash again and hung on, swearing under her breath. After six hours in this doorless, springless vehicle, she felt even worse than she had after the first week of the grueling six-month training course OMEGA put her through.

The head training instructor, a steel-eyed agent whose code name, Jaguar, described both his personality and his method of operation in the field, had brushed aside Maggie's rather vocal comment about sadists. When he finished with her, he'd promised, she could hold her own in everything from hand-to-hand combat to a full-scale assault.

At this moment, she would've opted cheerfully for a full-scale assault. It had to be less dangerous than rattling along at sixty miles an hour down a road that existed only in some long-dead mapmaker's imagination! In a vehicle that had rolled off a World War II assembly line, no less.

Another wild swerve brought the other passenger in the open cab crashing into her side. Maggie held her breath until

Richard Worthington righted himself, with only a single jab of his bony elbow in her ribs.

"Uh, sorry…" he yelled over the clatter of the crates in the truck bed.

"That's okay," Maggie shouted back. "What's one more bruise here and there?"

He grabbed at the frame to steady himself. "Will you ask the driver to pull over? I need to check the map. We should have passed that town by now, the one just over the Balminsk border."

"We did pass it, Richard. A half hour ago."

He stared at her blankly. "I don't remember seeing anything but a few houses and a barn."

"That was it. On the steppes, two houses and a barn constitute a town."

"But…but…"

"But what?" she yelled, struggling to keep the exasperation out of her voice. Two days of flying and six hours of driving with Dr. Richard Worthington, brilliant young physicist and klutz extraordinaire, had strained Maggie's patience to the limit.

"But that was where we were supposed to meet our escort."

"What?"

They bounced upward, then slammed downward, with the precision of synchronized swimmers.

"Uh, we'll have to go back."

Maggie closed her eyes and counted to ten.

They'd already lost almost half a day's travel time due to confusion among the airport officials when they landed and an extended search for the transit permits that Richard had, somehow, packed with his underwear. At this rate, they wouldn't make Balminsk's capital until late afternoon.

When Maggie opened her eyes again, Richard's earnest, apologetic face filled her dust-smeared lenses. Bracing one hand against the roof, she swiveled in her seat.

"Stop the truck, Vasili."

"No, no! She goes well. If we stop, she may not start again."

"We have to turn around and go back."

The broad-faced driver rolled his eyes toward Richard. "Do not tell me. This one lost another something."

"All right, I won't tell you. Just stop. We'll have to let the rest of the team know. When they catch up with us," Maggie added darkly.

Vasili's quick-silver grin flashed. Muttering something about old women in babushkas who should ride only bicycles, he swung the wheel with careless abandon. Maggie felt her kidneys slide sideways, and grabbed Richard's arm before the rest of her followed.

With dust swirling all around them, Vasili braked to a screeching halt and cut the engine. While it hacked and shuddered and wheezed, Richard climbed out of the high cab and turned to help Maggie down.

His hand felt surprisingly firm after the shaky, soul-shattering ride. They stood for a moment in unmoving relief, and then Richard lifted a hand to shade his eyes.

"How far back are the others, do you think?"

"A half hour as the crow flies. Or ten minutes as Vasili drives."

The smile that made him seem so much younger than his years lightened his face. "I have to admit, I hadn't anticipated quite this much excitement our first day in-country."

Maggie's irritation with him faded, as it always seemed to do when he turned that shy, hesitant look on her. He thought this was excitement? Well, maybe it was, compared to spending ten or twelve hours a day bent over a high-powered microscope, playing with protons and neutrons.

"I think I can do with a little less of Vasili's brand of thrills," she answered, smiling.

Rolling her shoulders in a vain attempt to ease the strain of the past few hours, Maggie glanced at her watch. At least this unplanned stop would give her a chance to contact Nate during the time parameters they'd agreed on. She scanned the rolling countryside for a moment, then nodded toward a low, jagged line of rocks a hundred yards away.

"That looks like an ignimbrite formation. I'm going to go take a look."

"I'll come with you. Those rocks could be dangerous. You might trip."

Right. *She* might trip. "No, thanks, I don't need an escort."

"You could twist your ankle or fall." Richard assumed an air of authority. "I'm responsible for the team's well-being. I'd better come...."

"Richard, I have to go to the bathroom."

"Oh." He blinked several times. "Yes, of course."

Plucking her backpack out of the truck bed, Maggie trudged off toward the low-lying formation.

She really did have to go to the bathroom.

That basic need attended to, she examined the chronometer on her left wrist. With its black band, chrome face and series of buttons for setting the date, the time and the stopwatch function, it looked exactly like a runner's watch. It also contained a state-of-the-art miniaturized communications device that produced and received crystal-clear, instantaneous satellite transmissions. Scrambled incoming signals so that they couldn't be intercepted. Was shockproof. Radar-proof. Urine-proof.

Maggie chuckled, remembering the lab director's stunned reaction when she'd relayed the information that several orphans had piddled in Jaguar's boot during a mission in Central America and put the highly sophisticated unit concealed there out of commission. This new, improved version, he had solemnly assured her and Cowboy a few days ago, would not fail. She punched in a quick series of numbers on the calculator buttons.

A few nerve-racking minutes later, a flashing signal indicated that her transmission was being returned. Eagerly Maggie pressed the receive button.

"Chameleon here, Cowboy. Do you read me?"

"Loud and clear. Are you in place?"

"Well, almost." She gave him a succinct but descriptive rundown of the adventures attendant upon traveling with Dr. Worthington. "How's it going at your end? Have you located the boom box yet?"

"No."

The clipped response was so unlike Nate's usual style that Maggie instinctively tensed.

"There's been a slight change in the mission parameters," he supplied, confirming her suspicion that something was wrong.

"What kind of change?"

For several long moments, he didn't reply. When he did, it was in a low, acerbic tone.

"Alexandra Jordan has decided to accept the president's gift of a stud, but not the four-legged variety."

"Come again, Cowboy? I didn't quite catch that last transmission."

"She's suggesting that I stand in for Three Bars Red."

Frowning, Maggie shook her wrist. Despite the lab chief's assurances, the transmitter had to be malfunctioning. Either that, or Nate was using some kind of code. Maybe he was under observation, Maggie thought, her pulse tripping. Maybe he was under duress.

"I'm not sure I understand what you're trying to tell me," she replied, listening intently for a hidden message in his words.

"Dammit, I'm trying to tell you that she expects me to single-handedly repopulate Karistan. Or at least a good portion of it."

Nate was definitely under duress, Maggie decided. But not the kind that would cause her to open the crate marked Geological Survey Equipment and roll out the specially armed helicopter to rush to his assistance.

"I'm sorry I'm a bit slow on the uptake," she said, still not quite believing what she was hearing. "Are you saying that she expects—? That you're supposed to—?"

"Yes, she does, and yes, I am." Nate gave an exasperated

snort. "At first I thought it was a joke, but apparently the entire unmarried female portion of the camp voted on the idea."

"They...they did?"

He caught the unsteady waver in her voice. "You won't think it's so funny when I tell you that I haven't had two seconds to myself in the last few hours. I can't even take a leak without some interested party showing up to inspect the plumbing. You wouldn't believe what I had to go through to slip away for this contact."

"Try me," she suggested, her lips quivering.

"Chameleon," he warned, "this is not— Oh, hell, here comes Ivana. Let Control know what's happened. I'll contact you later."

The transmission terminated abruptly.

For several seconds, Maggie could only stare at the watch. Then a huge, delighted grin split her face.

Cowboy was about to give the term *deep cover* a whole new meaning!

This was priceless. When the small, select fraternity of OMEGA agents heard about this, they'd never let him live it down.

Poor Nate, she thought with a hiccup of laughter. The woman who'd snagged his attention and masculine interest during the mission prebrief had just offered him up as the jackpot in the Karistani version of lotto. No wonder he didn't view the situation with his characteristic easygoing sense of humor.

Still grinning, Maggie forced herself to consider the implications to their mission of what she'd just heard. She didn't believe for a moment that Nate would let this bizarre development impact his ability to accomplish his task. He was too good in the field, too experienced, to be distracted, even by a camp full of women who wanted to...to inspect his plumbing. If Alexandra Jordan or any of the other Karistanis had possession of the decoder, Nate would find it. But he'd sure have his hands full while he was looking for it.

Her eyes sparkling with delight, Maggie punched in another code and waited for her OMEGA controller to acknowledge her call. This contingency was definitely outside the range of possible parameters David Jensen had defined in such detail during their mission-planning session. She could visualize the pained expression his handsome, square-jawed face assumed whenever something occurred that he hadn't envisioned or planned for. That didn't happen very often, which was why Doc ranked as one of OMEGA's best agents.

What she couldn't visualize, however, was Adam Ridgeway's reaction when David relayed her report. That just might be one of those rare moments when even Adam's rigid control would slip. With all her heart, Maggie wished she could be there to see it.

Still chuckling, she made her way out of the rocks a little while later.

"Are you ready to go?" she called, rounding the end of the truck.

"Not…quite."

Richard's reply sounded indistinct and muffled. Which wasn't surprising, seeing as he was lying spread-eagled in the dirt, with a rifle barrel held to his head.

Chapter 7

Maggie peered over the tops of her dust-smeared glasses at the murderous-looking brigand holding the rifle to Richard's head.

"Who are you?"

"He...he is the son of the Wolf," Vasili gasped from his prone position a few yards away, then grunted when another bandit prodded him viciously in the back.

Maggie folded her arms across her chest. "No kidding?"

Her phrasing translated as something along the lines of "You do not speak the joke to me?"—but it was close enough. Either the words or the nonchalance with which she spoke them seemed to impress the dark-haired, menacing stranger. Without relieving the rifle's pressure on Richard's skull, he smiled.

It wasn't much of a smile, Maggie noted. More a twist of lips already pulled to one side by the raw, angry scar cutting across his left cheek. Now that, she thought, comparing the scar to her own semitattooed chin, was definitely an attention getter.

"No, he does not make the joke," the brigand responded. "Who are you?"

Under her folded arm, Maggie's fingers deftly extracted the small, pencil-thin canister sewn into her jacket's side seam.

"I'm Dr. St. Clare," she stated calmly. "I'm with the UN nuclear facilities site inspection team, as are my companions. We're traveling under international passports, with guarantees of safe passage through Balminsk."

She didn't really expect these men to be impressed with the thick sheaf of papers signed by a battery of clerks and stamped with seals in a dozen different languages. Assuming, of course, that Richard could produce them again. Still, the longer she delayed using deadly force, the better her chances were of getting Richard and Vasili out of harm's way.

"Forgive me, Dr. St. Clare."

Maggie's eyes widened at the smooth, lightly accented English. To her considerable surprise and Richard's audible relief, the man stepped back. A nod from him sent Vasili's guard back a step as well.

"We were told the UN team would be in convoy. When we saw this lone vehicle stopped along the road, naturally we came to check it out."

Maggie sent Vasili an evil glare, which he ignored as he scrambled to his feet.

"Is this how you check things out?" she asked the leader.

The faint smile edged farther to one side. "Not as a rule. But when your companion attacked, we responded in kind."

Maggie's incredulous gaze swung to the attacker in question.

"They, uh, came up so quietly," Richard explained, dusting off his jacket front. "When I turned around and saw them behind me, I sort of freaked out."

With great effort of will, Maggie managed not to freak out, as well.

The leader gazed at the young scientist with something that might have been amusement. With that scar, it was hard to tell.

"The way things are in this part of the world, we take no chances, you understand."

"I'm beginning to," Richard admitted, a touch of belligerence in his voice.

The stranger's black eyes went flat, and his face hard under its livid scar. "The least spark will ignite a conflagration between Balminsk and Karistan. Surely you were told of this before you ventured into this remote area?"

"Yes, we were," Richard replied. "But we weren't told exactly where you fit into all this, Mr....Wolf."

"My father is known as the White Wolf of Balminsk. I am Nikolas Cherkoff. Major Nikolas Cherkoff, formerly of the Soviet transcontinental command."

Cherkoff! The pieces fell into place instantly for Maggie. So this was the son of the wild-eyed radical, Boris Cherkoff, who ruled Balminsk. The man whose blood feud with Karistan had kept this corner of the world in turmoil for decades. She'd been briefed that Cherkoff's son was in the military, but intelligence reports had last placed him at the head of an elite, highly mobile combat unit, the Soviet version of the Rangers. She wondered what he was doing here, then decided that the rawness of the jagged wound on his cheek probably had something to do with the fact that he now wore civilian clothes instead of a uniform.

"Formerly?" Richard asked innocently, echoing her thoughts.

"There is no longer any Soviet Union," he replied, his tone dispassionate. "Nor am I any longer on active duty. I will escort you to my father."

Maggie slipped the tiny lethal canister back into the slit in her jacket sleeve. The special weapons folks had assured her that the biochemical agent it contained was extremely potent, but localized and temporary. She was just as happy not to have had to use it on this hard-eyed major. She had a feeling he would've been twice as tough to handle once he'd recovered from a "temporary" disabling.

Cherkoff, Jr., relegated Richard to the truck bed and took

his place beside Maggie in the cab. Squeezed between his hard, unyielding body and Vasili's brawny one, she contemplated the interesting turn her mission had taken in the past few minutes. Now she had not only Dr. Richard Worthington and the unpredictable, warlike leader of Balminsk to deal with, she also had to factor his son into the equation.

She'd have to let Nate know about this new development as soon as possible—assuming he could manage to slip away from his bevy of potential brides to answer her call, Maggie thought with an inner grin.

Stifling a groan, Nate held up a hand. "No, thanks, Anya. No more."

The dainty, sloe-eyed woman smiled and pushed another plate piled high with steaming, dough-wrapped meat pastries across the folding table. Blushing, she said something in a soft, sweet voice that under any other circumstances would have completely delighted him.

"Anya speaks of an old…old…saying among the women here," Katerina translated, her forehead wrinkled with the effort to find the right words. "Keep the cooking pot full, and…and…even the stupidest of men will find his way home in the dark."

Despite himself, Nate laughed. "Sounds about right. I'd find my way through a blinding blizzard if I knew something like these dumplings were waiting at the other end. But I can't eat any more, Anya, I swear."

When Katerina relayed his words, the young widow cocked her head and looked him up and down. Her soft comment brought a burst of laughter from the group around Nate. He decided not to stick around for the translation this time. Ignoring a flutter of feminine protest, he eased through the circle.

"I'm riding out this afternoon, remember? I'd better go before I'm too heavy for Ole Red to carry."

As Nate made his way through the camp, the mingled irritation and embarrassment that had dogged him ever since

Alex dropped her little bombshell earlier this morning returned full-force. He felt like a fat, grain-fed steer ambling down the chute toward the meat-processing plant. The men grinned as he passed, nudging each other in the ribs. The women chuckled and looked him over as though they were measuring him for the cooking pot Anya had mentioned.

It didn't help his mood any to see Alex waiting for him across the square, wearing her long, figure-flattering coat over her bright red shirt, an amused expression on her face. And to think he'd wanted to keep a smile on the woman's face, he thought in derision.

Nate knew his present disgruntled feeling had a lot to do with the fact that she'd been discussing his merits as a possible breeder with all the other unmarried women in camp while he was weaving fantasies about her and her alone. Fantasies he had no business weaving. At least until this mission was over. But once it was...

Controlling with sheer willpower the sudden tightening in his loins at the thought of proving to Alexandra Jordan just how good a breeder he might be, Nate strolled across the dusty square.

"Been waiting long?"

"Only a few moments. I could see you were busy."

"Just finishing dinner." Nate kept his tone light and easy. He wasn't about to let on how disconcerting it was for a man to chew his food with half a dozen women watching every bite and swallow.

"Good," she responded. "You'll need your strength this afternoon to keep up with us."

Nate eyed the others who were drifting up beside her. Having learned from Wily Willie early on to measure a man by the size of his heart and not the length of his shadow, he didn't make the mistake of underestimating Dimitri or Petr or the big, beefy-faced man with jowls to match his sagging belly. Still, he had to have thirty, maybe forty, fewer years under his belt than any one of the Karistani men. He figured he'd keep up.

When they were all mounted, Alex swung her gray gelding around. "Are you ready to ride?"

Although her question was polite enough, there was no mistaking the challenge in her amber eyes. Or the amusement. Obviously she thought Nate's only alternative to this little excursion was to stay in camp and be force-fed more of Anya's dumplings.

She couldn't know that he wasn't about to let her out of his sight.

"Yes, ma'am, I surely am."

They rode at a steady jog across the high plains, dodging the ravines that scarred the steppes' surface at intermittent intervals. The morning sunshine faded slowly as clouds piled up, and a decided chill entered the air.

When Alex called a halt at a stream lined with feathery, silver-leafed Russian olive trees, Nate tipped his ball cap back and surveyed their small band. If any of the men slumped untidily in their saddles felt any strain from the long ride, they sure didn't show it. Nor did their shaggy, unshod mounts.

Sitting easy while Red watered, Nate eyed the Karistani's horses with new respect. Descendants of the tough little steppe ponies, that could gallop for an hour without stopping, last two days without food or water and remain impervious to the extremes of temperature that ravaged the steppes, the small, shaggy Dons weren't even blowing hard.

The beefy, red-faced rider caught Nate's appraising look and said something to Alex.

"Mikhail sees that you eye his mount," she translated. "He says it may be small compared to the red, but very agile."

"That so?"

"That is so. He wonders if you'd like to see what the Don can do. A small race, perhaps?"

Nate realized he was being given the first opportunity to "prove" himself.

"Mikhail much admires your hat," Alex added. "If you care to wager it, he'll wager his own in return."

That alone would have been enough to make Nate turn down the bet. He didn't particularly fancy the greasy black sheepskin hat the big, raw-boned man wore at a rakish angle. Nor was he in any particular hurry to play Alex's game. But he'd never been one to pass up a good race—or the challenge in a pair of gleaming golden eyes.

"Fine by me," he replied easily.

They used the stand of trees as a course for what turned out to be the Karistani version of a barrel race.

Weaving through the thicket with hooves pounding, Red stayed well out in front for the first few turns. A true cutting horse, he could wheel on a dime and give back nine cents change. He couldn't, however, duck under low-hanging branches and just about skin the bark from the tree trunks with every turn, as the smaller, nimble Don could. By the sixth turn, Red had lost the advantage of his size and speed. By the tenth, the Don held the lead.

Nate didn't begrudge Alex and Mikhail their grins when he crossed the finish line well behind the Karistani.

"That was some fine riding," he conceded.

Tugging off the ball cap, he tossed it to the victor. Mikhail stuffed his sheepskin hat in his pocket and donned his trophy.

Alex translated his laughing reply. "He says that all he knows of riding he learned from Petr Borodín."

Her casual tone didn't fool Nate for a moment. Sure enough, the balding, bag-eyed hero of the steppes was the next to suggest a little contest. It sounded simple enough. The first one to fill a pouch with the water trickling along the muddy bed and then return to the starting point would be the winner.

"Let me make sure I understand this. He wants to race to that little creek, fill one of these skins, and race back?"

Alex nodded. "That's it."

Nate glanced at the one-armed warrior, who winked and upped the stakes.

"He has a bottle of his best vodka in his bag," Alex commented. "He'll wager that against your watch."

"Make it my belt buckle, and he's on," Nate countered.

Red made it to the shallow ravine several lengths ahead of Petr's mouse-colored Don. Nate was out of the saddle and down on one knee in the muddy water before Red had come to a full stop. Glancing up at the sound of approaching hooves, he almost dropped the leather pouch.

While his mount galloped at full speed, Petr Borodín hung upside down from the saddle. Using only the strength of his thighs to hold him in place, he gripped the reins in his one hand and the strings of the pouch in his teeth. The leather sack trailed the water for a few seconds before Petr dragged himself upright. By the time Nate and Red had clambered up the shallow bank, their opponents were already back beside Alex.

Cowboy drew up beside them, shaking his head in genuine admiration. "I doubt if there are many two-armed rodeo trick riders who could do that."

"It's called the *djigitovka*," Alex explained, her eyes sparkling. "It's one of the many circus tricks the Cossacks of old used to perform to impress the Russians and other outsiders."

"Well, it sure impressed the hell out of me."

Grinning, Nate unhooked his belt and passed the silver buckle, with its brass stenciling, to Petr. The gap-toothed warrior promptly hung it from one of the frayed medals decorating his chest. Reining his mount around, he went over to display his trophy to the others.

"At this rate, I'll ride back into camp buck-naked."

Alex arched a brow. "Katerina and the others would certainly appreciate that."

"Think so, do you?"

A delicate wash of color painted her cheeks at his sardonic reply, but she let her glance roam over his body in a slow, deliberate appraisal.

"Yes. I think so."

That little flush went a long way toward shooting out the dents in Nate's ego. He felt a whole lot better knowing he had somewhat of the same effect on Ms. Jordan as she had on him. Crossing his wrists over the saddle horn, he decided to get this thing out in the open.

"I guess this is as good a time as any to talk about your little announcement this morning."

"There's nothing to talk about. My father would've defined it as a simple matter of supply and demand."

"They demand and I supply, is that it?"

The color crept higher in her cheeks, but she kept her head high. "That's it."

"You want to tell me how I progressed overnight from a potential rapist who had to be warned off with threats of being flayed alive to the prize in the Crackerjack box?"

"As Katerina informed me, it was time to reassess Karistan's needs. All of them."

"Come on, Alexandra. What's really behind all this nonsense?"

"What makes you think it's nonsense?"

"Give me a break, lady. This is the twentieth century, not the eighteenth. A woman today ought to be looking for something more in a mate than mere availability."

Alex sat back in the saddle, thinking of all the responses she could make to that statement.

She could tell Sloan that availability didn't rank quite as high on his list of qualifications as the strong arms Ivana had speculated about during breakfast this morning and Alex herself had experienced last night.

That Anya, sweet, pale-haired Anya, had gotten up with the dawn to light the cook fires, commenting on how much pleasure it gave her to prepare delicacies for someone with such a long, lean body and flat belly.

That, despite herself, Alex was coming to agree with Katerina. A smile in a man's eyes went a long way toward countering any less desirable traits he might have.

Instead, she simply shrugged. "Availability is as good a criterion as any other on the steppes. We have a saying here, that women must have the courage of the bear, the strength of the ox, and the blindness of the bat. Otherwise none would wed."

Nate's bark of laughter had the other men swinging around to stare. "For all that they're anxious to acquire husbands, seems to me that the women of Karistan don't hold men in very high regard."

"Oh, we like men well enough," Alex returned. "In their place."

Leaving Nate to chew over that one, she signaled that it was time to move out.

Whatever other "tests" Alexandra had planned for him quickly got shoved to the back burner.

They'd ridden only a few miles when Dimitri, who was in the lead, suddenly pulled up and signaled her forward.

Sitting easy in the saddle, Nate watched the dark-haired woman confer with her lieutenant. When she called the rest of them forward, her eyes were flat, and tight lines bracketed either side of her mouth.

"Dimitri has found some tracks he does not recognize," she told Nate tersely. "We will follow them."

Picking up the pace, she led the small band farther and farther east. Nate didn't need to consult the compass built into his chronometer to know they were heading directly toward Balminsk. Lowering his chin against the gathering wind, he wondered just what the Karistanis intended to do if they caught up with the riders who'd made those tracks. Given the shaky state of affairs between the two nations, he wouldn't be surprised to find himself in the middle of a firefight.

Nate glanced at Alex's back and felt a sudden clammy chill that had nothing to do with the wind. His jaw hardening, he battled memories of another cold, rainy day. A day when Belfast's streets had erupted with gunfire and a desperate, determined woman had died in his arms. Pushing that black memory back into the small, private corner of his soul where it permanently lodged, Nate edged Red up alongside Alex's gray.

A half hour later, the storm that had been threatening began pounding the plains ahead of them. Not long after that, Alex called a halt. Her mouth tight, she stared across the wide ravine that blocked their path. Although the stream that wandered through it was no doubt just a trickle ordinarily, now it was swollen and rushing with the rains that lashed the steppes.

When Dimitri called out a question, Alex eyed the far bank, then reluctantly shook her head.

Smart move, Nate acknowledged silently. He'd seen his share of bloated carcasses swept along on these gully-washers. While he didn't doubt Red's ability to swim the rushing torrent, he wasn't anxious to see Alex try it on her smaller mount.

When Dimitri rode back to confer with the others, Nate threw her a sidelong glance.

"You want to tell me just who we've been tracking these last few hours?"

She pulled her gaze from the black clouds scudding toward them and gave a little shrug.

"Whoever it was, we won't be able to track them any farther. Not with the storm washing the plains."

Her refusal to share even this bit of information with him didn't set well with Nate.

"You've all but invited me to become part of the family," he tossed at her. "Don't you think it's about time you tell me what the hell's putting that crease between your brows?"

She blinked at the uncharacteristic edge to his voice, but before she could reply, the first fat raindrops splattered on her shoulders.

"I don't think this is the time to talk about much of anything."

As if to punctuate her words, the storm erupted around them in awesome fury. Lightning snaked down and cracked against the earth, too close for Nate's comfort. The roiling black clouds spit out their contents, and the wind picked up with a vengeance, flinging the rain sideways, right into their faces.

The Karistanis, used to the violence of the steppes, buried

their chins in the high protective collars of their greatcoats and slumped even lower in their saddles. Nate dragged on the yellow slicker that had seen him through similar Wyoming storms. He wished he had his ball cap to keep some of the pelting rain out of his eyes.

"We'll take shelter among those rocks till it passes," Alex called above the howl of the wind, pointing to a line of black basalt boulders thrusting up out of the plains some distance away.

Nate nodded as she turned her gray and kicked him into a gallop. With the ravine on their right, they raced toward the dark, towering shapes. Dimitri and the others pounded behind them.

They weren't the only ones headed for the rocks, they soon discovered. Over the rumble of thunder, Nate heard the sound of hoofbeats coming from their left. He pulled his .38 out of the holster tucked under his armpit just as Alex whipped her rifle out of its leather saddle case.

"They're ours," she shouted in relief a second later, as a small band of riderless horses charged out of the rain. "Usually they graze south of here. The storm must have driven them across the steppes."

Within moments, the two bands had merged and were flowing toward the rocks. They'd almost made it when lightning arced to the earth just a short distance ahead of them.

Even Red, as well trained as he was, shied.

Thighs gripping, body thrusting forward, Nate kept his seat. The Karistanis, Alex included, did the same.

A quick glance over his shoulder showed Nate that the blinding flash of light had panicked the other horses. Manes whipping, tails streaming, they scattered in all directions. Through the sheeting rain, he saw a bay yearling head right for the ravine's edge. It went over with a whinny of sheer panic.

Nate whipped Red around. Following the rim, he searched the rushing, muddy water for some sign of the colt. A few moments later, its muzzle broke the surface. Even from this distance, he could see its eyes rolling in terror and its forelegs flailing uselessly as it was dragged back under.

Nate yanked his rope free and followed the course of the rim, waiting for the yearling to surface again. When it did, it had been carried to the far side of the gorge, well beyond his reach. Cursing, he watched the rushing water slam the colt into a toppled, half-submerged satinwood tree that was still tethered to the far bank by its long, snakelike roots. Over the roar of the rain he heard the animal's shrill cries, and then the brown water closed over its head once more.

"Sloan! What is it? What are you doing?" Alex brought her gray to a dancing halt beside him.

"You've got a horse down!" he shouted. "There! He's caught in that tree."

Shoving her wet hair out of her eyes with one hand, Alex squinted along the line of his outstretched arm. "I see him!"

Standing up in the stirrups, Nate searched the ravine in both directions. "Any place I can get across?"

She shook her head. "Not for another twenty kilometers or so. We'll have to jump it."

"The hell *we* will!" he yelled. "Red can carry me across, but that little pony of yours won't make it."

"He'll make it. Either that, or he swims!"

"No! Dammit, Alex, wait!"

The wind tore the words away almost before Nate got them out. His heart crashed against his ribs as he saw her race the gelding toward the ravine's edge. She bent low over its neck, until the line between horse and rider blurred in the driving rain.

Cursing viciously, Nate sent Red in pursuit. There was only a slim chance the bigger, faster quarter horse could catch the smaller Don before it reached the rim, but Nate was damn well going to let him try.

Ears flat, neck stretched out, Red gave it everything he had. Throwing up clods of muddy grass with each pounding stride, he closed the short distance. But the gray's lead was a few whiskers too long. With a thrust of its muscled haunches, it launched itself across the raging torrent.

In the split second that followed, Nate had the choice of drawing rein or joining Alex in her attempt to bridge the dark, ragged chasm. Without conscious thought, he dropped the reins and gave Red his head. The chestnut's massive hind-quarters corded. His rear hooves dug into the dirt. With a powerful lunge, he soared into the driving rain.

Chapter 8

The gray landed with inches to spare.

Red hit the grassy rim with a wider margin of safety and a whole lot more power. By the time Nate brought him around, Alex had already dismounted.

Swiftly she stripped off her heavy, swirling greatcoat and tossed it over her saddle before heading toward the edge. The rain immediately darkened her red shirt to a deep wine and molded it to her slender body in a way that would've closed Nate's throat if it wasn't already tight.

He ripped the rope from his saddle and threw a leg over the pommel. Catching up with her in a few long strides, he spun her around.

"Loop this around your waist," he barked, furious over the fear that had clawed at his chest when he saw her sail across that dark torrent.

She blinked at his tone, but saw at once the sense of an anchor line. While she fumbled with the thin, slippery hemp, Nate whipped the other end around one of the satinwoods that were still firmly rooted on the bank. Shoving the end through his belt, he tied it in a slipknot.

"Play the rope out with both hands as I go down," he shouted.

"Wait, Sloan. I'll go. I'm smaller, lighter. Those roots may not take your weight without giving way."

"They may not take either one of us. Just hold on to the damn rope!"

She flung her head back, throwing the wet hair out of her eyes. But either she decided not to waste precious moments arguing or she realized that smaller and lighter weren't real advantages when it came to wrestling a three-hundred-pound animal from a nest of branches. Gripping her end of the rope in both hands, she watched as he slid down the bank on one heel and one knee.

With a grim eye on his footing, Nate worked his way along the slippery, half-submerged trunk. The satinwood strained and groaned as rushing brown water pulled at its tenuous grip on the bank. The frantic, thrashing yearling, its eyes rolled back in fright, added his cries to the chorus.

"Whoa, youngster. Hang on there."

A fresh torrent swept over the tree, forcing it and the trapped animal under. Lunging forward, Nate grabbed a fistful of black mane. His muscles straining against the combined pull of the water and the colt's weight, he dragged its head back above the surface. Balancing one hip against a heavy branch, he held on to the plunging, flailing creature with one hand and worked the slipknot with the other. It took him a couple of tries, but he managed to get a loop over the horse's small head. That done, he tore at the branches that caged it.

The water rushed over the tree with brutal force. The branches sliced back and forth, slashing at Nate's arms like sharp serrated knives. His slicker and the denim jacket underneath protected him from the worst of the cuts, but he felt their lash against his neck and face. With each whip and tug of the muddy water, the tree fought its anchor in the bank.

The colt came free at last. While Alex used the fulcrum of

the rope to swim it to shore, Nate fought his way back along the shuddering trunk. He was halfway to solid ground when the satinwood groaned and its roots began to give way with a sickening popping sound. Cursing, Nate dived for the bank. His hands dug into the slick earth just as the tree pulled free of its last fragile hold.

When it went, it took a good chunk of earth along with it. Before Alex could scramble backward to safety, the ground she was standing on crumbled beneath her feet. With a startled shout, she slid down the steep slope on her backside and tumbled into the rushing, muddy water.

Nate threw himself sideways and grabbed at the rope still tethering her to the colt. The hemp tore across his palms with a raw, searing heat before he could get a good grip on it. Looping the rope around his wrist, he pulled Alex out of the swirling water. She crawled up the slippery bank on all fours, coughing and spitting.

Nate traded his hold on the rope for one on her arm and dragged her to her feet. "You okay?"

"Except for swallowing half the steppes," she said, choking, "I'm fine."

"Then I suggest we get the hell out of here before we end up swallowing the rest."

With the palm of his hand against her rear, he boosted her up. Once back on solid ground, she wrapped the rope he passed her around her gray's saddle, then backed it up slowly to guide the shaky yearling. Nate followed a few seconds later.

With the rain sheeting down around them and the thunder still rolling across the sky, Alex took a moment to soothe the shivering colt. Nate wasn't sure when he'd seen a sorrier-looking pair. The wobbly legged youngster shuddered with every breath, his sides heaving under his drenched hide. Alex herself wasn't in much better shape. The brave red tunic that had so impressed Nate this morning with its gold frogging and braid was now a sodden, muddy brown. Her pants clung to her slender curves like the outer wrapping of a cheroot, and her once silky, shining mane was plastered to her head.

But when she lifted her wet face and gave Nate a wide-eyed, spike-lashed look of triumph over their shared victory, Nate was sure he'd never seen anything quite as beautiful in his life.

He forgot the cold. Forgot the mud seeping down along his instep. The need to sweep her into his arms and taste the rain on her lips crashed through him. The fact that another bolt of lightning slashed out of the sky at approximately the same moment was all that held him back.

At the sudden flash, Alex ducked and buried her face in the colt's wet, muddy side. By the time she recovered from her reflexive action, Nate had himself once more in hand.

"If I remember correctly," she shouted, rising, "there's a ledge of sorts a little farther south. It has an overhang wide enough to shelter us."

"Lead the way."

Alex felt a jumble of confused emotions as she grabbed the gray's reins and mounted. She was wet to the bone and colder than sin, but swept with an exhilaration at having wrested a victim from the violence of the storm. The stark, unguarded look she'd seen on Sloan's face for a brief instant added to her tumult, layered as it was on top of the wrenching fear that had sliced through her when the tree gave way and almost took him with it.

Stretching up in the stirrups, she waved to the men watching from the other side, signaling them to go on. Dimitri acknowledged her wave with a lift of his arm, then turned and led the others toward the jagged line of rocks, still some distance away. Tucking her chin down against the rain, Alex headed south. The colt, still tethered by the rope, trailed at Red's heels as Sloan followed suit.

Within minutes, she found the stone shelf carved high above the raging waters. It was wide enough to take the three horses without crowding, and deep enough to cut off the slant-

ng, driving rain. Shoulders sagging in relief, Alex slid out of
he saddle and leaned her forehead against the gray's neck for
a few moments.

Sloan's voice filled the small space, carrying easily now
over the rain's tattoo. "Looks like we might be here awhile."

Alex lifted her head and stared out at the gray, sheeting
wall. "I've known these storms to last an hour...or a day."
One shoulder lifted in a shrug that rippled into a shiver. "On
he steppes, one never knows."

She turned away to loosen the gelding's girth. Although the
Don was hardy and tough, Alex had learned early to put her
mount's well-being before her own. Pulling a shaggy wool
hat from the coat she'd tossed over the saddle earlier, she
began to rub the gray down.

From the corner of one eye she saw Nate shrug out of his
slicker and toss it over his saddle. Shaking his head like a
big, well-muscled dog to rid it of the water, he lifted an elbow
to wipe his face on his denim sleeve. That done, he moved
to Alex's side and tugged the woolly hat out of her hands.

"I'll do that. You'd better go dry yourself off. You're wet-
er than he is." His glinting gaze drifted down her front. "A
whole sight wetter."

The gleam in his hazel eyes reinforced what Alex already
knew. Her thin wool tunic, one of the hottest-selling items
from her spring Militariana collection, clung to her skin like
a wet leaf. She didn't need to glance down to know that her
nipples were puckered with the cold and pushing against the
thin lace of her bra.

"Go on," he instructed. "Your lips are turning purple,
which makes an interesting combination with that chili-pepper
shirt."

Alex might have hesitated if a violent shiver hadn't started
at her shoulders and jiggled its way down her spine. It jiggled
down her front, as well, and the gleam in Sloan's eyes deepened.

The fact that she was uncomfortable aside, Alex had been
taught to respect the power of the elements. Only a fool would

ride out into the snows that blanketed the steppes in winter without knowing where to find shelter for himself and his mount. Likewise, those who worked the herds in the cold, wet rains knew better than to risk pneumonia in a land where medicines were precious and physicians rare.

Snatching her greatcoat from the saddle, she moved to the back of the shallow cave. The high-collared calf-length coat was modeled after the *cherkessa* that had protected her ancestors from heat, wet and cold alike. Alex had executed her design in a tightly woven combination of wool and camel hair similar to the fabrics used a century ago. Although damp on the outside, the coat's inner lining was dry and warm.

Keeping an eye on Nate's back, she peeled off her wet, clammy tunic. Her boots gave her some trouble, but eventually yielded to determined tugging. Numb fingers fumbled with the buttons to her pants and finally pushed them down over her hips. The thick felt socks she wore under her boots soon joined the heap of sodden garments. With another quick glance at Sloan's back, she decided she could stand the dampness of her lacy underwear.

A few quick twists wrung most of the moisture out of her clothes. They'd still be clammy when she put them on again, of course, but not sopping-wet. Alex set them aside, thankful that she'd be dry and warm for the duration of the storm, at least.

Wrapping herself more snugly in the heavy coat, she leaned her shoulders against the stone wall and watched Sloan work. His broad shoulders, encased in weathered blue denim a few shades lighter than his worn jeans, strained at the jacket's seams with each sure stroke. The jacket rode up as he worked, giving Alex a glimpse of a narrow waist and lean flanks. Admiration sparked through her for the corded, rippling sinews of his thighs and the tight muscles of his buttocks. Her interest in his physique was purely objective, of course. Assessing the line and shape of the human body was part of the job for a woman in her profession.

He wiped the thick wool hat over the gelding with slow

sure strokes that told her he didn't consider tending to animals a chore. When he finished the gray, he nudged it aside with one shoulder and went to work on Three Bars Red.

They were a lot alike, Alex mused, this tall, broad-shouldered man and the well-muscled stallion. Both exhibited a lazy, easygoing nature, although she'd seen them move with blinding speed when the occasion warranted. Neither showed the least hint of softness or aristocratic pedigree in the raw power of his body. They were built for performance, not show, she decided.

The thought sent a spear of heat to her belly.

For the first time, the possibility occurred to her that Sloan might actually "perform" the role she'd assigned him. As Katerina would say, he was much a man, this compatriot of hers.

Alex had no doubt that Dimitri and the men would agree he had proven himself this afternoon. The games they'd played with him earlier had been just that, tests of his temper more than of his horsemanship. She knew his good-humored compliance with their wagers and his unstinting praise for their skill had impressed them far more than if he'd won the races himself.

But it was the way he'd pitted himself against the raging waters for a spindly-legged creature he had no responsibility for or claim on that would win their respect. Among the Karistani, bravery was valued not so much for its result as for the fact it shaped a man's soul and gave him character. Whatever else he might have, Alex thought wryly, Nate Sloan certainly had character.

So why did the realization that he might choose one of the women who fluttered around him like pigeons looking for a nest leave her feeling edgy? Why did the idea of Sloan performing with Katerina or Anya or Ivana of the honey pot make her fingers curl into the thick camel-hair fabric of her coat?

Damp, frigid air swirled around Alex's bare feet as she asked questions she wasn't ready to answer. Slowly she slid down the wall to a sitting position and tucked her cold toes under her.

A few moments later, Nate gave Red a final slap. "That ought to do you, fella."

The chestnut lowered his head and nuzzled his broad chest. Nate knuckled the white blaze.

"Sorry, big guy. I don't have anything on me but some chewing gum."

"For pity's sake, don't give him that!" Alex pleaded. "I don't want to think what he could do with gum in such close quarters."

Nate laughed and pushed Red's broad face away. Catching the rope still looped around the colt's neck, he tugged it toward Alex.

"Here, you work on this one while I dump the water out of my boots. I'm walking around in the half of the steppes you didn't swallow."

Glad to have something to take her mind from her chaotic thoughts, Alex took the soggy hat from him and rose up on her knees. Her hands moved in smooth, rhythmic motions over the shivering animal while she murmured meaningless nonsense in its ear.

Nate sat on the stone shelf, his back to the curving wall at a slight angle to hers and hooked a foot up on his knee. He grunted as he tugged at his worn boot. It came off with a whoosh, spilling a stream of muddy water. A second small cascade followed a few moments later.

Since the man had dragged her out of a raging torrent, Alex decided she could be magnanimous. "Use the skirt of my coat to dry your feet," she tossed over her shoulder.

"Thanks, but there's no sense muddying it up any more. I'll use my shirt to dry off with. It's already half soaked and sticking to me like feathers to tar."

He shrugged out of his jacket, and Alex noted the businesslike shoulder holster he wore under it. Despite her father's aversion to firearms, she was no stranger to them. During her summers on the steppes, she'd learned to handle them and respect them. Sloan unbuckled the weapon and set it aside, then unbuttoned his blue cotton shirt.

Resolutely Alex kept her attention fixed on her task, ignoring the ripple of muscle and the slick sheen of his skin as he shook himself like a lean, graceful borzoi. He toweled his tawny hair, sending water droplets in all directions, then sat down again to tug off his socks.

By the time he tossed the shirt aside and pulled his jacket back on, Alex had finished with the colt. The animal whuffled softly and stuck its muzzle into her side, as if wanting to share her body heat. Evidently deciding she didn't have enough to spare, he ambled over to join the other horses. With a tired sigh, she sank back down.

Sloan's deep voice carried easily over the drumming rain. "Your turn."

"What?"

By way of response, he dug under her coat and located one icy foot. Grasping her heel firmly in one hand, he began to massage her numb toes with the other.

Alex jerked at the touch of his big, warm hands on her skin.

"Relax," he instructed. "I've had a lot of practice at this. From the time I was big enough to get my hands around a bottle of liniment, I'd work Wily Willie over after every rodeo."

He glanced up from his task, his mouth curving. "Willie generally collected a sight more bruises than he did prize money, you understand?"

"Mmm…"

That was the best Alex could manage, with all her attention focused on the warmth that was transferring itself from his hands to her chilled toes. He had working hands, she thought, feeling the ridges and calluses on his palms with each sure, gentle stroke. The kind of hands her grandfather had possessed.

"What did he do when he wasn't rodeoing?" she asked

after a few moments, more to distract herself from the feel of his flesh against hers than anything else.

"Willie?" The skin at the corner of Nate's eyes crinkled. "As little as possible, mostly. As long as he had enough money in his pocket for the entry fees at the next event and the gas to get us there, he was happy."

"And you? Were you happy?"

"What kid wouldn't be? I grew up around men who didn't pretend to be anything but what they were, which was mostly down-and-out cowhands. I was convinced that sleeping in the bed of a truck and feasting on cold beans out of the can was the only way to live."

"You slept in a truck?"

"When we had one," he replied, with a lift of one shoulder. "Willie was always selling it to raise the cash for entry fees. He and I were the only ones who knew how to wire the starter, though, so we always got it back at a reduced price when he was in the money again. Here, give me your other foot."

How strange, Alex thought, studying his face as he took her heel in his lap and worked her instep with his incredible, gentle hands. All the while he shared more stories of this character who had given him his name and his peculiar philosophy of life and not much more, apparently. Nate Sloan came from a background as nomadic as that of any Karistani, one he'd evidently enjoyed, despite the deprivations he made light of.

Alex hadn't thought about it before, but perhaps in every culture, on every continent, there were people who preferred change to stability, movement to security. People who felt restless when surrounded by walls, and crowded when within sight of a town.

With a grudging respect for Katerina's instincts, Alex admitted that her cousin had been right in her assessment of this man. Sloan seemed to possess many of the same characteristics as the Cossacks who had originally claimed the steppes—the stubbornly independent outcasts who'd fled Russian oppression and made the term *kazak* synonymous with "adventurer" or "free man."

This tall, self-assured man fit in here far more than she did herself, Alex thought, with a twist of the pain she'd always kept well buried. She was the product of two cultures, torn by her loyalties to both, at home in neither. Sloan was his own man, and would fit in anywhere.

"And now?" Alex probed, wanting to understand more, to know more. "Now that you say Willie's retired and settled on this bit of land you have in..."

"Wolf Creek."

"In Wolf Creek. Do you always just pick up and travel halfway across the world as the mood or the opportunity strikes you?"

His hands shaped her arch, the thumbs warm and infinitely skilled as they massaged her toes. "Pretty much."

"You've never married? Never felt the need to stay in Wolf Creek?"

"No, ma'am," he drawled. "I've never married. Why? Does it concern you? Are you worried that I might be woman-shy and upset this little scheme of yours?"

"I worry about a lot of things," she responded tartly. "That's not one of them."

He caught her glance with a sardonic one of his own. "I might not have the experience Three Bars Red has, but I'll surely try to give satisfaction."

At the sting in his voice, Alex hesitated. "Look, Sloan, I know I may have pricked your ego a bit this morning by offering you up like a plate of pickled herring, but...but you don't understand the situation here."

Strong, blunt-tipped fingers slid over her heel and moved up to knead her calf. "Try me."

Alex bit her lip. For a few seconds, she was tempted. With an intensity that surprised her, she wanted to confide in this man. Wanted to share the doubts and insecurities that plagued her. To test her half-formed plan for Karistan's future against the intelligence he disguised behind his lazy smile.

With a mental shake, Alex shrugged aside the notion. One of the painful lessons she'd learned in the past few weeks was that responsibility brought with it a frightening loneliness. She couldn't bring herself to trust him. To trust any outsider. Not yet. Not while there was still so much danger to her people and to Karistan. And not while Sloan had his own role to…to perform in the delicate balance she was trying to maintain for the next few days, a week at most.

While she debated within herself, his hands continued their smooth, sure strokes.

"You're using me as a diversionary tactic, aren't you, Alexandra?"

She shot him a quick, startled glance. Had the man read her mind?

His eyes locked with hers. "I'm supposed to draw the friendly fire, right? Keep Katerina and the others occupied until you resolve whatever's putting that crease in your brow? No, don't pull away. We can talk while I do this."

"Maybe you can," she retorted, tugging at her leg. "I can't."

Alex wasn't sure, but she thought his jaw hardened for an instant before he shrugged. "Okay, we'll talk later."

It wasn't the answer she'd expected, but then, Alex never knew quite what to expect of this man. Frowning, she tugged at her leg. "Look, maybe this isn't such a good idea."

He relaxed his hold until her calf rested lightly in his palm. "Why so skittish, Alexandra?" he taunted softly. "We established the ground rules last night, remember? I won't touch you…unless you want it. Or unless I want to risk getting my hide stripped by that short-tailed whisker brush you tote."

"I wouldn't be so quick to dismiss the *nagaika*, if I were you," she retorted. "The Cossacks of old could take out a gnat's eye with it…at full gallop."

A rueful gleam crept into his eyes. "After seeing Petr Borodín in action this afternoon, I don't doubt it."

Belatedly Alex realized that his hands had resumed their stroking during the short exchange. Had he taken her failure to withdraw from his hold as permission to continue? Or had she given it?

With brutal honesty, she acknowledged that she had. His touch was so gentle, so nonthreatening. So soothing. Slumping back against the wall, she gave herself up to the warmth he was pumping through her veins.

The minutes passed. Rain drummed on the stone roof above them. An occasional roll of thunder provided a distant counterpoint to the snuffling of the horses. The faint scent of wet wool and warm horseflesh filled Alex's nostrils.

Gradually it dawned on Alex that Sloan's gentleness was every bit as seductive as the raw strength she'd tasted in his arms last night. The slow, sure friction of his big hands generated more than just heat. Prickles of awareness followed every upstroke. Whispers of sensation came with each downward sweep. Telling herself that she was crazy to let him continue, Alex closed her eyes.

Only a few moments more, she promised herself. She'd hold on to this strange, shimmering feeling that pushed her tension and her worry to a back corner of her mind for just a little longer.

Only a little while longer, Nate told himself. He'd only touch her a little while longer.

Although it was taking more and more effort to keep his hold light, he wasn't quite ready to let her go. He couldn't. Despite the heat that warmed his skin and the slow ache that curled in his belly.

When her dark lashes fluttered down against her cheeks, a tangle of emotions twisted inside Nate. Emotions he had no business feeling.

He should be using this enforced intimacy to draw some answers out of her, he reminded himself brutally. She still stubbornly refused to confide in him, but she was coming to trust him on the physical level, at least. It was a step. A first step. Something he could build on. Something his instincts told him he could take to the next, intimate level…if he was the kind of man she thought he was. If he was the stud she proclaimed him.

At that moment, he sure as hell felt like one. He'd spent enough of his life around animals to respect the breeding instinct that drove them. And to know the raw power of the desire that sliced through his groin as he stared at her shadowed face.

Fighting the ache that intensified with each pulse of the tiny blue vein at the side of her forehead, he stilled his movements.

"Alexandra?"

The dark lashes lifted.

"I think you ought to know that massaging Wily Willie's aches and pains never gave me a whole set of my own."

It didn't take her long to catch his meaning. Eyes wide, she tugged her leg out of his hold.

As her warm flesh slid from his palm, Nate cursed the sense of loss that shot through him. Settling back against the stone wall, he raised one leg to ease the tight constriction in his jeans and rested his arm across his knee.

With Alex watching him warily, he repeated a silent, savage litany.

This woman was his target.

She was the focus of his mission.

He was here to locate a small black box and extract it from her. Not the shuddering, shimmering surrender he was beginning to want with a need that was fast threatening to overwhelm both his common sense and his self-restraint.

Christ! He had to get himself under control.

Forcing his eyes and his thoughts away from the woman sitting two heartbeats away, he made himself focus on the mission. He'd made a little progress this morning, but not much. With Katerina and Anya and the others as willing, if unwitting, accomplices, he'd pretty well searched the entire camp. If Alex had the damn thing in her possession, he was willing to bet it wasn't hidden in any of the goathide tents.

A frustration he didn't allow to show grabbed at his gut. It was two parts physical and one part professional, with a whole lot of personal thrown in. The agent in him didn't like the fact that his progress was so slow. As a man, he was finding the fact that Alex couldn't bring herself to trust him harder and harder to deal with.

As he settled back against the stone wall, Nate hoped to hell Maggie wasn't running into as many complications on her end of this mission as he seemed to be.

Chapter 9

Oh, Lord, Maggie thought with an inner groan. As if this operation weren't complicated enough!

Reaching across the table, she eased a cloudy, half-full glass out of Richard's shaky grasp.

"But we're not fin... We haven't finush..." He blinked owlishly. "We're not done with the toasts."

"I'm sure President Cherkoff will understand if we don't salute the rest of the nations represented on the UN team. At least not until they arrive tomorrow."

She set the glass out of Richard's reach and glanced at the man with the shock of silver hair and the gray, almost opaque eyes. Those eyes had sent an inexplicable shiver along Maggie's nerves when the White Wolf of Balminsk received them a half hour ago.

"We've been traveling for three days," she offered as a polite excuse. "We haven't slept in anything other than a vertical position in all that time. We must seek out our beds."

President Cherkoff curled a lip in derision, as if in recognition of the fact that Dr. Richard Worthington would be horizontal soon enough, with or without the benefit of a bed.

Maggie stiffened at the look, although she had to admit, if only to herself, that Richard was rather the worse for wear. She hadn't needed his ingenious aside to know that he'd never tasted vodka before. When the first shot hit the back of his throat, his brown eyes had rounded until they resembled one of Vasili's threadbare truck tires. His Adam's apple had worked furiously, but, to give him his due, he'd swallowed the raw liquor with only a faint, gasping choke.

Unfortunately, with each of the interminable toasts their host insisted on, Richard had managed to get the vitriolic alcohol down a little more easily. In the process, he seemed to have lost the use of his vocal cords. Maggie should've had the foresight to warn him to sip the darn stuff instead of letting himself be pressured into following their host's example and throwing it down his throat.

"One last salute," Cherkoff ordered in heavily accented English. "Then my son will show you to your quarters."

It was a test. A crude one, admittedly, but a test nonetheless. Maggie recognized that fact as readily as Major Nikolas Cherkoff, who stood just behind his father. The livid scar slashing across the major's cheek twitched once, then was still.

Richard stretched across the table to retrieve his glass. The clear liquid sloshed over his shaky hand as he raised it shoulder-high.

"To the work that has brought you here," the White Wolf rasped. "May it achieve what we wish of it."

Since Cherkoff had made no secret of the fact that he bitterly resented the UN's interference in the affairs of Balminsk, Maggie wondered exactly what results he wished the team would achieve. She'd been briefed in detail about Cherkoff's reluctant compliance with the Strategic Arms Reduction Treaty. Only the fact that his country teetered on the brink of collapse had forced him to comply with the START provisions at all.

Once part of the breadbasket of the Soviet Union, Balminsk was now an *economic* basket case. During their ride across the high, fertile plains, Maggie had learned from Vasili that the huge combines that had once moved through endless wheat fields in long, zigzagging rows had fallen into disrepair, with no replacement parts to be had. The rich black chernozem soil now lay fallow and unplanted.

As they drove through the deserted, echoing capital, Maggie had seen only empty store windows and equally empty streets. A casual query to Major Cherkoff had elicited the flat response that prices in this small country now doubled every four weeks. A month's salary wouldn't cover the cost of one winter boot…if there was one to be bought.

From her briefings, Maggie knew most experts blamed Balminsk's problems on President Cherkoff's mismanagement and the unceasing war he'd conducted with his hated enemy, the old headman of Karistan. Unlike Karistan, however, Balminsk had at last ceded to economic pressures.

In return for promises of substantial aid, Cherkoff had agreed to allow the UN to inspect and dismantle the missiles occupying the silos on the Balminsk side of the border. But the old hard-line Communist wasn't happy about it. Not at all.

Even Richard sensed the hostility emanating from the ramrod-stiff man across the table. Blinking to clear his glazed eyes, he lofted his glass higher.

"To…to the work that brought us here."

Throwing back his head, Richard tossed down the rest of the vodka. He swallowed with a gurgling sort of gasp, blinked rapidly several times, then turned to look at Maggie.

As did the White Wolf of Balminsk.

And Major Nikolas Cherkoff.

Suppressing a sigh, Maggie pushed her thick, black-framed lenses back up the bridge of her nose with one forefinger and lifted her half-full glass. She downed the colorless liquid in two swallows, set the glass back on the table and gave the president a polite smile.

Behind that smile, liquid fire scorched her throat, already searing from the cautious sips she'd taken after each toast. Raw heat shot from her stomach to her lungs to her eyelids and back again, while her nerve endings went up in flames. Yet Maggie's bland smile gave no hint of how desperately she wanted to grab the water carafe sitting beside the vodka bottle and pour its contents down her throat.

The White Wolf bared his teeth in response and waved a curt dismissal.

With Richard stumbling behind her, Maggie followed the major from the dank reception room. Once out of the president's line of sight, she slipped two fingers under her glasses to wipe away the moisture that had collected at the corners of her eyes. Dragging in quick, shallow breaths, she brought her rioting senses under control and began to take careful note of her surroundings.

From the outside, Balminsk's presidential palace had appeared a magical place of odd-shaped buildings, high turrets and colorful, onion-shaped domes. Inside, however, long strips of paint peeled from the ceilings and brown water stains discolored the walls. The cavernous reception room they'd been shown into boasted ornate carved pillars and moldings, but the gilt that had once decorated them was chipped and more verdigris than gold. The empty rooms they now walked through hadn't withstood the passage of time any better. Maggie's boots thumped against bare, sadly damaged parquet floors and sent echoes down the deserted corridors.

After a number of convoluted turns, the major stopped in front of a set of doors guarded by an individual wearing a motley assortment of uniform items and a lethal-looking Uzi over one shoulder. At Cherkoff's nod, the guard threw open the doors and stood to one side.

"It is not the St. Regis," Nikolas said, "but I hope you will be comfortable here. There are enough rooms for the rest of your team members when they arrive."

Richard mumbled something inaudible and tripped inside. Maggie paused on the threshold, tilting her head to study the major's lean face. Just when had this enigmatic, scarred man been inside that venerable landmark, the St. Regis?

"I spent two years in New York City," he said in answer to her unspoken question. "As military *chargé* with the Soviet consulate."

Before Maggie could comment on that interesting bit of information, he bowed in an old-fashioned gesture totally at odds with his rather sinister appearance.

"Sleep well, Dr. St. Clare."

Maggie stepped inside the suite of rooms. The door closed behind her, and she heard the faint murmur of voices as the major issued orders to the guard to stay at his post.

Her eyes thoughtful, she strolled across a small vestibule lined with an array of doors. In the first room she peered into, a magnificent nineteenth-century sleigh bed in black walnut stood in solitary splendor in the middle of the floor. Her battered metal suitcase was set beside it. There wasn't another stick of furniture to be seen. No chair, no wardrobe, and nothing that even faintly resembled a sink. After a quick search through several other similarly sparse rooms, she finally located Richard.

He was standing in an odd, five-sided room, staring out a window that showed only the wall of an opposite wing and the gathering darkness.

Tugging off her heavy glasses, Maggie slipped them into her shirt pocket. "Richard, have you discovered the bathroom yet?"

"N-no."

Her heavily penciled brows drew together at his mumbled response. "Are you all right? Can I get you something? I think I have some Bromo-Seltzer in my bag."

He hunched his shoulders. "No. Thanks."

"Richard, if you're going to throw up, I wish you'd find the bathroom first."

"I—I'm not going to throw up."

Maggie sighed. Crossing the dusty parquet floor, she gave his shoulder a consoling pat.

"Look, you don't have to be embarrassed or macho about this. That was pretty potent stuff you chug-a-lugged back there. I'm not surprised it's making you sick."

"It...it's not making me sick...exactly."

"Then what?" Maggie tugged at his shoulder. "Richard, for heaven's sake, turn around. Let me look at you."

"No, I don't think I should."

"Why not?"

"It's...not...a good idea."

Alarmed at the low, almost panicky note in his voice, Maggie took a firm grip on his arm and swung him around. He stood rigid and unmoving, his brown eyes pinned on the blank space just over her left shoulder.

Frowning, she searched his face. His dark hair straggled down over his forehead, and he was a little green about the gills, but he didn't look ill enough to explain his unnatural rigidity or the way he kept swallowing convulsively. Unless...unless the damned White Wolf of Balminsk had slipped something other than vodka into his glass.

"Richard, what's the matter?" Maggie asked sharply. "What's wrong with you?"

"It's not an unexpected physiological reaction," he said through stiff lips.

"What is?" She shook his arm. "Tell me what you're feeling!"

"In...in clinical terms?"

"In any terms!" she shouted.

He swallowed again, then forced himself to meet her eyes. "I—I'm aroused."

"You're *what?*" Involuntarily, Maggie stepped back. Her gaze dropped, and then her jaw.

Dr. Richard Worthington was most definitely aroused. To a rather astonishing degree.

"I'm sorry..." His handsome young face was flaming. "It's the vodka. Apparently alcohol has a stimulating and quite unexpected effect on my endocrine system."

Maggie dragged her stunned gaze away from his runaway

endocrines. Wetting her lips, she tried to ease his embarrassment with a smile.

"Gee, thanks. And here I thought it might have been this road-dust cologne I've been wearing for the last six hours."

His agonized expression deepened. "Actually, you have a very delicate scent, one that agitates my olfactory sense."

"Richard, I was kidding!"

"I'm not. I find you very excitatory. Sexually speaking, that is. Er, all of you."

Maggie gaped at him. She was wearing boots that gave her the grace and resonance of a bull moose making his way through the north woods. Her pants were so stiff and baggy, not even the roughnecks on her father's crew would have pulled them on to wade through an oil spill. The heavy, figure-flattening T-shirt under her scratchy wool shirt just about zeroed out her natural attributes, and there was enough charcoal on her eyebrows to start a good-size campfire. Yet this young man was staring at her with a slowly gathering masculine warmth in his brown eyes that made her feel as though the artists at Glamour Shots had just worked their magic with her.

It was Maggie's turn to swallow. "I think we need to talk about this."

"Not if it makes you feel uncomfortable," Richard replied with a quiet dignity.

It wasn't making *her* feel uncomfortable, Maggie thought wryly. She wasn't the one with a bead of sweat trickling down the side of her neck and the endocrine system working double overtime.

Although it obviously took some effort, he managed a small, tight smile. "You don't have to worry. I won't attempt anything Neanderthal. But you must know how I feel about you."

Astounded at his mastery over a vodka-filled stomach and rampaging hormones, Maggie shook her head.

"Well, no, as a matter of fact. I don't."

He lifted one hand and traced the line of her cheek with a

gentle finger, gliding over the semitattoo on the side of her jaw.

"I think you shine with an inner beauty few women possess, Dr. St. Clare…Megan. A beauty that comes from the heart. I've seen you swallow your impatience with me time and again these last few days. You've never once undermined my authority with the team, or let the delays and inconveniences bother you. I've heard you laugh in that delightful way you have when the others were simmering with irritation, and seen your eyes sparkle with a joy of life that makes my breath catch. You're a kind person, Megan, and a very beautiful woman. And I'm sure you're a most proficient geologist," he tacked on.

Kindness wasn't exactly high on the list of most desired qualities in an OMEGA agent. And, in Richard's case, at least, beauty was definitely in the eye of the beholder.

But Maggie sighed and let her chin rest in his warm palm. That was the longest, most coherent string of sentences she'd heard the young physicist put together at one time, and probably the sweetest compliment she'd ever receive in her life.

"Just how many women have you really known, Richard?" she asked softly. "Outside the laboratory, I mean?"

The shy smile that made him seem so much younger than his years tugged at his lips. "Aside from my mother? One, really. And I didn't particularly impress her, either. In fact, I've only heard from her once in the three years since we met. But that doesn't mean I don't fully appreciate what I feel for you."

Maggie didn't make the mistake of dismissing his emotions lightly. For all his seeming ineptitude, Richard was a highly intelligent man. And one whose self-restraint she had to admire. She doubted she'd exhibit the same rigid control after several glasses of potent vodka if she was locked in a room with, say…

Unbidden, Adam Ridgeway's slate blue eyes and lean, aristocratic face filled her mind. Maggie pulled her chin free of Richard's light hold, frowning at the sudden wild leaping of her pulse. She must have been more affected by that one glass of raw alcohol than she'd thought.

"We'll talk about this tomorrow, after the vodka has worked its way through your, ah, system."

"Megan…"

"Get some sleep, Richard. The rest of the team should arrive early in the morning. When they do, you'll want to update them on your meeting with Cherkoff and review the schedule for our first day on-site."

He accepted her reminder of his responsibilities with good grace and stood quietly as she left.

With a silent shake of her head, Maggie made her way to her own room. Good grief. She'd better make sure Richard avoided any more ceremonial toasts. That rather spectacular display of his endocrine system would definitely rank among the more vivid memories she'd take away from this particular mission, but it wasn't one she wanted him to repeat on a frequent basis. Not when she needed to focus all her concentration on nuclear missiles and hostile, hungry wolves.

Maggie stopped just inside the threshold to her room and eyed the thick, feather-filled comforter piled atop the curved bed. Imagining how wonderful it would be to sink down into that fluffy mound, she sighed. Later, she promised herself. Later, she would strip down to her T-shirt and panties and lose herself in that cloud of softness.

Right now, however, she had a mission to conduct.

Closing the door to her room, she sat on the edge of the bed and punched Cowboy's code into her wristwatch. While she waited for him to respond, she opened the suitcase and rummaged through her possessions. By the time she'd tugged off the plaid shirt and bulky pants and pulled on a black turtleneck and slacks, Nate still hadn't returned her signal. Grinning, Maggie wondered if he was having difficulty slipping away from a potential bride who wanted to inspect his plumbing.

David Jensen, on the other hand, responded immediately.

"OMEGA Control. Go ahead, Chameleon."

"Just wanted to confirm that I'm in place, Doc."

"I've been tracking you. You made good time, despite the initial delays."

Maggie's grin widened. She would've bet her last pair of clean socks David had plotted the digitized satellite signals to know exactly when she'd arrived in Balminsk's capital. With his engineer's passion for detail, he wouldn't let her and Cowboy out of his sight for a second. His precision in the control center certainly gave Maggie a sense of comfort.

In response to his comment, she dismissed the hair-raising, heart-stopping hours in Vasili's truck with a light laugh. "Our driver is in training for the first Russian Grand Prix. He made up for lost time. I couldn't raise Cowboy, Doc. Have you heard from him?"

"One brief transmission, several hours ago. He said something about losing a race to a one-armed acrobat and heading toward Balminsk."

"He's heading here?" Maggie's heavy brows drew together.

"He was. I now show him stopped 27.3 miles from the border. He's been at that position for several hours. There are satellite reports of heavy weather in the area, which may explain why he's holding in place."

"Well, the weather's fine here," Maggie replied. "I'm going out to reconnoiter."

"Roger, Chameleon. Good hunting."

"Thanks, Doc."

Maggie knelt on one knee, surveying the contents of her open suitcase. She didn't need to scan it with the infrared sensor concealed in the handle to know the various objects inside had been handled by someone with a different body-heat signature from hers. If the White Wolf hadn't thought to order a search, his son would have. Unless the searchers were a whole bunch more imaginative than OMEGA's special devices unit, though, they wouldn't have found anything except some plain cotton underwear, thick socks, another plaid shirt or two, some essential feminine supplies, a Sony Walkman with a few tapes, and the geological books and equipment Maggie had considered necessary for her role.

Pursing her lips, she studied the various items, trying to decide which had the most value in a country whose economy was in such shambles that black-marketing and barter were the only means of commodity exchange.

A few moments later, she opened the door to the suite. The guard pushed his shoulders off the opposite wall, his bushy brows lowering in a suspicious scowl.

"Good evening, my friend," Maggie said in the Russian dialect predominantly used in Balminsk. "Does your wife have a fondness for perfumed body lotion, perhaps?"

Okay, Maggie thought as the guard sniffed the small black-and-white plastic squeeze tube, so some people might not consider Chanel No. 5 Body Creme an essential feminine supply. She did. But she'd decided not to risk agitating Richard's olfactory sense any further.

Three hours later, Maggie and the guard wound their way back through the dark, deserted corridors of the presidential palace. Her mind whirled with the bits and pieces of information she'd managed to collect.

She hadn't expected the few residents of Balminsk she'd encountered to open up to an outsider, and they hadn't. Exactly. But a few country-and-western tapes, a confident smile and her ease with their language had helped overcome their surly suspicion to a certain degree.

At her request, the guard had taken her to what passed for a restaurant in Balminsk. He'd explained to the proprietor of a tiny kitchen-café that the *Amerikanski* was with the UN team and wished to sample some local fare after her long trip. The ruddy-faced cook had shrugged and shown her to the only table in the room. The other customers, all two of them, had crowded to the far end of the table and shot Maggie frowning glances over their bowls of potato soup.

The soup was thin and watery and deliciously flavored. Maggie followed the other patrons' example and sopped up every drop from the bottom of her bowl with a chunk of crusty black bread. Her first bite of a spicy, meat-filled cabbage roll had her taste buds clamoring for more, but the empty pot on the table indicated that she'd exhausted the café's supply of menu items. Luckily, the light, crispy strips of fried dough drenched in honey that the cook served for dessert satisfied the rest of her hunger. So much so that she had to force down a minuscule cup of heavily sweetened tea.

The patrons of the tiny café mumbled into their cups in answer to her casual questions. When she inquired as to their occupations, they responded with a shrug. It was only through skillful questioning and even more skillful listening that Maggie learned anything useful. Like the fact that the brawny, muscled man in blue cotton work pants and a sweatshirt proclaiming the benefits of one of the Crimea's better known health spas was a modern-day cattle rustler. It slipped out when the cook made a comment about needing more Karistani beef for the *peroshki*.

The low-voiced discussion that followed gave Maggie a grim idea of how desperate Balminsk's economic situation really was. With so many other hot spots in the world demanding the West's attention, it was entirely possible the economic aid package Balminsk had been promised might arrive too late to prevent widespread starvation during the coming winter. Unless the men of this country took action of their own to prevent it. If that action resulted in a renewal of the hostilities that had ravaged Balminsk and Karistan for centuries, so be it.

From what Maggie could glean, that action would come soon.

As she followed the guard back through the palace, she knew she needed to talk to Cowboy, fast. Slipping her escort a Randy Travis cassette for his troubles, she lifted the latch on the door to the team's suite and eased inside. Richard's room was bathed in dark stillness, punctuated at regular intervals by a hiccuping snore. Smiling, Maggie opened her own door.

She'd taken only two steps inside when a hard hand slapped over her mouth. In a fraction of a heartbeat, her training kicked in, and she reacted with an instinctive sureness that would've made even the steely-eyed Jaguar proud.

Her right elbow jabbed back with every ounce of force she could muster. Her left ankle wrapped around one behind her. As her attacker went down, Maggie twisted to face him.

A single chop to the side of the neck sent him crumpling to the floor.

Chapter 10

Maggie made herself comfortable on the sleigh bed while she waited for Nikolas Cherkoff to recover consciousness. Holding her .22-caliber Smith and Wesson automatic in her left hand, she used the other to break off bits of the crispy dough strip she'd brought back as a late-night snack.

As she nibbled on the savory sweet, she kept a close watch on the major. She had far too much experience in the field to take her eyes off a target, even an unconscious one, which was probably what saved her life a few moments later.

Cherkoff, Sr., might be known as the White Wolf, but Cherkoff, Jr., possessed a few animal traits all his own. His lids flew up, and his black eyes focused with the speed of an eagle's. Curling his legs, he sprang to the attack like a panther loosed from a cage.

"One more step," Maggie warned, whipping up the .22, "and the White Wolf will have to sire a new cub."

He pulled up short. In the stark light of the overhead bulb, his scar stood out like a river of pain across his cheek.

"So, Dr. St. Clare," he said at last. "It appears we've

reached what the military would call a countervailing force of arms."

Maggie arched a brow. "It doesn't strike me as particularly countervailing. I'm the only one with a weapon here. Unless you have something hidden that my search failed to turn up...and I conducted a *very* thorough search."

Thorough enough to discover that Nikolas Cherkoff's face wasn't the only portion of his anatomy that bore the scars of combat. Maggie hadn't actually seen phosphorus-grenade wounds before, but Jaguar had described them in enough detail for her to guess what had caused the horrible, puckered burns on the major's stomach. And she didn't think he'd taken that bullet through the shoulder in a hunting accident.

He jerked his chin toward her left hand. "Do you really think a weapon of that small caliber can stop a man of my size and weight before he does serious damage?"

"Well, yes...when it's loaded with long-rifle hollow-point stingers, which, as I'm sure you're aware, do as much tissue damage as a .38 special."

His black eyes narrowed dangerously. "Do you care to tell me what a UN geologist is doing with such a weapon?"

"I might, if you tell me what you're doing in said geologist's room."

His jaw worked at her swift, uncompromising response. "I came to speak with you."

"Really? And you attack everyone you wish to speak with?"

"Don't be foolish. Naturally, I was alarmed to find you gone. So when a figure dressed all in black...and of considerably different proportions than the one I expected...stepped into the room, I reacted accordingly."

Maggie had to admit her knit slacks and turtleneck were a bit more slenderizing than the baggy tan pants and thick wool shirt, but she wasn't ready to buy his story of mistaken identity. She kept the .22 level.

"What did you wish to speak to me about, Major?"

He didn't respond for several seconds. "Your team goes from Balminsk to Karistan, does it not?" he said at last.

"It does."

"I came to warn you. You travel into harm's way."

Maggie regarded him steadily. "Why?"

"Why what?"

"Why do you warn me? What's in this for you?"

At her soft question, he went still. Like an animal retreating behind a protective screen, he seemed to withdraw inside himself, to a place she couldn't follow and wasn't sure she wanted to even if she could. Black shutters dropped over his eyes, leaving behind an emptiness that made Maggie shiver.

As the seconds ticked by, the deep, gut-level instincts that the other OMEGA agents joked about and Adam Ridgeway swore added to the silver strands at his temples, stirred in Maggie. She chewed on a corner of her lower lip for a few endless moments, then rose.

Lifting the hem of her turtleneck, she slid the .22 into the specially designed and shielded holster at her waist.

"Tell me," she said quietly, walking toward him.

The scar twitched.

She laid a hand on an arm composed entirely of taut sinew and rock-hard muscle. "Tell me why you came to warn me."

With infinite, agonizing slowness, Cherkoff looked down at her hand. When he raised his head, his eyes were as flat and as desolate as before, but focused on her face.

"Balminsk is a series of catastrophes waiting to happen. If not this week, then the next."

"And?"

He spoke slowly, his voice harsh with effort. "And I've seen enough of war to know that this time, when our world explodes with guns and bullets, the wounds could be fatal. To us. To Karistan. To any caught between us."

"Cowboy, this is Chameleon. Do you read me?"

Nate hunkered down on both heels and pressed the transmit button.

"I read you, Chameleon, but talk fast. I've got about a minute, max, before someone notices Red and I have taken a slight detour and comes looking for us.''

Maggie's voice filtered through the darkness surrounding Nate. ''I'm in Balminsk's capitol. I'm convinced they don't have the decoder here. But I'm also convinced that all hell's about to break loose.''

''What kind of hell?''

''A raid on Karistan is imminent, but I can't confirm when or where. My source is convinced that it will reopen hostilities and escalate into something really nasty, really fast.''

''Is your source reliable?''

''I think so. My instincts say so.''

''That's good enough for me,'' Nate muttered.

''Any progress in finding the decoder on your end?''

Nate's jaw clenched. ''No.''

A little silence descended, and then the sensitive transmitter picked up Maggie's soft caution.

''Things in this corner of the world are turning out to be a lot more desperate than any of the intelligence analysts realized. Be careful, Cowboy.''

''I know. I've got my boots on.''

''What?''

Nate allowed himself a small smile. ''When the corral's this full of horse manure, Wily Willie always advised pulling on a good pair of boots before going in to shovel it out. I'm wearing my Naconas. Make sure you keep those clunkers of yours on.''

He could hear an answering smile seep into Maggie's voice. ''I will. I promise.''

''And keep me posted, Chameleon.''

''Will do.'' She paused, then added in a little rush, ''Look, I think I might be able hold them off at this end for a few days. Two, maybe three, at the most. Will that help?''

''It wouldn't hurt,'' he returned. Two, possibly three, more days to work his target. To break the shell around her. To learn the desperate secret she hid behind that proud, self-contained exterior. It wouldn't take him that long, he vowed to himself. And to Alex.

"What have you got in mind?" he asked Maggie.

"The team is scheduled to go down into the first silo tomorrow. Uh...don't be alarmed if you hear reports of a low-grade nuclear fuel spill."

The hairs on Nate's neck stood on end. "Good Lord, woman!" he shot back. "That's not something you want to fool around with!"

"Oh, for Pete's sake. I'm not going to actually *do* anything. But maybe I can make some people think I did."

"Chameleon!" Nate caught his near shout and forced himself to lower his voice. "Listen to me! Don't mess around down in that silo. Those missiles are old and unstable. You don't know what you're dealing with there."

"I may not, but one of the world's foremost nuclear physicists is leading this team, remember? I'm fairly sure I can convince him to cooperate."

"Why the hell would he cooperate in something like this?"

"It has to do with endocrine systems, but I don't have time to go into that right now. Just trust me, this man knows what he's doing."

Nate almost missed her last, faint transmission.

"I hope."

When Maggie signed off, Nate remained in a low crouch, staring at the illuminated face of his watch.

She wouldn't, he told himself. Surely to God, she wouldn't. With a sinking feeling, he acknowledged that she would.

Holy hell! Maggie intended to fake a nuclear fuel spill! Nate shook his head. He'd just as soon not be around when she tried to explain this one to Adam Ridgeway.

Contrary to the trigger-happy Hollywood stereotype, OMEGA agents were highly skilled professionals. They employed use of deadly force only as a last, desperate resort. Most had used it at one time or another, but no one ever spoke of it outside the required debrief with the director. Eventually a sanitized version of the event would circulate so that other agents could learn from it and, hopefully, avoid a similar lethal position.

Within that general framework, OMEGA's director gave his operatives complete discretion in the field to act as the situation warranted. Still, Nate suspected Maggie might have to do some pretty fast talking to convince Ridgeway the situation warranted what she had in mind.

Whatever the hell it was she had in mind!

Nate's stomach clenched as he considered the awesome possibilities. He rose, feeling as twisted and taut as newly strung barbed wire. Maggie's transmission had added a gut-wrenching sense of urgency to the edgy tension already generated by the hours Nate had just shared with Alex on the shallow ledge.

Instead of easing after he'd settled back against the wall and put some space between himself and his target, his desire had sharpened with every glance of her black-fringed eyes, deepened with every movement of her bare flesh under her coat. By the time the storm's violence had subsided enough to allow safe travel, Nate's physical and mental frustration had left him feeling as surly as a kicked mongrel, and twice as ugly.

The long ride hadn't improved his mood. An hour after they rejoined Dimitri and the others, a silent signal had pulsed against the back of Nate's wrist. His impatience had mounted as he waited for an opportunity to shake his companions and answer the signal. He knew he had to do it on the trail, if possible. Once he returned to camp, it would be even harder to slip away from Ivana and Anya, not to mention Katerina.

The Karistani campfires were distant pinpoints of light against the velvet blackness before he managed a few moments alone. Dimitri had halted beside a blackened, smoldering tree split lengthwise by lightning. When Alex and the others clustered around to examine the storm's damage, Nate had used the cover of the colt's restless prancing at the end of its tether to slip away.

He'd known he had only a few moments, and he'd used them. Now he had to deal with what he'd learned from Maggie.

As Nate moved toward Red, standing patiently nearby, tension gnawed at him.

Where the hell was that decoder? How would it come into play if Balminsk launched an attack? And what was he going to do with, or to, Alexandra if Maggie couldn't hold off the raiders?

Despite the cool night air, sweat dampened his palms. How could he protect Alex? Especially when the blasted woman didn't want protection. She took her responsibilities as *ataman* of this tattered host so fiercely, so personally, that Nate didn't doubt she'd be in the middle of the action. His gut twisted at the thought.

Reins in hand, he stopped and stared into the distance. The star-studded Karistani night took on a gray, hazy cast. The open steppes narrowed, closed, until they resembled a fog-shrouded street. The vast quiet seemed to carry a distant, ghostly echo of automatic rifle fire. The sound of panting desperation. A low grunt. The gush of warm, red blood...

The soft plop of hooves wrenched Nate from his private hell.

Instantly he registered the direction, the gait and the size of the horse that made the sound. The tension in him shifted focus, from a woman who'd been part of his past to a woman he damned well was going to make sure had a future.

The metallic click of a rifle bolt being drawn back sounded just before Alex's voice drifted out of the night.

"I hope that's you, Sloan. If it is, you'd better let me know in the next two seconds."

"It's me," he replied, in a low, dangerous snarl, "and the name's Nate."

She didn't respond for a moment. When she did, her tone was a good ten degrees cooler than it had been.

"Before you take another step, I suggest you tell me just why you separated from the rest of us...and why you suddenly seem to have a problem with what I call you."

Nate wasn't in the mood for threats. He took Red's reins, shoved a boot into the stirrup and swung into the saddle. Pulling the stallion's head around, he kneed him toward the waiting woman. Her face was a pale blur when he answered.

"It's like this, *Alexandra*. If you Karistani women insist on sneakin' up on a man while he's tryin' to commune with nature, I figure you ought to at least call him by his given name."

Her chin lifted at his drawling sarcasm. "All right, *Nate*. I'll use your given name. And you won't disappear again. For any reason."

She might've thought she was calling his bluff, but he smiled in savage satisfaction at her response.

"You know, Alex, Wily Willie always warned me to chew on my thoughts a bit before I spit them out. You don't want me to disappear on you again? For any reason? Fine by me. From here on out, sweetheart, you're going to think you've sprouted a second shadow. You'd better look over your shoulder before you...commune with nature, or with anyone else."

Nate smiled grimly when he heard a familiar sound. The short whip cracked twice more against her boot top before she replied in a low, curt voice.

"You know that's not what I meant."

"Well, *you* may not have meant it, Alexandra, but *I* sure did."

It didn't take Alex long to discover Sloan did mean it.

Without a word being spoken between them, he and Dimitri somehow exchanged places. The tired, stoop-shouldered lieutenant fell back, and Nate took his position at Alex's side as though he belonged there.

The small band rode into camp an hour later. The temperature had dropped, and the wind knifed through their still-damp garments with a bone-chilling ease. Her hands numb, Alex could barely grip the reins when she at last slid out of the saddle.

A small crowd gathered to meet them and hear what news, if any, they brought. While the men took charge of the horses and the women pressed mugs of hot tea into their hands, Katerina drifted to Nate's side to welcome him back personally.

"You...you wear the wet!" she exclaimed, plucking at his jacket sleeve. She glanced around at the rest of the small party. "All of you."

Anya, her pale hair dangling down her back in a fat braid, clucked and murmured something in her soft voice.

"Come," Katerina urged, tugging on Nate's arm. "Anya says the water is yet hot in the steaming tent. She left the fires...how is it? Stroked?"

"Stoked," Alex supplied between sips of hot, steaming tea.

The thought of Nate being hustled to the small tent that served as the camp's communal steam bath almost made her forget the shivers racking her body. Like most of their European counterparts, the Karistanis had few inhibitions about shedding their clothes for a good, invigorating soak. Alex herself had long ago learned to balance her more conservative upbringing in the States with the earthier and far more practical Karistani traditions. But she knew that few Americans took to communal bathing. Folding her hands around the mug, she waited to watch Sloan—Nate—squirm.

If the thought of stripping down in front of strangers disconcerted him, he didn't show it.

"Thanks, Katerina," he responded with his lazy grin. "We could use some thawing-out. But the steaming tent won't hold us all. Let Dimitri and the others go first. I'll take the next shift...with Alexandra."

Katerina sent Alex a quick, frowning glance over the heads of the others.

"It is not...not meet for you to bathe with an unmarried woman," she said primly to Nate.

Ha! Alex thought. If he'd suggested Katerina go into the steam tent, she would've joined him quickly enough.

The cattiness of her reaction surprised Alex, and flooded her with guilt. Deciding she'd had enough for one day, Alex passed Anya her mug.

"I'll leave the second shift to you," she conceded to Nate, not very graciously.

"God keep you until the dawn, Alexandra Danilova."

"And you...Nate Sloan."

Alex rose with the sun the next morning and walked out into
the brisk air. The wind had taken on a keenness that brought
a sting to her cheeks and made her grateful for the warmth of
her high-collared, long-sleeved shirt in soft cream wool, which
she wore belted at the waist. Its thick cashmerelike fabric defied
the wind, as did the folds of her loose, baggy trousers. Fumbling in her pocket for a box of matches to light the charcoal
in the samovar, she saw with some surprise that the brass urn
was already steaming.

"Will you take tea, *ataman?*"

Turning, she found Dimitri waiting in a patch of sunlight
beside the tent. Gratefully Alex reached for the tin mug he
offered.

"Thank you. And thank you, as well, for lighting the samovar."

"It was not I," he replied. "The *Amerikanski,* he did so."

Alex folded her hands around the steaming mug, her spine
tingling in awareness. Nate had been up before dawn? To light
the samovar? Involuntarily she glanced over her shoulder, half
expecting, half wanting, to see him behind her.

Dimitri picked up his own mug, then gave a mutter of disgust as tea sloshed over the sides. Seeing how his stiff hands
shook, Alex felt a wave of compassion for this loyal and well-
worn lieutenant.

"Why are you awake so early?" she asked. "Why don't
you wait until the sun takes the chill from the winds to leave
your tent?"

"Until the sun takes the stiffness from my bones, you
mean?" His pale, rheumy eyes reflected a wry resignation. "I
fear even the summer sun can no longer ease the ache in these
bones."

Alex felt a crushing weight on her heart. "Dimitri," she said
slowly, painfully, "perhaps you should go to the lowlands for
the winter. You and the others who wish it. This...this could
be a harsh time for Karistan."

"No, my *ataman*. I was born on the steppes. I will die on the steppes." His leathered face creased in a smile. "But not today. Nor, perhaps, tomorrow. Drink your tea, and I will tell you what Gregor learned from listening to his wireless in the small hours of the night."

As the lieutenant related an overheard conversation between two shortwave-radio operators in Balminsk, a band seemed to tighten around Alex's chest.

"And when is this raid to take place?" she asked, her eyes on the distant horizon.

"Gregor could not hear," Dimitri replied with a shrug. "Or the speakers did not say. All that came through was that Karistani beef must provide filling for *peroshki*, or many in Balminsk will die this winter."

"I suppose they care not how many Karistani will die if they take the cattle!"

"It has always been so."

Alex swallowed her bitterness. "Yes, it has. Although it will leave the camp thin, we must double the scouts along the eastern border. Make sure they have plenty of flares to give us warning. Send Mikhail and one other to move the cattle in from the north grazing range. I'll bring in those from the south."

Dimitri nodded. "It is done."

He threw the rest of his tea on the ground, then half turned to leave. Swinging back, he faced her, an unreadable expression on his lined countenance.

"What?" Alex asked. "What troubles you?"

"If the raiders come and I'm not with you," he said slowly, "keep the *Amerikanski* close by you. To guard your back."

Alex stared at him in surprise. "Why should you think he cares about my back?"

The somber light in his eyes gave way to a watery smile. "Ah, 'Zandra. This one cares about most parts of you, would you but open your eyes and see it. You should take him to your bed and be done with it."

Her face warming, Alex lifted her chin. "Don't confuse me

with Katerina or Ivana. I'm not in competition for this man's...services.''

"Nevertheless, sooner or later he will offer them to you. Or force them on you, if he's half the stallion I think he is."

His pale eyes fastened on something just over Alex's left shoulder, and he gave a rumble of low laughter.

"From the looks of him this morning, I would say it may be sooner rather than later."

He strolled away, leaving Alex to face Sloan.

Gripping her tin mug in both hands, she swung around. As she watched him stride toward her, she realized with a sinking sensation that she wasn't quite sure how to handle this man. The balance between them had shifted subtly in the past twenty-four hours. Alex felt less sure about him, less in control.

She didn't understand why. Unless it was the determined glint in his eyes. Or the set of his broad shoulders beneath the turned-up collar of his jacket. Or the way his gaze made a slow, deliberate journey from the tip of her upthrust chin, down over each of the buttons on her shirt, to the toes of her boots, then back up again. By the time his eyes met hers once more, she felt as though she'd been undressed in public...and put together again with everything inside out.

"Mornin', Alexandra."

"Good morning, Sl—Nate."

"I like your hair like that." A smile webbed the weathered skin at the corners of his eyes. "Especially with that thinga-mabob in it."

Alex fingered the French braid that hung over one shoulder, its end tied with a tasseled bit of yarn and horsehair. The compliment disconcerted her, threw her even more off stride.

"Thank you," she replied hesitantly.

"You ready to ride?"

She tipped him a cool look. "Ride where?"

"I talked to Dimitri earlier. You need to bring your cattle in."

"That so?"

His smile deepening, he reached for a mug and twisted the spigot on the samovar.

"That's so."

It was only after his soft response that Alex realized she'd picked up one of his favorite colloquialisms. Good Lord, as if her jumble of Karistani, North Philly establishment and Manhattan garment-district phrasing weren't confusing enough.

Disdaining sugar, he sipped at the bitter green tea. "How many head do we have to bring in?"

Alex hesitated. She didn't particularly care for this air of authority he'd assumed, but it would be foolish to spurn his help. Any help. With the feeling that she was crossing some invisible line, she shrugged.

"A hundred or so from the north grazing. Mikhail will bring those to the ravine. There are another thirty, perhaps forty, south of here."

"We're going after them?"

She forced a reluctant response. "I guess we are."

He set aside his mug and stepped closer to curl a finger under her chin. Tilting her face to his, he smiled down at her.

"That wasn't so bad, was it?"

When she didn't answer, he brushed his thumb along the line of her jaw. "Listen to me, Alex. It's not a sign of weakness to ask for help. You don't have to ride this trail all alone."

"No, it appears she does not."

Katerina's voice cut through the stillness between them like a knife.

Alex jerked her chin out of Nate's hold as her cousin let the tent flap fall behind her and sauntered out. Tossing her cloud of dark hair over one shoulder, she glared at them both.

Apparently the peace between her and her cousin was as fragile as the one between Karistan and Balminsk, Alex thought with an inner sigh. Anxious to avoid open hostilities with the younger woman, she suggested to Nate that they saddle up.

Chapter 11

Within two hours, Alex and Nate had driven the cattle into the ravine where their small band merged with the herd Mikhail and his men had brought down from the north. Leaving the beefy, red-faced Karistani with the black Denver Broncos ball cap on his head in charge, Alex insisted on returning to camp immediately.

They were met by Katerina and Petr Borodín, who was practically hopping up and down in excitement.

"You will not believe it, *ataman!*" he exclaimed in Karistani as they dismounted. "Such news Gregor has just heard over his wireless!"

Alex's heart jumped into her throat. She thrust her reins into Katerina's hands and rushed over to the thin, balding warrior.

"What news, Petr? Tell me! What has happened? We saw no flares. We heard no shots."

"There's been some sort of accident in Balminsk. No one knows exactly what. The radio reports all differ. The head of the team says it is cause for concern."

"What team?" she asked sharply.

Petr waved his one arm, causing the medals on his chest to clink in a chorus of excitement. "The team that checks the missiles. From the United Nations."

"They're there, then," Alex murmured, half under her breath.

Petr cackled gleefully. "Yes, they are there, and there they will stay. This team leader has said that Balminsk's borders must be closed, and has called in UN helicopters to patrol them."

"What!"

"No one may travel in or out of Balminsk, until some person who checks the soils...some geo...geo..."

"Geologist?"

"Yes, until this geologist says there is no contamination."

"Oh, my God."

Her mind whirling, Alex tried to grasp the ramifications to Karistan of this bizarre situation. If what Gregor had heard was true, no raiders would ride across the borders from Balminsk, at least not for some days. But neither would anyone else!

The one person she'd been waiting for, the one whose advice she'd been counting on, was stranded on the other side of the border.

"You want to let me know what's going on here?"

The steel underlying Nate's drawl swung Alex around. "There are reports of an accident in Balminsk."

His eyes lanced into her, hard and laser-sharp. "What kind of an accident?"

"No one quite knows for sure. The reports are confused. Something about soil contamination."

"Anyone hurt?"

Alex relayed the question to Petr, who shook his head.

"Not according to reports so far. But supposedly they've closed the borders until a geologist with the UN team verifies conditions. No one may go into or out of Balminsk for several days, at least."

"Holy hell!" Nate raked a hand through his short, sun-streaked hair. "I hope she's got her boots on," he muttered under his breath.

Katerina sauntered forward, her dark eyes gleaming. "So, cousin, this is good, no? We have the...the reprieve."

"Perhaps."

"Pah! Those to the east have worries of their own for a while. I? I say we should take our ease for what hours we may."

"Well..."

"As the women say, my cousin, life is short, and only a fool would scrub dirty linens when she may sip the vodka and dance the dance."

Strolling forward, Katerina hooked a hand through Nate's arm and tilted her head to smile provocatively up at him. "Come, I will show you the work of my aunt, Feodora. She paints the...the...*pysanky*."

"The Easter eggs," Alex translated, fighting a sudden and violent surge of jealousy at the thought of Katerina sipping and dancing with Nate.

"Yes, the Easter eggs," her cousin cooed. "They are most beautiful."

Lifting her chin, Alex gave Nate a cool look. "You should go with Katerina. My aunt is very talented. One of her pieces is on permanent display at the Saint Petersburg Academy of Arts."

Nate patted the younger woman's hand. "Well, I'd like to see those eggs, you understand. But later. Right now, I'd better stick with Alexandra and Petr. We need to find out a little more about what's happened in Balminsk."

Katerina pursed her lips, clearly not pleased with his excuse. With a petulant shrug, she flipped her dark hair over one shoulder.

"Stay with them, then. Perhaps later we will play a bit, no?"

"Perhaps," he answered with one of his slow grins, which

instantly restored Katerina's good humor and set Alex's back teeth on edge.

"Come, Petr," she snapped. "Let us go see what additional news Gregor may have gleaned."

Alex turned and headed for the camp. With the sun almost overhead, she didn't cast much of a shadow on the dusty earth. But Sloan's was longer, more solid. It merged with hers as they strode toward the tent that served as the Karistanis' administrative center.

For the rest of the day, Gregor stayed perched on his shaky camp stool in front of his ancient radio. Static crackled over the receiver as he picked up various reports. The residents of the camp drifted in and out of the tent to hear the news, shaking their heads at each confused report.

No Karistani would wish a disaster such as Chernobyl on even their most hated enemy—and it was soon obvious that the accident in Balminsk was not of that magnitude or seriousness. It kept the White Wolf trapped within his own lair, however, and that filled the Karistanis with a savage glee.

Long into the night, groups gathered to discuss events. The tensions that had racked the camp for so long eased perceptibly. Having lived on the knife edge of danger and war long, the host savored every moment of their reprieve. It was a short one, they acknowledged, but sufficient to justify bringing out the vodka bottles and indulging themselves a bit.

By the next morning, an almost festive air permeated the camp, one reminiscent of the old days. One Alex hadn't seen since her return.

The Karistani were a people who loved music, dance and drink, not necessarily in that order. In the summers of Alex's youth, they had needed little excuse to gather around the campfires at night and listen to the balalaika or sing the lusty ballads that told of their past—of great battles and warrior princes. Of mythical animals and sleighs flying across snow-blanketed steppes.

On holy days or in celebration of some triumph, the women

had cooked great platters of sugared beets and spicy pastries. Whole sides of beef had turned on spits, and astonishing quantities of vodka had disappeared in a single night. Karistani feasts rivaled those rumored to have been given by the Cossacks of old, although Alex had never seen among her mother's people quite the level of orgiastic activity that reputedly had taken place in previous centuries.

As she and Nate walked through the bright morning sunlight, blessed by a rare lack of wind, she saw signs of the feverish activity that preceded a night of revelry.

Alex herself wasn't immune to the general air of excitement. For reasons she didn't really want to consider, she'd donned her red wool tunic with the gold frogging, freshly cleaned after its dousing in the storm two nights ago. Her hair gleamed from an herbal shampoo and vigorous brushing, and she'd dug out the supply of cosmetics she usually didn't bother with here on the steppes. A touch of mascara, a little lipstick, and she felt like a different woman altogether.

One Sloan approved of, if the glint in his eyes when he met her outside the tent was any measure. Ignoring him and the flutter the sight of his tall, lean body in its usual jeans and soft cotton shirt caused, Alex strode through the camp.

Anya stood at a sturdy wood worktable, her sleeves rolled up and her arms floured to her elbows, slamming dough onto the surface with the cheerful enthusiasm of a kerchiefed sumo wrestler. Her pretty face lighted up as she caught sight of Nate, and she called a greeting that Alex refused to translate verbatim. It never failed to astound her that Anya—pale, delicate Anya—should have such an earthy appreciation of the male physique.

Ivana, honey pot in hand, came out of the women's tent as they approached. Alex translated the widow's laughing invitation for Nate and Ole Red to join her on an expedition in search of honeycombs, and Nate's good-natured declination.

Secretly pleased, but curious about his refusal, Alex tipped her head back to look up at him. "Why don't you go with her? I have things I must do. I don't need you on my heels every minute.''

Sloan hooked his thumbs in his belt, smiling down at her. ''You know, Alexandra, Wily Willie used to warn me to be careful what I wished for, because I just might get it. You wanted me to stick close? I'm stickin' close.''

Alex wasn't sure whether it was the smile or the soft promise that sent the ripple of sensation down her spine. To cover her sudden pleasure, she shrugged.

''I'm beginning to think your Willie has Karistani blood in his veins. He has as many sayings as the women of this host. One of which,'' Alex warned, ''has to do with skinning and tanning the hide of a bothersome male. At least if one makes a rug out of him, he can be put to some use.''

Laughter glinted in his hazel eyes. ''Ah, sweetheart, when this is all over, I'll have to show you just how many uses a bothersome male can be put to.''

The ripple of sensation became a rush of pleasure. He'd called her ''sweetheart'' several times before. At least once in anger. Several times in mockery. But this was the first time the term had rolled off his lips with a low, caressing intimacy that sent liquid heat spilling through Alex's veins. The sensation disconcerted her so much that it took a few moments for the rest of his words to penetrate.

''When what is all over?'' she asked slowly.

The laughter faded from his eyes. ''You tell me, Alex. What's going on here? What have you got planned?''

They stood toe-to-toe in the dusty square. The camp bustled with activity all around them, but neither of them paid any attention. The sun heated the air, but neither of them felt it.

''Tell me,'' he urged.

Alex wanted to. She might have, if one of the women hadn't called to Petr at that moment, asking him if he thought it safe for her to go collect wild onions for the beefsteaks without escort. The question underscored the impermanence of these few hours of reprieve, and brought the realities of Alex's responsibilities crashing down on her.

"I...I can't."

She turned to walk away, only to be spun back around.

"Why not?"

His insistence rubbed against the grain of Alex's own strong will.

"Look, this isn't any of your business. Karistan isn't any of your business."

"Bull."

She stiffened and shot him an angry look. "It's not bull. I'm the one responsible for seeing these people don't starve this winter. I'm the one who has to keep the White Wolf away from our herds."

"There's help available. The president..."

"Right. The president. He's so caught up with the troubles in the Middle East and Central America and his own reelection difficulties that he doesn't have time for a tiny corner of the world like Karistan."

"He sent me, didn't he?"

"Yes, and Three Bars Red." Her lip curled. "As much as we appreciate the offer of your services, Karistan's problems need a more immediate fix."

"Then why the hell didn't you take the aid package that was offered?"

"You know about that, do you? Then you ought to know what this so-called package included. No? Let me tell you."

Alex shoved a hand through her hair, feeling the tensions and worries that had built up inside her bubble over.

"Some fourth-level State Department weenie came waltzing in here with promises of *future* aid...*if* I agreed to open, unannounced inspections of Karistan by any and every federal agency with nothing better to do. *If* I converted our economy and our currency to one that would 'compete' on the European market. *If* I agree to an agricultural program that included planting rice."

Sloan's sun-bleached brows rose in disbelief. "Rice?"

"Rice! On the steppes! Even if my ancestors hadn't turned over in their graves at the thought of our men riding tractors instead of horses, these lands are too high, too arid, for rice, for God's sake.''

"Okay, so some bureaucrat didn't do his homework before he put together a package for Karistan..."

The blood of her mother's people rose in Alex, hot and fierce. "Let's get this straight. No one's going to *put together* anything for Karistan, except me. I didn't ask for this responsibility, but it's mine."

He took her arm in a hard grip. "Listen to me, Alex. You don't have to do this alone."

She flicked an icy glance at the hand folded around the red of her sleeve, then up at his face. "Aren't you forgetting the ground rules, Sloan? You won't touch me without my permission, remember? Unless you want to feel the bite of the *nagaika*.''

His fingers dug into her flesh for an instant, then uncurled, one by one. Eyes the color of agates raked her face.

"You better keep that little horsetail flyswatter close to hand, Alexandra. Because the time's coming when I'm going to touch a whole lot more of you than you've ever had touched before."

He turned and stalked away, leaving Alex stunned by the savagery she'd seen in his eyes. And swamped with heat. And suddenly, inexplicably frightened. She wrapped her arms around herself, trying to understand the feeling that gripped her.

She could remember feeling like this only once before. One long-ago summer, when the half-broken pony she was riding had thrown her. She'd been far out on the steppes, and had walked home through gathering dusk with the echo of distant, eerie howls behind her.

With a wrenching sensation in the pit of her stomach, Alex now realized that Nate Sloan loomed as a far more powerful threat to her than either the gray wolves of the steppes or the White Wolf of Balminsk. Not because she feared him or the look in his eyes. But because her blood pumped with a hot,

equally savage need to know what would happen if...
when...he touched her as he'd promised.

Swallowing, she watched him brush by Katerina with a nod
and a curt word. Her cousin's brows rose in astonishment as
she, too, turned to stare after him.

No wonder Katerina was surprised. The Sloan who strode
through the camp was a different person than either she or
Alex had thought him.

This wasn't the dusty outsider who'd laughed when she
threatened to teach him to dance, Cossack-style.

Nor the man who'd warmed her frozen toes with his hands,
and her heart with his tales of his improbable youth.

This was a stranger. A hard, unsmiling stranger who radiated anger and authority in every line of his long, lean body.
One who challenged her as a woman as much as he now
seemed to challenge her authority.

Alex gave a silent groan as a scowling Katerina made her
way across the square. Still shaken by the confrontation with
Sloan, she was in no mood for more of her cousin's dark
looks.

"So, cousin. The *Amerikanski* stomps through the camp
like a bear with one foot in the trap, and you, you pucker
your lips like one who has eaten the persimmon. You fight
with him, no?"

Alex ground her teeth. "Can't a person have a single conversation or thought in this camp without everyone watching
and commenting on it?"

"No, one cannot," Katerina retorted. "You know that! Nor
can one spend every waking moment with a man and not raise
comment. Why has he stuck to you like flies to the dungpile
these last few days?"

Alex twisted her lips at the imagery.

Katerina mistook the reason behind that small, tight smile.
Planting her hands on her hips, she glared at Alex.

"So, it appears you change your mind about him, no? Is
that why you dress yourself in your prettiest tunic? Is that

why you wear the lipstick? Do you now think to take him to stud yourself?''

"Don't be crude, Katerina.''

"I, crude? I'm not the one who proposed such a plan. You *said* you didn't want him, cousin. You *said* one of us was to have him.''

Alex's temper flared. "You may have him, Katerina, I told you that! If you're woman enough to hold him.''

Katerina stepped back, her eyes widening at the sharp retort.

Alex wasn't about to stay for the next round in this escalating war between them. She'd had enough of Katerina. Enough of Nate Sloan. Enough of this whole damned cluster of goathide tents and curious aunts and cousins and aged, bent warriors.

"Tell Dimitri I'll be at the ice cave. And you, my cousin, may go to—go to join the rest who cook pastries and pour vodka!''

Whirling, Alex strode to the north pasture. In three minutes she had a snaffle bit and saddle on her gray. In five, she was heading for the retreat that had been her special place since childhood.

With the feel of the gelding's pounding hooves vibrating through her body and the sun beating down on her shoulders, Alex rode across the plains.

For an hour or so, she would leave the camp behind. She would leave her responsibilities and her worries and her cousin's animosity. She would pretend, if only for an hour or so, that she was once again the thin, long-legged teenager who had galloped across the steppes as though she owned them.

When she reached a line of low, serrated hills, Alex guided the gelding toward a rocky incline. Halfway up, she found the narrow, almost indiscernible path between tumbled, sharp-sided boulders. After a few moments, Alex reined the gray in on a flat, circular plateau surrounded by boulders and dismounted.

"Well done, my friend."

She gave the gray's dusty neck a pat, then slid her rifle from its case and pulled the reins over the animal's head to let them drag the ground. Trained by Petr himself, the gelding would not move unless or until called by its rider.

For a moment, Alex paused to look out over the rim of tumbled rocks. High, grassy seas stretched to the distant horizon. Gray-green melted into blue where earth and sky met. From this elevation, she could see the jagged scars in the surface, the sharp ravines and deep gorges carved by centuries of rains and swollen spring rivers.

She could see, as well, a distant horseman patrolling a small, barbed wire compound. Inside that wire, beneath a grassy, overgrown mound, was a cylinder of steel and death.

The missile site looked so innocent from this distance and this height. A slight bulge in the earth. A patch of shorter grass in a sea of waving stalks. Miles from the deserted launch facility that straddled the border between Karistan and Balminsk.

From her research, Alex knew that the U.S. missile sites scattered across Montana and Utah and Wyoming were just as isolated, just as remote. Just as innocuous-looking. Linked by underground umbilical cords to launch facilities hundreds of miles away, the weapons themselves were protected by an array of sophisticated intrusion-detection systems.

In more peaceful times, cattle had grazed near the Karistani site and scratched their backs on those twists of barbed wire. Soldiers in Soviet uniforms had come to inspect the warheads and the intrusion-detection systems. Now the soldiers were gone, and only a lone Karistani rider patrolled the site. Watching. Waiting. As they all waited.

Sighing, Alex turned toward a crack in the stone wall behind her. Angling sideways, she edged through the opening and left the twentieth century behind.

She stood in a high-ceilinged cavern lighted by narrow fissures in the cliff overhead. The air was cool, the temperature constant. It was an ice cave, her grandfather had told her when he first brought her here, so many years ago. It had been cut into the rock by long-ago glaciers, and had been used by hunters and travelers down through the ages.

As her eyes grew accustomed to the gloom, Alex sought the faint, fading splotches of color on a far wall. Propping her rifle against the stone, she went over to examine the paintings. She had too much respect to touch them. She wouldn't even breathe on them. A team of paleontologists from Moscow had examined them some years ago, promising funds to study and protect them. But these pictographs, like so much else, had fallen victim to the disintegration of the Soviet state.

One of Alex's goals, when—and if—she secured Karistan's future, was to protect this part of its past.

Her fingers itched for her sketch pad as she studied the outline of a shaggy-humped ox, an ancestor of the yak that had migrated centuries ago to Tibet and Central Asia. She drank in the graceful lines of a tusked white tiger, similar to those that had inhabited these parts long before encroaching civilization drove them east to Siberia. And the artist in her marveled at the skill of the long-ago painter, who'd captured in just a few strokes the determination of the naked, heavily muscled hunters moving in for the kill.

Alex walked farther into the cavern, to where the chamber divided into smaller, darker tunnels. There were more paintings in these spokes, she knew, and a few piles of bones.

The hunters had wintered here, according to the paleontologists. They'd eaten around fires in the main cavern, stored their supplies of meat and roots in the tunnels, wrapped their dead in hides and left them in the small, dark fissures because the ground was too frozen for burial. If they'd believed in burial.

Ducking her head, she entered one of the narrow tunnels. Enough light came from the main chamber behind her to show her the way, although she'd been here often enough to know it even in the dark. She was halfway to her special place when a faint rattle made her pause.

She glanced over her shoulder, listening intently. Was

someone or something in the main cavern? It couldn't be
Dimitri, or anyone else from camp. They would call out to
her, signal their presence.

An animal? A bear, or one of the silver foxes that made
their lairs in the stony precipices?

No, her horse would have whinnied, given notice of a predator's approach.

A rodent of some kind, a cave dweller whose nest she had
unwittingly disturbed in passing?

Another chink of stone against stone told her that whatever
came behind her was too large to be rodent.

Instinctively Alex dropped to a crouch and balanced on the
balls of her feet. Her arms outstretched, fingertips pressing
against cool stone, she peered through the dimness.

Only shadows and stillness stretched behind her.

Her heart began a slow, painful hammering. Her eyes
strained.

One of the shadows moved. Came closer. Took on the
vague outline of a man.

Alex didn't waste time cursing her stupidity in leaving her
rifle in the cavern. Her grandfather had taught her not to spend
energy on that which she could not change. Instead, she must
concentrate on that which she could.

All right, she told herself. All right. Someone was between
her and the Enfield. Someone who had seen the gelding outside. Someone who now stalked her with silent, deliberate
stealth.

Alex took a swift inventory of her weapons. She had the
bone-handled knife in her boot. And the short braided whip
looped around her wrist. And the fissures along the tunnel to
conceal herself in.

The dim shadow, hardly more than a notion of movement
along the dark wall, drifted toward her.

Her breath suspended, Alex eased upright and flattened her
back against the stone. Moving with infinite caution, she
inched her shoulders along the wall until the left one dipped
into a crevice.

When her left side fit into the opening, Alex wanted to sob with relief. Instead, she swallowed the fear that clogged her throat and carefully moved her body into darkness. She didn't let herself think what might be behind her. If there were bones, they could do her no harm. If there were pictographs painted on the slick, cold stone, she'd explore them some other time. Assuming she lived to explore another time.

She didn't have any illusions about what could happen to her if the man coming toward her had, somehow, slipped across the border from Balminsk.

For many years, just the threat of her grandfather's retribution had laid a mantle of protection over the women of the host. Justice was swift and sure to any who violated a Karistani woman. But the wars, the killings, the mutilations—by both sides—had stripped away the thin veneer of civilization of the people of this area.

They were descended from the Cossacks. Some from the Tartars, who took few prisoners and made those they did take beg for death. That so few of the Karistani men survived today was evidence of the savagery and the hate the wars with Balminsk had generated.

The shadow merged with the darkness of the tunnel. Alex couldn't see anything now. Nor could she hear anything. Except silence and the pounding of her own heart.

She sensed the intruder's presence before she saw him.

Her fingers gripped the knife's bone handle. She held it as her grandfather had taught her, with the blade low and pointed upward to slash at an unprotected belly.

A low growl drifted out of the darkness.

"I'm going to get stuck if I go much farther into this tunnel. You'd better come out, Alex."

Relief crashed over her in waves. Followed immediately by a wave of fury.

"You fool!" She slid sideways through the narrow aperture. "You idiot! Why didn't you call out? Let me know who you were? I was about to gut you!"

"You were about to try," he said, with a smile in his voice that sent Alex's anger spiraling.

"You think this is funny? You think it's something to laugh about?"

"No, sweetheart, I don't. I was just remembering the first time we met. Best I recall, you used about the same terms of endearment."

"Don't *sweetheart* me, you damned cowboy. I ought to..."

"I know, I know." He reached out and gripped her wrist, twisting it and the knife downward. "You ought to gut me and tan my hide. Or boil me in fish oil. Or feed me to the prairie dogs. You Karistani women are sure a bloodthirsty lot."

"Sloan..."

"Nate," he reminded her, using the hold to tug her closer.

"Let go of me."

"I'm just keeping that rib-tickler out of our way while we settle some things between us."

"There's nothing to settle."

With a smooth twist of his arm, he had Alex's wrist tucked behind her and her body up against his.

"Yes, Alexandra Danilova, there is."

"Sloan..."

The arm banding her to him tightened. "Nate."

"Let me go."

Even in the dim shadows, she could see the glint in his eyes. "Did anyone ever tell you that you're one stubborn female?"

"Yes, as a matter of fact. My grandfather, twice a day, every day I spent with him. Now let me go."

"I don't think so."

The soft implacability in his voice sent a shiver dancing along Alex's nerves.

"Aren't you forgetting the *nagaika?*"

His breath fanned her lips. "I guess I'll just have to take my licks."

"Sloan... Nate..."

His lips brushed hers. "It's too late, Alexandra. Way too late. For both of us."

Chapter 12

Ever afterward, when she thought about that moment of contact in the dark, narrow tunnel, Alex would know it was Sloan's combination of gentleness and strength that shattered the last of the barriers she'd erected around herself.

He was a man who knew his strength, and wasn't afraid to show gentleness. His mouth moved over hers with warm insistence. Tasting. Exploring. Giving a pleasure that stirred a response deep within her.

At first, Alex refused to acknowledge it. She held herself stiff and unmoving, not fighting, not cooperating.

At first, he didn't seem to mind her lack of participation. He drew what he needed from her lips, like a thirsty man taking a long-awaited drink.

All too soon, the situation satisfied neither one of them. Alex made a little movement against him, as if to pull away, and discovered that his hand had already loosened its grip on her wrist. She'd been held, not by his strength, but by his gentleness.

Though she knew she was free, she didn't move. She

should, she told herself. She should push away from the seductive nearness of this man. She should go outside, back to the camp. Back to her responsibilities.

At the thought, something deep within her rebelled. For weeks now, she'd carried this burden that had been thrust on her. For weeks, she'd sublimated her own life, her own desires, for those of the others. A sudden, totally selfish need rose in her. She wanted a few more minutes with Nate. She wanted to lean into his power. She wanted his arms around her. His mouth on hers.

Oh, God, she wanted him.

With the admission came a molten spear of heat. She was woman enough to recognize the heat for what it was. And honest enough to acknowledge what she intended to do about it.

Reaching up on tiptoe, she wrapped her arms around Nate's neck and brought his head to hers.

This was right.

The moment she tasted the hard, driving hunger in his kiss and felt her own rise to meet it, she knew this was right.

Here in the darkness, in the cold splendor of the caves where her ancestors had found shelter and perhaps survival, the primitive urge that surged through her was right. And natural. And shattering in its intensity.

He was made for this. She was. Their bodies fit together at knee and thigh and hip. She had to stretch a bit, he had to bend a little, but they managed to make contact everywhere that mattered. Her blood firing, she arched into him. His mouth ravaged hers. Her hips ground against his.

She wasn't sure whether it was minutes or hours later that he speared both hands through her hair, holding her head still as he dragged his own back. She waited unmoving, her breath as ragged as his.

Calling on every ounce of discipline he possessed, Nate willed himself to control. This was crazy. Insane. He hadn't intended for this to happen when he followed Alex across the plains, spurred by the twin needs to protect this stubborn woman and to know where she was going. He hadn't intended to let his desire to hold her, to drink in her taste and texture, get out of hand like this.

But even as he fought his own pumping desire, he felt hers in the ragged, panting breath that washed against his throat and the hard nipples that pushed through the red wool of her blouse.

Any hope of control shattered when she arched her lower body into his with an intimacy that sent a white-hot heat through his groin.

"I want you, Nate," she whispered. "Just for a little while, I—need you to hold me."

She did. More than she realized. Even more than he himself had realized until this instant. Nate heard the vulnerability in her voice, the aching loneliness.

With stunning intensity, a dozen different forces collided within him. The driving male urge to mate that had him hard and rampant. The masculine impulse to claim the woman who'd haunted his nights and filled his days. The purely personal and far more urgent desire to lose himself inside this shimmering, complex, compelling creature that was Alex. The simple need to give her pleasure.

He'd hold this woman…for a whole lot longer than the little while she'd asked for.

"I want you, too, Alexandra. I have since the first moment I met you. But not like this. Not in the darkness and the shadows."

She made a murmur of protest.

"I want to see your eyes dilated with pleasure and your mouth swollen from my kisses. I want to see your forehead."

"What?"

"Just come with me."

He wouldn't, couldn't, take the time to tell her now that his entire being was concentrated on erasing every damn worry line from her face and replacing them with a flush of pleasure.

When they slipped through the opening in the cliff face,

the bright, dazzling sunlight blinded them. Alex stumbled and would have fallen if Nate hadn't caught her with an arm around her waist and swung her back against the cliff face. Pinning her body to the stone with his, he took up where they'd left off in the dark cave.

Nate couldn't have said how long it was before hard, hungry kisses and the friction of their clothed bodies against each other weren't enough...for either of them.

Her mouth locked with his, Alex slid her hands inside his jacket and peeled it over his shoulders. While her tongue played with his and he drank in her soft little sounds of pleasure, her fingers groped at the buttons on his cotton shirt.

With one arm still wrapped around her waist to cushion her from the rock wall, Nate tugged at the high collar of her red top. Frustrated at the small patch of soft skin her collar gave him access to, he put just enough distance between them to fumble with the buttons on the tunic.

Alex leaned against the wall, her mouth satisfactorily swollen and her forehead free of all lines, while Nate worked the gold frog fastenings that marched with military precision down the front of her blouse. He soon found himself cursing under his breath at the elaborate fastenings. They looked impressive, but they were hell for a man with hands the size of his to get undone. Impatient, he worked the last one free and shoved the soft red wool down to her elbows. When he saw the bra that cupped her breasts, Nate didn't know whether to grin or to groan.

He'd held that bit of lace in his hands the night Red raided Ivana's honey pot, and spent more than one sweat-drenched hour wondering how it would look on Alex's body. None of his imaginings had ever come close to reality, he discovered as he stripped away the rest of her clothes.

She was glorious. As slender and smooth as a willow sapling. Long-legged as a newborn colt, but far more graceful. Her skin gleamed with ivory tints and satin shadows in the sunlight. Dusky nipples crowned her small, high breasts, and the triangle at the juncture of her thighs was as dark and as silky as her mane of tumbling sable hair. But if Nate had been allowed only one memory to take away with him of that moment, one vivid impression, it would have been her eyes. Golden and glorious, they held no hint of fear, no shadow of worry. Only a smiling invitation that made him ache with wanting her.

"I want to see you, too," she murmured, sliding her hands inside his shirt. "All of you."

By the time Alex had managed—with Nate's ready assistance—to rid him of his clothing, she was liquid with need.

He was magnificent. Lean, finely honed by exercise or work, each muscle well-defined under supple skin lightly furred with soft golden hair. His body showed evidence of the hard youth he'd told her of that day when the storm cocooned them on the shallow ledge. There were long white scars that traced back to his rodeo days, she suspected. Hard ridges of flesh. And a small round patch of puckered skin on the right side of his chest.

Alex had spent enough summers on the steppes to recognize a bullet wound when she saw one.

"When did you get this?" she asked, her voice husky.

"A long time ago."

Her fingers traced the scarred flesh. "How?"

His hand closed over hers, trapping it against his skin. "It doesn't matter. It's part of my past. At this particular moment, I'm more concerned about the present."

Alex felt a rush of dissatisfaction that Nate would shut any part of himself off from her. The feeling was irrational, she knew. At this point in time, she probably had many more secrets tucked away inside her than he did.

With a sudden, fierce resolve, she shoved aside the past and refused to think about the future. He was right. For this slice of time, at least, there was only here. And now. And Nate.

She slid her hand free of his loose hold and let it travel slowly down his chest. Across his smooth-planed middle. Over his flat belly. With the tip of one nail, she traced the length of his hard, rampant arousal.

Her eyes limpid, she smiled up at him. "I don't think you have to be too concerned about the present."

He half laughed, half groaned.

Alex closed her fingers around his rigid shaft, then blinked in surprise when he pulled away.

"Wait," he ordered softly. "Wait a moment."

He turned and hunkered down to dig through their pile of discarded clothing. While Alex admired the smooth line of his tanned back and his tight white buns, he emptied the pockets of his jeans. He tossed an old pocketknife, what looked like a half-empty package of chewing gum and a handful of coins on top of her crumpled tunic before he found what he wanted.

Straightening, he walked back to her side.

Alex fought a feeling of feminine pique as she stared at the foil packet. She should've known someone with Nate's laughing eyes and rugged handsomeness would be prepared for just these circumstances.

"Do you always carry an emergency supply?" she asked, a hint of coolness in her voice.

He propped an arm against the cliff and used his free hand to tip her head back.

"Always, sweetheart. Wily Willie taught me that a man isn't a man if he doesn't protect his spread, his horse, and his woman."

"I can imagine which one came first with Willie," she retorted, refusing to acknowledge the shiver that darted down her spine at his use of the possessive.

"I never had the nerve to ask," he responded with a grin. "But I can tell you which comes first with me. You, Alexandra Danilova Jordan. You, my wild, beautiful woman of the steppes."

When he bent to nuzzle her neck, Alex arched against him. His teeth and his tongue worked her flesh, causing explosions of heat in parts of her body well below her neckline. The unyielding stone wall held her immobile, unable to withdraw any part of herself from him even if she'd wanted to.

And she didn't.

Sweet heaven above, she didn't.

When his hand shaped her breast and tipped it up for a small, biting kiss, she gasped and lifted herself higher. When he suckled the aching nipple, streaks of fire shot straight from her breast to her loins. When one of his hair-roughened thighs parted hers, and a hand slid down her belly to delve into the moist warmth at her center, Alex buried her face in his neck to muffle her moan.

Sometime later, he rasped softly in her ear, "Look at me, Alexandra."

She shook her head, keeping her face against his neck. She didn't want to see, to think, to do anything but feel the exquisite sensations his hands and his mouth were bringing her. And return them in some way.

"Alex, I want to see your eyes."

"I...I thought it was my forehead," she gasped, wriggling desperately as his thumb pressed the nub of flesh between her thighs.

"Whatever," he growled.

She brought her head back, her eyes narrowed against the sun and her own spiraling pleasure. Wanting, needing, to give in return, she matched him stroke for stroke, kiss for kiss.

When she felt as though she were about to drown in the waves of sensation that washed over her, he stepped back to tear open the packet and sheathe himself.

Then his strong, square hands circled her waist.

Holding her back away from the rough cliffside, he lifted her, and brought her down onto him. Alex gave a ragged groan as his rigid shaft entered her slick channel. Her muscles tightened involuntarily, then loosened to accept him.

Fierce masculine satisfaction flared in his eyes for a moment, before giving way to an emotion Alex might have tried to identify if she hadn't been caught up in a whirling, spinning vortex of pure sensation. Using his muscled thigh, his straining member, his hands and his mouth, Nate stoked the fires within her, fanning the leaping flames, until at last she exploded into shards of white light and blazing red heat.

When the spasms that held her rigid subsided, Alex slumped against his chest. Which was when she first realized he hadn't climaxed. Or, if he had, he didn't give any evidence of it that she could tell.

"Oh, Nate," she murmured breathlessly. "I'm sorry. I can't... I've never..."

She swallowed, and tried unsuccessfully to force her limp muscles to move. "Just give me a little while."

He managed a grin and eased himself out of her. "Isn't that usually the man's line?"

"Yes, well..."

Alex wet her lips, not wanting to confess that she'd never before exploded into so many pieces, and wasn't sure exactly how to put herself back together.

"It's okay, sweetheart," he assured her, brushing a strand of limp hair from her forehead. "I'll live."

At his words, Alex felt a mix of guilt and satisfaction and responsibility. She wasn't the kind of woman to take and not give.

"I want you to do more than just live, Nate. You just made me feel as though I was..."

His eyes glinted. "Yeah?"

"Flying across the steppes on a wild pony," she told him with a wry smile. "I want you to fly, too."

"Well, I wouldn't mind a little flying, you understand, but I'm afraid my emergency supply won't make it through another ride across the steppes."

She gave the supply in question a quick inspection, then sent him a look of inquiry.

"I don't want to risk tearing it, Alex. I won't add to your worries."

She tilted her head, unused to having decisions taken out of her hands so summarily. After a moment, she put her palms on his chest and pushed him away.

"Fine. We won't risk it. You just sit on that boulder over

there, and I'll show you how the women of Karistan solve a problem like this."

"Alex…"

"We have a saying," she told him, shoving him toward the low, benchlike rock. "One passed from mother to daughter for centuries."

"I'm not sure I want to hear this."

Hands on his shoulders, she pressed him down.

"A man may be more difficult to trap than a wild goat," Alex purred, "but he's far easier to milk."

Later, much later, when they had trapped and milked and flown across the steppes to everyone's mutual satisfaction, Nate dragged on his jeans. In no hurry to see Alex's long, slender legs covered up, he dug only her panties and his jacket out of the pile of scattered clothing.

After wrapping the warm felt-lined denim around her shoulders, he settled down with his back against the cliff and took her on his lap. Resting his chin on the top of Alex's head, Nate stared out at the vast, endless vista.

For a while, the only sounds that disturbed the stillness were the occasional shuffle of the horses as they shifted in and out of their sleepy dozes and the distant call of a hawk circling far out over the plains. The sun hovered just above the line of boulders at the edge of the rocky plateau and bathed the grass below in a golden hue.

Alex pulled the front edges of the jacket closer. The thin felt lining carried traces of Nate's scent, warm and masculine and comforting. As comforting as the feel of his rock-solid chest behind her and the arms wrapped loosely around her waist.

She shifted on his lap and felt a stone dig into one bare heel. Wincing, she rubbed her foot along the rocky ground to dislodge the sharp pebble, then glanced around the bare, rocky plateau. The place probably wouldn't rate on anyone's list of the top ten most romantic rendezvous. No soft bed with silken sheets. No dreamy music or chilled champagne. Not even one of the thick, cushioning wolf pelts the Karistani women had been known to tuck under their saddles when they rode off to bring food and other comforts to their men riding herd at some distant grazing site. But at that moment, Alex felt more bonelessly, wonderfully comfortable than she'd ever felt in her life. She wouldn't have traded Nate's lap and the open, sunswept plateau for all the silk sheets and wolf pelts in the world.

"Just imagine how many people never see anything like that," he murmured above her.

She lifted her head from its tucked position under his chin and looked up to see his eyes drinking in the vast, empty distance.

"It calls to you, doesn't it?" she asked with a hint of envy.

He glanced down at her. "It doesn't call to you?"

Alex turned her face to the open vista, frowning. "It used to. Sometimes, at night, I think it still does. But..." She gave a little shrug. "But then I decide it's just the wind."

He tightened his arms, drawing her closer into his warmth. "You were born here, weren't you?"

"Yes."

"And?" he prompted.

"And I grew up as sort of an international nomad," she answered lightly. "I spent the summers in Karistan. In the winters, I attended school in North Philadelphia."

"And now that you're all grown up? Very nicely grown up, I might add. How do you live now, Alex?"

"Until a few weeks ago, I commuted between Philly and Manhattan. With occasional trips to London and regular treks to Paris for the spring and fall shows thrown in."

"Not to Karistan?"

She stared out over the empty steppes. "No, not to Karistan. I hadn't been back here for almost ten years when my grandfather died."

He shifted, bringing her around in the circle of his arms to look down into her face.

"Why?"

"What is this?" Alex returned. "Are we playing twenty questions? We don't have time for games, Nate. I need to get back."

She curled a leg under her, intending to push herself off his lap. His arms held her in place.

"Tell me, Alex. Tell me who you are. I want to know."

She turned the tables on him. "Why?"

"A man wants to know all he can about the woman he's going to be riding across the steppes with."

Alex caught her breath at the steely promise in his voice.

"Tell me," he urged. "Tell me who you are."

Alex hesitated, then slowly, painfully articulated aloud for the first time in her life the doubts she'd carried for so long.

"I don't know who I am, Nate. I guess I've never really known. I've always been torn by divided loyalties."

"Yet when the chips were down, you came back to Karistan."

"I came back because I had to. I stay because…"

"Why, Alex?"

"Because Karistan's like me, caught between two worlds. Only its worlds aren't East and West. They're the past and the present."

She stared up at him, seeing the keen intelligence in his eyes. And something else, something that pulled at the tight knot of worries she'd been holding inside her for so long.

His thumb brushed the spot just above her eyebrows. "And that's what's causing this crease? The idea of leading Karistan out of the past and into the future?"

The knot loosened, and the worries came tumbling out.

"I know I may not be the best person to do it. I've made some mistakes. Well, a lot of mistakes. Maybe I should have accepted the aid package. Maybe I should have agreed to the conditions that State Department weenie laid out. I've lain awake nights, worrying about that decision."

"Alex…"

She twisted out of his arms to kneel beside him. "But I couldn't do it, Nate. I couldn't give away the very independence my grandfather fought for. I couldn't just hand over the trust he passed to me.''

She broke off, biting down on her lower lip.

Nate didn't move, didn't encourage her or discourage her by so much as a blink. With a gut-twisting need that had nothing to do with his mission to Karistan, he wanted Alex to trust him. Not because he'd convinced her to. Because she wanted to.

She chewed on her lip for long, endless seconds, then pushed herself to her feet.

''Wait here,'' she told him. ''I...I want to show you something.''

Alex scrambled up. Pausing only to pull on her pants and boots, she slipped through the narrow entrance in the cliff wall.

Chapter 13

Nate got to his feet slowly. As he watched Alex disappear through the dark entrance to the cavern, he tried to decide what to call the feeling that coiled through him.

Not lust. He knew all the symptoms of lust, and this wasn't it.

Not desire. Holding Alex wrapped in his arms and hearing her open up had taken him far beyond desire.

What he felt was deeper, fiercer, more gut-wrenchingly painful.

He turned to stare out over the steppes, thinking about what she'd knowingly and unknowingly revealed in the past few minutes. He suspected that Alex herself didn't realize how deep the conflict in her went.

Nate himself had never known a home, as most people knew it. He'd never wanted or needed one. Rattling around with Willie in their old pickup had filled all his needs. Even after the authorities caught up with them and forced Willie to leave Nate with family friends during the school year, he'd snuck away whenever possible to hitchhike to whatever dusty, noise-filled town was hosting the next rodeo.

He'd never put down roots, and he'd never felt himself pulled in different directions by those deep, entangling vines. Alex had roots in two different worlds, but nothing to anchor them to.

Everything in Nate ached to give her that anchor. She was so strong, so fiercely independent, and so achingly lost in that never-never land of hers. With every fiber of his being, Nate wanted to give her world a solid plane. Instead, he knew, he was about to tear it apart.

His savage oath startled the horses out of their sleepy dozes. Ole Red tossed his head, chuffing through hairy lips as he came more fully awake and threw Nate an inquiring look.

"Hang loose, fella. We'll be heading back to camp soon."

The words left a bitter taste in Nate's mouth, and he turned once more to stare out at the empty vastness of the steppes.

A rattle of stone at the cave's entrance announced Alex's return a little while later. He swung around as she emerged into the waning sunlight and hurried toward him, his heart constricting at the sight of her.

Her hair tumbled over her shoulders in a dark, tangled mass, and the lipstick she'd worn earlier had long since disappeared. She looked like a refugee from a homeless shelter in those baggy pants and his oversize jacket. But as he watched her come toward him, bathed by the glow of the setting sun, Nate could finally give a name to the feeling knifing through him.

He loved her, or thought he did. The emotion wasn't one he had a whole lot of practice or familiarity with.

The thought of what he was about to do to that love curled his hands into fists. When she stopped beside him, he didn't have to glance down to know that one of the items she held in her hands was a small black box.

"My grandfather passed these to me when he died," she told him breathlessly.

A small metallic chink drew Nate's reluctant gaze to the

tarnished silver snaffle bit she held up. The D-rings to which reins would have been attached were carved in an intricate design, as ornate as any museum piece.

"This was used by a long-ago *ataman* of our host," Alex said, her voice low and vibrating with pride. "He led five hundred men against the Poles at Pskov, in 1581, when the steppes were still known as the Wild Country. The czar himself presented this bridle bit in recognition of that victory."

Her mouth twisted. "The same czar tried to reclaim it not two months later, when he decided the Cossacks had grown too powerful. The plains were awash with blood for years, but the Cossacks held the Wild Country. They chose to die before they would give up their freedoms. No Cossack was ever a serf. Not under the czars."

Her hands closed over the tarnished silver bit. Nate saw the fierce emotion in her eyes, and for the first time understood the power of the forces that pulled at her.

"Scholars say true Cossackdom died after World War I, when long-range artillery made horsemen armed with rifles obsolete. The Cossack regiments were absorbed into the Soviet armies, and the red bear spread its shadow over the steppes. The hosts disintegrated, and people fled to America, or to Europe, or China. Except for a few stubborn, scattered bands."

She drew in a ragged breath. "My grandfather's father led one of those bands, and then my grandfather. Rather than see his people exterminated during Stalin's reign of terror, he accepted Moscow's authority. But he never gave up fighting for them, never stopped working for Karistan's freedom. Our men died, one by one, in the last battles with the Soviet bear, and with the wolves of Balminsk, who wanted to take the few resources left to us."

Nate caught the shift in pronouns that Alex seemed unaware of. In her short, impassioned speech, she'd shifted from *his* people to *our* men. From *them* to *us*. The roots that pulled at Alex went deeper than she realized.

"When the Soviets planted their missiles on our soil, they

didn't care that they made Karistan a target for the West's retaliation. But in the end, those missiles will give us the means to keep the freedom we won back.''

Lifting her other hand, she uncurled her fingers. ''This has more power for Karistan than the Soviets or the West ever intended it to have.''

Nate didn't look down, didn't look anywhere but into Alex's eyes. ''What do you intend to do with it?''

A flicker of surprise crossed her face. ''Don't you want to know what it is?''

''I know what it is, Alex.''

She stared at him, her brows drawing together in confusion. ''How do you know? How could you?''

As with most moments of intense drama, this one was broken by the most mundane event.

A deep, whoofing snuffle made both Alex and Nate glance around. Red had ambled across the rocky plateau and was now investigating the articles of clothing still scattered on the ground.

''Get out of there.''

The stallion's ears twitched, but he ignored Nate's growled command. One big hoof plopped down on the braided *nagaika*. Nosing Alex's bra aside with his nose, he lipped at the red wool tunic.

''Red! Dammit, get out of there! Oh, hell, he's after the package of chewing gum!''

Still confused, still not quite understanding the inexplicable tension in the man who had only moments before cradled her in his warmth, Alex watched Nate stride across the plateau.

''Come on, Red, spit out the paper! I don't want to have to shove a fist down your windpipe to dislodge it if it gets stuck.''

As Nate tried to convince Red to relinquish his prize, the sun sank a little lower behind the rim of boulders. A chill prickled along Alex's arms that wasn't due entirely to the rapidly cooling air. Feeling a need to clothe herself, she tucked the silver bit and the black box in her pants pocket, then shed Nate's jacket to pull on her red top.

Kneeling, she reached for the short braided whip no steppe horseman ever rode without. Her fingers brushed over the handful of loose coins and the old pocketknife that Nate had dug out of his jeans earlier. When she touched the bone handle of the knife, she gave a start of surprise.

The first thing Nate noticed when he finally convinced Red to give up the wadded paper and gum and swung around were the tight, grooved lines bracketing Alex's mouth.

The second was the pocketknife resting on her upturned palm. Although he couldn't see any movement, Nate knew the knife was vibrating against her palm.

"If I thought you were the kind of man to go in for kinky sex toys, I'd say this is another one of your emergency supplies." Her lips twisted in a bitter travesty of a smile. "But then, I don't really know *what* kind of man you are, do I, Sloan?"

"Alex…"

"This is some kind of a device, isn't it? An electronic homing device of some kind?"

"Close enough."

"What set it off?"

He met her look. "The decoder."

"You bastard."

The way she said it sliced through Nate like a blade. Without heat. Without anger. Without any emotion at all. Except a cold, flat contempt.

"That's what you came to Karistan for, isn't it? The decoding device?"

He hooked his thumbs in his belt. "Yes."

"That's it?" she asked after a long, deadly moment. "Just 'yes'? No excuses? No explanations? No embarrassment over the fact that you just used me in the most contemptible way a man can use a woman to get his hands on what he wants."

"No, Alex. No excuses. No explanations. And I didn't *use* you. We used each other, in the most elemental, most fundamental way a man and woman can. What we had... What we have is right, Alex.''

Her lip curled. "Oh, it was right. It was certainly right. You're good, Sloan, I'll give you that. If there's a scale for measuring performance at stud, I'd give you top marks. I suspect not even Three Bars Red is in your class. But I hope you don't think that one—admittedly spectacular—performance is enough to convince me to give you this little black box.''

They both knew it wasn't a matter of giving, that he could take it from her any time he wanted. They also knew he wouldn't use force against her. Not yet, anyway, Nate amended silently.

"I'm going to mount and ride out of here,'' Alex told him, spacing her words carefully. "I'm going to ride back to camp. You and that damned horse of yours will be out of Karistan by dawn, or I'll shoot you on sight.''

"Then you'd better keep your Enfield loaded, sweetheart. I'll be right behind you. Like a second shadow, remember?''

"Sloan...''

"Think about what happened here during the ride back to camp, Alex. It had nothing to do with that decoder. When you work your way past your anger, you'll admit that. You're too honest not to. Think about this, too.''

There wasn't anything gentle about his kiss this time. It was hard and raw and possessive. And when Alex wrenched herself out of his arms and stalked to her gelding, Nate could only hope that the glitter in her eyes was fury, and not hatred.

He stood beside Red while Alex worked her way down the steep incline. His every muscle was tense with the strain of wanting to go after her. But he knew she needed time. Time to work through her anger and her hurt. Time to get past this damned business of the decoder.

But not too much time, Nate vowed grimly.

He was halfway back to camp when the chronometer pulsed against his wrist with a silent signal. Nate glanced at the code and reined Red in.

"Cowboy here. Go ahead, Chameleon."

Maggie's voice cut through the shadowy dusk, tense and urgent. "I think you ought to know the horse poop just got deeper at this end. In fact, it's over my boot tops at this moment. Hang on. I'm going to code Doc in. He needs to hear this, too."

The few seconds it took for her to call up OMEGA Control spun into several lifetimes for Nate. His eyes narrowed, he searched the shadows ahead for a sign of Alex.

"This is Doc. Thunder's here, too, listening in. Go ahead, Chameleon."

The sensitive transmitter picked up Maggie's small, breathy sigh. Nate couldn't tell whether it was one of dismay or relief at the news that Adam Ridgeway, code name Thunder, was present in the Control Center. Nate suspected Maggie was already dreading the debrief she'd have with the director when this mission was over, but there wasn't anyone either one of them would rather have on hand when the horse manure was about to hit the fan. Which it apparently was.

"Okay, team, here's the situation," Maggie reported. "Cherkoff, Sr., dug up a team of Ukrainian scientists with some radiation-measuring equipment of their own. He had them flown in this afternoon. When their equipment showed no evidence of soil contamination, he insisted on watching while we remeasured with ours. He wasn't too happy when he discovered we'd exaggerated the readings a bit."

"Fabricated them, you mean," Thunder put in coldly.

"Whatever. In any event, Richard—Dr. Worthington—was forced to rescind the order closing the borders."

"Hell!"

"I'm sorry, Cowboy." Maggie paused, then plunged ahead. "There's more. Since the soil samples showed clear, the White Wolf also insisted that the silos be inspected. Richard and I were the first ones to go down. Turns out we were the only ones. We're, uh, still here."

"Are you all right?" Adam's sharp question leaped through the air.

Nate glanced down at the chronometer in surprise. As one of OMEGA's old-timers, he'd worked for Adam Ridgeway for a goodly number of years. He knew that the safety of field operatives overrode any mission requirement as far as the director was concerned. But Nate had never heard that level of intensity in Ridgeway's voice before. He wondered if Maggie had caught it, as well.

Evidently not.

"We're fine," she assured Adam blithely. "We're just sort of…trapped here. Richard's working on the silo hatch mechanism right now. He thinks it's been tampered with."

"Cherkoff," Nate growled.

"Exactly." Her voice sharpened, took on a new urgency. "Look, Cowboy, I don't know how long it will take us to get out of here. In the meantime, I can't control what's going on topside. But I do know the Wolf's fangs were bared last time I saw him. He's out for blood. Any blood. If not that of the capitalist scum he hates so much, then that of the Karistanis, whom he hates even more."

"Guess it's time we pull his fangs," Doc interjected. "Your play was more effective than you realized, Chameleon. It bought enough time for me to deploy a squadron of gunships from Germany to a forward base in Eastern Europe. They can be in orbit over Karistan in…one hour and fourteen minutes. Less, if the head winds drop below twenty knots."

The tension at the base of Nate's neck eased considerably. "Well, now, with that kind of firepower, this might just turn out to be an interestin' night. Sorry you're going to be stuck down in that hole and miss it, Chameleon."

"Try not to start the party without me, Cowboy. I'll get out of here yet. Hey, I'm sitting on a couple of megatons of explosives, aren't I?"

Three startled males responded to that one simultaneously. Nate and David conceded the airwaves to Adam, who gave Maggie several explicit instructions, only one of which had to do with sitting on her hands until they got an extraction team to pull her and Worthington out of that damned hole.

Nate signed off a few seconds later, his eyes thoughtful. With a squadron of AC-130 Spectre gunships backing him up, he could hold off anything the White Wolf threw at Karistan, with plenty of firepower left over.

What he wouldn't be able to hold off was Alex's fury when he told her that the United States, in the person of Nate Sloan, was preempting every one of her options when it came to deciding Karistan's future.

There was no way he could leave that decoder in her hands, not with tensions about to escalate from here to Sunday. Nor could he stand by while Alex put herself in harm's way. She was good, too damn good, with that Enfield and that knife of hers, but she didn't have Nate's combat skills or even Maggie Sinclair's training. Somehow, he had to convince her to trust him enough to see them through the battle that was about to erupt.

Wishing Maggie was here to assist in what he feared would be a dangerous situation, Nate smiled grimly at the thought of her and Alex together. Talk about a combination of brains, beauty, and sheer determination.

When this was all over, Nate promised himself silently as he kneed Red into a gallop, he was going to enjoy watching those two meet.

When this was all over, Maggie promised herself a half hour later, she was never, *never,* going down into anything round and dark and sixty feet deep again.

Flattening her palms against the concrete wall behind her, she stayed as far back as possible from the edge of the narrow catwalk that circled the inside of the silo like a dog collar. Craning her neck, she peered up through the eerie greenish gloom.

Richard had managed to activate one of the auxiliary lights in the silo. It had just enough wattage to illuminate the huge, round, white-painted missile a few feet from Maggie's nose and to show the vague shadow of Richard's boots above her.

The boots were perched on the top rung of the ladder that

climbed the height of the silo. An occasional grunt told Maggie the young scientist was still wrestling with the manual levers that were supposed to open the overhead hatch when the pneudraulic systems failed.

"Any luck?" she called into the echoing murkiness. The boots swiveled on the ladder as he bent to peer down at her.

"The hatch cover won't budge."

"Richard, be careful. Don't twist like that. You might— Oh, my God!"

Horrified, Maggie saw one of his boots slip off the rung completely. He jerked upright to clutch at the ladder, causing the other foot to lose its hold, as well. While his hands scrambled for a grip on the slippery metal, his shins whacked against the lower rungs.

Instinctively Maggie grabbed for the rung nearest to her. There were only three feet of space between the concrete wall and the gleaming surface of the missile. If she hung on to the ladder with one hand and braced the other against the missile, she might be able to break Richard's fall with her body.

"I'm...I'm okay," he called out a moment later. "I'm coming down."

Swallowing heavily, Maggie reclaimed her spot on the catwalk. Richard had told her that the narrow steel platform encircling the silo could be raised and lowered to allow maintenance on the missile. At this moment, however, it hovered some forty feet above ground zero, as he had ghoulishly termed it.

She edged sideways to make room for Richard on the metal platform. His face, tinted chartreuse by the light, scrunched up in frustration.

"I simply don't understand why the hatch won't open. The manual systems are completely independent of the pneudraulic lifts."

He slumped back against the concrete wall, making Maggie quiver with the need to grab at him. Those big feet of his could slide off the narrow catwalk just as easily as the ladder.

"Can't you think of something to make it work?" she

snapped, her eye on the minuscule distance between his feet and oblivion.

"Why don't *you* think of something?" he shot back. "You got us into this. God, I can't believe I let you talk me into faking a nuclear fuel spill!"

Maggie arched a brow. "As I recall, you didn't need much talking."

"I must have been out of my mind!" He speared a hand through his hair. "That's what happens when the endocrine system fluctuates. The overproduction of bodily fluids, particularly the hormonal serums, can upset the chemical bal—"

"Look, could we finish this discussion some other time? We've got other things to worry about right now besides your hormonal serums."

He leaned his head back against the wall for a moment, expelling a long, slow breath. When he faced Maggie again, his green face was softened by a look of apology.

"I'm sorry, Megan. I shouldn't blame my lapse in judgment on you. I'm not usually swayed by illogic, nor do I normally indulge in irresponsible acts. But you're...well, you must know you're impossible for any man to resist. And when you mentioned this ruse might delay an attack on Karistan, I felt obligated to help."

Maggie wasn't sure whether to be offended, flattered, or amused. Deciding on the latter, she gave him a small grin.

"Maybe you won't think it was so irresponsible or illogical when I tell you that our little ruse worked. We bought enough time for a squadron of Spectre gunships to deploy from Germany."

His face settled into a thoughtful frown.

"I thought I heard you talking while I was up on the ladder," he said slowly. "To receive that kind of information, I must assume you have some kind of a satellite transceiver on your person. A small, but powerful one. With at least twenty gigahertz of power to penetrate this level of concrete density."

"Something like that."

"Then I may also assume you're not a geologist?"

"Not even a rock collector," she admitted.

"Who are you?"

"I can't tell you that. But I can tell you that there's a team on the way to Balminsk to get us out of here." Her grin faded as the realities of a possible hostile extraction filtered through her mind. "I don't suppose you know how to use a .22?"

She reached under her shirt and slipped her Smith and Wesson out of the holster nestled at her waist.

"I know how to use a .22, a .38, a .45, and any caliber rifle you care to name," Richard replied quietly.

At her quick, startled look, he lifted one shoulder. "I'm no stranger to violence. I shot a man when I was six years old. In the kneecap. By luck, more than by aim, but it disabled him enough for me to get away. I made sure luck wouldn't be a factor in my aim after that."

Maggie stared up into his green-tinted face. Richard might have lost the tip of his pinkie when he was kidnapped as a child, but he'd gained a confidence few people would exhibit with the threat of violence staring them in the face. Without a word, she passed him the .22. He checked the magazine with careful expertise, then tucked it into his jacket pocket.

Maggie assembled the arsenal of other weapons supplied by OMEGA, then propped her shoulders against the wall beside Richard. She glanced up at the shrouded tip of the missile, shivering a bit as she thought of the warhead encased in the cone.

"Isn't it ironic that we've got all that explosive power within a few feet of us and we can't use it to blow that hatch?"

Richard followed her line of sight, then looked up at the circular steel silo cover. "I suppose we could," he said slowly. "Blow it, I mean."

"*What?* No, I don't think that's a good idea. Really, Richard, I was just making small talk. You know, the idle chitchat everyone indulges in when they're stuck in a nuclear missile silo."

He pushed his shoulders off the wall and leaned over to peer down into the murky depths. "It could be done," he murmured.

Maggie grabbed his arm and hauled him back. "Richard, listen to me! This is *not* a good idea!"

"Just how much do you know about physics, Megan?"

"I remember exactly two things from high school! One, for every action there's an equal and opposite reaction. Two..." She waved a hand wildly. "I forget the second. Richard, I swear, if you go *near* that warhead I'll...I'll..."

"I have no intention of touching the warhead." He wrapped his hands around her upper arms. "I'm talking about imploding the pneudraulic systems. They're simply mechanisms, really. Quite similar in concept to hydraulics."

"Oh, that helps."

He grinned, his white teeth startling in his green-tinted face. "When gas pressure trapped in the pneudraulic cylinder expands, it forces up the lift, which in turn raises the hatch. The more gas, the greater the force when it expands."

She eyed him suspiciously. "So?"

"So this missile has three stages. Three separate rockets, to launch the warhead into an orbital trajectory."

"So?"

"So each of those stages has a separate motor."

"So *what*, Richard?"

"So the motors require periodic inspection and maintenance. Which is done through their separate hatches. Which lift via pneudraulic canisters. Four per hatch."

He gave her a little shake.

"Don't you get it? The second-stage motor is only about four feet below where we're standing. If you hang on to me while I reach over the edge of the catwalk, I can open the hatch and extract the gas canisters. I'll then insert them into the lifts for the overhead hatch cover. With that extra firepower, we can blow the lid right off this silo."

The absolute certainty in his dark eyes almost convinced

Maggie. She glanced sideways at the white shell of the missile and repressed a shudder.

"Are you sure there won't be any, uh, secondary explosions when the lid goes?"

"Positive. That sucker will shoot straight up in the air. The energy from the canisters will expel upward with it. Trust me."

Maggie groaned. "Oh, Richard! Don't you know those are the last two words a woman wants to hear when a man's trying to talk her into something she knows she shouldn't be doing in the first place!"

Chapter 14

Nate kept Red to a hard, pounding gallop. He was still some miles from the Karistani camp when he caught sight of a dim figure ahead. His jaw hardening, he urged the stallion to even greater speed.

At the sound of drumming hoofbeats behind her, Alex twisted to look over her shoulder. She couldn't fail to identify Red's distinctive silhouette, even in the gathering dusk. Realizing that there was no way her gray could outrun the faster, stronger quarter horse, she pulled her mount around.

Nate was out of the saddle in a swift, surefooted leap, and he grabbed her reins, almost jerking them out of her hands. The startled gelding tried to dance away.

"Let go of my mount!"

"No way, lady. We need to talk."

Her mount skittered sideways, its hooves raising a small cloud of dust.

"We've talked all we're going to! Let go of the reins."

Her angry shout added to the gray's nervousness. Jerking its head back, it reared up against Nate's hold. As Alex fought for balance, her arm swung in a wild arc, the braided whip slicing through the air.

When the *nagaika* descended, Nate raised a forearm. The tail hissed viciously as it whipped around his jacket sleeve. With a twist of his wrist, he caught the stock in his fist and gave it a hard yank.

Tethered by the loop around her wrist, Alex tumbled out of her saddle. With a startled cry, she landed in Nate's arms.

He held her easily, despite her furious struggling, and drew her up on her toes. "Listen to me, Alex. It turns out there wasn't any spill in Balminsk. The borders are open again."

She stopped jerking against his hold. "What? When?"

"An hour ago, maybe less."

She stared up at him, the planes of her face stark in the rising moonlight. Her breath puffed on the cool air in little pants as she fought to take in the implications of his news.

Nate's fingers dug into her arms, unconsciously communicating his own tension. "That means the situation here could get real nasty, real quick."

"Is that why you came after me? To warn me?"

"That's one of the reasons."

"Or because you wanted to secure the decoder?"

"That, too," he told her with brutal honesty. "It's not something you need to be worrying about in the middle of a firefight. Left unsecured, something like that could make matters escalate out of control."

She went utterly still. Shock widened her eyes to huge golden pools. "Escalate? My God, do you think I would allow that to happen? That I would try to…to actually arm the warheads? Even to save Karistan?"

"Of course not, you little idiot. But hasn't it occurred to you that the White Wolf might be after something other than cattle? That he might just want to get his hands on that bit of electronic gadgetry? You may not be planning to hold the world as a nuclear hostage, but he would."

"He couldn't."

The absolute certainty in her voice made Nate's eyes narrow. "Why not?"

She wrenched out of his hold. "Because the device is useless. I disabled it weeks ago."

"Come on, Alex! We're not talking about a TV remote control here. You don't just unscrew it and take out the batteries."

In answer, she dug into her pants pocket, pulled out the small black box and heaved it at him.

"Jesus!"

Nate jumped to catch the device, fumbling it several times, like a football player bobbling a poorly thrown pass. Although his rational mind told him there was no possibility of any disaster occurring if he dropped the thing, his subconscious wasn't taking any chances.

Alex watched his performance with a tight, derisive smile. "For your information, it *is* very similar to a TV remote control. I contacted an acquaintance—actually, the son of an acquaintance—and he told me how to open the casing and remove the transistors."

"I don't believe this! You've been talking about nuclear devices with the son of an acquaintance!"

"Richard's a brilliant young physicist and engineer."

"Richard?" Nate froze, the decoder clutched in both hands.

"Dr. Richard Worthington."

"How do you know him?" He rapped the words, his mind racing with all kinds of wild possibilities.

"Not that it's any of your business, but his mother bought some of my early designs when I was just launching my own line. She invited me to their home—more of a fortress, really—and Richard had dinner with us. When I came back to Karistan, I called him for advice. He arranged to be part of the UN team so he could assess the situation and give me some suggestions regarding the nuclear reduction treaty."

"Why in hell would you trust him, when you don't trust the representatives of the State Department?"

"Maybe because he has some ideas for Karistan's future that don't include growing rice!"

"Christ!" Nate muttered, hefting the black box in his hand. "I can't believe it. You've been bluffing all along. Remind me to stake you in poker against Willie one of these days. You'd clean him out."

She sent him a look of mingled resentment and wariness. "I only need a few more days. Just until Richard gets here."

It was as close as someone with her proud background would come to begging, Nate realized. She still simmered with anger over his deception, still eyed him with wariness and resentment, yet she would put aside her personal feelings in the face of the responsibilities she carried. The tightness around Nate's chest ratcheted up another notch.

Slowly, he held out his hand. As she reached for the small device, his fingers wrapped around hers.

"Even if I wanted to give you those few days, Alex, I can't. I'm not the only one who's called your bluff. The White Wolf has, too. If the reports I got tonight are accurate, you've just run out of time."

Her face paled, and Nate lifted their intertwined hands until hers rested on his breastbone.

"You're not alone in this. Not by a long shot. There's backup firepower on the way. And until it arrives, I'm going to take a real active role in the camp's defense." His hand tightened around hers. "I want your word you'll do exactly as I say, at least until help arrives."

"I can't just turn over leadership of the host to you! Not now, not when…"

"I'm not asking you to abrogate your responsibilities. I know you wouldn't, in any case. But I've got more experience in what's coming down. Let me do this. Let me help you, Alex."

She tugged at her hand. "Why? Why should you do this? You accomplished your mission. You got what you came for. Why don't you get out of here while you can?"

"Oh, no, Alex. I'm not leaving. And I haven't got everything I came for. Not by a long shot."

He stood a heartbeat away, his face tipped with shadows and his long body radiating a tension that matched hers.

"I didn't realize when I rode onto the steppes that I was looking for you, Alexandra Danilova. I sure as hell didn't know I'd find you. But I was, and I did. And now that I have, I'm not about to lose you."

They rode back to camp at a fast, ground-eating gallop.

Her mind whirling, Alex tried to absorb everything she'd learned, everything she'd felt, in the past few hours. The thought of Americans coming to Karistan's aid sent a rush of relief through her, tinged with the faintest touch of bitterness. Relief that her ragged band of warriors would have assistance in whatever occurred tonight. Bitterness that, once the crisis was over, the gunships would return to their base and Karistan would again face an uncertain future.

Alex didn't pretend to be any kind of an expert in world affairs, but she knew that this tiny country couldn't claim a superpower's attention for very long. There were too many crises all over the world, too many trouble spots erupting into war. U.S. forces were spread thin as it was. She couldn't expect them to stay in Karistan, not without an inducement.

The only inducement for keeping the West's attention on Karistan, the only bargaining chip she'd had, was those missiles and the wild card of the decoder. She'd played that wildcard as long as she could, knowing someone might call her bluff at any moment.

Someone had.

She slanted a quick glance at the man beside her. His face was taut with concentration, his eyes were narrowed on the dark plains ahead. He absorbed the impact of Red's pounding stride with an unconscious coordination.

Alex tried to whip up some of the anger and resentment she'd felt when she left the plateau outside the cave. The sense of betrayal. The conviction that Nate had used her to get to the decoder.

She made a moue of disgust at her own choice of terms. Nate was right. He hadn't used her, any more than she had used him. They'd come together in a shattering explosion of need that had nothing to do with his mission to Karistan and everything to do with the attraction that arced between them. Had arced since the first moment they'd faced each other at either end of her rifle.

Alex had told herself she wanted to draw from his strength, if only for a few hours. Take comfort in his gentleness, if only for an afternoon. But now, with the world about to explode around them, she could admit that a few hours hadn't been enough. Not anywhere near enough.

He'd promised that they'd finish what was between them when this was all over. Alex tucked that promise away in a corner of her heart, knowing that it would give her something to hold on to in the desperate hours ahead.

When they rode into camp, the horses lathered and blowing, she felt a sharp sense of disorientation. The muffled laughter and sounds of singing took her by surprise. It took her a moment to remember that when she left, Anya had been happily rolling out pastries and Ivana had gone to collect honeycombs. So much had happened in the past few hours that the bright, sunny morning filled with the promise of a reprieve seemed a lifetime ago.

"So, cousin," Katerina called out, coming forward. "It is time you returned."

Her dark eyes shifted to Nate and seemed to go flat and hard for a moment. Alex dragged the reins over the gray's head, preparing to inform her cousin this was not the time for jealousies between them, but then the younger woman gave a small, defeated sigh.

"We have meat roasting, and fresh bread," she said, her shoulders sagging. "Come, you must be hungry."

"There's no time to eat," Alex responded. "We have news

from the east, and it's not good. Tell Dimitri I must speak with him, if you would, and spread word for the men to gather their weapons. I'll meet with everyone in the square in ten minutes.''

She turned to pass the reins to one of the men who'd appeared at her side. For an instant, the enormity of what was about to happen washed over her. Her hand trembled, the leather leads shook.

A strong, steady hand took the reins from her grasp. Giving both Red and the gray into the care of the waiting man, Nate stood before her.

"Remember, you're not alone in this."

She flashed him a quick, uncertain look.

"You'll never be alone again, Alex," he told her quietly, then took her arm and turned her toward the camp. "Let's go talk to Dimitri."

The gray-bearded lieutenant listened without comment as Alex quickly outlined the situation.

"So," she finished, "if the White Wolf leads a force of any size into Karistan, these Spectre gunships with their infrared scopes will detect them and give us warning. If only small bands come, from different directions, as they have done in the past, they'll be more difficult to detect. Then we must rely, as we have before, on our sentries to signal the alert and our men to hold the camp until Nate calls in the air cover.''

"We can hold them off until the gunship arrives, *ataman*." Although Dimitri spoke to Alex, his eyes were on the man standing at her shoulder.

With a wry smile, Alex translated his words for Nate. Since the moment the aged lieutenant had joined them, she'd felt the subtle shift of power from her to Nate. Not so much a lessening of her authority as a recognition that another shared it. Dimitri knew these gunships would come because of the man beside her. He understood that the *Amerikanski* could control and direct their firepower. Whether she wanted to or not, she now shared the burden that had been given her.

As the two men bent over the sketches Alex had drawn of the camp's defenses, Katerina stepped out of the shadows.

"What if we do not fight with the men of Balminsk?"

"What are you saying?" Alex asked sharply.

"What if we give them that which they seek? What if we end this ceaseless feud?"

"You would have me just hand over our cattle? Our grazing lands?"

"We...the women...we don't wish to see more bloodshed. We want none of this, 'Zandra."

"It's only this night, Katerina. Just this night. You'll be safe. You'll go to the ice caves, with the other women, until it's over."

She shook her head. "It is already over. We don't wish to live like this anymore. We take the children and we leave in the morning for the lowlands."

Alex felt Nate's presence behind her.

"Do we have a problem?"

Slowly, her heart aching, Alex translated for him.

For Alex, the few hours were a blur of tension and terror, relief and regret.

Nate organized the men. Petr Borodín, who had won renown and a chestful of medals for his activities as a saboteur during World War II, took fiendish delight in helping Nate plant what he called perimeter defenses.

Dimitri sent men with flares and weapons to guard the cattle, while others saddled the horses and tied their reins in strings of six, as had the Cossacks of old, to make it easier to lead them through battle if necessary.

Mikhail and a heavily armed squad shepherded the women and children to the protection of the ice cave...all except Katerina, who refused to leave. She would stay, she insisted, because she was of Karistan. For this night, at least.

Alex herself oversaw the distribution of the pitiful supply of arms and ammunition. A few grenade launchers her grandfather had bartered with the Chinese for. A Pakistani shoulder-held rocket launcher, still in its protective Cosmoline coating. The miscellaneous collection of rifles.

She told herself that the gunships hovering somewhere far overhead would make the difference. That their firepower was swifter, surer, more devastating. The thought gave her little comfort.

When the first, distant *whump-whump-whump* came out of the sky, Alex thought the attack had come. Desperate determination and an icy calm overlaid the churning fear in her stomach. Following Nate's terse order, she took a defensive position on a low, rolling hill at the rear of the camp, just above the stream. Katerina crouched beside her, unspeaking, a pistol in her hand and a flat, unreadable expression on her face.

A dark-painted helicopter skimmed out of the darkness from the east. Its searchlights swept the camp like flashlights swung from a giant hand. They illuminated a lone figure standing in the middle of the square. His rifle to his shoulder, old Gregor squinted along the barrel at the hovering aircraft.

"No!" Nate raced out of the darkness, into the undulating circle of light. "No! It has UN markings!"

Although Gregor didn't understand the words, Nate's urgency communicated itself, and he lowered the rifle. They stood together while the hovering helicopter settled in the dusty square.

When Richard clambered out, his eyes wide and his body jackknifed to avoid the whirling rotor blades, Alex recognized him at once. But she didn't recognize the long-legged brunette who jumped out behind him and was promptly swept against Nate's side in a bone-crushing squeeze. The woman whipped off her glasses and waved them in the air as she and Nate ducked away from the rotor blades, talking urgently.

As she strode across the square, Alex caught snatches of the woman's comments. "Blew the hatch...small explosion, nothing to worry about... Right behind us, about fifty strong. Heading right for the camp... This is no cattle raid, Cowboy.

I'm going back up in the helo. Richard and I devised a few small surprises that might delay them a little.''

Nate whirled at Alex's approach. "There's no time for long introductions, sweetheart. Things are moving too fast. But you know Worthington.''

Alex sent the young scientist a quick smile. "Hello, Richard.''

"Hello, Sandra. Sorry it took me so long to get here. We had...uh, an unexpected delay.''

The tall, confident brunette in lumberjack's clothing stepped forward. "I'm Nate's partner. I've been hoping to meet you.'' Her generous mouth quirked. "You wouldn't know it to look at me right now, but I'm a great admirer of your work. Look, I've got to get back in the air, but maybe when this is all over, we can talk.''

As drawn by the woman's vitality and confidence as she was unsettled by the easy camaraderie between her and Nate, Alex nodded. "When this is all over, we'll definitely talk.''

The brunette flashed Nate a cheeky grin and a thumbs-up, then headed for the helicopter. "Come on, Richard. Let's get this hummer up and see if those little canisters work as well from the air as they did from the bottom of a silo.''

The helo lifted off in a wash of swirling air and whining engines. Her stomach twisting, Alex turned to Nate.

"Tell me what we face.''

In brief, succinct phrases, Nate related the bald facts. Small, separate groups had slipped out of Balminsk, avoiding surveillance. They'd converged some twenty miles from the camp. Were heading this way. The gunships were in the air, closing fast.

"It's going to be tight, but we should be able to keep the attackers occupied until the real firepower arrives.''

"Nate—''

Whatever she would have said was lost in the sudden, distant boom of an explosion.

Nate whipped around, his eyes searching the impenetrable darkness. When he turned back, his eyes held a wry smile.

"That was one of Petr's booby traps. A satchel charge. It'll cause more confusion than damage, but at this point, confusion will work for us as well as anything. Get Katerina, Alex, and take cover. This could be an interestin' half hour."

Ever afterward, Alex would remember the events of the next few moments as a blur of confusion, shouts, and sudden, gripping fear.

She was halfway across the square when another explosion sounded, then another. She whirled, watching Nate freeze beside Dimitri as they strained to peer through the darkness beyond the barricades. And Petr, his bald head shining in the moonlight as he held a rifle tucked in his armpit.

Oh, God, she would remember thinking. Has it come down to this? Have all her grandfather's hopes for Karistan, all her own plans, come down to this last, desperate hour?

Another explosion. And then the sound of drumming hooves.

Alex raced across the square to Katerina, her stomach twisting at the blank emptiness on the girl's face as she calmly, mechanically, loaded a magazine clip into an automatic rifle. No fear. No terror. She'd done this before. Many times. She was so young, yet she'd seen so much death. And was about to see more.

As she closed the distance to her cousin, Alex thought of her father. Of the way Daniel Jordan had stood by his principles in the face of the hawk-eyed chieftain's vitriolic scorn. He'd insisted guns weren't the answer for Karistan, but he'd had no other.

Once again, the forces that had pulled at Alex for so many years ripped at her soul. Who was right? *What* was right?

Pulling Katerina behind the shelter of an overturned van, Alex slid a hand in her pocket and gripped the silver bridle bit in a tight, hard fist. Her knuckles nudged the small black box.

When Katerina turned her head and met her cousin's eyes,

Alex's disparate worlds seemed to rush toward each other like two comets hurtling through the heavens.

When Nate shouted a warning and Alex slewed around to see him standing tall and commanding, in charge of a battle he had no stake in, no responsibility for, her separate worlds collided.

And when a lone rider hurtled out of the darkness and soared over the barricades a few heart-stopping moments later, she knew what she had to do.

"Hold your fire!"

Her command rang through the camp, echoing Nate's.

For a few moments, no one moved. They were all caught up in the drama of watching the rider yank his mount's head around and bring it to a dancing, skidding, shuddering stop.

When the uniformed man dismounted, the scar on his face stood out in the moonlight, as did the cold expression on his face. He searched the shadows, then fastened his gaze on Nate.

"I am Cherkoff. I have ordered the men of Balminsk to hold outside the mine field you have planted while I come to speak with you."

Nate walked out into the center of the square. Slowly, deliberately, he measured the stiff figure.

"No," Nate replied, "you come to speak with the *ataman*."

Alex heard the soft response as she came up behind Nate, Katerina at her side. The splinter of private joy his words gave her helped shatter the tight knot of pain at what she was about to do.

"The *ataman* is here," she replied.

Cherkoff turned to face her, his dark eyes piercing, his shoulders rigid in his brown uniform with red tabs at the shoulder denoting his rank.

"You have something my father wishes to possess."

"No, I have not."

A muscle twitched at the side of his jaw. "You don't understand the depths of my father's hatred."

Alex swallowed. She understood it. Her grandfather had passed her the same hatred.

"Why have you come?" she asked him. "And wearing that uniform?"

"I wear it," the major said slowly, as though each word were dragged from his heart, "because it is a symbol of what was before."

His hand lifted to the leather strap that crossed one shoulder, holding his service holster and pistol. His fingers brushed a gleaming buckle.

As Alex watched, her breath suspended, he lifted the strap's end, undid the buckle and removed the holster. Opening his fist, he let the weapon fall to the ground.

"It's time to put this past behind us. I would speak with you about the future, and about this device you hold that so incites my father's fury."

Katerina stepped forward. "I have the device which you seek. You will speak with me."

Chapter 15

"All right, let's get down to some serious negotiations here."

Maggie pushed the black glasses up the bridge of her nose and shrugged off the weariness of a long night and frantic morning. Folding her arms on the scarred surface of the table, she waited while the two officials who'd been standing by in Germany ever since the crisis over the decoder first surfaced took their seats. They'd arrived just moments ago, aboard the transport that would take Maggie and Nate back to the States. Before that plane lifted off, the parties gathered in the dim, shadowy tent needed to reach agreement.

The State Department representative, a big, burly man in a crumpled navy suit and white shirt, looked Maggie up and down.

"Just who are you?" he asked coolly. "And what authority do you have to participate in these negotiations?"

"She's Dr. Megan St. Clare," Alex supplied from her seat next to Maggie's, her tone several degrees colder than the official's. "She's here at my request, and that of my cousin,

Katerina Terenshkova. As is our technical advisor, Dr. Richard Worthington."

A thin, well-dressed woman in her mid-forties seated beside the State Department official peered across the table. "Richard Worthington? From MIT?"

"Well, I, uh, consult with several institutes."

The woman, a midlevel bureaucrat with the Nuclear Regulatory Agency, frowned. "This is highly irregular, you know. Negotiations like this are quite sensitive. We don't generally allow outsiders to participate."

"You are in Karistan," Alex reminded her with a lift of one brow. "You're the outsider here. My cousin and I will decide who does and does not participate."

The woman blinked, then sat back. "Yes. Of course."

The burly State Department rep, who looked as though he'd be more at home roaming the back streets of D.C. than the corridors of the granite federal building in Foggy Bottom, frowned.

"Before we begin, I understand you have a certain device which we'll take possession of."

Alex turned to Katerina, who dug into the pockets of her skirts. She pulled out the decoder and dropped it on the table with a loud clatter.

The officials winced.

"Here, take it," Maggie urged, pushing the thing across the table with a cautious finger. Since her hours in that dark silo with Richard, she didn't want anything associated with nuclear matters within her sight. Ever again.

She picked up the papers torn from Alex's sketch pad, which were now filled with the figures they'd hurriedly put together in the small hours of the night.

"All right, here's the bottom line. We estimate that the total cost to dismantle all nuclear weapons in Balminsk and Karistan at approximately three billion dollars."

"What?"

"That includes a system to verify the warheads' destruction, and compensation for the enriched uranium that will be extracted.''

''Now see here, Dr. St. Clare...''

''It also includes approximately ten million dollars,'' Maggie interjected ruthlessly, ''to establish a science and technology center here. The center will bring in outside expertise—researchers, technicians, and their support staffs.''

''Perhaps a hundred men or more,'' Katerina murmured, her eyes gleaming. ''My aunts will be most pleased.''

A wave of red crept up the State Department rep's bull-like neck. ''This is absurd.''

Richard cleared his throat. ''Uh, no, actually, it's not. This is exactly half what the United States offered the Ukraine less than a year ago as inducement to sign the Strategic Arms Reduction Treaty. The Ukraine had fewer missiles, as I'm sure you're aware, giving the Karistanis the advantage of 6.4 times the throw weight.''

The woman across from Maggie jerked her head up. ''Dr. Worthington! We don't negotiate treaties dollar for dollar based on throw weight. It's highly irregular!''

''There is more,'' Katerina added. ''The major, he has the thoughts about con...con...''

''Conventional arms,'' Nikolas supplied, coming forward out of the shadows at the back of the tent to stand behind Katerina's chair.

She sent him a slow, provocative smile over one shoulder. ''*Da!* Nikolas will talk with you about such conventional arms, so we may protect our borders when the missiles are gone.''

''Now wait just a minute...''

The blustering official faltered as Nikolas Cherkoff placed his hands on Katerina's shoulders and leaned into the light. His scar livid against his cheek, he bared his teeth in a smile.

''No. No more waiting. We have waited long enough for peace in this land. We will proceed.''

Several hours later, Maggie stepped out of the black tent and wiped an arm across her forehead. ''Whew! That was almost as nerve-racking as being trapped in a hole with Richard.''

''I can imagine,'' Alex replied, her eyes on the two stiff-backed bureaucrats who were stalking toward the aircraft that squatted like a camouflaged quail on a flat stretch of plain just outside camp.

A ripple of sound inside the tent caught Maggie's attention. The young scientist gave an indignant sputter, Katerina a teasing laugh. For a crazy moment last night, when she first saw Richard approached by a young woman with a cloud of dark, curling hair, a sultry smile and a chest that drew his eyes like a magnet, Maggie thought—hoped!—that Katerina might go to work on Richard's endocrine system. But either the physicist's hormonal serums went out of whack only with older women, or Katerina wasn't interested in awkward young scientists. After a brief greeting to Richard, she'd never taken her eyes, or her hands, off Nikolas Cherkoff, and the young scientist had stuck to Maggie like gum on the bottom of a shoe.

Maggie sighed, deciding she'd just have to take Richard in hand when they got back to the States and introduce him to more older women.

Why did her life seem to grow more complicated after each mission? If she wasn't collecting German shepherd-size blue-and-orange-striped iguanas, she was taking charge of organizing a brilliant physicist's love life.

Hearing Cherkoff's quiet voice, Maggie turned to Alex. ''Do you think your cousin and the major will keep the peace between Balminsk and Karistan?''

''They will, if Katerina has anything to say about it, and my cousin is a most...persuasive woman.'' She paused, and gave Maggie a tired smile. ''I don't know how to thank you for your help last night. And this morning. I thought I drove a pretty hard bargain with my suppliers when I negotiated for materials, but you made me realize I'm still in the minor leagues.'' Her smile became a little forced. ''Nate told me you were good. One of the best, he said, although he failed to specify at what.''

Maggie caught the faint, almost imperceptible hint of acid in her voice, and decided to ignore it. Until Nate and Alex worked out whatever had driven him away this morning, she wasn't going to get in the middle.

"No thanks are necessary," she said with a grin. "Unless…"

"Yes?"

"Unless you might have a dress or two in your tent that would fit me. One of your own designs, maybe, that I could purchase at a reasonable price."

Alex gave her a quick once-over. They were about the same height, although Maggie carried a few more inches on her curving frame than Alex did.

"I think I might just have something."

"You wonderful person!"

"In cashmere."

Maggie groaned with pleasure.

Alex's eyes sparkled in response. "Dyed a shade of burnt orange that will pick up the glossy highlights in your hair and always remind you of the steppes at sunset."

Maggie tugged off her glasses and tucked them into the pocket of her plaid shirt, staring at this Alex. No wonder Cowboy had disappeared to lick his wounds this morning. If he was hit as hard as Maggie suspected he was, it was going to tear him in two to leave this vibrant, glowing woman behind.

"Thanks, Alexandra. I'll admit I wasn't looking forward to flying back to the States and facing my boss for a mission debrief wearing this outfit. It's going to be tough enough without feeling like I just crawled out of…of a silo."

At the mention of flying, the smile faded from Alex's eyes. She lifted a hand and toyed absently with one of the small tassels decorating the yoke of her swirling fitted greatcoat.

"You're leaving this morning?"

"In a couple of hours. Richard wants time to inspect the missiles on Karistan's soil before we leave."

"Is Nate going with you?"

Maggie gave her a level look. "Yes. And Three Bars Red, evidently. Nate asked me to have the pilot rig a stall for him. He said that you weren't satisfied with the stud's, er... performance."

Maggie had to bite her lip to hold back a grin. The memory of Nate's choked voice when he'd told her just which stud Alexandra had decided to accept on behalf of Karistan was one she'd always treasure.

"It's not his performance that's the problem," Alex replied in a tight, small voice, then gave herself a little shake.

"Red's already covered half the mares in Karistan," she continued. "We just can't seem to keep him in the pastures and out of the tents. Not if he gets a whiff of anything sweet. He destroyed my aunt Feodora's latest *pysanky*—Easter egg— when he..."

Alex broke off at the sound of muffled thunder from outside the camp. Frowning, she glanced over her shoulder. The thunder rolled closer, then separated into the pounding tattoo of hooves drumming against the earth.

It happened so quickly, Alex had no time to react. One moment she was standing in the open square beside Maggie, staring at the barricades still ringing the camp. The next, Red came soaring over the low wall, ears flat, nose stretched out, legs tucked. He landed with a fluid grace and flowed into a smooth gallop.

Nate was bent low over the stallion's neck, his eyes on Alex, one hand gripping the reins.

In the same instant Alex realized what he intended, she knew she couldn't stop him. Instinctively, she stumbled backward, without any real hope of getting away.

Nate leaned lower, his arm outstretched. It wrapped around Alex's waist with the force of a freight train and swept her up as Red thundered by. Her thick coat padded most of the impact, but her bottom thumped against a hard leg, then a hip, before he dragged her across his thighs.

She grabbed at his jacket and wiggled frantically to find purchase.

"Are you crazy?" she shouted, gasping for breath. "What is this?"

"Just a little circus trick I picked up from Peter the Great. Hang on, sweetheart."

Alex did, with both hands, as Red slewed to one side and then the other, weaving through the tents with the agility of a world-class cutting horse. He cleared the barricade at the opposite end of the camp with the same flying ease.

Her hair whipping her eyes, Alex caught a glimpse of Petr's startled face behind them. And Dimitri's grinning one. She heard a distant shout, a surprised oath, and then nothing but the sound of Red's steady gait and the wind rushing in her ears.

Nate didn't slow, didn't stop to let her find a more secure seat. Holding her against his chest with one iron-hard arm, he took Red across the steppes.

When at last he drew rein beside a low outcropping of rock, Alex had regained some of her breath and most of her equilibrium. Still, she was forced to cling to him with both hands as he kicked a boot out of the stirrup, swung his leg over the saddle horn and slid off Red with her still banded to his body.

She shoved at his shoulders with both hands, leaning back to look up at his face.

"Were you just trying to impress me with a last demonstration of your horsemanship?" she panted. "Or is there a point to this little circus trick?"

"Oh, there's a point. Which we'll get to in a few moments. After we straighten out a couple of things between us."

Alex wasn't sure she cared for the hint of steel under his easy tone. It was as hard and unyielding as the arms that held her.

"First," he said, "you want to tell me just what Katerina

was doing with that decoder? I just about blew it when she pulled it out last night.''

''I gave it to her.''

His eyes narrowed. ''Why, Alex?''

''I closed my ears to what the women were trying to tell me,'' Alex admitted, still breathless and shaky. ''When I saw you caught in the middle of the feud that my grandfather had helped perpetuate for so long, I realized I was trying to hold Karistan to his vision, instead of shaping it to theirs.''

''I'd say you did some pretty fair shaping this afternoon. I just talked to two very uptight bureaucrats at the plane.''

She managed a smile. ''With Maggie's help. I still can't quite believe I haggled over nuclear warheads like a horse trader bringing a new string to the bazaar.''

The knowledge that she'd just bought Karistan a future went a long way toward easing the ache in Alex's heart. Not all the way, but a long way.

''What's the second thing?'' she asked, staring up at Nate's lean, sun-weathered face. Alex knew that the little pattern of white lines at the sides of his eyes would stay in her memory forever. And the gold-tipped sweep of the lashes that screened those gray-brown eyes. And the small half smile that lifted one corner of his lips. ''What else do we have to get straight between us?''

''I love you, Alex. With a love that doesn't know any borders, or states, or cultures. I want to bind your life to mine, but not your soul. That has to stay free. That's what makes you unique. And wild and proud and too damn stubborn for your own good. It's also what makes you the woman I can't live without. I figure I've got about two hours until I have to go back to the States to wrap up some loose ends, but then I'll be back. And when I come back, I'm staying. We're going to do some serious flyin' across the steppes, my darlin'. For the rest of our lives.''

She didn't move, didn't speak, for long, endless moments. ''You'd live here, with me?''

''I'd live in the back of a pickup with you, Alexandra Danilova. Or in North Philly, or Wolf Creek, or Parsnippety, New Jersey. I never needed an anchor in this world until I met you. Now you are my anchor."

Alex felt her separate halves shimmer, then splinter into a hundred smaller and smaller pieces, until the different worlds that had pulled at her for so long disappeared in a shower of dust. With a feeling of coming home, she slid her arms around Nate's neck.

"The decoder wasn't all I gave Katerina," she whispered. "I also passed her the silver bridle bit, the one the czar presented to my ancestor. The one my grandfather gave to me."

It was Nate's turn to go still. He stared down at her, his skin drawing tight across his cheeks as he waited for her to continue. This had to come from her, he knew. As much as he wanted to pull it out, or force it out, or kiss her until she breathed it out between gasps of raw passion, he knew it could only come from her.

"Katerina's stronger than she thought she was," Alex said softly. "She has the strength of the steppes in her, and the wisdom of our people's women. She's of my grandfather's blood. She should be *ataman* of this host."

"And you, Alex? What do you want to be?"

Her eyelids fluttered for a moment. Nate could count each black, sooty lash, see each small blue vein. Then the lids lifted, and her glorious, golden eyes called him home.

"I want to be your anchor, Nate."

Alex thought he'd kiss her then. Her heart thudded painfully against her breastbone with anticipation. Her breath seemed to slow, until she forgot to draw in any at all.

Instead, his lips curved in one of those lazy, crooked grins that set her pulse tripping and sent a liquid heat to her belly.

"Which brings us to the point of my little circus act, as you called it."

Tugging her arms from around his neck, he set her to one side. Dazed, Alex watched as he untied a rolled bundle from behind the saddle. He walked a few steps into the high grass, then knelt on one knee.

Alex raised a hand to shove her hair back. "What are you doing?"

Even as she asked the question, she knew the answer. Desire, hot and sweet and instantaneous, flooded through her.

"I'm making us a bed," he replied, confirming her hopes.

She swept the open, windswept plain and endless blue sky with a quick glance. "Here?"

"Here. Katerina told me that when a woman of the steppes chooses a man to take to her bed, she'd best be sure the bed is movable, because it's a sure bet the man will be. I figured it works both ways."

"Kat—Katerina told you that?"

The leather laces gave, and a thick, shaggy wolf pelt gleaming with silvery lights rolled out onto the thick grass.

"Uh-huh. Right after she reminded me that the Cossacks of old didn't take a whole lot of time for courting. They just swooped down and carried their brides off."

Tucking the knife back in his pocket, he spread one of the feather-soft mohair blankets that kept the Karistanis warm, even in the bitterest of winters, on top of the wolf pelt. That done, he squatted on one heel and grinned up at her.

"Come here, Alex. Come, shed your clothes and your worries and your inhibitions, and fly across the steppes with me."

She took a half step, then hesitated.

"Still have some doubts?" he asked with a little twist of pain at the crease that etched a line between her eyes. "Some worries?"

"One," she murmured, taking a slow step toward him.

"Tell me. Share it with me."

Her fingers touched his, then slid across his palm and folded around it.

"I'm just hoping you don't have any chewing gum in your pockets. I don't want Red nosing under the blanket at…an inopportune moment, to get at it."

Laughing, Nate tumbled her to the blanket.

If Alex had thought this joining of their bodies and their

hearts would be a gentle one now that they'd torn down the barriers between them, she soon realized her mistake.

It started easily enough. His hands worked the buttons on her coat with lazy thoroughness, while his mouth played with her, touching, tasting, rediscovering. Her fingers worked their way inside his jacket, planing across the wide spread of his chest. With each outer layer shed, however, their legs tangled more intimately. With each touch, their bodies caused more friction.

By the time Nate tore the last button loose on her tunic and yanked it open, his breath was a river of heat against her skin.

By the time Alex fumbled open the snap on his jeans and pushed them down over his lean hips, her fingers trembled with the need to feel the warmth of his flesh.

Nate crushed her into the mohair, his body hard and urgent against hers. Alex opened for him her arms, her mouth, her legs.

They twisted together, straining against each other, aching with want and with need. Nate buried both hands in her hair, anchoring her head while his mouth slanted across hers.

Alex arched under him, grinding her pelvis into his until at last frustration and need made her twist her hips and thrust him off.

Panting, she propped herself up on one elbow. "The women of Karistan have a saying about a situation like this."

"Oh, no, Alex..." he groaned, flopping back on the blanket. "Not another one. Not now."

"Oh, yes, another one." She slid a leg across his belly, then pushed herself up. Planting both palms against his chest, she straddled his flanks.

"Once a woman decides where it is she goes, she must simply mount and follow the sun across the steppes until she gets there."

Steadying herself against his chest, Alex lifted her hips and mounted.

Later, much later, when Alex had followed the sun until it exploded in a million shards of light and Nate had flown across the steppes twice, they lay wrapped in a cocoon of mohair and body heat, cooling sweat and warming sun.

Pressed against the shaggy pelt by Nate's inert body, Alex slid one foot along the blanket to ease the ache in one hip joint from her splayed position. Her toes slipped off the edge of the blanket and into the rough grass. She smiled, remembering another rocky bower under another open sky.

"Nate?" she murmured against his ear.

"Mmm?"

"I love you. I'll live with you in the back of that pickup, if you want, or in Parsnippety or Wolf Creek or wherever. But do you suppose we might invest in a bed, or at least a real mattress? And make love on something other than the hard ground once in a while?"

He lifted his head, and Alex's heart contracted at the wicked gleam in his eyes.

"If we're going to do as much flying across the steppes as I think we are, sweetheart, we'll invest in a whole houseful of beds. One for each room."

He brushed a kiss across the tip of her nose. "One for the attic."

Another kiss feathered along her cheek. "One for the back porch."

Alex gasped as he withdrew a bit and bent to reach her lips. "One for the…"

"Never mind," she breathed, arching her hips to draw him back into her depths. "This wolf pelt seems to be working just fine."

Chapter 16

The hazy September sun added a golden glow to the smog hovering above Washington's noontime streets. In offices on both sides of the Potomac, senior-level officials and lobbyists just back from their power lunches shed their tailored jackets and settled down to return their stacks of phone messages before starting their afternoon round of meetings. It was a well-established routine, one respected and adhered to by most denizens of the capital.

In one particular office on a quiet side street just off Massachusetts Avenue, however, the routine had been disrupted. OMEGA's director had called an immediate meeting with two of his operatives.

While she waited for Adam Ridgeway to finish with a phone call, Maggie perched on a corner of his receptionist's desk, swinging a foot encased in one of Alexandra Jordan's supple, cream-colored calf-high boots. The boot, with its decorated tassels edging the top, just skimmed the hem of her flowing umber skirt. A matching tunic in the same burnt orange draped her from shoulder to hip, and was banded at the wrist and neck with wide strips of corded piping in cream and gold. Maggie rubbed her hands up and down her arms, luxuriating in the sinful feel of the finest, softest cashmere against her skin.

She'd used the transport's tiny bathroom to wash both her eyebrows and her hair in a shallow stainless-steel sink. The shoulder-length brown mass now hung shiny and clean in its usual smooth sweep, and her brows were restored to their natural lines.

But Adam's receptionist, Elizabeth Wells, nibbled on her lower lip delicately as she stared at the kidney-shaped blemish on Maggie's jaw.

"Are you sure it will fade, dear?"

"The guys in Field Dress say it will," Maggie replied, a little doubtfully. Her faith in the wizards of the wardrobe was severely shaken. The formula that was supposed to dissolve the ink they'd injected under her skin had only dimmed it to a purplish hue.

Forgetting the blemish in view of more pressing concerns, she swung her foot. "Are you sure Adam said he wanted to see us as soon as we arrived at the headquarters? Usually he talks to us after the debrief."

Kind, matronly Elizabeth sent her a sympathetic look. "He took a call from the president just moments before you and Nate landed. The notes he gave me to transcribe from that conversation include some rather inflammatory remarks from the director of the Nuclear Regulatory Agency. And a highly agitated senior official from the State Department is on the line right now."

"Oh."

Sprawled with his customary loose-limbed ease in an antique chair set beside Elizabeth's desk, Nate grinned.

"Maggie, sweetheart, this next half hour might be one of those scenes Willie says looks a whole lot better when you're peering at it through the rearview mirror instead of the windshield."

Maggie laughed and tucked the sweep of her hair behind

one ear. "I just hope it's only a half hour. Neither one of us has slept in the last thirty-six. What's more, we just shared a twenty-four-hour plane ride with a horse. I need a bath and some sleep, preferably at the same time."

When Elizabeth's intercom buzzed a moment later, she lifted the receiver, listened a moment, then nodded.

"Go on in, dear. You too, Nate."

Maggie edged off the desk and smoothed her hands over her hips. The soft cashmere settled around her in elegant, body-hugging lines. She might not have had recourse to her perfumed body lotion to counter the effects of Red's companionship, but at least she looked better than she smelled. A *lot* better.

When Maggie walked into the director's office a few steps ahead of Nate, Adam felt his shoulders stiffen under the wool of his tailored navy wool blazer. With considerable effort, he refrained from reaching up to tug at the Windsor knot in his crimson-and-gray-striped Harvard tie. He stood quietly behind his desk, absorbing Maggie's vivid impact.

Sunlight streaming through the tall windows behind him highlighted the golden glints in her chestnut hair and picked up the sparkle in her wide brown eyes. It also illuminated every one of the soft peaks and valleys of her body, displayed with stunning, sensual detail in a sweater dress that caused Adam's fingers to curl around the edge of his mahogany desk.

He returned the two agents' greetings calmly enough, and waited until they were seated in the wingback chairs in front of his desk before taking his seat.

"I realize that it's somewhat unusual to call you in before the debrief in the control center," he began. "But there are certain matters that need clarification immediately."

Opening a manila folder centered on his desk, he pulled out a hand-scribbled note. "Before the president calls the rather substantial campaign contributor who offered Three Bars Red to Karistan in the first place, he'd like to know why Alexandra Jordan turned the stud down. Was his performance unsatisfactory?"

Maggie folded her hands in her lap and waited gleefully for Nate's response. She hadn't had the nerve to mention "performance" matters in front of Cowboy during the trip back, not with Alexandra Jordan curled in his lap for most of the way.

Nate gave Adam one of his easy grins and sidestepped the issue.

"Let's just say Karistan has more pressing matters to attend to right now than horse-breeding."

"So I understand," Adam responded, turning to Maggie. "One of which is establishing a science and technology institute at the cost of…"

Maggie swallowed a groan as he extracted a sheet filled with rows of neatly typed figures.

"…of eight million dollars. A price, I'm informed, that was negotiated by a certain Dr. St. Clare."

She gave a small shrug. "Well, we were asking for ten million."

"I suppose you have a good reason for entering into negotiations on behalf of a foreign government…against your own."

Maggie hesitated, then leaned forward, trying to articulate the feeling that had crept over her with chilling intensity during her hours in that silo.

"If a future graduate of that institute finds a way to make nuclear power obsolete, the world will be a safer place for everyone. Eight million dollars will be a small price to pay. That stuff's scary, Adam. Especially when you're locked down in a hole with it."

"I see. Perhaps that explains why you decided to blow the silo hatch, causing a wave of unsubstantiated reports of a nuclear explosion to ripple across the globe?"

Maggie sat back, nodding. "Yes, that explains it. That and the fact that Cowboy needed me."

"Our forces were pretty thin in Karistan, Adam. We were real relieved when Maggie and Richard Worthington showed up."

Instead of placating OMEGA's director, Nate's quiet contribution caused an unexpected reaction. Maggie held her breath as Adam's blue eyes frosted over until they were positively glacial.

"Yes, let's discuss Dr. Richard Worthington."

He slid the typed list inside the folder and pulled out a faxed copy of a memo. "This is an interagency request for the permanent assignment of a geologist to Dr. Worthington's team. At his own insistence, he's been assigned as the chief inspector for the START treaty provisions. He will be traveling extensively all over the world for the next few years, inspecting silos."

Maggie shuddered at the thought of Richard—sweet, clumsy Richard—climbing down into an endless series of silos.

"This request has the highest national priority," Adam added. "Since the geologist in question is one Megan St. Clare, the president has asked me to favorably consider it."

"I was expecting this," Maggie muttered.

"You were?"

"Yes. It has something to do with endo—" She glanced at Adam's rigid face and waved a hand. "Never mind."

"I need an answer for the president," he reminded her.

"Look, Adam, when you turn this request down would you include a suggested alternate name? I know a geologist who's worked with my father. She's superbly qualified. A widow with no children, so she'll be able to travel. And she's just a couple years older than I am," Maggie finished, with a private, satisfied grin.

"You're assuming I'm going to turn down a personal request from the president?"

Maggie met Adam's eyes across the acre of polished mahogany that served as his desk. What she saw in them caused a tight curl of pleasure.

"No," she replied softly, the smile in her eyes for Adam alone. "I'm not assuming that you'll turn it down. I know you will."

Nate glanced from one to the other. Then his lazy drawl broke the silence. "If that's all, Adam, I need to go upstairs and get with Doc before the debrief. He's got some questions for me."

Adam stood and tucked the ends of his tie inside his blazer. "That's all I needed you for, but you don't have to rush your session with Doc. He's planning to stand by after the debrief for an extended session with you and Maggie."

Nate shook his head as he pushed himself to his feet. "Can't do it. I've got to make this debrief as quick as possible. I'm on borrowed time here, folks."

He hooked his thumbs in his belt, grinning. "Alexandra's picking Willie up at the airport in two hours, and then they're going to put their heads together. About wedding clothes. Unless I want to find myself walking down the aisle in Willie's unique concept of formal wear, all decorated with Alex's thingamabobs, I'd better go protect my interests."

"Since I'm going to be giving you away, ask her to design something for me," Maggie begged.

Nate's blond brows lifted. "*You're* giving *me* away?"

"I am. Alex says it's a custom among the Karistanis. The women of her host have a saying, something about only a woman being able to make sure the man is where he is supposed to be when."

"I might have known," Nate groaned.

"Oh, by the way," she added, sailing toward the door, "one of my responsibilities in this role is to call out a list of your positive and negative character traits, so the bride can decide whether she'll accept you or not. I've already made up the lists, Nate. One of them is *really* long."

She almost made it out the door on the wake of Nate's laughter.

"Just a moment, Maggie. I'm not quite finished with you." Adam nodded to Nate as he walked around the corner of the desk. "We'll join you upstairs for the debrief in a few moments."

Nate gave her an encouraging wink and left.

Maggie ascribed the sudden weakening in her knees to the fact that she'd been without sleep for the last thirty-six hours. It had nothing to do with her body's reaction to the controlled grace of Adam's movements or the overwhelming impact of his nearness. Or to the way his eyes seemed to survey every square centimeter of her face before he spoke in that cool Boston Brahmin voice of his.

"You will never…*never*…again attempt to blow anything up when you're locked inside it. Do I make myself clear, Chameleon?"

Since he was standing two heartbeats away and Maggie drew in the spicy lemon-lime scent of his aftershave with every breath, it would've been hard for him to be any clearer.

Still, she wasn't about to let Adam know quite the impact he was having on her hormonal serums. Keeping her voice cool and her eyes steady, she returned a small smile.

"Loud and clear, Chief."

For a moment, she thought he was actually going to admit that he was furious.

Fascinated, Maggie watched a tiny muscle at the side of his jaw twitch. To her profound disappointment, the twitch subsided.

"Good," he said quietly.

Well, maybe next time, she thought.

Summoning up a cheeky grin, she tipped him her version of a military salute, the one that always brought a pained look to his aristocratic features.

"By the way," she tossed over her shoulder as she headed for the door, "remind me to tell you about the interesting uses the women of Karistan have for yak oil sometime."

*   *   *   *   *

Since you loved
DANGEROUS TO HOLD,
we have two other treats in store.

Merline Lovelace's fast-paced,
exciting quartet of the original
CODE NAME: DANGER
series concludes with

DANGEROUS TO KNOW

In stores from Silhouette Books in July, 2002.

Meanwhile, available this month is a brand-new
assignment from the Omega files.

Don't miss
HOT AS ICE
Intimate Moments #1129

Turn the page for a sneak peek....

Prologue

"*I* hear her!"

The figure swathed from head to foot in bright orange Extreme Cold Weather gear whooped with joy. "She's punching through!"

His companion spun in a circle, searching the endless, unbroken surface of the polar ice cap. A dozen different shades of white dazzled his eye, shielded though they were by protective goggles. The blue white of the ice. The downy, cloud-soft drifts of glistening snow. The hazy, gray white of the sky that merged with the horizon.

"I don't hear anything!"

"Listen!"

The frustrated listener threw back his hood. He risked losing an ear to biting wind that dropped the outside temperature to almost thirty below, but he was too eager to care at that moment. Then he, too, gave a shout of glee as a series of sharp cracks rifled through the air.

Suddenly, a scant forty yards away, the ice cap erupted. Huge white slabs pushed upward. Groaning, they rose straight into the air before toppling over with a crash. A mo-

ment later the tip of a black conning tower poked through the crack.

"How do you like that! She's right on target."

Both men grinned. Sophisticated navigational equipment had guided the USS Hawkbill from Hawaii, but good old-fashioned muscle power had provided her surfacing site...a large X shoveled in the ice.

The two oceanographers raised their hands and clapped fur-lined mitts in a jubilant high five. After months at the remote laboratory 165 miles north of Point Barrow, Alaska, they were ready—more than ready!—for a fresh infusion of supplies and outside conversation. Still grinning, they watched as the submarine's conning tower rose a foot. Two feet. Ten.

The hulking body of the sub appeared, rolling great chunks of ice off its sides. When the hatch atop the conning tower opened and a hooded sailor appeared, the two scientists rushed forward.

"Boy, are we glad to see you!" the senior scientist shouted. "We're down to the last battery for the Underwater Observation Buoy."

"We brought the spares you requested." Bulky and awkward in his protective gear, the seaman climbed down the iron rungs riveted to the conning tower. "We'll start unloading immediately."

"We'll help. Jack, bring up the snowmobile."

Eager to get the valuable equipment unloaded and hauled back to the collection of huts connected by air-heated tunnels that formed the United States Arctic Oceanographic Research Station, the lead oceanographer threw an impatient glance over his shoulder.

"Jack! The snowmobile!"

His partner didn't move. Frozen in place, he gawked at one of the huge slabs of ice tossed up by the sub.

"What's got into you, man?"

His breath clouding on the frigid air, the senior scientist stomped across the ice. Irritation creased his forehead under his ski mask.

"Why are you just standing there? We've got a hundred tasks to get done before we... Oh, my God!"

His eyes bugged. Disbelief rose up in great, choking waves to close his throat, cut off his breath. Stumbling to a halt, he gaped at the helmeted figure staring back at him through five feet of ice.